THE THUNDERBOLT AFFAIR

By

Geoffrey Mandragora

Rosswyvern Press

This is a work of fiction. Names, characters, businesses, places, events and incidents are either the products of the author's imagination or historical persons and events used in a fictitious manner. Any resemblance to actual persons, living or dead, or actual events is purely coincidental.

ISBN:
978-0-9857907-0-7

For Nevi
A real-life Eastern European genius

Acknowledgments

I wrote a book. It was entertaining and somewhat interesting. With the help of some extraordinary individuals it fleshed out to a much richer story. Starting with my first reader, Robin Raymond, the details of the characters expanded to become very engaging individuals. Then it passed through the hands of Megan Mcintosh and Liz Springer; two people whose attention to detail and quick minds made me work very hard. They deserve all the credit for the things that work right. I, however, am solely responsible for inaccuracies, mistakes and errors.

Prologue – April, 1884

"Volunteers. The man said he wanted volunteers only," Corporal Wesley groused. "I don't recall volunteering."

"Shut yer gob." Sergeant Beam replied. "You're a bloody Royal Marine, you volunteered at least once."

The ten men in the rented steam launch were tired and bedraggled from the long trip along the shoreline. They had ridden in the open boat through a miserable cold rain that was just tapering off. The trip started from New York Harbor, headed to the mouth of the Quinnipiac River in Connecticut. So far, all they had to show for it was wet clothing and frayed tempers. The small deck was close quarters, but the tiny cabin would accommodate only four, if everyone was friendly. Besides, the smell from putrefying bilge scum that, combined with the rolling waves would turn the strongest sailor's stomach.

Commander Peter Waite listened as the men complained and checked the time on his pocket watch. He grunted, examined the sky with an experienced eye, then squinted at the shoreline where the mouth of the river was just coming into view. They were barely two miles from their ultimate destination and, despite the gloomy weather, they would be on time for the rendezvous.

"Yeah, I volunteered to serve in the Queen's uniform," Wesley continued. He plucked at the dank civilian clothes he wore under his slicker. "My best mufti kit and look at it."

"Don't concern yourself," the sergeant replied. "It'll probably have bullet holes in it by the time we're through."

"Cold water," said Petty Officer George Grant, his voice tinged with Cornwall roughness. "That's the ticket for getting those nasty blood stains out of your clothes." His voice held the sound of experience.

Corporal Wesley glared at the compact sailor whose skin had turned to leather under the tropical sun. The non-com displayed the cool manner of competency that marks a veteran. He certainly seemed familiar with the .476 caliber Enfield Mk II revolver tucked inside his jacket. The commander seemed similarly confident in his ability with a revolver. The

1

four marines on board had never fired their venerable Martini-Henry carbines in anger, having been assigned to embassy duty in the United States.

"I thought you damn limeys were supposed to be tough," spoke up Adam Greer, the man in charge of the four Americans on board. "For a Pinkerton, this is just a nice day out." He took off his derby hat, which the damn limey kept calling a bowler, and used his finger to reshape the slowly drying brim. He resisted the urge to tweak the drooping ends of his long mustache. He and his men wore long oilskin dusters that covered their velvet-collared frock coats, the preferred outer garment for concealing Sam Colt's best, the .45 caliber single action Peacemaker, a very reliable piece of hardware for the men who would be first in the assault.

"How long?" he asked the British officer.

Commander Waite eyed the map, which he had folded so that only the river route was showing. "About ten minutes."

The Pinkerton grunted, drew off the damp duster to reveal the just-as-damp coat underneath and his men followed suit. As he did so, he reached into his coat pocket and extracted the paperwork that made this bit of business legal. Well, mostly legal.

At the heart of it, it was just a property repossession. John Holland, as agent for the Delamater Iron Company, built a custom boat, but upon completion the customers decided stealing it was better than making the final payments. Turned out they didn't know how to run the thing and the customers almost wrecked it, so they went back to the Delamater Company to make a deal. The chief engineer professed to go along, but actually offered the boat to the Royal Navy, who needed a Yankee hand to collect. The Pinkertons contacted the customers and arranged a meeting to exchange cash for "instructions."

All nice and simple, except the customers were the Fenian Brotherhood, a group of Irish rebels living in the United States, and the bomb throwers weren't likely to take kindly to this action. They would most likely be armed to the teeth, even if they were not expecting trouble, *and* the damn boat had some sort of artillery piece on board that they kept calling a dynamite gun, whatever the hell that was.

"Your men are ready?" the commander asked, as he and the marines climbed out of their rain gear.

"Always," the Pinkerton replied. He earned a frown in response.

"You will have to do the talking." Waite continued, "One word from any of our men and the ruse is discovered."

"Yeah, the jig's up; got it. But I won't be able to keep it up long, 'cause I don't know nuthin' about no damn boats."

"Well, you can fake being a sailor, better than I can fake being an American."

"You got that right." He rushed to add, "No offence, but you talk like that pouncey boy in 'British Blondes'. And that one," he jerked his thumb at Grant, "sounds like a vaudeville Long John Silver."

Waite grinned and then addressed the marines. "All right, sergeant, get your men below decks."

"Aye, aye." Sergeant Beam turned to his men. "You heard the man, down below." The men grumbled as they packed into the malodorous cabin.

"Stay down," the commander ordered. "We don't want any chance of them seeing you through the windows."

Petty Officer Grant shoveled more coal into the steamer and checked the pressure. If they were going into battle he wanted to ensure he had a full head up.

"Coxswain, everything cleared?" the commander asked.

"Aye, sir."

"Then make way up the river at half speed."

In a few minutes, they saw the smoke from a steam tug in the distance, and within minutes, they pulled within shouting distance.

"That steam tug's not your boat, is it?" Greer asked.

"No."

"Don't see it." said the Pinkerton, with a note of concern.

"It's only thirty feet long; most likely behind the tug." Waite frowned. They had discussed how to proceed if the boat was not present and there were few good options.

Tommy O'Connor peered at the approaching launch through the fancy binocs that had been in the boat when they nicked it; a theft so easy that it seemed a lark at the time. Born and raised in Brooklyn, New York, the ginger-haired lad took his Irish heritage very seriously and was proud of his position in the Fenian Brotherhood. But Tommy was near beside himself in frustration. The elders were fighting over the finances and were on the verge of just leaving the weapon that they paid for in the hands of the fat cat Holland. That is, until John J. Breslin himself, asked Tommy go and get what was rightfully theirs. So, on a moonless night last November, Tommy rented a steam tug and, along with Young Pat and two other Fenians, accompanied their leader down to the docks at the Morris and Cummings pier and gave the guard a forged letter.

Apparently no one thought it odd that Holland wanted his craft moved under cover of darkness. They just tied the boat to the stern, added Holland's little "pleasure boat" for good measure and steamed off. With the two boats in tow, the Fenians had their procession nearly to Whitestone Point when the plan fell apart. The unattended smaller boat started sinking. The tow rope to the small boat snapped, the jolt nearly jerking the deck from beneath his feet. Tommy was just about to dive into the water, as if he could do something. Breslin laid a reassuring hand on his shoulder. "We got what we came for."

Tommy's reverie was interrupted by a man on the approaching launch waving at him. "Pat," Tommy called. Two men looked up in anticipation while Tommy removed his worn grey workman's flat cap and waved back. He used his other hand to smooth out his bristly hair. "Not you Paddy," he said. "Young Pat, come here."

Pat levered himself off the deck where he had been half drowsing. "They coming?" he asked with a hint of an Irish accent, tempered by years of living in New York.

"Yeah," Tommy replied. His name was Irish, but his voice was pure Brooklyn. "Looks to be four of them, with a two-man crew and they don't look like sailors to me."

Concern tinged Pat's voice. "Do they look like coppers?"

"No, they look like bankers—derby hats and fancy coats."

"Well the Delamater Company said they was sending engineers." Pat replied. "I wouldn't put it past Holland . . ." he started in an irate tone.

"Yeah, but Holland's not running the show, now is he?" Tommy interrupted. "We're dealing directly with the company and they made it clear they just want money." He inspected the approaching steam launch for any sign of aggression. The incoming craft slowed, coming to a stop about ten feet away under the deft control of a tall fellow at the wheel.

Tommy walked to the bow, cupped his hands, and yelled, "You from the Delamater Ironworks?"

One of the men, wearing a derby hat and a long drooping mustache, leaned over the bow of his craft. He cupped his hand and shouted, "You have the money?"

Tommy held up a mailbag. The Fenian Brotherhood promised John Holland a final payment of $1,500, which brought the financial dispute to a head. Tommy and his pals had raised a third of that, and offered it to the Delamater Company. Two days later, a representative contacted them saying they would honor an agreement.

The man with the mustache waved forward and the steam launch crept toward the bow of the tug where a gangplank was extended. Once it was in place, the four men boarded the tug, and the tall sailor at the wheel handed the helm to a shorter, darkly tanned man, and fell in with the boarding party.

"Let's see it," the man with the mustache demanded as he stepped on the deck.

Tommy sprung the snap link holding the bag closed and pulled apart the top to show the contents.

The man in the derby grunted satisfaction and extended his left hand for the bag. He exaggerated the turn of his body so that his coat momentarily obscured his right hand.

Tommy handed over the bag and the man drew back, his right hand emerging from the coat with the Colt Peacemaker, the hammer already drawn back.

"This can be right peaceable," he said with exaggerated affability, "if'n you don't do anything stupid."

The rest of the Pinkertons produced their weapons. Young Pat on the upper deck by the wheelhouse, grabbed a sawed-off shotgun from under the railing, but froze as a rifle shot rang out.

The compact sailor called out from the other boat in a Cornish accent, "Next shot takes yer bloody head clean off."

Pat looked up to see four riflemen in the other boat with their weapons trained on him. He took the shotgun and held it in one hand, raised it over his head, then laid it on the deck, and put his hands back in the air.

The Pinkerton glanced up to see if the Fenian had complied. Tommy, in the split second distraction, made a dash for it and ran across the narrow deck, jumping in the cold river. The city boy was not much of a swimmer, but suddenly very motivated, he made a lot of splashing, moving away from the boat. When no one shot or pursued him, four more men joined him.

Commander Waite rushed across the boat as if making a belated chase, but then stopped, "It's here!"

The Pinkerton looked at the remaining two men on deck. "You boys with them, or hires?"

The older one shrugged. "We're sympathetic, but we work for the skipper." He jerked a thumb at the wheelhouse. As if in response, the wheelhouse door opened and the captain stepped out, his hands over his head. "Don't want no trouble," he announced.

The lead detective gently released the hammer and holstered his revolver. "No one wants any trouble. Just come on down here." After checking that his men were fine, the detective picked up the heavy canvas and leather mail bag and walked across the tug to join the commander on the far rail. The two men peered over the edge.

"What in tarnation is that damn thing?" said the detective, "Some sort of ironclad?"

The tugboat captain clattered down the boat's ladder, and the Pinkerton tore his eyes from the strange boat and faced the skipper. "Your boat for hire?" he asked in a calm, even voice.

"I got a choice?" The captain matched his tone.

The Pinkerton chuckled. "Man's always got a choice." He tossed the bag so it landed at the captain's feet. "Ever been to New York?"

A quarter of a mile away, the five Fenians staggered from the water and Paddy collapsed to his knees, still gasping for air.

"We'll get some men; we'll take it back." Tommy swore.

"Leave it," Paddy coughed out, his thick brogue nearly incomprehensible to the Americans. He took a deep breath. "The 'ole damn boat thing was a' arseways gobshite idea fro' the git. It pract'ly bankrupted the Brother'd; we'd be mite thick to be tossin' any more time o' gelt inta it."

"But it's our boat!" Tommy screamed, his hands clenched in impotent rage.

"Well, screw them," Young Pat said and spit on the ground, "it's their boat now."

5

Chapter One – March 1887

I am chagrinned to admit my part started in a cheap sailor's pub, just outside Whitechapel. A glass of gin was three pennies and, as I had recently gone from half pay to suspended pay while I awaited the court of inquiry, the price set well with my purse. Besides, my inclination was for oblivion rather than genteel company or surroundings. Whiskey, and now cheap gin, were the only things that kept my blind eye from seeing the dead and dying amid the flames, or hearing their screams amid the rush of black water. If I imbibed enough, it could even dull the "hysterical" pain that burned across my back and down my left arm almost to the stump of my wrist. That was what the learned doctors called it, unable to determine the cause. I've learned not to admit it still exists to avoid bearing the label "hysteric," that they slapped on my mother. My father was greatly relieved when she finally succeeded at suicide. My naval revolver weighed heavy in my pocket and as many nights, I considered giving him the same relief by applying the device to my temple.

The night was cold; thick yellow fog clung to the streetlamps as my wandering led me to the Fouled Anchor pub. The thick air seemed to leech the illumination from the lanterns in the cramped space, leaving a shadowy atmosphere of flickering half-light that smelled of tar and the stink of burning coal, the scent clinging to the sailors serving on the "black gang" that stoked the great coal fires.

I was bundled into a corner where my sketchbook of mechanical drawings would not arouse undue attention. I held it down with the stump of my left wrist while I drew refinements to the device I envisioned. Before the accident, I was considered quite handsome. I was among the tallest in my class at university, standing near unto six feet, and I was renowned for playing rugby. My chest was broad and my limbs were stout. My thick hair is still black and my remaining eye is blue. Although I have endeavored to keep up my strength, my frame has become more compact.

My mind wandered as I considered my reduced fortunes compared to those of the British Empire. I cannot put my finger on exactly when things started to go bad for each of us, but I have felt for some time that all history, not just my life, has not worked out the way it should. The string of defeats in North and South Africa, starting with the Zulu disaster and followed by invasion of our colonies by native warriors, threatened to collapse the realm. Even our proud navy started to implode as quiet, private internal divisions became fractious public business and led to a complete restructuring of the military. The restructuring seemed to be holding, but many people resented some of the rough compromises arranged to placate different factions.

A hush fell over the room as a gentleman walked in. I had assumed a conventional sailor's woolen jacket with a knitted watch cap to blend in with regular seamen, and the eye patch and missing hand went a long way to complete the impression. But the man in the elegant frock coat and top hat stood out like a swan that had blundered into a nest of crows.

He stood as if he were quite comfortable in his surroundings, accustomed to the ways of rough men, though not a party to them. To my eye, he seemed to be a former ship's captain, tall and craggy as if he were carved from granite, with steel grey muttonchops along the side of his face. He carried a serviceable walking stick with nonchalant grace, and had about his neck a thick red and grey striped tie that resembled an old-fashioned cravat. As he looked purposefully around the room, even the hushed conversations fell to complete silence and men turned away from his hawk-like gaze.

He spied me and although I looked away, his eyes narrowed and he made his way directly to me.

"Is this place free?" he inquired, nodding to the seat across from me. I shrugged.

He removed his topper and set it on the table as he sat down. "You can be a hard man to find, Commander Rollins."

"Commander was a brevet rank." I said as I held the cup of gin in my hand and tilted it up to study it. "Senior lieutenant and not even that for much longer."

I had received the temporary rank to fill in as an engineering officer, a specialty still in short supply among the senior ranks. This is the reason I would be retained on active duty despite my injuries, even if I became a disgraced perpetual lieutenant.

He produced a card identifying him as Michael Cooper-Smythe.

"I have come from the admiralty," he said, with a voice accustomed to command.

"I had guessed." I looked him in the eye. "You are far too tidy to be a bill collector."

He pursed his lips.

I looked around the room at sailors pretending to ignore us while actually straining to hear what we said.

"I *attempted*, to find you at the officer's mess, but they had not seen you in some time," he said slowly. "It seems there is some business about an arrears."

I looked down at my tin cup. "I'll pay it soon," I promised with more confidence than I felt.

7

"No need. I took the liberty of settling your account."

My jaw dropped in surprise, and my eyes narrowed in suspicion. "Thank you for your generosity. I will ensure—"

"I then sought you at your lodging." He talked over my words as if he didn't hear them. "The landlady was most anxious to find you; it seems there was a bit of an arrears there, as well."

I started to speak, but he waved me silent.

"I took the liberty of settling that, too." He tapped the table by my drink. "I can even settle your tab here if need be."

I lifted the tin mug and drank. "No need. Cash up front only."

"Quite," he said, his voice amused.

"I would assume there is a purpose to your generosity?"

"No generosity involved; it will be deducted from your pay." His smile was not friendly, but predatory. "I have been charged to make certain that you report to the admiralty tomorrow at 1000. The board of inquiry will render its final verdict."

"It isn't scheduled for weeks."

"Schedules change," he said as he nonchalantly shrugged one shoulder.

Such a sudden change felt ominous. I drew in a deep breath and let it out slowly.

"Am I to testify?" I picked up the cup and swirled the contents.

He frowned and shook his head. "There will be no need. We have your deposition, as well as testimony of the rest of the crew."

I set the cup down with a bang that drew more attention than I wanted. "But you are saying that I may not speak on my behalf."

"I am saying that there is no need for you to put any further statement into the record." His voice was as cold as steel and intense as live steam

I could barely keep the hurt and anger out of my voice. "The initial—"

He raised a hand and his voice lowered in volume, though not intensity. "The initial inquiry board was in a quandary concerning the veracity of your version of events. The statements by the officer of the watch, and the captain, seemed to indicate that your version should be discounted; that your injuries may have clouded your recollection."

I bit my upper lip. That was a tactful way of putting it. The captain had said that I lied. That was when my pay was suspended.

"My memory is crystal clear," I said.

Cooper-Smythe sighed. "You misunderstand. The testimony of the crew, particularly the chief engineer and his mates, has borne out your tale."

I looked at him, unable to comprehend.

He picked up the tin cup and sniffed at it, disdaining the quality of the liquor, before moving it away from me. "You will need to be in full uniform, sober, and attentive in the morning."

8

I nodded dumbly.

He rose, retrieved his top hat and sat it upon his head. "The court is in a hurry because you are needed to fill a very particular vacancy, and they want you to report to your new billet as soon as practicable."

He tipped his hat at me. "I must wish you luck, commander. You are going to need it."

For the first time in months, I returned to my lodgings at 22 Connaught Square before the streetlamps were extinguished. I was greeted at the door by the landlady, Mrs. Hawn, who I'd been dodging for almost a month. Her apron had been freshly starched in the morning, but now it sagged a bit and was smudged by a light dusting of flour; otherwise she was crisp in appearance and manner as when she was a nurse in the Crimean War, over twenty years before. Her welcoming smile let me know that the man from the Admiralty had at least spoken the truth about making good on my arrears.

I arose early the next day and made my ablutions, including shaving for the first time in days, before dragging my uniform from the wardrobe, and proceeding to brush it properly. The buttons had become very tarnished. It took much longer than I expected to restore them to a proper polish.

The dark blue uniform still had the three stripes of gold braid denoting my brevet rank. I briefly considered removing the third, but I had never been formally stripped of the rank, and I decided that if they wanted to degrade me, they could work for it. I regarded myself in the mirror. The coat hung loosely on me as I had lost flesh in the last year, but I decided that I could pass muster, as long as one disregarded the missing hand and eye. As a final touch, I retrieved the seaman's hook from the bottom of the wardrobe where I had thrown it in disgust six month ago. I slid the leather cuff over my stump and laced it on tightly.

The hearing was scheduled at the building commonly referred to as The Old Admiralty or, more properly, the Ripley Building. It was a three story, U-shaped, surprisingly plain-looking brick building located in a cluster of five buildings between Whitehall and the Mall.

Upon entering, I removed the new style peaked cap and carried it stiffly under my left arm as I walked to the designated chambers. I joined Captain William "Jab" Clarke, formally master of Her Majesty's Steamship (experimental) *Indomitable*, and Senior Lieutenant Richard Gaither, formally the fifth officer of the same.

The good captain acknowledged my presence by inclining his head; just enough to glare at me down his aristocratic nose. His face was one born to be chiseled into marble monuments, but so far, he had failed to distinguish himself as a junior officer, and the ill-fated *Indomitable* had been his highest command.

Gaither, on the other hand, had distinguished himself early, but fell victim to a tropical fever while serving in India. He survived the fever but never really regained his previous stamina or acumen, and was fated to remain forever a lieutenant. The illness left an indelible mark on his body, leaving him unnaturally thin with folds of flesh on his face and dark sunken eyes. Those eyes narrowed at my approach and he studied me as if I were a vagrant who wandered into a proper neighborhood. His jaw clenched in disdain.

After a few awkward, if not actually hostile minutes of silence, the door to the inquiry chamber opened and Gaither, who had served as officer of the watch that night, was summoned.

He returned less than five minutes later. He carefully closed the door to the chamber and addressed the captain in his harsh raspy voice, a sound that did not carry so well through the speaking tubes, or even across an open deck. "They just asked me to reaffirm my deposition, and then dismissed me."

Captain Clarke nodded.

The clerk of the court announced, "Will Captain William Clarke please present himself to the board." While the sentence was framed as a request, it was spoken as a command.

Captain Clarke rose stiffly, marched into chambers, and he, too, walked out after just a few minutes. I took note that his braid was still in place. He ignored me and turned to Gaither.

"It seems that our boilermaker has moved into the 'Old Boy Network.'"

Gaither nodded and then looked daggers at me.

The captain turned to me. "Education cannot make you a seaman, and it certainly cannot make you a gentleman." He strode out with Gaither on his heels.

I was summoned and marched into the hearing chamber. The room was enormous; the walls decorated with large oil paintings depicting Trafalgar, the battle of the Nile, Drake at Cadiz, and the defeat of the Spanish Armada. There was no furniture save for the ornately carved wooden table, behind which sat four serving captains and Admiral Wainwright of the First Fleet, acting as the president of the board. I knew two of the men, but the others were strangers to me. I had served as a lieutenant under Captain Raymond "Streak" Stevens (so called because of an incident during his middie cruise involving white paint and an admiral's daughter). I also knew Captain Arthur "Tug" Wilson by reputation.

I stopped ten feet from the table and saluted. The admiral was a tall lean man with thick, snowy white hair and matching bushy eyebrows. On the table in front of him was a new style peaked cap that he chose to wear, even though he'd only set foot in the academy as an instructor. In front of all the officers were ink-stained manila folders, stuffed with papers and photographs.

Admiral Wainwright returned the salute and spoke for the board. "Senior Lieutenant Rollins, please step forward."

He paused for a moment and frowned. "I see you are still wearing commander's rank."

I was actually terrified to stand before these accomplished officers, knowing that they were going to pass judgment without my testimony and without any chance for appeal. Cooper-Smythe, whose card was still in my pocket, had indicated that I was to be exonerated, but from the stern faces looking at me I could scarce credit it. Squaring my shoulders I tried to stand tall and sound-stout hearted, even though the shift in my shoulders triggered the painful spasm down my arm.

"I have not received notification that it had been revoked." The words came out a trifle more defiant than I intended.

The admiral leaned forward to rest his elbows on the table, steepling his fingers, and tapping them against his chin as he looked me up and down, then nodded. "Very well."

There was momentary gleam in his eye, but from his stoic countenance I could not tell if it was amusement or irritation. He nodded to Captain Wilson, who was keeping the record. "Please amend the record to denote that *Commander* Ian Rollins has reported."

The admiral motioned me to approach. I stepped forward until I was less than a foot from the table. On the surface before me were a fountain pen and a document I recognized as a copy of the official secrets act.

"Please sign."

I took the proffered pen and signed without reservation. I had signed the same paper over a dozen times in the last year and perhaps a hundred times in my career. The projects I have been working on are all experimental and extremely confidential. I had no qualms about signing, but I did not understand *why* I was signing, as all court martial proceeding are supposed to be open. In fact, I fully expected to read the result of this hearing in the daily shipping news.

"You will acknowledge that these proceedings are closed, and you will not divulge anything about them."

I nodded slowly.

"Please answer verbally."

The Admiral nodded toward Captain Wilson, looking to ensure my reply was entered into the record transcription.

It suddenly dawned on me how unusual it was for a serving captain to be doing a clerk's task. "I so acknowledge," I said.

A door opened to my left and Mr. Cooper-Smythe slipped into the room. The members of the board could obviously see him, but they took no notice.

"I must impress upon you the confidential nature of this inquiry," the admiral continued. "You have signed the official secrets act, and now I will inform you that the judgment of this court is rendered classified. You may not now, or at any time in the future, discuss the result."

"I don't understand."

This time I could plainly see amusement twinkling in the admiral's grey eyes. "You do not understand the meaning of 'classified'?"

"No sir," I replied. "I do not understand why court records would be, or could be, classified."

He leaned back in his chair and jabbed a finger at me in a short choppy motion. "Because the captain and the rest of the crew have been given a fabricated resolution."

I stared at him, as stunned as a midshipman at his first gunnery exercise when the eight-inchers go off and the deck rocks with the recoil. "Beg pardon?" I choked out.

He leaned forward and mouthed the words slowly. "We lied to the captain." His voice was tinged with anger. "The official findings and records will be adjusted to match the lie." His face clouded with barely concealed contempt.

I gaped at him, still not comprehending.

He leaned back, and tapped his forefingers together. "Due to the actual findings, and the nature of your new assignment, you will need to know the truth." The admiral picked up the folder in front of him.

"The official verdict, for the public record, is that Seaman Willard, who perished in the accident, mishandled the steam valves going to the experimental steam turret, resulting in a fast-moving fire that asphyxiated the engineering staff and ultimately destroyed the ship."

I nodded. The steam turret had been laid on a decommissioned wooden-hulled steamship. The ship was a Frankenstein's monster whose only purpose was to test an automatic turning and aiming system. However, it could sail, so it was assigned a crew and recommisioned as the HMS *Indomitable*, holding that name until Her Majesty's Royal Navy could launch a new gunboat. Tradition demanded that names such as "Indomitable" always be in commission.

"Allow me to review your deposition." He studied the papers in front of him, squinting to make out the faded writing. "You had retired to your cabin, which you shared with the ship's doctor, and were about to repair to bed, when you felt something wrong in the ship?"

I nodded, and then remembered the transcript. "Yes."

He looked up from the paper. "Could you elaborate?"

I looked up and down the panel; their eyes watched me intently. "There was something odd in the way the ship moved, the noises it made."

"I see." The admiral seemed satisfied with my answer and returned to the papers. "You then went to the bridge, to find the officer of the watch embroiled in a disciplinary matter."

"Yes sir, a drunken sailor on watch."

"Since the watch officer was engaged, you took it upon yourself, as acting third officer, to use the ship's Chadburn telegraph to signal the engine room for a status report."

"Yes, sir."

"And the telegraph returned a signal of green?"

"Yes, sir." I hesitated, even though the signal had been green.

"But that wasn't good enough for you?"

"It was too fast." I paused for breath and arranged the facts in my head. "Sir, even if the chief engineer had just finished doing a survey of all systems, I would still expect a delay of one or two minutes. Under normal conditions, I would not expect a reply for five to ten minutes."

"And that made you suspicious, so you hastened to the boiler room."

"Yes, sir."

The admiral scanned the paper in front of him. "And there you found the section in flames, half the watch crew dead, the rest overcome by smoke and flame."

He put down my deposition and picked up another paper. "Have you been allowed to see the other depositions?"

"No, sir. I have also been ordered not to discuss the incident with anyone."

"According to the chief engineer, he regained his senses to find you dragging bodies out of the boiler room, until the boiler exploded."

"That makes it sound very heroic, but I just moved the men with a pulse out to the corridor and telegraphed the bridge."

"Quite so. Your actions saved three men from the boiler watch, and the rest of the crew."

I stood silently.

He picked up another deposition. "Except, the officer on duty and the captain maintain that you recklessly ran into the boiler room because of imagined distress, interfered with the watch crew, and caused the fire."

I stood mute.

"Captain Clarke goes on to speculate that you may have been drunk, or possibly helped yourself to some of the medicinals that your roommate stocked."

I started to protest, but he just kept talking.

"Our investigation shows that you acted correctly. More than that, your actions leading up to the discovery of the fire show a special sense of seamanship. The fact that you instinctively knew there was something wrong, that intimate 'feel' for the ship and crew only the best officers develop, goes to your credit, especially given the unusual course of your career. There are many serving officers who believe an officer like yourself, after taking leave from the service to pursue a scientific degree, loses the feel of the sea, and cannot develop the necessary instincts to command a ship. "

"I am familiar with that sentiment."

The admiral nodded, and made an inviting gesture to Mr. Cooper-Smythe, who approached the table.

"I have just a couple of questions." He leveled his gaze at me until he was sure he had my full attention. "Who telegraphed 'green' to the bridge?"

Suddenly startled, I looked at the members of the board, as if they may have the answer, then looked back. "I think that I was under the impression that it was an error." I spoke carefully not wanting to wrongly accuse anyone. "The last report had been green, and I thought perhaps the device malfunctioned from the fire and repeated the last status."

"But it worked fine when you sent the fire alarm?" Cooper-Smythe pressed.

I did not know what to say.

Cooper-Smythe addressed me in his unhurried way, as if he were now speaking for the board. "We have determined that the fire and explosion were, in fact, deliberate sabotage and without your quick action, it would never have been known."

I stood open-mouthed in shock. My jaw worked for a moment, until words came out. "Who is this 'we'?"

The admiral spoke up. "Mr. Cooper-Smythe here is with the clandestine branch of the Naval Intelligence Division."

"There is no clandestine branch," I said, and then stopped when I realized how stupid the remark sounded to my own ears. The division had only recently been created from the Foreign Intelligence Committee and was publicly recognized to have two branches—foreign intelligence and mobilization.

Cooper-Smythe explained, "The board here will release an official verdict of misadventure, and we will, unfortunately be forced to besmirch the name of Seaman Willard. Once the affair is truly settled, we will correct the record, of course."

The admiral took over. "Your actions have been determined to uphold the highest traditions of the royal navy. You will be reinstated and confirmed in the rank of commander. However, you need to know this: the experimental steam-ship was destroyed by an agent of the German Empire."

I looked up, even more startled.

"But this can never be known. You cannot reveal this to anyone. Besides besmirching Willard, we will not be awarding the Albert Cross to you at this time, though you deserve it."

"But why me?" I blurted out, "Why am I above the suspicion of the board, especially after the captain's deposition?"

"Because, our investigation covered the background and movements of every man aboard that ship," said Cooper-Smyth. "Every officer is effectively a suspect, except you."

"Because I was injured?"

"No, because we can account for every second of your time, leading up to the fire. You are the only one we can trust to assist. And–we need your expertise on another matter."

The admiral turned to Captain Wilson. "Is there anything you would like to add?"

The captain looked up from his notes and studied me.

I looked back at those cool blue eyes set in a dark wind-burned face half covered by a full, well-groomed beard. I had heard of Captain

Wilson's exploits in the Mediterranean. He earned the Victoria Cross at the battle of El Teb. If other ships had been able support his actions, or exploit the gains he made, we would still hold North Africa.

"No," he replied with a tight smile. "I suppose he will do."

The admiral pushed back from the table and waved for Captain Wilson to stand. "Continue, by all means, captain."

"Commander Rollins, your decision to pursue a technical education after the academy separates you from most of the officer corp."

I nodded.

"The secrecy of this court and rumors about the *Indomitable* will also create a rift with your fellows. So, you are now being asked to do something that will forever separate you."

He turned his head to address the board, "We will give him one last chance to decline."

The admiral started to speak, but I interrupted. "With all due respect, I cannot imagine how I could be more apart than I am at this point."

"Excellent, because you will be working for me, and I expect you to shake things up." Captain Wilson's face maintained the tight smile, but there was a glint of mischief in his eye. "What you will be working on is underhanded, unfair, and damned un-English."

"I see."

"Odds are, this assignment will kill you. If you survive, and are ever captured by the enemy, you will be hanged on the spot."

I looked from Captain Wilson to Mr. Cooper-Smythe. "I do not think I would make a very good spy."

Captain Wilson raised his head and gave a barking laugh. "No, your duties will be much more complicated than mere skullduggery."

Chapter Two

I arrived back at my lodging with my head spinning and a set of orders that I was not to open, let alone read. All the way home I inspected the way the bright red wax seal of the Admiralty office was affixed to the heavy envelope, turning it this way and that to see how I might gain access to the papers undetected.

Captain Wilson, my new commanding officer, merely explained that he would call for me in the morning at 0900 at my lodgings, and accompany me to my new assignment. He informed me that I would not be leaving the city of London immediately as my duty lay at the Port of London, and he hinted at the possibility of independent command. When I asked him if he was referring to a ship or one of the port facilities, he just laughed and asked if I could swim.

It was nearly time for tea, so I removed the hook from my sweaty stump, but this time I cleaned it well and placed it on a shelf. I idly wondered if there was something I could line the leather cuff with that would be more comfortable, but still be secure.

During my enforced idleness, my personal routines and good habits became lax. I worked at reapplying myself, and just as I finished brushing my uniform coat and hanging it in the closet, I heard an insistent knock at the door. Puzzled, I turned toward the entry. Mrs. Hawn was the vigilant guardian of the street entrance, hence no one should be at the door of my flat without being announced. Besides Mrs. Hawn never pounded on my door in such a manner, even when I owed her money.

I opened it to find a man dressed in a rough grey sack suit, a long cotton kerchief tied around his neck, his nervous fingers crumpling a cloth cap. He stood about medium height, though his frame was bent from age. He had a crown of snow white hair around an acre of pink scalp. His eyes were a muddy sea green; his squashed nose was red veined and pockmarked.

"Beggin' yer pardon, yer Lordship," he began in a hesitant voice.

"Good God, Jenkins," I interrupted. "I am no more a lord than I am king of Araby. I believe your wages were current when you left?" I understood how he passed the venerable Mrs. Hawn. After I was brevetted a commander, Captain Clarke insisted I hire a valet, even though it was financially challenging, as my brevet rank paid the same as a senior lieutenant. But despite my protests, Jenkins was foisted on me. Do not mistake me: Jenkins, when sober, was a mostly serviceable valet and very entertaining with tales of his several years as a shipboard steward for a most remarkable admiral. I suspect some of the tales are even true—maybe.

But he was very fond of drink, and gambling, and women of uncertain virtue. As a person, I kind of liked him, but I am not the sort of person who is comfortable with a valet.

"Beggin' yer pardon . . ." he began again, and paused. "Commander Rollins, I am seekin' a position."

"Excuse me?"

He fidgeted, but continued on, more confident. "I hears . . ." I could see his concentration as he made the "h" sound. It was not natural to him and he tried to remember to enunciate. "I hear that you have been fully promoted, so you will be needin' a valet." He had practiced his ending "g" when he was with me, but he seemed to have backslid.

I frowned. Truth be told, I did not want a valet. "I thought you found another position."

He drew himself up to full height. "Indeed sir, I found a position. There are good people who recognize the value of my service."

"Well, then." I made to say good bye and close the door.

He blocked it with his hand. "He is a Methodist, sir."

"Who?"

"My new employer, sir."

I saw the conflict and suppressed a chuckle. "I gather he does not look fondly on drink?"

He sighed. "Or on any other joy o' life, sir. I think it's his goal to make this life so miserable, that you'll jump at any chance for the next. Free with a Bible verse, he is, and ready to point out me sins, for me own good."

I looked down at the stump of my left hand, and thought how much easier my life would be with someone to do a few of the chores. And, I knew Jenkins's faults already. There is something to be said for dealing with the devil you know.

"Very well, you may start by cleaning the sitting room."

He brightened considerably. "Thank you, sir. Might I start tomorrow? I will need to clear accounts with the Methodist."

"Of course," I replied. I suspected that he would also be clearing accounts with a certain pub at the end of the block.

That night, I fidgeted in my bed for some hours, unable to find a comfortable position. I finally fell into a restless slumber, only to awake with a start. My breath came in short gasps, and my heart pounded in my chest. A scalding finger tracked down my arm with a network of agony that seared the cords of my muscles. The smoke and fire was so thick in my head that I had to physically shake my skull and rub my eyes before I was convinced the flames were not real. Gin removes the pain, but I do not know if it actually keeps away the dreams or I sleep so deeply I do not recall them. For now I just hoped I hadn't called out in my sleep, or a frantic Mrs. Hawn would be knocking at my door.

Hours later, I managed to doze slightly until dawn progressed further. I arose to find my shaving water and towel prepared. I arranged myself into a dressing gown, an affectation I usually avoided, but Jenkins would tut-tut me if I appeared in my shirtsleeves. Once I stepped out of my chambers, I appreciated the gown as the spring morning was unusually cool and no fire had been set.

I found Jenkins in the sitting room, brushing my uniform coat, and I have to admit it already looked much better for his effort. He was working industriously, if a bit unsteadily, and there was an air of old whiskey and beer about him. The sack suit was not in evidence and he wore his inside clothes, striped trousers with a woolen waistcoat under a short black jacket. He sported a tightly knotted blue-and-black striped tie over a white shirt with a boiled front, collar, and cuffs.

"The kettle is on to boil, and the paper is on the table." His speech was slightly slurred.

"Thank you." As if to underscore his words, a faint whistle sounded from the small gas stove by the cupboard.

"Have a seat, I'll fetch that, sir."

By the time I lifted the paper, he carried in a small tray bearing a bone china cup and a steaming teapot with the teaball steeping, and set it on the table for me. "Will Mrs. Hawn be bringin' breakfast?" he asked as he filled the cup.

"I will have to have a word with her. I am afraid the larder is bare."

"As you're busy, if you like, I could have a word with her." He looked at me expectantly.

I took his meaning and extracted some banknotes from my dressing gown. "I think, for the time being, we should get by if she could provide a hot breakfast and a cold luncheon. I will be dining at the mess for a bit."

"Understood, sir."

I finished my tea in silence.

There was a polite knock on the door.

"Come in," I called out. Jenkins shot me a look of disapproval and walked over to answer the door properly.

"It's just Mrs. Hawn," I protested.

Jenkins opened the door the proper distance. His personal habits might be dubious, but as valet, he knew the proper way to do everything.

I heard Mrs. Hawn's voice.

"Carriage here for the commander."

I looked at my watch; the captain was early. I hurriedly strapped on my hook, waving away Jenkins's offer of assistance with more anger than was called for, but I did allow him to assist me with my coat. I put on my hat, slipped my still-sealed orders into my portfolio, which I tucked under my arm, and grabbed my case. The designs I had been working on were near completion and provided comfort, so I decided to keep working on them as the occasion presented itself.

I stepped out into the crisp morning air. The smell of bread baking and the fresh breeze gave temporary relief to the air of coal ash and horse that hung over the city. Captain Wilson was pacing by a hansom cab, though not as if he were impatient, but rather too excited to sit still. We clambered aboard and the horses set off.

I extracted the sealed orders. "May I read them now?"

"Not presently. There is one more thing I need to know about you, and you need to know about yourself, before I can share much more concerning your assignment. Today is actually going to be a sort of test. If you pass, then the orders stand. If not, they never existed." That enigmatic statement brought an end to conversation.

The Port of London is the largest in the world and extends more than eleven miles, stretching from the center of the city to the North Sea. A longer ride than I expected brought us out past the East India Dock to the Thames Ironworks and Ship Building Company located near Leamouth. I had not been to the port in the last two years. The squat grey buildings and the massive dry docks had been augmented by what appeared to be a lighthouse rivaling what had been London's only lighthouse, the experimental one just the other side of Bow Creek at Trinity Buoy Wharf. Unlike that traditional pile of stone, this edifice was built atop one of the foundry works. It seemed to be constructed of a lattice work of iron beams, apparently painted with a bronze color that stood out starkly from the industrial grey sooty structures. I also noted that two smoke-stacks had been built much higher, so that soot would blow away from the structure.

The carriage rolled down to the dock. We passed through a guard of red-jacketed Royal Marines and stopped by the wharf.

Forty men stood to attention as we alighted from the coach.

Captain Wilson waved his hand first to the men, then to the seemingly empty dock. "This may be your new command," he said quietly, his lips pressed together in a tight smile.

"How likely?"

He licked his lips. "First, you have to get through today." He nodded again to the empty dock. "I assume you are looking forward to seeing her?"

I looked at the men lined up for inspection. Thirty common and able seamen, three lieutenants, one senior lieutenant, and one crusty old salt I took to be the coxswain, or most senior enlisted sailor. They stood rigidly face front, but I could feel their eyes sizing me up.

The captain gestured again at the empty dock.

I suspected that there was some joke at my expense, but I walked over to the seemingly unoccupied boat slip anyway, expecting maybe to see a pinnace or other small craft down low.

My breath caught in my throat at the first sight of the thick layers of flat grey paint covering a watertight hatch atop a small tear-shaped cupola that jutted roughly two feet out of the water. Two steps more and the neat lines of the craft came into view. A sense of childish glee rose inside me, fighting against a crushing realization of what was expected of me.

To me, the boat was beautiful, a marvel of engineering. It was awash, only the top of her rounded hull broke the surface of the water. I could see the cupola was situated more toward the stern of the craft, which was marked by long narrow wings and a huge propeller that I could barely see in shadows. Thirty feet long, six feet wide, and barely moving in the tide.

For a moment, I heard not but the gentle lapping of water against this incredible vessel.

"A submersible," I breathed out. I'd heard the navy had acquired one, but I never expected to actually see it, let alone be involved with its activity.

"Aye," the captain said. "Allow me to present Her Majesty's Submersible *Holland Ram*."

"*Holland Ram*," I repeated, my mind trying to focus. "That is an odd name, I heard we acquired one from America, or is it Dutch?"

There was an peculiar twinkle in his eyes. "It is an odd tale, but Holland is the name of the man who built it, and it is American."

I shook my head slowly in wonder. "How did it get here?" I imagined the craft crossing the Atlantic, but no, it must have been towed.

He smiled. "We stole her." He frowned. "Probably legally." His manner led me to believe he wasn't going to say any more.

I looked back at the men, still standing at rigid attention, their faces forward, but I knew they were taking in everything. "Seems a large crew for such a small boat."

"The craft takes three at a time," Wilson explained. "Every man jack you see has been down at least ten times. We will need to build up a cadre of experience if I am to command the Royal Navy Submersible Fleet."

"Can you have a fleet with one boat?"

He smiled wolfishly and the mischievous gleam was back in his eye. He tapped a finger to the side of his nose. "You know as much as you need to know until you are presented with orders."

Turning, he waved to the man wearing the rank of senior lieutenant, who in turn selected another lieutenant and a rating, and then the three men started towards us.

I turned back to the *Ram* and bit my lip in apprehension. Reading about the exploits of Captain Nemo was one thing, but the thought of actually sinking below the waves in such a device made my stomach twist. My heart pounded just a tad too fast and my mouth went unusually dry. I was glad that the captain had not told me in advance, as I realized this was something best done quickly, before I had too much time to think about it.

"Commander Rollins," the captain interrupted my reverie. "May I present your first officer, Lieutenant Heinrich Graf?" The senior lieutenant saluted.

I startled a bit at the name and the captain came to my rescue. "The lieutenant's family made itself *persona non-grata* in the German Empire some years ago."

I returned the salute. Graf was a name frequently used by German nobles who lost their titles when leaving the empire for various reasons. He was a solid-looking, very serious man in his middle thirties with light brown hair, blue eyes, and a waxed mustache. The most startling thing about his appearance was a slightly curving scar that ran along his left cheekbone and ended just before his ear. He had a similar scar on the left side of his forehead and another, much fainter mark on the right side of his brow.

"Mensur fencer?" I asked. "Heidelberg?"

"Mensur, yes," he replied, sounding a little surprised. "Heidelberg, no." He spoke without an accent, but in slightly stilted English. "My family fled to England while I was a child. My father is the one who trained at Heidelberg. There is a Mensur club here in London, which is where I took up the sport."

I did not know why it should surprise me that such a club existed, as there were many societies devoted to all manner of physical culture in London. It is just that I always thought of Mensur as the stupidest form of martial activity. The participants hack at each other with sharpened swords, wearing only their shirt sleeves and eye covers. The goal appeared not to win or avoid injury, but suffer with the most grace.

"Do you fence?" he asked.

"No, at Edinburgh I studied with two German engineers."

"Ah," he replied vaguely." He turned to introduce a slightly younger blonde man with clear blue eyes, carrying a strong leather case on a strap over his shoulder. "This is Lieutenant Bartley. He will be driving the submersible today."

I shook hands with both men.

Lieutenant Graf addressed the captain. "How is Commander Waite doing?" His voice indifferent, as if asking a formally required question.

"Coming along nicely," Captain Wilson said. "He is expected to be released home, shortly." He turned to me. "You will want to remove your coat."

I hesitated a second, but when Lieutenant Bartley removed his, I followed suit. I am not unduly shy, but I had to admit that standing in front of my potential command in shirtsleeves was discomfiting. The rating quickly stripped off his uniform tunic to reveal the traditional striped shirt.

As soon as Bartley was out of his coat, he opened the case he carried and produced a set of finely made Italian Porro-prism binoculars. I eyed them with some pleasure, admiring the craftsmanship of the sturdy set. Perhaps it is not completely normal, but I find a well-crafted instrument or device to be almost as alluring as a lady's well-turned ankle.

"The binoculars are useful for conning the sub, and necessary for sighting the main gun."

I nodded as if I understood, but suppressed a moment of panic. If binoculars were necessary for any reason, how the devil was I going to use them?

Captain Wilson seemed to be reading my thoughts. "The binoculars are preferred not for stereoscopic vision, but rather for field of view. You can scan more of the horizon quickly. I suspect you will find ways to compensate."

"You have done your walk-through?" Lieutenant Graf asked Bartley.

"Aye," he replied, looking over at the rating. "We went through the checklist. All systems warm, in standby ready."

Lieutenant Graf seemed satisfied. "You may take command."

Bartley saluted and beckoned me to accompany him.

The seaman, who had not been introduced, deployed a gang walk from a set of rails, pushing it with small effort, allowing the far end to drop down until it clanged upon the top of the sub. He smiled mirthlessly at me and spread his hand out toward the vessel. "Mindful of your step, sir. It is a bit slippery on the conning tower."

He indicated the cupola sitting above the water and I made a mental note to get the captain to give me a full briefing on the terminology. "Thank you, Seaman . . .?"

"Able Seaman Weber, sir."

The craft bobbed slightly under my weight as I moved carefully down the steeply sloped gangplank. I paused for a minute to look out over the river, and took a deep breath. At this point of its course, the Thames is tidal, daily flushing away effluvia of the city and, early in the day, it smelled like the ocean. Well, like a part of the ocean where several things tended to rot.

When I was solidly on the conning tower, the seaman followed me on board, slipped nimbly past me, and deftly opened the hatch. "Pardon sir, you'll have to go first, and work your way to the very front."

I nodded and started to lower myself through the tiny opening. I had to squeeze my shoulders together as I passed into the tiny cramped compartment. I supported myself by pressing most of my weight on my good hand and steadied my bulk with the hook, but a fiery thread began to trace down my arm. There was no ladder or such awaiting me, but my legs swung free until they came to rest on a metal surface and I allowed my weight to settle there to ease my arm. Ducking inside, I saw I was squatting on a sort of seat made of sheet metal and I eased myself off to set my feet on the iron deck. Every inch of the hull seemed to be crammed with equipment and valves, but I managed to squeeze down between an air compressor on my left, and on my right, the most unexpected thing—an electric motor. I saw one demonstrated at school, and tried my hand at building one as a lark, but even the best were terribly inefficient, and I would think completely inadequate to power a boat.

Another set of legs swung through the hatch, so I worked my way forward as instructed. I understood why I had to go first—the space was so narrow that we would have to crawl over top of each other, although at the very front there was at least room to turn about.

A moment later, the rating climbed off the chair and stood between the compressor and motor. He closed a switch on the top of the motor and an indicator light came on. In the glow, he saw me eyeing the device. "You wouldn't have liked the first engine, sir," he said, shaking his head. "It was an oil burner, two cylinders, and had about fifteen horsepower. The air heated up right quick in those days."

Bartley slid in, squatted on the seat, and looked at me expectantly as he closed the hatch with a loud clang. The only light came from the four small, rectangular portholes on the conning tower, and the faint amber indicator light on the motor.

I guess he was satisfied by what he saw.

"Sir," Bartley said with a grim smile, "just to let you know, many people have an unpleasant reaction when the hatch is closed."

"I understand."

"It is also common for people to discover an unexpected antipathy to being underwater."

"I will keep that in mind."

"Just so you know, sir, there is no shame in being unable to stay submerged: Captain Wilson himself is unwilling to go under."

"Really?" I blinked in surprise.

"I mean," he said, his voice an uncanny mimic of the captain's, "to command submersibles as a fleet, not ride in the damned things."

I chuckled in spite of myself.

He arranged himself comfortably on the seat.

"This is the HMS *Holland Ram*," he began, "it is powered by an electric motor, which can produce twenty horsepower. Top speed of six knots on the surface, and eight knots submerged."

I looked at the motor again: I could scarce credit the claim of twenty horsepower. "I don't suppose there is a dynamo on board to power the motor?"

"That is a state secret, sir. You will be briefed as soon as you have completed a familiarization cruise."

"And you seriously expect me to believe she runs faster under water?"

"Truth, sir. The propeller is overlarge and on the surface it rides too close to the top and catches air so it is not as efficient."

I nodded. I could believe that.

"Then, if you are ready?"

"Aye," I replied. I was beginning to understand why we removed our coats. The air was getting a bit close already, or was that my imagination? I was unaware if I had any "antipathy" for being enclosed underwater, but I knew I had no head for heights, and the first symptom was the feeling of being unable to get adequate air.

Bartley grasped two upright control levers and craned his neck up to look out the ports. "Moorings away. Bring up the power."

"Aye, aye, captain." Weber closed a switch on the bulkhead.

Swan incandescent lights came on. I found their faint glow much more appealing than the Edison imports. In the dimness, I could see several more details of the boat. The captain's chair was actually situated directly over the main differential gear, with a large flywheel directly behind it. As I turned to face the front of the boat, I could see pipes and valves on my left, a rack of six-foot long cylinders with bulbous tapered noses and a fin assembly at the rear. I patted one out of curiosity.

"That would be our armament," Bartley said. "Those are dummy rounds for the compressed air gun."

I ran my hand down the smooth cylinder. The nose end tapered into a threaded, empty hole.

I addressed Weber. "You do firing drills with these?"

"Aye. Once every six month. Live fire once a year."

I fingered the opening again. You practice fitting with fuse and detonator?"

"Aye. We have inert fuses and detonators up there." He motioned to a large grey box fixed to the bulkhead just above the rounds.

I looked down and saw something that looked very much like a standard cannon breach.

"Compressed air fires one of those things about 1000 feet," Bartley explained, following my gaze. "The real ones are loaded with dynamite. You're standing in the gunner's station." Bartley touched a finger to his brow and gave a casual salute to the rating. "Weber here is actually the best gunner in the unit."

The rating smiled at the praise.

"Now, then," the lieutenant continued. "Weber, if you would give me reverse, one-eighth power."

"Aye, aye."

I heard the gears mesh under the captain's chair as Weber engaged the drive. The boat lurched beneath my feet and edged backwards away from the pier. We started slowly to avoid cavitation, which makes the propeller inefficient, but picked up speed after the blades bit the water. Once again, my emotions were working at cross purposes. On one hand, I was living out a Jules Verne adventure, but I do not think Verne imagined the smell in the close quarters. There was a reek of oil, despite the electric motor and the air was thick with the lingering odor of overheated men.

The two-man crew worked with practiced ease. The lieutenant gave commands in a calm unhurried voice as Weber replied with the traditional "Aye, Aye." One "aye" acknowledged the command, the second to declare it would be completed.

The lieutenant deftly swung the boat around. "Engine neutral," he said. As the boat slowed to a stop, he ordered, "Ahead, one-eighth." The boat lurched slightly again as Weber engaged the lever that moved the gears, and we were soon moving forward, into the harbor. He ordered the engine to three quarter power and we traveled in silence at a nice clip for about fifteen minutes. I had several questions, but I could see the concentration on both men's faces. Bartley held the levers firmly in his hand, keeping the sub moving smoothly awash, while Weber occasionally turned valves. I later learned the valves were necessary to balance the ballast before diving to make the sub more manageable under water.

At length, Lieutenant Bartley addressed me. "Are you prepared for your first dive?"

"Looking forward to it. Is there anything I need to do?"

"Just brace yourself," Bartley replied. "I think Weber has it just about right; the *Ram* is set for neutral buoyancy." He tapped the control lever on his left. "We will dive with planes alone." He smiled. "Brace now." He pushed the lever forward and the deck smoothly dipped to a sharp thirty degrees.

"Heads up!" Weber shouted, and I jerked my head to the left just in time to see the box above the dummy warheads slide forward and detach itself from the bulkhead. As it tipped, two fuse-detonator sets spilled from the unsecured lid. I instinctively tried to grab them, but I fumbled with my hand and hook, and they fell to the deck. I did manage to stop the falling box.

I braced the heavy box with my body and heaved against it, trying to set it back in its place while Bartley smartly leveled the craft.

"Weber." Bartley voice was part command and part inquiry.

The able seaman worked his way forward, took hold of the end of the box, and together we jockeyed it back to the bracket that had come loose. A broken bolt fell from the support and hit the deck with a sharp ping. Weber inspected the hole where the broken bolt came from, retrieved it, and jammed it into place as a temporary fix. I bent to retrieve the fallen items, picking up one with my good hand, while I set my foot on the other to keep it from rolling on the deck.

Weber took the first from me and opened the top of the box to place the device in the wooden cutout that housed it. I bent down to pick up the last one, grabbing it at the narrowest part close to the nose with my good hand, and froze. The very tip felt unnaturally warm against my skin. I held it firmly to the deck to keep it from moving, bent down very close and sniffed. The familiar smell of acid crinkled my nose.

"Lieutenant, we have a problem," I said, my voice sounding in the cramped chamber.

"Sir?"

"These rounds may be dummies, but this detonator has a live fuse. From the smell of the acid, it's armed."

"Weber, what the devil is a live fuse doing on board?"

Weber just looked at that lieutenant with wide eyes.

"It is worse than that," I continued. "I am not certain of the exact armament you use, but from my experience, this feels like an active detonator."

Chapter Three

To his credit, Bartley did not appear to panic, although Weber instantly went white as a sheet.

I continued to examine the fuse. This type had a timer composed of a glass tube filled with acid. When the tube broke, the acid would eat though its container, and ignite a drop of fulminate of mercury. The device would make an annoyingly aggressive pop, like a giant firecracker. The fuse was molded into a detonator which had a wad of nitrocellulose, or guncotton. This was a so-called "low explosive." It exploded with less force, and was intended to set off a much larger charge of dynamite. However, in this enclosed space, the small explosion would still be devastating.

I wrinkled my nose as the caustic vapor emanated from the regulator.

"How long is the timer?" I asked.

It was standard for this type of munition to be equipped so that if it missed its target it would still blow up, and not become a hazard later. The timer would be initiated by a sharp blow like the propellant blast from a gun. Since the *Ram's* gun used compressed air for the propellant—with a less sudden shock than guncotton—the fuse was set to activate upon a lower initial impact, like falling four feet to the steel deck of the sub.

"Six minutes. Be careful, it will also detonate on contact."

I picked the thing up cautiously with my good hand, and stabilized it with the hook. I was less worried about the contact detonator as it would be set for fairly high resistance so it would only explode when it hit something really solid.

"Can we surface and just chuck it out the hatch?"

I saw his brow furrow in concentration as he tried to figure out the timing. He gave a small shake of his head. "Better idea." He looked at the rating. "Weber, what is the gun compression status?"

Weber glanced at a gauge. "I have full compression."

"Make the round ready for firing. We'll just shoot the damn thing to the bottom."

Weber unceremoniously took the detonator from my hand and squeezed up beside me to deftly affix the device to the outermost round.

He addressed me as he wedged himself back to the side of the projectile.

"Is the tube clear?" He must have noted the confusion in my eyes. "Check the sight glass on the side of the breech. Is it empty?"

I looked to the indicated apparatus. "Aye. Sight glass empty."

"Then open the breech."

The breech block was a thick steel plate fitted into a heavy groove at the back of the gun so that a lever slid it into place to close the breech after loading. I grasped the handle firmly, and yanked it down, noting that it slid more easily than an ordinary gun.

Weber undid the latches that held the round down. I edged myself to the side and then gingerly reached for the nose of the projectile, carefully supporting the weight of the dummy warhead as Weber grabbed the main body.

He supported most of the awkwardly balanced fifty-pound weight as I carefully guided the projectile into the tube. When the round clicked into position, I raised the breech block.

"Loaded," Weber called out, his loud voice boomed in the small compartment and betrayed his relief.

"Flood the tube," Bartley commanded, his voice calm as he fell into the familiar ritual of gunnery practice.

Weber reached for a valve and spun it quickly. There was a hissing, gurgling noise that lasted half a minute. I saw the sight glass fill with water. When it reached the top I called out, "Tube flooded."

"Open tube cover." Bartley's command was almost simultaneous with my report.

Weber grabbed another valve and tried to turn it. It did not budge. He gripped with both hands; corded muscles bulged in his forearms under the effort.

"Bloody Jesus, it's stuck!"

"Curb the blasphemy, Weber," the lieutenant replied, his voice preternaturally calm. To my ear, it indicated a great effort of will.

"What happens if the detonator goes off in the tube?" I asked.

His answer was so quick that it was obvious we were thinking along the same lines.

"It would depend what gives out; the outer cover, the breech block, or the compressed air tanks."

Bartley thoughtfully gnawed at his upper lip. "Commander Rollins, how much time do you think is left on that fuse?"

"I would say no more than two minutes."

"Then make yourself ready, and fire at my command."

Weber paled a bit, and then met my eyes with grim resignation. He pointed with his forefinger. "That would be that lever over there, sir."

Bartley sat bolt upright, his posture signifying his resolve. "Weber, pass out belts please."

"Bottles as well?"

I looked at him quizzically, but no explanation was forthcoming.

"I shouldn't think so."

Weber opened a compartment behind the compressor and brought out three cork life belts. As he handed one to me, he spoke quietly, "Leave it a bit loose, you'll want it to ride up a bit when you hit the water."

"Gentlemen, please blow all ballast."

Weber pointed at a wheel just above the air compressor, and then grabbed its twin above the motor.

We both spun the wheels as quickly as we could. There was a great roar as compressed air filled the ballast tanks and the boat began to pitch wildly. I felt the sub list to my side as Weber deftly spun his valve much faster than I. I grunted and spun harder, trying to compensate. The boat pitched again, but began to stabilize as it moved upward. I moved back to the firing lever, and stood by.

"I am angling the planes up. Brace yourselves." He craned his neck to look outside quickly. His intent was to get the bow as close to the surface, or even above the water to lessen the back pressure on the outer cover. If the compression blew out the tiny hatch, the concussion would do less damage. "The detonator will explode when it hits the tube cover. Prepare yourselves." He craned his neck to look out again.

"Fire now."

I pulled the lever switch, promptly covered my right ear and my left as well as could with my stump, and opened my mouth to mitigate the explosive pressure wave. There was a howl of compressed air, followed by a split second of silence, like a stutter, when the rushing air couldn't find a place to go. Then came the bang.

The craft jerked as if it ran into something. A control wheel caught me in the ribs on my way to the deck; the breath was knocked from my body as I crumpled in the constricted space.

There was a secondary lurch as the great differential gear disengaged, and we started to drift.

Water sprayed over me for a second from the sprung breech block, and then slowed to a trickle.

Weber had been thrown against the air compressor and was bleeding from a gash in his forehead. He dragged himself upright.

"Status report," Bartley demanded.

I was still trying to draw breath as Weber steadied himself and moved forward to stand over me. He pressed his ear to the forward bulkhead. "I hear a little gurgling, sir."

"Ballast chamber or compressed air tank?"

He listened at a few more places.

"I'd like to say compressed air tanks."

"Start the compressor."

Weber moved away. I was finally able to pull myself up and pressed my ear to the bulkhead. I heard a slight hiss, and reported it.

Bartley nodded and spoke to Weber, "See if you can engage the gear. Give me forward one-quarter."

Weber adjusted the motor for quarter speed and hauled on the gear lever.

I felt the boat lurch sharply, and then start to come about.

"We are on the surface, but the nose feels sluggish. I fear we are taking on some water." Bartley made an adjustment to the diving planes. "The stern is riding a little high, making it slow going, but I still have rudder control. Commander Rollins, do you hear more hissing or more gurgling?"

I closed my eye and pressed my ear to the iron. "More hissing."

He mulled that over for a moment. "Weber, hold the controls a second."

Weber complied as Bartley climbed up on his chair and pushed the hatch to full open and latched position so that if the boat did begin to sink we would be able to exit. Resuming his seat, he took the levers back. "Weber, full power, if you please."

Captain Wilson sat behind his desk and rubbed his face in his hands. He looked up, and carefully regarded the three of us. "You will tell no one the particulars that we have discussed."

Bright sunlight shone through the large mullioned windows that looked out over the docks, illuminating the spacious office of dark mahogany and brass. Behind us, there was a small fireplace with a pair of Queen Anne chairs and a matching table. In front of us was an intricately carved desk burdened with thick piles of documents and books, behind which sat the captain with his own burdens.

He continued to rub his face, then his temples, finally running his fingers through his hair, and clasped them at the back of his head. He sat slouched in that pose for several minutes with his eyes closed. Finally, he sat up straighter and addressed Lieutenant Bartley.

"You will tell the men that you hit something."

The incident on board had gone unnoticed by any observer. The tiny bang of the detonator, which resounded so loudly to our ears, had not carried to shore, although when the *Ram* returned to the dock it was obvious something was amiss. One of the forward compressed air tanks had sprung and filled with water, giving the craft a lop-sided appearance, but with all the ballast tanks emptied, the boat was in no danger of sinking. We reported to the captain and immediately repaired to his office for a full accounting. We spent the better part of an hour standing in front of his desk, each of us giving every detail of the incident.

"Aye," Bartley acknowledged with a sigh. "We've hit things before."

I quirked an eyebrow at him. "You have?"

He nodded. "We hit submerged logs frequently, but the sub has a ram hull, so usually it just makes a loud thump and that's about all. But last year we hit a big one right at the base of the conning tower and . . ." he shrugged.

"And what?"

"And Commander Waite is recovering nicely," Captain Wilson said.

The captain turned to Weber. "Can you keep your mouth shut?"

The rating made a gesture of crossing his heart, and then mimed spitting at the floor.

Wilson seemed to accept this. "All right then, Weber, you are dismissed."

The rating turned and left.

As soon as the door closed behind him, Wilson turned on Bartley, his face grim and his eyes blazing. "You will make enquires—discrete enquiries. Only Commander Rollins and I are to know anything about your activities."

"Lieutenant Graf?"

"He does not need to know. If that changes I will tell him, understood?"

"Aye, sir."

"I want you to find out about anyone who had access to those fuses." He paused to think for a second, "That includes sailors, dockhands, marines, munitions clerks, or quartermaster—anyone, military or civilian."

"Aye, sir."

The captain stood up from his desk and strode to the widow to look out at the activity in the shipyard. "The last live fire exercise was more than two weeks ago. No fuses should have been anywhere near the boat."

Bartley bowed his head in thought.

Captain Wilson, expecting a reply, turned around.

"The Americans?" Bartley suggested after a second.

"What Americans?" I asked.

"Last week two fellows from the Zalinsky Pneumatic Dynamite Gun Company paid us a visit," Captain Wilson spoke slowly. "They manufactured the *Ram's* gun and they have just undertaken a contract to build a pneumatic gunship they are calling a 'dynamite cruiser,' the *Vesuvius.*"

"Yes, sir," Bartley nodded. "And they were specifically looking at the fuses and detonators. In fact, they brought us some new prototypes that we were asked to test."

"Was the fuse on the *Ram* one of the new ones?"

"I couldn't tell you, sir."

"Find out what happened to those new ones." He nodded at the young man. "Bartley, you are dismissed."

Once we were alone, Captain Wilson waved me to the conversation area and bade me sit. "You may look at those orders now, if you desire." He brought two short tumblers, set them on the table, and produced a bottle of twelve-year-old Scotch from his desk. He poured us each about an ounce.

He sat quietly across from me for a second as I read my official assignment, then picked up his glass and raised it in salute. "To your first dive."

Too far apart to clink glasses, I returned the salute and sipped gently at the smooth liquor for a moment.

"I think you suspect why you are being brought in to command. This is the first obvious case of sabotage, but there have been a series of accidents of suspicious nature."

"Like the boiler room of the *Indomitable*."

"Like Commander Waite's collision. Too many things had to go wrong to do as much damage as occurred."

"What happened?"

"We will be getting to that, but you have a lot more material to catch up on first. The Admiralty believes that that a gang of German agents has infiltrated the Royal Navy, or at least a few strategic shipyards, and that they are trying to delay progress on our newest equipment. "

"Why you don't just replace everybody, make a clean sweep?"

"Don't think we haven't considered it. We have replaced a number of dockworkers, but there are problems. First, the more people we bring into the program, the more people learn some of our dearest secrets."

"Like what runs the electric motor?"

"That is one bit of restricted knowledge."

"I must say that electrical motor was amazing. But you would need a bank of lead acid batteries bigger than the boat to power it."

"The motor and the batteries were invented by a very young Serbian fellow working for the French. He quit the Edison Company office in Paris and was determined to move to America. However, I caught up with him at his mother's funeral in Gospić, and convinced him to come here instead. You will be meeting him soon. He and his assistant will be covering your technical training." He rubbed the side of his nose. "The battery is nothing compared to . . . other things. The other reason we don't replace the sailors is that we went through the entire navy and found only fifty volunteers. The ones we have left are all that completed the initial training. I honestly do not know where we would get replacements."

"Perhaps we can do with half as many; the craft only takes a crew of three."

Wilson grimaced and used his bottom teeth to gnaw at his mustache until he came to some sort of decision.

"Has today's incident put you off on the idea of command?"

"No, sir. If anything it has made me quite keen."

He drank the rest of his whisky and stood abruptly. "Follow me. It is about time for you to see exactly what we are up to here."

I drained my glass and scrambled to my feet. I was surprised by how fast the good whisky went to my head, leaving me slightly dizzy and a little flushed. I grabbed my leather portfolio with my sketchpad and followed.

The Thunderbolt Affair

We strode across the shipyard through a cordon of marine guards to the dry dock. The enormous wooden building was one of the largest enclosed ship-building facilities in the world, nearly forty feet high by sixty feet across and ran for a length of almost 300 feet. An entire "*Shannon*" class cruiser could be built indoors. The long west wall bordered the river and it was designed to be removed in sections so that the ship under construction could be launched sideways into the river, where the bottom had been dredged clear to make room for it. As we approached the mammoth structure, I could hear the muffled clash of heavy industry in the distance.

"In here is the next step in our plan for a submersible fleet." Wilson pointed to a sign erected in front of the building that read "Submersible Tender Ship Construction."

"Tender," I said slowly, my mind speculating on the potential. "A purpose-built ship to support the submersible?"

"*Conventional* thinking is that submersibles are by necessity small, with limited independence and that they will need to be accompanied by a surface ship." He said "conventional" with obvious distaste. "A tender could tow it over long distance and keep it resupplied. The design we were considering would make it possible for the tender to actually take the submersible on board."

"Of course," I replied. I admired the simple, but reasonable conclusion to the logistical difficulties of a submersible.

"That is the conventional thinking," he said with a smile and a knowing light in his eyes.

He ushered me into the cavernous building, and the noise increased tenfold. Quiet banging that I was vaguely aware of became a staccato of metal clangs, scraping metallic sounds, and grinding noises that assaulted my ears as the smell of heated steel assaulted my nose. We stood on the lip of a depression dug into the ground nearly twenty feet. In the center of the hollow, the huge frame of a mighty craft stretched away from me, over half of its mass covered in thick steel plates. The structure was supported by hundreds of wooden poles that were laid in a crisscross angle so the keel was held off the floor. It did not take an experienced eye to know that the object under construction was not designed to be a submersible tender.

Small teams of workers were carefully fitting the steel plates to the sturdy frame of the craft while others fastened them into place with half-inch red hot steel rivets. As one man used the massive iron back plate to keep it snug, a partner used the heavy peening hammer to secure it. I marveled at so much steel. Builders were only starting to use such plating for battleships.

The craft was clearly inspired by the comparably tiny HMS *Holland Ram* and looked to be over 120 feet long, twenty feet abeam, and twenty-six feet tall. The frame of the conning tower rose an additional four feet. Sitting on the dry dock rails, it looked for all the world as if they were making an airship out of steel.

"My God," I exclaimed.

Wilson chuckled. "She has yet to be christened, but by everyone's initial reaction, she may well be called the 'HMS *My God*.'"

"Where . . . who . . . the design?" I was completely overwhelmed by the sight, but tended to blame the swallow of whisky for my inability to communicate.

"Designed by John Holland himself. Of course, he thought he was being paid to indulge in a mental exercise at the behest of the Admiralty, designing a boat for a power plant that does not yet exist. Our Serbian electrician and his tinkering assistant filled in some of the gaps."

"Who knows about this? Have any unusual accidents happened here?"

"These dock workers know, of course. We pay them extra to keep quiet. We use only men who have a reputation for keeping their mouth shut, but with hundreds on a work crew . . ." He frowned and shook his head.

"Does *my* crew know?"

"Some have voiced speculations, but the only ones in the know are your officers and the coxswain."

"How long until it's ready?" The frame seemed very complete to me.

"They need to install the interior decking, which is more of a challenge than we expected," his voice was strained with understatement. "Then we must mount the engines, and of course, finish plating the hull." He sighed. "Less than two months, another reason we needed you on board as soon as possible."

The captain let me gaze for a while, then patted me on the shoulder. "You will see the specifications soon enough; we have another matter to attend to." He beckoned me and I reluctantly left the construction. We exited through a side passage that led toward the foundry building with the outlandish tower perched upon it. We stepped outside to a short breezeway between the structures. Up close, I could see that the tower, built in a lattice design, was not built on top of the building, but rather two of the four legs straddled the corner. I later learned that the other two legs were built inside the building. It rose sixty feet above the harbor and was crowned with a round structure about thirty feet in diameter, with a railing all around the top. From where I now stood I could see the bronze coating was not paint, but a sort of plating. I left the breezeway to go and inspect it more closely, but the captain waved me back.

"Time for that later," he said. We went through a side door into a corridor that did not actually go into the depths of the building, but ended at a wall with a sliding door. The captain pushed the door open with little effort to reveal a second cage-like door which he shoved open as well, and bade me enter what looked like a well-appointed cupboard. I nodded in recognition. I had seen a drawing of a lift, but had not encountered one before.

The Thunderbolt Affair

The captain stood by a control that resembled the round body of a Chadburn ship's telegraph with one control lever, but instead of many positions on the indicator face, it had merely "up and "down." Captain Wilson took control while I closed the doors. He moved the handle and we began to rise.

I looked up.

"We are heading for the primary development laboratory for this project. This is where you will receive your technical briefings and learn about the revolutionary power plant." The car came to a stop and Captain Wilson paused for a moment. "Be certain to address him as 'doctor.' We arranged a degree from Cambridge as a bribe to get him here."

I nodded as he slid open the cage door and we stepped into insanity.

There were two people amid the clutter. One, in a relatively clear area in the corner by an exhaust fan, was wearing a technician's leather apron while operating a carbon arc welder, using the big carbon rod to join pieces of some metal mechanism. Thick dark goggles covered half the person's face while a heavy kerchief covered the mouth and nose. A cap protected the worker's hair from tiny sparks that leapt about the work.

"Careful," the other person spoke, looking up from piles of paper on his desk. His voice was a thickly accented tenor. "She is working with zinc plating."

I knew all too well the effect of breathing zinc fumes and have suffered from the horrible symptoms that foundry workers called "zinc flu."

"Dr. Tesla," Captain Wilson was not the least bit put off by the man's manner, "I would like to present Commander Rollins."

The man turned his sharp dark eyes back to the papers. "Tesla is busy. Come back tomorrow." The room was almost uncomfortably warm, but Dr. Tesla wore a grey suit with a starched white shirt and black bow tie. His hair was thick, and though he used some sort of pomade to control it, several strands stuck straight out. His mustache was thick and as black as coal, but the rest of his face was shaved so closely that it almost glowed. His manner was self-assured and hard to reconcile with his youth. The man appeared to be no older than twenty-five, and I later learned that he was barely twenty-one. By that age, he had already invented a revolutionary electric motor, performed many experiments with alternating current, and now invented a new way of powering his engine.

"Commander, this is Dr. Nicola Tesla, the inventor of the electric motor you so admire."

I stepped forward, setting my portfolio on his desk before offering my hand. "Dr. Tesla, I cannot tell you how much I am impressed by your device."

Tesla glared at me for a second, then accepted my hand. His grip was hesitant. "And do you know enough to be impressed? Or are you like a savage impressed by fire and silly tricks?"

"Dr. Tesla, Commander Rollins will be replacing Commander Waite."

Tesla waved his hands in the air. "Bah, useless."

I looked into his eyes expecting him to elaborate.

He waved his hand at me and spoke to the captain. "Is she as useless as the Commander Waite?"

The captain scratched the back of his head. "The commander here is a technical officer. He has a degree in mechanical engineering from Edinburgh."

Tesla slapped himself in the forehead. "Ah, the man has a degree," he said. "I suppose she thinks he understands what we are doing?"

I noticed he had the eastern European habit of confusing pronouns.

"Not now, but I am willing and able to learn."

He dismissed me with another wave. "Not very probably."

Completely without hesitation or any indication of awkwardness, he flipped open the cover of my portfolio as if he owned it. I made an abortive attempt to stop him, but he jerked the sketch pad away from me and waved me back.

He sat there for several seconds, his sharp eyes flitting across the paper as he first nodded to himself and then shook his head slightly. He pursed his lips. "Is this your work?" he asked in a much quieter voice, toning down the bombast.

"It is," I admitted, discomfited by having another person see what I considered so intimate.

He extended his lower jaw so that his teeth worried at the end of his mustache. "She might not be so worthless after all." He looked at some more of my drawings, then he looked at my hook, and the stump of my left wrist. "This is most interesting. Not my area of expertise, though. Danny, come here and look at this."

Danny waved him away.

"*Neh, neh, neh,*" he spoke emphatically in Serbian; sounding like a staccato "nay-nay-nay." "Danny, you will want to see this."

Danny took a visibly patient breath, shut off the current to the carbon rod, and stood up. I assumed that when Tesla referred to his assistant as "she," it was simply pronoun confusion, but there was a heavy utilitarian dress under the leather apron, and she pulled off the cap to release long dark hair that spilled in soft curls over her shoulders. When she removed the kerchief, I found myself staring into eyes so dark brown they appeared black, but with a spark of mischief in them. She was possibly a decade older than the absurdly young doctor, but still moved with as much energy as a teen.

"Miss Tesla." The captain greeted her with a smile and a slight bow.

"Captain Arthur," she replied, with a friendly nod.

Wilson's eyes blinked in resignation at the way she used his first name, and he turned to me. "Commander Rollins, may I present Danjella Tesla, the doctor's cousin and assistant."

She smiled politely at me, then moved around the doctor's desk to look at the papers. Her brow furrowed as she regarded them.

"These are remarkable," she said slowly in a voice not so heavily accented. "You have even specified the metals for the winding springs." She looked at me again, as if seeing me for the first time and her eyes seemed to evaluate everything about me in one long gaze. I imagined I saw a twinkle in her eye. I assumed I must have imagined it. I had often seen that twinkle in a woman's eye before, that hint of attraction; but since the number of my eyes had been divided by half, not so much.

"It is merely a thought exercise," I explained, unwilling to talk about my hopes.

She held up her hand for silence, then tapped the paper with her slender finger. "No, no, this is . . . ingenerate? Ingenuine? Some word like that."

"Ingenious?" Tesla suggested.

She ignored him and brought her hand to her mouth. "May I make one suggestion?"

Tesla broke in, "Danny, he makes devices. Used to work with my mother to create kitchen gadgets, things of cogs and gears. Now she thinks bigger. Makes very complex things."

"I would be honored for any suggestions."

Her manner became very business-like and she picked up a fountain pen from the desk. She pointed with the pen, "These gears here, this linkage, makes the system stop as soon as it meets resistance."

"Why yes, that is the design."

"But what if you wish to grip something more thoroughly? If you change linkage like this. May I?"

I nodded and she made a few pen strokes on my drawing. "Replace these gears with springs to reopen, then you can override the linkage incrementally."

I was overwhelmed. It took me six months to conceive of the linkage, and she improved it in seconds.

Tesla looked at the drawing, nodding. "Tesla approves of this one."

I imagined the captain gave a sigh of relief.

Tesla looked at me appraisingly. "You should do something for the eye, too," he laughed, as if it were some private joke.

Miss Tesla held up my drawings again, and then pressed them to her chest. The movement revealed that under the leather apron she was not as tightly corseted as the current fashion dictated. I flushed as I realized my attention was wandering.

"May I hold on to these for a bit?"

I felt a flash of anxiety and a momentary desire to refuse, but she continued "I will make certain to get them back to you by the end of the day."

"Certainly." I tried to speak nonchalantly, but to my ears it sounded like a nervous croak.

"Doctor," Captain Wilson interrupted, "if we can plan for the commander's training regimen."

I seized on the opportunity to distract myself from the anxiety I felt over my portfolio. "Please, Dr. Tesla, I really would like to know how you power the electric motor. It must be some sort of battery, but I cannot imagine."

He tapped the side of his head. "Imagination is the key, guided by knowledge. What are the problems with batteries?"

"Everything." I held up my fingers as I listed the major points. "They are inefficient, they lose their charge when stored, they take more energy to charge than they store, and they take damned—" I stopped myself, having momentarily forgotten there was a lady present. "And they take a blessed long time to charge."

Tesla held up a finger in acknowledgement and walked over to a large glass vat filled with a thick sludge that was light grey in color. He pointed to it. "This is my battery."

I looked dubiously at the material, and then scratched my head as a thought nagged at a memory until I suddenly realized what I was seeing. "This is the electrolyte to a flow battery! Like the one introduced by Charles Renard last year."

Tesla managed to look both chagrined and impressed at the same time. Miss Tesla covered a smirk with her hand.

The flow battery invented by Renard was introduced in France the previous year. Renard used it to power the army airship *La France*, whose propeller was driven by an electric motor.

"Renard's battery is primitive," Tesla declared. "I have gone far beyond that toy." He strode to another work bench and pulled the cover off a large rectangular container made of heavy glass. It was about one foot wide, and just as tall, and two and a half feet long, glowing dimly with a strange blue luminescence. I could see a series of copper plates, two heavy duty copper lugs covered with glass insulators, and a port on either side with ceramic plugs screwed in. The threads cut in the thick glass reflected the pale blue glow of the electrolyte.

Tesla pointed. "The lugs in the front, they deliver 240 volts at 50 ampere for six hours."

I wanted to exclaim "that's impossible," but I held my tongue. After all, something was powering the *Ram*. Instead I asked, "I suppose the ports are for refilling the electrolyte?"

"Exactly, we pump the discharged electrolyte out and re-energize it separately."

"I can see the utility, but certainly it still takes a lot of energy and time to charge."

"That is the secret." Tesla replied, his eyes gleaming. He tapped himself on the chest. "And that is Tesla's invention, not Renard," he swiped his finger in front of him as if he were crossing out the name on an imaginary chalk board. "Not Edison." He swiped the finger again. "This process can re-energize electrolyte in different ways; very slowly with a tiny trickle of current, or almost instantaneously with super high voltage and current."

"What can produce that kind of electricity?"

He held his hands above his head and wiggled his fingers while making a sound like thunder, and I realized that I was looking at lightning in a bottle.

Chapter Four

I sipped at the whiskey, savoring the pleasant burn while I studied the cut glass tumbler in which my drink was served at the officers' mess. It felt much more solid in my hand than a tin mug. The liquid inside was easier on my tongue and throat than three-penny gin, and it went straight to my head. I set the glass down on the small pedestal table that sat between us.

Captain Wilson held up the bottle in silent question, but I shook my head and put my hand over the glass. He invited me to dine with him at the port officers' mess and secured a private room for us. The amount of post prandial-whiskey he'd poured already was much more than the ceremonial tot in his office.

"I need all my wits just to get a sense of everything I've seen today and all that is happening."

"Very well." He smiled, and poured himself just a touch more.

We were sitting in the center pair of four comfortably upholstered wing-back chairs of fine burgundy brocade arranged in a loose semi-circle facing the cold fireplace, unneeded on the unusually warm spring night. The remains of our supper were cooling on the table behind us.

I returned to our conversation. "So you are saying that everyone in the unit had unrestricted access to the *Ram*, even after the other accidents?"

He gritted his teeth and shook his head, partially in regret. "All the officers would go down there when they had a chance, to sit in the seat and get used to the controls. Everyone was encouraged to go down and lock themselves in, even at night. We wanted everyone to be completely familiar with the boat, able to orient themselves, and find every control in the dark. However, now we are keeping a marine guard right on the pier, not just by the gates, and they are to log all visitors."

"You have to understand that this is the most egregious, the first truly overt act of sabotage, we have encountered. Until now, with one exception, the things we have seen have caused little damage and so far, no loss of life." He knocked on the wooden table. "And I'm not convinced that our incident with Commander Waite was anything other than an accident. I just cannot get a grip on what the saboteur is trying to do. His actions have not really hurt the program, barely even slowed it down, he is just managing to confuse us."

"And if that is his goal?"

"To what end?" He shook his head silently.

"Tell me about the submersible. You said there was a story. How did we acquire it? "

Wilson snorted and drained the last of his drink. "It is one of those stories, that if it didn't really happen no one would believe it. The boat was built at the Delamater Iron Company by an American, John Holland, probably the most experienced submersible maker in the world. The man is quiet keen on those boats." He raised a skeptical eyebrow as if he were not certain that the subject was something a man should be keen about.

"Such a craft has to be expensive: I cannot credit the Admiralty laying out funds for such."

"As I said before, we stole it." He stopped and considered his words for a moment, "Or stole it back; it depends on your point of view. The original name of the boat was *The Fenian Ram.*"

"Sounds vaguely Irish."

"Vaguely; it was commissioned by an American group that supports Irish independence, the so-called Fenian Brotherhood."

"Of course, I have heard of them." I tapped at the whiskey glass on the table. "I'm afraid the drink has made me a bit slow. But why on God's earth, or sea, would they want a submersible?"

"They were better at raising money than making plans. They got in contact with Mr. Holland and asked him to build a submersible that would be able to harass British shipping. I don't know precisely what they had in mind, but I expect they thought that this would somehow lead to Irish independence."

"Well, of course," I replied, but I could not conceive of any plot or plan wherein a single sub could modify Crown policy.

"When the thing was just about complete, there was a disagreement among the Fenians; in fact, the organization split up about the same time. One faction decided that they had a moral right to the craft, and stole it and another mini-submersible, and hid the *Ram* in New Haven, Connecticut, where they stuck it in a shed. Then they had a problem."

"Getting it across the Atlantic?"

"No," he chuckled, looked down at his empty glass, and then set it near mine on the table. "It seems none of the Fenians ever bothered to learn how the bloody thing worked. You've seen for yourself that it is quite complex."

"Have you driven the *Ram*?"

He barked with laughter. "You know better than that! I am certain that Lieutenant Bartley informed you of my dislike for being *under* the waves."

"He may have mentioned it."

He chuckled and waved his hand dismissively. "Of course he did. The men call him 'Blatherskite Bartley,' as the man never met a rumor he didn't like. Fortunately, he sticks to gossip and has managed to keep his mouth shut about our projects."

His face grew serious and I saw a strange shadow in his eyes. "I went down one time, which was plenty. I thought I would be enthralled, but I couldn't take the smell, the heavy air."

I knew exactly what he meant.

"Although," he said wistfully, "I might have to give the new boat a trial. Anyway, the Fenians went back to Holland to make a deal. He was very angry and his first reaction was to tell them to piss off, but then he had a better idea. He agreed to meet with them to schedule training, but then turned to our embassy in New York—assuming that passing the boat on to us would rile the Irish blackguards. He gave the naval attaché, your predecessor Commander Waite, all of the information he had on the Fenians and arranged a meeting with the boat. We sent out a squad of marines with Pinkertons, and took the boat. We gave Holland a small fee and he trained Waite and Petty Officer George Grant, now your coxswain, to sail and shoot it."

"How did you come to be so inspired by this device? While you are a sailor from the old school, you seem very sympathetic to the academy men, but it seems odd to me that you would be so enthused."

His eyes took on a fierce expression. "I am a captain in the Royal Navy," I could hear the capital letters in his voice. "The navy that has been the greatest navy in the world for centuries. We have kept it that way by staying one step ahead of the French, the Germans, and the Russians, and now we better stay ahead of the Japanese." He smacked his fist on the table for emphasis. "The rest of the world is innovating and we are dithering. The French and the Americans are already building submersibles. Germans are building airships, and we are floundering around in a stolen boat and arguing about whether or not to start a school of ballooning, let alone an air corps! If we hesitate, the rest of the world will own the skies and the seas, and we will be stuck on our little island. Right now, right this minute, Dr. Tesla gives us an edge, and I mean to exploit it."

I sat dumbfounded at this sudden passion.

There was a discreet knock on the door.

"Come," Captain Wilson called.

The door opened just enough for Mr. Cooper-Smythe to slip his rugged frame through. He was still dressed as severely as our last two encounters, and if it weren't for the fact that his apparel was clean and well-tended, I would believe he never changed his clothes.

I started to rise, but Captain Wilson waved me down and with the same motion waved Cooper-Smythe over to what was apparently a prearranged meeting.

Captain Wilson indicated the bottle of whiskey as the clandestine agent sat down, but he declined with a shake of his head.

"Inquiries are being made," he said.

"I should hope so," I retorted.

42

He looked at me, his hard eyes boring into mine for a split second before he continued. "Inquiries are being made to the Admiralty about the submersible."

"And who is inquiring?"

"The German naval attaché from their London embassy, Kapitän Mueller; the damn fellow wants a ride in it."

"Seriously?"

Cooper-Smythe rubbed his face in his hands. "Yes, the request is going through channels." He pulled a silver case from his jacket and offered us each a cigar, which we both declined. He shrugged and lit one for himself.

"What do we know about this Mueller?" Wilson asked as Cooper-Smythe puffed on the cigar to get it going.

"Precious little." His reply was oddly slurred as he kept he cigar clenched in his teeth. Apparently needing to elaborate, he took the cigar from his mouth. "He is a confidant of Little Willie, so he is no friend to England." He used the irreverent nickname for Kaiser Wilhelm's grandson, also named Wilhelm.

I knew young Wilhelm nurtured a list of real and imagined injuries caused by the British, despite the fact that his mother was English and his grandmother was Queen Victoria.

"Any news about Friedrich?" Rumors about the health of Crown Prince Friedrich, the heir apparent of the German empire, had been bandied about in the press for months.

"It is not generally known, and this information should not be spread, but my sources tell me that the problem with his throat is a malignancy. He may not live to be crowned, leaving us with Little Willie."

"Certainly Bismarck will keep him in line?" Captain Wilson asked rhetorically. The infamous Iron Chancellor all but governed the empire.

Cooper-Smythe shook his head in a weary manner. "The mess we made in Africa has emboldened the empire. As we speak, they have renewed their colonial aspirations at the Cape of Good Hope, intending to have a major base of operations there by fall."

He didn't say, but we all knew that in case of hostilities, Germany would be in a position to cut us off from India and our trading houses in Hong Kong and Macao.

"But Bismarck has been pushing for a more domestic policy, not expansion." Wilson said.

Cooper-Smythe gestured dramatically with his cigar. "Bismarck's influence may be waning."

There was another discreet knock at the door. I glanced at the empty chair and wondered if there was to be another visitor.

"Come," Wilson called again.

Instead of another caller, the door opened to reveal one of the mess stewards. His white jacket was crisply starched, contrasting with my sadly wilted uniform. Most of my postings were shipboard and I was used to a uniform that needed serious refreshing at the end of the day. In my rare beach assignments, I was called upon to do design and office work, and either did not put much wear on my clothes, or had adequate time to change for dinner. This assignment promised to be very hard on my clothing since I would go from boat to shipyard to foundry to office, all in a day's work. To keep up this pace, and maintain standards, I was going to have to invest in more uniform coats. Or something.

The steward nodded politely. "Pardon the interruption, but the commander's cab has arrived."

I rose and brushed at my forlorn coat, trying ineffectually to improve its appearance. I turned to Captain Wilson and offered my hand. "Thank you sir, for bringing me on board."

He grinned and rose to take my hand in a firm grasp. "Do not thank me. As things go, you may not live to regret it."

I shrugged and tucked my portfolio under my arm, less bulky without my sketch book— though I still had a few pages I'd scribbled on. Miss Tesla promised the return of the rest by day's end, but as yet she had not sent it to my office and I was hesitant to go in search of her. Grabbing my hat, I let the steward lead me out through a short hall to the main club room of the mess. The spacious room had three fireplaces, and many comfortable leather chairs for reading. There were also several tables for officers to while away time with friendly, and not so friendly, games of cards. I almost made it across the room when a high, slightly slurred voice rang out.

"Commander Rollins." Captain Clarke, late of the *Indomitable*, managed to make the rank of commander sound like a slur. "I hear you have found your berth on a submersible." He grimaced as if the word itself were painful to contemplate, let alone speak out loud.

I turned toward his voice to find him sitting in a wing-backed chair, a copy of the *Times* in his lap, and a glass of whiskey in his hand. His uniform was quite crisp.

"Good evening, captain." I replied. I stayed civil, and didn't rise to his bait.

"Good evening? Is that what you have to say to me?"

He rose unsteadily to his feet, the paper spilling unheeded from his lap. "You burn my ship to the waterline, and they give you a *promotion*? Look at you, have you no pride, sir?"

He wrinkled his nose as if I smelled bad, and he might have had a point as I was acutely aware that the odor of oil and grease lingered.

"What sort of 'academy' did you graduate from? They taught you bollocks about seamanship, precious little about machines, and apparently nothing about standards. So far the only thing to come from the 'academy' is cronyism. 'The Old Boy Network'— the whole system of school mates covering up incompetence."

He stepped toward me and stabbed an angry finger at my chest, emphasizing his words. "The proper education for a ship's officer is on a *ship*. When he goes to his next assignment, he is judged by his *ability*, his seamanship, not by what school he attended or who he knows."

The room had gone silent and he suddenly seemed aware of the attention we were receiving. The card players weren't even pretending to look at their hands. He looked heavenward and sighed, then regarded me with his lip twisted into a sneer.

"Well, at least they gave you the right command. Commander Rollins here is an expert at sinking ships."

I could feel several pairs of eyes sizing me up. I am sure that some knew what sort of boat I was assigned to and they certainly had opinions that I would soon hear, but for right now, they were enjoying a bit of penny-dreadful drama at my expense. Captain Clarke stepped even closer and motioned me toward him as if he wanted to have intimate speech. I could smell the whiskey on his breath. He covered the side of his mouth with his hand as if to hide his words, but his voice carried into the room.

"Allow me to impart some professional wisdom, from a life spent at sea." His voice projected exaggerated sincerity. "The trick about commanding a submersible isn't the ability to sink the damned thing. The trick is that you are supposed to bring the damnable thing back up!" He laughed as if he made a very clever jest. "I hear your first act was to try and leave it on the bottom. Well, good riddance is what I say. The damn thing should be scuttled and any officer that is so depraved to volunteer for such a wretched business should be drummed out of the navy."

The steward stepped between us. "Beggin' yer pardon, sir," he said to Captain Clarke. "I has me orders to get the commander here out to his cab."

Clarke glared at the interruption.

The steward beckoned to another steward, his voice very calm. "Perhaps sir, you would like a refill? On the house, sir."

The captain turned to look at the glass he had left on the table and took a moment to focus on it. The steward took the opportunity to take me by the elbow, leading me away at a fast clip. As we exited the club room, he spoke, "My apology, sir, but that whisky will have to appear on your bill."

I started to say something, but he continued. "Otherwise, it comes out of my pay. And it seemed the only way to avoid more unpleasantness."

"I see."

His brow clouded as his speech came out a bit more forthright than I would have expected, "No, you don't. The captain has been here nearly every night since he was beached, unable to find a ship, and has been freely condemning 'that damned incompetent boilermaker,' which I suspect means you."

"I can validate your suspicions."

The steward led me to the front. I felt a slight shiver that I attributed to the weather and although it had been warm, it was now turning cool as the sun disappeared.

"I would not presume," the steward said, "to tell you your business, but I would be circumspect about visiting the mess." Having said his peace, he departed.

I turned toward the drive where a hansom cab awaited and the cabbie tipped his topper at me.

"22 Cannaught Square," I instructed the driver, who sat in the high seat in the back where he could look out over the short roof of the compact cab. I stepped between the cab and the horses to settle in the spacious leather seat, big enough for two, or three, if they were friendly. This one was equipped with a sort of a folding half-door at my feet that I could close to keep mud from splashing up from the street as the horse trotted along. I established myself, grateful for a lap rug left there for the passengers.

We set off at a steady trot back toward the main gate of the port. I was thinking about the long day when I noticed a light that shimmered through the thickening fog. It was very high up and could only be coming from Tesla's workshop, atop the tower. Did the eccentric man work late into the night?

I knocked at the small trap door above my head, my hook turning my simple gesture into a sharp impatient rap. The cabbie opened it. "I may have left something at work. Would you mind taking me over to that foundry building for a moment?"

"Aye, guv'ner, ta the foundry it is." He flicked the reins and smoothly closed the trap door.

Minutes later, I alighted from the cab and handed the driver a few coins to wait. I crossed to the building, returned the marine guard's salute, and had entered the hall toward the lift when I saw its door open. Danjella Tesla stepped out. I felt unaccountably nervous and nodded my head in greeting. "Miss Tesla, you are working late?"

She smiled at me. "Commander, it is my cousin. How you say, he burns the midnight eel? Ore? Some word like that."

"Oil?" I ventured.

She looked at me sharply. "I speak strange, I know. And Nicola corrects me, but I would prefer that— if you understand me well, to just—let it pass." She sighed then brightened a bit and smiled. The leather apron and goggles had been replaced with an attractive red velvet jacket and matching hat. The jacket did not hide the fact that she was not tightly bound. She also cleaned the carbon smudges from her face and added a touch of rouge to her lips, making her expression much more cheerful.

I nodded.

"How is the doctor?"

She laughed as if I'd made a joke.

"What is so funny?"

"Nicola, he makes a small joke with Captain Arthur."

"I do not understand."

"Nicola comes home after his mother dies; he is distraught. His mind is searching for distraction and he is becoming obsessed with Thomas Edison, the man who owned the company he worked for, and with Niagara Falls."

"Captain Arthur follows him from Paris, wants him to come to England to make his motors." She tapped her finger to the side of her head. "He thinks he knows who Nicola is. Nicola is brilliant, and he knows that. But the men Captain Arthur spoke to said that he was vain and arrogant, and that he envied their degrees. So, the captain comes to Gospić just as Nicola needs a project. Captain Arthur approached my cousin expecting the vain, arrogant scientist he heard about—'The Great Tesla' as if he were some music hall conjurer. His attitude amuses my cousin and, *voilà*, 'The Great Tesla' is created. He became the arrogant bombastic character the captain expected."

I chuckled. "Well, your cousin has certainly grown into the role."

"It amuses him, and I have to admit it amuses me. Mostly."

"And what are you doing in England?"

She shrugged, not with Gallic ambivalence, but rather with Eastern European fatalism. "There was a great sadness for me in Serbia; he offered to take me and here I am. I am useful, working with devices. And when Nicola is engaged in something, and when he is—" her brow creased in thought— "animated? agitated? Some word like that. He needs grounding, like one of his electrical experiments."

"I see."

"And you, Commander Rollins?"

"Please," I said; surprised by my own forwardness, "call me Ian."

She quirked an eyebrow at me. "And you, Ian?"

"No, I meant—" I stopped talking as she waved me quiet. I meant for her to call me Commander Ian, like she called Wilson "Captain Arthur."

"Ian is a good name, I like it. So, you are working late?"

"I just finished dinner at the officers' mess." I continued. "Then I saw the light and thought to take a look."

"Well, I am glad to see you. I am afraid I was remiss in getting your papers back to you. I am finished with what I wanted. They are back upstairs; should I fetch them for you?"

In truth that would have made me feel better, but instead I replied, "No problem, they can keep until morning."

She flipped back her lapel to glance at a watch pinned there. "I am waiting for my companion, and I shall be going home."

"Companion?" I asked.

"Yes, a Mrs. Livingstone. Nicola arranged for her to share my lodgings and generally ensure that I am, how you say? Guided? Guarded? Some word like that."

I nodded again. "And Mr. Livingstone?"

"Apparently he was a drunkard—" she started ticking off on her fingers, as if reciting some list she memorized— "a layabout, a cad, a bounder, a rogue, a wastrel, and a scoundrel who had the bad grace to die three years ago at this foundry. Apparently, he was working to fit a boiler plate when it fell on him."

I flinched. I had seen the results of too many accidents like that.

She sighed deeply. "I can at least believe the man was a drunkard."

"Why is that?"

"I have been living with that woman for just about a year." She took a deep breath and held her hand to her face. "And I very much need a drink."

Her expression looked so forlorn I barely repressed a chuckle, which earned me an angry pout, accompanied by a glint of humor in her eyes.

The door opened behind me and the marine motioned to Miss Tesla. "She has arrived."

We stepped outside. A four-wheel growler carriage was parked next to my hansom and a stout, sober woman of indeterminate age stood by the door. She was dressed in a black jacket and skirt of a severe cut with a small bustle in the back. Her hair was coarse black, going to iron grey, and pulled back into a bun so tight it made her eyebrows seem permanently arched in surprise. She topped this with a prim, flat straw hat that I would normally associate with a school teacher. It was decorated in funerary fashion with a black velvet band.

Miss Tesla greeted her with a nod. She turned to me. "Ian, may we give you, um . . . a ride? A trip? Some word like that."

Mrs. Livingstone frowned, either at the informality or the offer, perhaps both.

"I have my own."

"Nonsense." She waved away my objection. "Cabbie! Ian, the commander here, he will be going with us."

"Very good." The man tipped his hat and departed.

I nodded in concession. "Thank you, Miss Tesla."

"Really, Ian," she said with a shy smile. "Danjella, or Danny, if you prefer."

Mrs. Livingstone could stand it no further. "Miss Tesla," she remonstrated, "this informality with this . . . this *sailor*."

She sighted down her slightly bulbous nose and carefully scrutinized me from my cheap shoes to my wilted coat to my eye patch. Her already stressed eyebrows rose at the sight of my shirt cuffs, grease stained from my trip on the *Ram*. Her lip twitched—in fear? Curiosity? Some strong emotion crossed her face when she took notice of the hook.

"This familiarity is unseemly and I shall have to report this to your cousin."

Danjella smiled sweetly. "Mrs. Livingstone, would you be a dear and shut up?" She turned to me with a puzzled smile. "That is correct— 'shut up'? I seem to think 'shut down' would make more sense."

I started to say something, and my mouth moved, but there was no sound. Danjella was no shrinking violet, and even with her chaperone she was definitely in charge.

The older woman glowered at her and then at me. She puffed her cheeks in indignation and without a further word, turned to step into the carriage.

Danjella rolled her eyes at me and mimed taking a drink.

"Where to, sir?" the driver inquired.

I called out my street and number, and offered my hand to assist Danjella into the carriage. She took my hand with a playful squeeze, and levered herself up to sit facing forward next to her companion, while I clambered up the step and sat opposite. The growler carriage was a smaller sort of brougham, and when the horse pitched forward, my knees brushed against Danjella's with the lightest touch. It sent electricity equivalent to one of her cousin's batteries through me. This accidental contact elicited a scandalized "Hrumph" from Mrs. Livingstone, while Danjella simply turned her knees slightly aside to provide more room, demurely folded her hands on her lap, and cast her hypnotic dark eyes down at them. But for just a moment, her eyes flicked up and met mine, and I thought I saw a trace of amusement? Amazement? Some word like that . . .

We rode on in companionable silence for several minutes.

"Ian?" Danjella said as we approached my residence. From the sidewise glance she gave Mrs. Livingstone, I presumed her primary purpose for using my given name was to tweak her companion. "I was wondering, have you ever been to a music hall? Or the theater?"

I was momentarily at a loss for words, as this was not a question I expected.

"I have, upon occasion, but not recently."

"I have been so curious. I cannot go without appropriate escort, and Mrs. Livingstone, she has an allergy? Antipathy? Some word like that, against . . ." she paused, her brows creased in concentration. "Against fun. In any form."

Mrs. Livingstone gave another, "Hrumph."

I was not sure how to respond, so I kept quiet.

"I rather think that you should invite me to one or the other," she said with a smile.

I was saved as the carriage came to a stop.

"I am afraid that I must take my leave." I scrambled out of my seat and fairly jumped into the gathering gloom of the narrow street.

I heard Danjella say something unintelligible.

I turned back, "I'm sorry, what was that?"

She leaned out over the rail beside the door of the carriage. "I was just agreeing that you are afraid." She waved as the carriage pulled away.

I tipped my hat to the ladies and watched as the cabman smartly cracked the reins and brought the horses to a trot. I watched the cab until it reached the end of the block, made my way to the front stoop, and fumbled for my key.

As I noted earlier, I am not unduly shy, but my relations with women have changed, and I am unusually conscious of the change. I felt admiration for Danjella, and I supposed her attention was out of some misplaced pity. Also, it would not go well if I made my attraction known, especially if it caused trouble with her cousin.

Pondering imponderables, I fumbled and dropped the heavy brass key so that it bounced off the doorstep, forcing me to turn and stoop to get it. Turning thus, I noticed a hansom cab pulling away from the curb down the block. Perhaps my nerves were a bit on edge, but it seemed to me to be moving at an unusual speed for city driving. I imagined it must be trying to catch up to Danjella's growler. The feeling intensified as the driver appeared to avert his face on passing, leaving me the fleeting impression of a sharp-faced man.

I thought my nerves must be far more on edge than I supposed, as a feeling of immediate threat to Miss Tesla settled upon me. I looked up and down the street, and up into the sky to identify any real cause for alarm before taking a deep breath. I could not let my apprehension take control of me. What use would I be jumping with alarm any time I spied a carriage moving quickly? Besides, the only possible action I could take would be to rush to her dwelling to see if she arrived without difficulty, and I had no earthly idea where that was.

I took control of myself, determined that it was indeed my imaginings, and bent to recover my key.

Jenkins was waiting, a kettle ready to boil in case I wanted tea, and a wineglass was set at the table, if that was my inclination. There was a covered dish on the table and I recalled that I told him I would mess at the port. He lifted the lid to reveal a small selection of cheeses.

I nodded approval. "I will have a glass of port, if you please." I began to unstrap the hook.

I assumed that his first order of business having been left with cash would be to stock spirits, and I was not mistaken.

"Very good," he replied and fetched a bottle.

Setting aside the leather cuff, I rubbed my wrist to regain some circulation, and put the hook on the shelf. I picked up the plate of cheeses, moved across to an overstuffed chair by the fireplace, and set the plate on a side table before collapsing into the warm comfort of the armchair.

Jenkins poured the port. "How was your day, sir?"

"Incredible," I replied, "in the truest meaning—'beyond belief.'"

"I could not help but notice that you were delivered by a brace of ladies."

"You noticed that, did you? Did you notice a hansom cab that seemed to be following them?"

His eyes shifted left then right in concentration. "I believes I saw a hansom cab, but I do not recall that it seemed to be following anyone;

rather, it dropped a chap down the block. Although it did move out quickly, probably trying to get somewhere where it was likely to pick up a fare; not many people heading out from here tonight."

I nodded. It was most likely the cab was in a hurry to get to Soho to return genteel reprobates to their proper side of town, or to Drury Lane to pick up higher class reprobates.

"I recall the night the admiral was delivered home by a brace of, well um, women."

"Oh?"

"Yes, he was slightly worse for drink when he was accosted by two female pickpockets."

"Good heavens."

"Yes, but apparently they found him so charming that after relieving him of the burden of his wallet, they used his money to hire a cab and deliver him home."

"Rather civilized of them." I rose, walked over to the wardrobe, and pulled out my uniform dress coat. It was not an ornate mess jacket, which would be beyond my means and for which I had little use, but it was a bit more civilian-looking version of my workaday. It had a slightly deeper neckline and the rank stripes were gilt, but most importantly, it was crisp and clean. The only odor emanating from it was the camphor of mothballs.

"Jenkins, I need you to run this over to the tailor's and have commander's stripes sewn on. Who knows, I might be going to the theater some evening."

I could see a question burning in his eyes, but he was too proper to ask, or perhaps it was that he was too sober on this occasion. Instead, he just said, "Certainly, is there anything else?"

"Why?"

"Beggin' yer pardon." He motioned for me to put on my coat, and I obliged. He grabbed a handful of cloth on either side, demonstrating how poorly the coat hung on my frame. "If you intend to make a romantic impression . . ."

"I see, but . . ."

He tut-tutted and strode off to return in a minute with a packet of pins. He bade me raise my arms and expertly pinned the coat, fitting to my shape.

I struggled out of the coat and handed it to my valet. "Well, while we are at it, see if the fellow can make me something like this." I opened my portfolio and removed a page I'd taken from my sketchbook.

He frowned at it. "It does look somewhat like a uniform, but is it regulation?" He chuckled at his own joke. There were ten pages in the navy manual about officers' uniforms (less for ratings) so each officer was left to secure his own kit, leaving very little that was actually uniform.

"I do not know. The manual does not specify a submersible commander's uniform."

Jenkins's eyes nearly popped out. "A what?"

I filled him in on my new command as he just stared at me.

Finally, he sighed, picked up my sketch and the coat. "I will see to these, sir."

"Also," I concluded, "I will a need a knee-length set of white drawstring trousers and a white short sleeved jersey. And, inform Mrs. Hawn that after tomorrow I will be forgoing a hot breakfast."

"Oh?"

"Yes, I find that I am out of shape and I will start practicing calisthenics in the morning."

That night I slept more soundly, only rousing once, imagining I heard a smoke-thickened voice crying out my name in the darkness.

Chapter Five

The second day of my new assignment was busier, but also far more tedious. I started the day by meeting each of my junior officers individually, and then met with them collectively for lunch.

I learned that Lieutenant Hanley, a ginger fellow with a florid face who looked much older than his twenty-five years, was saving money to buy some land and hoped to marry next spring. Lieutenant Bertram, on the other hand, was married and a strict Methodist who extolled the virtues of being a teetotaler and carried a Bible at all times. He seemed as if he would have been right at home with Jenkins's former employer.

I failed to learn much more about William Bartley, except to confirm that he was the most senior of the three junior lieutenants, despite his boyish looks. The time I allotted for his interview was spent discussing other pressing issues. We got off track when he informed me that he was able to confirm that one of the prototype fuse sets brought by the Americans was indeed missing, while all the standards munitions stocks were accounted for. It seems that since the American fuses were received without official paperwork, their handling had been inexcusably lax, widening the pool of suspects.

Which brought me to my interview with Lieutenant Graf.

He reported to my office at the appointed hour and knocked soundly three times on the frame of the open door.

"Come in, and close the door," I invited.

He strode to within a foot of my desk and saluted. His movement was so stiff and correct he could have been an automaton. Although, in fairness, his stiffness could also have been due to the excess of starch in his shirt; his collar appeared so sharp that if he let his chin down, it might have sliced his throat. His trousers had a similarly severe crease, and his coat had been brushed and pressed so that it looked as if it were brand new, an appearance belied by small touches of careful mending.

I returned the salute and told him to be at ease, then gestured to a chair by my desk. "Please have a seat."

He took the proffered chair but sat stiffly on the edge as if still at attention. His face was a study in stoicism and his determined eyes met mine. I smiled in an attempt to put him at ease, and he returned just a hint of a frown, barely drooping the carefully shaped tips of his mustache.

"Is something bothering you, Lieutenant?"

He worked his jaw for a moment as if he had something pressing to say, but was reluctant to actually say it. "It is customary to speak to the senior officers first," he finally said.

I shifted my head slightly to see him better with the right eye. "While I am not so certain that is customary, I will concede that it is more common," I said in slow conciliatory voice. "Perhaps I should have discussed it with you first, but I prefer to speak to people without preconceptions. If these men are going to be my officers, I need to get a feel for them."

He started to interrupt, but I waved him down and spoke in a slightly sharper tone.

"And if you are to serve as my executive officer and de facto co-commander, you will need to understand my ways."

This was my first private conversation with Graf. We had not discussed the concept of the structure Captain Wilson had in mind, but I was certain that he was fully aware of it. I would be in overall command of the unit, but Lieutenant Graf and I would each lead our own crew. The new boat would be going on short patrols, maybe as short as a week, and then it would swap crew and go back out, allowing only minimal time for port maintenance.

"I value your input and we will spend far too much time discussing and evaluating the officers and men. But for now, allow me to get to know them."

"As you wish," he replied, in a tone that spoke volumes of disagreement.

I softened my manner to ease the conversation into a more productive interview. "What about you? What can you tell me about yourself?"

He inclined his head. "What would you like to know?"

He was determined not to make this easy. "Are you married?" I hoped that by moving the conversation away from the professional area, he might unbend.

"Yes, sir, six years." His words were just answer enough that I could not accuse him of impertinence.

"Any children?"

"Yes, sir. Two girls."

I stared at him as if he had not answered the question, a technique I'd picked up from one of my professors.

It did not work. Instead of elaborating, he simply inquired, "Anything else you want to know sir?"

I drummed the fingers of my right hand on the desk. "Are you always this reticent, or is it me?"

"I don't know sir." His voice grew sharper, "Are *you* always so reticent, or is it *me*?"

I stopped drumming and leaned forward. "Meaning?"

His eyes flashed as the floodgates opened. "Meaning that something happened yesterday. You spent an hour with the captain and Bartley and now Bartley is acting strange and snooping around the munitions storage." He clenched his fists, "I am your second in command and no one sees fit to tell me anything."

I sighed, seeing him sit possibly even stiffer than before. "It's true that the captain has Bartley looking into a confidential matter . . ."

He started to speak, but I pointed at him and did not stop speaking. "That is the captain's affair and you would have to take it up with him. As for the time we spent with Captain Wilson, you may have noticed we hit something and damaged the *Ram*, and he had a little something to say about that."

The lieutenant almost smiled and edged back into his seat a bit.

"I imagine that he had something to say all right," he said. "But I did see the damage; that was an odd collision." His voice implied suspicions that he was not ready to address directly.

I understood his misgivings and decided to acknowledge them just as indirectly.

"Nevertheless, until stated otherwise, that is what it was, a collision."

He nodded. "Will that be all, sir?"

I frowned and thought about it for a moment. It would be easier to send him away and work at winning him over later, but I now had my initial impression of my officers and so I asked him, "What is your impression of the lieutenants?"

He hesitated for just an instant, and his eyes narrowed. "For the most part, they are good men."

"Excepting whom?"

"You misunderstand me. They are all mostly good, but like all men they each have their weaknesses. I am sure that you picked up on some of those." His tone suggested that he suspected nothing of the sort.

"What sort of weaknesses?"

"Bertram's problem with the bottle should be very evident."

I gawked at him, trying hard not to show my surprise. "The Bible thumper?"

"Yes." He gave a thoughtful nod. "He tries to stay to the straight and narrow. I suspect that his temperance lectures are meant for himself, and his wife declares that he 'fights the good fight.' I am certain that he is sober most of the time, but when the thirst hits him, he changes, becomes a very angry and frustrated man. His wife will bring the children and visit my family."

"Oh, good God." I closed my eyes for a second. "And Hanley?"

"He suffers from a certain melancholia. He will go for days at a time in a cloud of despair, and during these episodes bears watching because he is forgetful and easily fatigued."

"While he did appear to be a glum sort, I was under the impression he was looking forward to getting married."

"He is, that is what he despairs about. The girl has been ill, and I fear she is consumptive."

I shivered. Consumption is not a disease that I would wish on anyone, and I do not know how I would bear it if a loved one was so afflicted. But what Graf described as a weakness, I took as a strength that the man would stand by someone in such a state.

"And Bartley?"

"Aside from his habit of gossiping like a washerwoman, he is keeping a mistress."

I laughed aloud. "On a lieutenant's pay? Surely you can't be serious?"

"I am serious," his tone was almost, but not quite, defensive. "The man comes from money and I have seen him wager more on one hand of cards than I see in a month, then pay up and buy a drink for the winner. At least he does not wager what he cannot afford to lose." He slowed down his speech to make a point. "That is the coxswain's problem. But Bartley is only in the navy because of family tradition and he will not inherit unless he serves. I think he volunteered for the submersible program as a petty act of rebellion."

"Well, he seems a good sort."

Graf sighed heavily. "I will admit that I wanted to jolt you a bit about the nature of the men in your command. Describing the lady in question as Bartley's 'mistress' may be an exaggeration. He calls court on an actress several nights a week, and he even talks about that too much."

"And what about the men?"

He swept his hand dismissively. "That is the coxswain's concern. They do what they are told when they are told; that is the best and least we can expect from them."

An awkward silence stood between us.

"And my weakness?" I asked warily.

He regarded me with narrowed eyes, his brow creasing in thought.

"Permission to speak freely, sir?" he asked in the most uncertain voice I'd heard from him.

"I insist upon it."

"Yours is the worst weakness for an officer. You do not understand the last thing I said about the men; you do not understand that they, the common sailors, are tools. You should use them, command them, do not seek their approval; that only makes you look weak. Do not court their loyalty, for they have precious little to give."

I listened to him, tight-lipped. "I disagree. I believe that we can earn their loyalty and their respect, and we should make the effort."

"I have watched you here, and have talked to your former colleagues."

"You have gone to lengths."

"I care about this project. My reputation and career is tied to it and I have to know that the man they passed me over for command is fit." He paused as if he had said too much, but I nodded for him to continue.

"I am surprised you have not made inquiries about me. But everyone I talk to about you, tells a distressingly similar story. Senior officers do not understand you, and you are well-liked by the men in your command."

"I think that being respected by my men should be one of the things I am most proud of."

He shook his head, "It is nothing to be proud of; it speaks of the greatest weakness in an officer. You bear the burden of making life-and-death decisions for other men: you cannot be their friend. You have to enforce discipline and not be overly familiar. Permissive officers get their men killed. To be frank, I think that I will handle my crew far better than you will handle yours." He sat back in his chair, evidently satisfied he'd had his say.

"It would appear that we are at an impasse. I cannot agree with your opinion, but I must concede that I do understand it." I rose from my desk and extended my hand. "I do not expect you to agree with me on all things; I just ask that you work with me and support my goals, and I will work with you to the same degree. Thank you for meeting with me."

Understanding that the meeting was over, he stood as well and took the proffered hand.

"Lieutenant Graf," I said as I looked him in the eye. "It will be interesting to work with you."

He made a better show of camaraderie at luncheon, but I suspect he was making a brave face for the other officers. After the meal, I repaired to my office to deal with the most necessary and most distasteful part of an officer's duty— paperwork, in triplicate.

By late afternoon, I had ensured that the men would get paid, signed for supplies for the *Ram*, ordered more supplies, accounted for the damages to the sub, and filled out a form to order more forms. My fingers were ink-stained and I had a smear on one cuff from the sheets of carbonated paper used to make copies. I stacked the remaining pages neatly and put on my jacket to take a short trip.

There is a horse-drawn trolley that travels the length of the port on a regular schedule. I stepped aboard near the foundry works and rode for about five miles to where a small set of barracks had been built to house the marine detail at the port, and my men.

I walked in unexpected. According to the training schedule, this afternoon was listed as a cleaning day and I found the men vigorously scrubbing the barracks, thin mattresses airing on lines outside, and the coxswain striding around purposefully, keeping his eyes on the work and making sure that the men attended to every detail. One sailor stepped back from the airing line, and dusted his thick scarred hands against each other. One quick look would tell you that his nose had been broken more than a few times. His left ear stood out trumpet-like and was accented by thick scars around his right eye. As his eye met mine, he jumped to attention and hollered in a thick gravelly voice, "Attention on deck!"

I waited a moment for the rest of the men to come to attention and for the coxswain to report with a salute. Returning the salute, I gave the command, "As you were."

"I will be in the area the rest of the day," I announced, to let them know they could ignore my presence and not jump to attention every time they saw me.

I addressed my petty officer, "May I have a moment of your time?"

"Certainly, sir," he replied in a booming voice. Like most of the senior enlisted men he talked a little too loudly most of the time, partly from being used to shouting orders over the roar and hiss of a steam engine or across a parade ground, but mostly from spending too much of his career around the big guns.

We retired to his office; a small room where he had his bunk, a plain pine desk with three rough chairs, a locked wardrobe and his sea locker.

"Well, sir," he said, "What can I do for you?"

"Tell me about the men."

He actually preened a bit, which I saw as a signal that he was proud of his unit. "Well, they're a good lot. I think they are coming along nicely." His voice was offhand, but the gleam in his eyes spoke volumes.

"Who is the pugilist?" I inquired.

"Oh, Smith? Looks a fright, don't he? But he's reliable. Not as sharp as some, if you take my meaning, but you can trust him."

We spent another hour as he filled me in on some details and I made suggestions for the training schedule.

I began my third day at the barracks, feeling better rested. Although I still awoke to voices calling me in my sleep, I was getting better rest than I had in the last several months. Perhaps having something worth waking up for is better than a cup of gin to help you sleep.

It was 0600 when I arrived at the port, and took the trolley back to the men's quarters. I was traveling in my standard uniform, but packed in my case were the white cotton trousers and jersey Jenkins picked up for me, which just happened to be the uniform the men wore for calisthenics.

It may seem strange that I would consider such a uniform and still be uncomfortable appearing in shirt sleeves in front of my men in a command situation, but sport is different. It just is.

I timed my arrival carefully and got off the trolley when I expected the barracks to be empty. The man detailed as charge of quarters, Seaman Charles, did a double glance at my appearance, and then snapped to attention. "Sir!"

"At ease." I waved him back into his seat. "I need to use the coxswain's office for a minute."

He nodded to a door across the way. I started to head there when I saw him motion to another man seated in a chair around the corner, another sailor who had been detailed as runner and the CQ was evidently going to send word of my arrival.

I pointed at the runner as I passed. "Stand fast."

He blinked at me. "Aye, sir," he replied and sat back down. I went into the sparsely furnished office, stripped down, and swiftly changed into my exercise clothes, leaving my case and portfolio on the plain wooden desk. I then carefully unscrewed the iron hook from the wooden base of its leather cuff. Thus prepared, I went back to see the CQ. "Where do the men take exercise?"

He stared at me, his eyes wide. "The parade ground is out the door to the left, sir." His voice was uncertain, as if he should not be giving out the information. "Right past the last building, there is an open field."

"Very good." I nodded and left.

I reached the designated spot just as the men progressed to double intervals and without hesitating, I stepped out from the building. The formation faced me, the coxswain roughly ten feet from my position. His compact frame was strong and wiry for a man his age, with just a bit of a potbelly pushing at the front of his jersey.

"All right," his voice boomed across the field. "You bloody bastards, you are one sorry excuse for a navy unit. I've seen smarter moves from a poxed whore." His head snapped to the left and he singled out one of the men. "And you, Jonas, what the bleeding Jesus do you think are you looking at?"

Jonas was the first to see me, but by now the whole unit was staring at me, mouths agape.

"I think they are staring at me, petty officer," I called out in an amiable tone, loud enough to carry the field.

The coxswain spun around; and only his eyes betrayed any surprise at all, and then only a little. He frowned at my attire. "Beggin yer pardon sir, I'll be with you in a minute. I'm uh . . . exercising the men."

"I know," I continued, pitching my tone as if this were a casual conversation that just happened to be loud enough for everyone to hear. "I am afraid that I've been rather sedentary this last year and I have decided to join you."

"Join us?" the coxswain replied, his eyes now showing true surprise. Such an action was not only uncommon, it was unheard of, which is the reason I told no one of my intention. While Jenkins might accept that I wanted to exercise in the morning, he would have been apoplectic if he thought I was going to do it with the men. He might be yet.

The coxswain shook his grey head. "Sir, I don't think . . ." he began clearly trying to speak sense to the crazy officer standing before him.

I held up my hand. "Every man here is expected to know and perform the job of any other man, correct?" I gave him a sideways glance as I faced the men, my good hand and my leather bound stump held behind my back as if I were giving a lecture.

"That is the nature of a sub crew, sir."

"It follows that I, as the commander, should be able to do so as well.

59

At least to the same level, if not higher, correct?"

He nodded his head in reluctant agreement.

"How am I to know what the men are supposed to be capable of, and what I need to be capable of, unless I train with you, at least as far as is practicable?"

Petty Officer Grant gritted his teeth, the exasperated look of a professional sailor asked to put up with the eccentric whims of a deranged officer. He sighed deeply and gazed at the men who were intently watching the exchange. "Then, if you please sir, fall in."

I fell in to the far right position of the front row.

The coxswain rubbed his hands together. "All right lads," he said in quieter voice that was more gentle in tone, but still carried the field. "If you would be so kind as to get into position for jumping jacks."

I raised my hand and took one step forward.

The coxswain looked at me, and closed his eyes for a moment. He was struggling to maintain outward control. "Yes, sir?"

"I seem to notice . . ." I said, adopting the overly loud casual tone I'd used earlier, ". . . a, shall we say, change of manner? I am not here to change what you are doing, or to tell you how to do your job. This is your formation and your training, and if I am in your formation, I expect you to lead that training in your accustomed manner and to treat me as any other. Do I make myself clear?"

He stared at me with pursed lips for several seconds as he mulled over my words. "Are you sure you really mean that, sir?" he said with forced patience.

"Yes, I do." I said, with as much sincerity as I could muster.

It was his turn to sharpen his tone. "Then the first thing; you are an officer, show up for calisthenics, don't show; that's yer bloody business. But you show up late for my formation again, you will do ten press ups for every minute late, just like any other man."

"Absolutely. How many do I owe for today?"

He smiled slightly. "We'll let it pass today." A wicked grin crossed his lips and his eyes gleamed. He shouted at me as if I were a new recruit. "Now, shut yer bloody gob and get yer arse back in line!"

By the time I got back to my office, I ached; knowing I was going to ache more. What I wanted was a hot soak and some liniment to rub on my elbow to try to ease the pain shooting from that joint to my stump. The hurt in my back could be managed by standing stiff, but I needed to use that arm, and each movement sent an electric line of pain from my shoulder to my wrist. Nevertheless, I skipped ointments and breakfast, and made sure to be properly attired, fully anticipating being called to Captain Wilson's office as soon as he heard of my morning escapade. I surmised he would go about it one of two ways. If he was not overly alarmed by my behavior, he, or his aide, Ensign Robeson, would call me directly to his office. But if he felt that I was completely out of line, he might send word that he would call for me later, at some indefinite time to allow me to sweat and consider my actions. Apparently, there was a third option I had not considered.

The captain himself barreled into my office through the open door. Without preamble, he thundered, "In my office, now!" He turned and strode from the room. I stepped quickly to follow him as he stormed through the entire building to his office, far on the other side. Sailors, workers, and managers dodged aside as we plowed through. When we reached his office, he bade me enter first, and then followed, slamming the door. I stood at attention in front of his desk while he made his way around and sat down.

I started to salute, formally reporting, and he waved it away. He slouched in his chair, looking far more tired than angry. After a moment, he propped himself up. "Well, then," he said in a voice far calmer than his manner indicated, "that should let everyone know that I am furious with you."

I stared at him, astonished.

At the look on my face, he gave a tight smile and shook his head, then waved toward a chair. "Sit down and tell me what you think you are doing. I assume there is some purpose to your actions."

I collected my thoughts for a second. I had expected this interview and had prepared my arguments, but the abrupt nature of my summons had discomfited me.

"Fifty years ago, we could press any man off the street and turn him into a sailor. We could have him doing deck work in a few hours and in the rigging in a few days."

He nodded.

"Back then, we maintained discipline with rum and the lash. We did not need the sailor's ingenuity, or initiative, only his obedience. It seems to me, sir, sailors are now required to have far more skills, and the training we give them will have to be an investment. We need brains and motivation, and I think that one tool is demonstrating a respect for what they do, and showing our willingness to go through the same."

There was a moment of silence as Wilson mulled this over. "I don't know," he replied with a shake of his head. "Sailors haven't changed as much as you seem to think."

"But they will have to. We are doing something totally new, creating a new class of sailor; not a mariner, but a sub-mariner. The way we crew and operate a submarine is going to blur the distinction between officers and seamen. We must create a system that allows for flexibility, but that does not lose that distinction."

He slapped his hands together and rubbed his palms in thought. "And you allowed a petty officer to swear at you in front of your men to sharpen that distinction?"

"No sir, I encouraged it. Follow my logic for a moment."

"I will try, but I must admit I am at sea."

"I was still technically in command of the formation, being the senior there, but I delegated complete control to the person who had the responsibility for that activity."

"I see some of your point."

"It is simply an extension of what we are already doing. If I go out on the *Ram* tomorrow with Bartley driving, who is in command? Of the *Ram* itself?"

"That would be Lieutenant Bartley. While you would be technically in command, the driver is responsible for the sub."

"Exactly, just as I am technically in command in the coxswain's formation, but I defer to his area of expertise. The men are going to have to understand on a visceral level not only who is in command, but also who is in charge of any given operation."

Captain Wilson sighed and seemed to concede the point.

"In addition, I need to know my men very well, and they need to know me. Our lives will depend upon it. I believe that limited training with them will help that."

"Are you going to order your officers to do so as well?"

I reluctantly shook my head and sighed. "I do not think I will order them to go to calisthenics; that would not go over well, and it would not do for morale for the men to see their officers in such straits. But I do plan for some training to put officers under the temporary authority of a subordinate."

He leaned forward over his desk, steepling his fingers and resting his bearded jaw on them. "You have put me in an awkward position." He pensively tapped the fingers against his chin.

"If I tell you not to train with the men, half of them will think you didn't come back because it was too hard, and the rest will think you did it as a lark and it will erode their respect. So, for morale, I have to either relieve you completely, or let you continue with your madness."

"Yes, sir."

He looked at me with a grim smile. "Which you damn well knew would happen if you just went ahead without mentioning your hare-brained plan."

"Yes, sir."

He rocked his head back and let out a barking laugh. "Joke's on me, I suppose. I wanted you because you would shake things up, and you are succeeding beyond my wildest dreams."

He continued, his voice sounded wistful. "I don't suppose you could have a talk with the coxswain and request him not to swear at you specifically?"

"Have you never had a coxswain swear at you?"

He laughed at an apparent memory. "Not in front of the men."

"I don't think that will be a problem. I suspect he was just trying to gauge how serious I was."

The captain took in a very deep breath. "I am letting you get away with this, but I am giving you a direct and lawful order that you will discuss with me any future 'non-traditional training,' understood?"

"Yes, Sir."

"Then you are dismissed." I turned to leave, but he stopped me. "One last thing . . ."

"Yes, sir?" I asked over my shoulder.

"I have a reputation to maintain and as far as everyone else is concerned, I have spent the last few minutes verbally flaying your hide. Try to look properly mortified when you leave my office."

"Very good sir," I put on my most sincere frown. "Should I cry, sir?"

He snorted. "Good god, man, stiff upper lip; you are still British. Now, get out."

Lieutenant Graf caught me in the hallway, the stiffened tips of his mustache bristling. "What have you done?"

"Took some exercise."

He waved a finger in my face. "After our talk yesterday, I was hoping you could take a hint. Your naïve notion of egalitarianism is deadly."

"Lieutenant, attention!" I ordered harshly.

He snapped to so quickly his heels clicked.

"You are granted a certain leeway as my exec, but the plain fact is that I am in command." I pointedly looked at the captain's closed door. "Still in command. And while I may respect your attitude, you will not conflict with me in a disrespectful manner."

He glared at me.

"We will discuss this later. I will not do you the indignity of marching you through the building, but rather I will send for you when it is convenient for me."

He could sweat a bit. I turned to walk away from him.

"At ease," I said, still facing away from him.

I was not finished with the day's ration of disapproval; I still had to go home to Jenkins.

I walked into a dimly lit sitting room with no tea kettle ready to be put to the boil or wine glass laid out. A brooding Jenkins sat by the cold fireplace, slouched with his legs crossed at the ankles and his arms sullenly crossed against his chest.

"Good evening."

Jenkins glared at me. "Will I need to seek another position?"

"I mistake your meaning."

"Are you still on active duty?"

"Oh, yes."

He jumped to his feet in righteous indignation.

"Did you really let a petty officer tell you to 'shut your bloody gob and get your arse back in line'?" His eyes widened with incredulity. "In front of your men?"

"No, I didn't let him," I explained in a stern voice. "I actively encouraged him. I was making a point."

"You were making something. And you did nothing?"

I looked Jenkins right in the eye and said very seriously, "I did do something; I shut my bloody gob and got my arse back in line."

He stared at me for a second, then snorted in spite of himself and buried his face in his palm. "As your valet I am mortified," he said as he looked up at me. "But as a former petty officer and steward, gad, I'd love to have seen that. Reminds me of the time the bo'sun caught the admiral with his sister . . ."

"The Admiral's sister?"

"Oh no, sir, the bo'sun's sister. That was a pretty piece of swearing, it was. And the Admiral took it with good grace, he did."

Chapter Six

My fifth morning at the shipyards began with the same routine I had established, even though Saturday was only scheduled as a half day of work for the men. The gangs at the Ironworks would labor throughout the weekend because the riveting of the control house decking structure was behind schedule.

I reached the point where I was not so sore or enervated after physical training; in fact, there was color in my cheeks and my wind was improving. The activity even eased the old pain. I was not building the powerful muscles I sported in my rugby days, but was happy to notice more endurance and greater flexibility.

After cleaning up at the barracks as best I could, I changed into my customary uniform and traveled back to my office. My first order of business would be to head to the smaller dry dock at the far end of the pier and look in on the condition of the HMS *Holland Ram* as it went through repairs for the damage from the "collision." From there, I fully expected to spend the rest of my morning in the larger dry dock familiarizing myself with the bridge while the support struts were riveted in. The deck of the conning tower was to be made of oak, a decision that was argued for on the basis that it was far cheaper than the iron or steel used in the rest of the craft and that a deck fire was not a serious concern on a submersible. Nevertheless, I believe the debate was settled on nostalgic and esthetic grounds.

The first few times I visited the works, I wore my customary full kit, but found myself sweltering from the heat. Between the humid spring air, augmented by the warmth from the foundry works, I was awash in sweat in minutes and Jenkins complained bitterly about getting the salt stains out of my coat. I was loathe to go about in shirtsleeves, so I designed myself a compromise and, leaving the wool coat in my office, I put on my new acquisition. *The tailor's done tolerably well*, I thought as I shrugged into the black double- breasted waistcoat. It was made of heavy linen that was far cooler, if not as grand as my naval frock coat. It came up as high in front as my customary uniform. It was closed with the brass buttons of an officer's uniform, although there were no sleeves on which to sew the rank. I idly thought of reviving the use of epaulettes for rank and in a moment of whimsy, I imagined myself with the great fringed shoulder ornament of a commander in Nelson's fleet.

Thus attired, I made my way across the docks on my morning rounds. The HMS *Holland Ram* looked forlorn, braced up out of the water on a network of more than dozen wooden pilings; several of the rugged iron plates on her fierce ram bow were missing and a few left in place were sadly warped. I was very surprised to find the only person present was Nicola Tesla, sketching on a small notepad.

I watched him for moment disinclined to interrupt his train of thought, until he paused and look back up at the *Ram*. "Good morning, Dr. Tesla," I said.

He regarded me with a rueful shake of his head and an almost shy smile.

"Danny tells me that you have been talking, so between us, it is just Nicola, no?" He extended his hand as if it were our first meeting. As I gripped it, his face relaxed and for a moment I saw through the exceptionally gifted inventor to the extraordinarily young and isolated man.

"What are you drawing?"

"Oh, just where to put the electrodes," he replied casually, as if I were supposed to know what he was talking about.

"I'm sorry—electrodes?"

He frowned at me for a moment as he read the total confusion in my face. "For the plating." He studied my expression. "I see; have you not been told about the plating?"

"No," I said slowly. In a corner of my mind, I vaguely remembered the word 'plating' in one of the technical bulletins, but could not recall the context.

"You are going to galvanize it?" I said.

"*Da*," he replied.

"Why?" I looked at the flat grey coating as I attempted to understand the logic behind the decision. "The lead paint is better than zinc to prevent corrosion."

"*Neh, neh, neh.*" His face twisted in distaste. "Not zinc, the plating."

I understood the first words were in Serbian, but for all my comprehension, the latter might as well have been. "I am still not understanding."

He considered for a moment. "The plating, like the tower," he said, referring to the substance responsible for the shiny bronze color of the iron struts.

"It is a coating that Danny and I devised from a Russian process. It must be placed on very thick, because it does corrode in seawater, although very slowly."

"Then why use it?"

"It is an absurdly effective electrical conductor that keeps my laboratory well-grounded for my lightning experiments, and . . ." He raised a finger in the air and paused for effect. It was my first glimpse of the "Tesla persona" this morning.

"And," I said, in not completely feigned exasperation.

". . . as it slowly corrodes in seawater . . ." he continued, shaking his finger in the air.

It hit me like a blindside flanker. "It generates electricity."

He looked a bit deflated. "*Da,*" he nodded, laying his finger along the side of his nose. "For the R*am,* with no energizer on board, we will just be measuring the current for tests, but for the 'other,' the greater surface area should allow the onboard energizer to take back some of its own."

I imagined the *Ram* shining underwater like a goldfish as I left Nicola to his drawings. I made my way to the huge building where I spent too much of my time, desiring to learn every part of the new construction. Each day I poured over the work plan and compared it to the blueprints, constructing the ship in my mind's eye. I fully desired to be able to envision the boat before it was finished, as completely as I could envision my missing hand. Staring at the frame, I could imagine the broad tear-shaped conning tower with the incongruously delicate-looking rail around the edge, the great fore and aft diving planes, and the two massive propellers that would drive her. The heavy bronze blades were just above the hatch for the diver's lockout chamber in the stern; too damn close to the chamber, in my opinion, if any diver ever needed to enter or exit the craft in motion.

I was grateful for my modified uniform as the weather turned ever warmer. The portable forges which kept the great steel rivets glowing cherry red made even the huge space of the foundry so stifling, that despite my abbreviated attire, sweat dampened my shirt and trickled down my back. Many in the work crews despaired of their clothing and worked shirtless, covered only by heavy leather aprons that protected them from the occasional piece of fiery rivet sprawled off from the impact of the massive peening hammer. An occasional curse would ring out when such a sizzling bit found a patch of bare flesh.

I was in good spirits as I stood on the scaffolding and reviewed the day's expected progress. I looked down to watch as a big man crawled into a small space between plates, far too tight to allow the use of a steam hammer, squeezing a heavy backing plate in with him. Wincing, I saw his mate hold a glowing rivet in iron tongs and thrust it into the same cramped spot. The first man guided it to the hole, braced it from behind with the plate as the second peened the great rivet with a six-pound hammer. The project was creeping along. It was at the critical juncture where the front of the bridge decking frame was being fitted into place to support the most complex part of the bow, the huge cargo doors that would allow the sub to be loaded with full-sized torpedoes.

Many navies had tried to build a submersible that accommodates these deadly fish, long used only on small, swift, steam launches. So far, only an American had been successful, mounting one external tube to the outside of the *Nordenfeldt I*; however, the design was not all that impressive and the American navy allowed the boat to be sold to Turkey. This boat, on the other hand, had big teeth, a magazine with six torpedoes and two internal tubes.

As I climbed down the scaffolding, raised voices from the visitor's entrance caught my attention. They were loud enough to be heard over the clanging staccato of peening hammers. Alarmed, I started that way at a determined trot. Upon reaching the entrance, I beheld a man in a top hat and swallowtail coat yelling at the top of his lungs, waving a threatening walking stick at the riveting crew foreman, Jonathon Wells.

The red-faced man was haranguing the foreman, attempting to order him to do something. I could not immediately tell if his complexion was the result of the heat or his apparent passion.

"What is this about?" I demanded, in a voice that had been trained by shouting over the rumble and howl of a ship's boiler.

The man turned on me, waving his walking stick at me in a contemptuous manner. I snatched it out of his hand and threw it to the ground. I repeated myself, quieter, but with more intensity. "I said 'what is this all about'?"

His red face turned purple.

"Who the hell are you?" He made a show of looking me up and down and smirked in disapproval. "What concern of it is yours?"

I returned his gaze, and answered in a calm level voice. "I am the commander here, and this is most definitely my concern. Now, for the last time, what is going on here?"

The man looked at my costume and seeing no insignia of rank, he spoke with disbelief, "If you are indeed an officer, I hold that you are no gentleman. In fact, you look quite the pirate—Long John Silver himself." He seemed pleased with his wit.

I turned to John Wells. "What happened?"

The stranger started to answer. "This man has the temerity—"

"Not you," I interrupted sharply, waving him silent with my hook without looking at the man. "John, you tell me."

"I must protest . . ." The man blustered.

"One more word and I shall have the marines put you under guard. Do not test me." I turned my good eye to him for a second, then turned back to John Wells. "What happened?'

John rubbed at some grease on his hands and spoke with his eyes downcast. "This man 'ere, he's Mr. Wilkins; 'e's with the company."

"That would be the Thames Ironwork and Shipbuilding Company?"

"Aye, sir. So yesterday, sir, he brings us a set of revised blueprints for the decking structure. It calls for us to reduce the steel rivets by a third."

I turned to the man. "Why?"

"I assure you that we have properly calculated the stresses involved and the new design is sufficient." He picked lint off his coat.

"I was just telling the gentleman 'ere, that I could not accept the changes without direct orders from Captain Wilson. Or yourself, sir."

I looked at Wilkins, exasperated. "Again, why?"

He looked at me as if I were mentally slow. "We are getting behind schedule and tying up manpower for unnecessary rivets is expensive."

I nodded. That I understood. "Wells here is correct; he should not accept changes unless approved by me or the captain." I turned back to the foreman. "Wells, do you have the original blueprints?"

Wells handed them over. I looked at the diagram and checked that the rivet was standard navy specification.

I addressed Wilkins. "May I see the new plan?"

Wilkins pointed at a cylindrical leather case that had been dropped on the floor. One of the men standing around snatched it off the ground before I could and handed it to me. As he did, I glanced around and saw that we need not raise our voices to be heard. The building was far from quiet, but activity slowed to a virtual crawl as most of the men were watching.

I removed the plans from the case, spread them out, and looked at them, slowly shaking my head as I noted the weakened structure.

"This is absurd." Wilkins said, "Listen up, Jack. Don't pretend you even know what you're looking at."

I glanced up, and smiled at the man, ignoring his implication that I was a common "jack tar." "My engineering degree comes from Edinburgh."

"I suppose if such a man as yourself is going to claim a degree, he should claim such a school," he said.

"Please define 'such a man' and 'such a school'."

"Are you slow, or have not the wit to work it out?"

I regarded him carefully, enjoying the rising fire of righteous anger, but knowing that I needed to tamp it down.

"If you intend to slander me, please have the courage to do it directly, not by implication," I said.

His eyes burned and looked to burn me as well. He was standing with his chest puffed out, shoulders squared, resting like a boxer on the balls of his feet, and seemed on the verge of doing me some violence. The effect was ruined somewhat, by the sweat running down his face, which made him look like some vicious small dog left out in the rain.

I regarded the blueprints again. "The contract calls for navy specs." I hadn't seen the contract but it was a safe bet. "This is not navy spec. Are you attempting to breach the contract?"

"Good gad, are you now claiming to be a lawyer as well?" He waved his finger in my face. "You humbug, I shall report you to your superiors."

I handed the two rolls of plans to Wells. "Good idea. Wells, get a marine up here and have him escort this man out of my area and up to Captain Wilson. Also, you go along with both sets of blueprints."

I turned back to Wilkins. His face completely recovered from purple rage, and now appeared merely flushed with the heat. "Captain Wilson is neither an engineer, nor a lawyer, but I am certain he will have both available.

"And one more thing." I crooked a finger at him as I stooped to recover his walking stick. I very politely offered it back to him. He pursed his lips, strode over and made to seize it from me, but with timing learned on the practice field, I avoided his grasp and stepped inside his reach to thump the knobbed end of the stick against his chest. Not hard, just enough to get his attention. I spoke quietly, my voice firm. "If you ever wave a stick at any man under my authority again, I shall take it from you and thrash you soundly with it."

He grabbed the stick, intending no doubt to jerk it from me, but I held on to it for a moment, to show that I could. I waited until he used his whole body to wrench it away, and I let go.

He stumbled back a step, then regained his balance. His mouth opened and closed, then he addressed me, his voice low and menacing. "The next time I see you and have a stick in my hand, I shall beat you like the pox-ridden cur you are."

He gathered up his dignity, resettled his top hat, feigned indifference as he leisurely brushed his now-damp coat before turning his back to me, and striding past the waiting marine.

I sighed and looked around to see that just about all of the work in the dry dock had now come to a standstill. I spied another foreman from a different riveting team; my mind raced to remember his name. "Mr. Billings . . ." I ventured.

"Billers," he corrected.

I winced. "Sorry, Billers,"

He waved away my error.

I clasped the hook behind my back with my good hand as if I were on the deck of a ship. "Put the men back to work, if you please."

"Right, then." He turned around, his voice bellowed across the room. "You bunch, back to work." He waved his arms emphatically at the men too far away to hear and soon everyone was back to their assigned tasks.

I wanted to get back to examining the day's work, but I decided it might be prudent to go back to my office and get my uniform together for the expected summons. I hoped that Wilson would not find it necessary to fetch me himself, this time.

I had broken starch on a fresh shirt when there was a knock at my office door. I had not expected the captain to call for me so quickly. I opened the door, fully expecting a sailor waiting, and found Danjella standing outside. A bit flustered by her finding me with my fresh shirt still unbuttoned, I gaped at her for a second, and pulled the shirt closed as I reached for my jacket. She smiled and demurely lowered her eyes and held up a hand to halt me.

"Please adjust your shirt, but leave the coat." She held up a tailor's tape measure, "You would have to take it back off. I need to look at your forearm."

I looked down at the hook.

Her eyes still modestly looking at the floor she continued. "Your design, it will not be ready for some time and you cannot pilot the *Ram* with one hand, so I come up with an intermediate step."

Still looking down, she held the tape measure between the thumb and forefinger of each hand, pulling it taut.

"If I may?" Her voice was still demure in tone, but I could see a hint of amusement in her features.

I turned around and buttoned my shirt. I had become quite adept at doing this simple task with one hand, but when I imagined her watching my back, I fumbled egregiously and spent several awkward moments. Finished, I turned back to her and nervously rolled up the shirt sleeve, then paused, not knowing how to proceed.

I would rather be dragged naked before her, tortured by all the unspeakable horrors of hell, than bare the scarred bit of ruined flesh that remained of my wrist. I looked back at her; she smiled reassuringly and tugged at the tape measure again. Resigned, I put my fingers to the lacing and tried to untie it without betraying emotion, though fire burned my cheeks, and while my rational brain argued for calm, other parts gave in to humiliation. The laces gave way, and I offered her the most naked part of my body. I dared not look at her face because the slightest touch of disgust would destroy me.

"Much better than I expected," she muttered. "It is well formed and robust."

Danjella deftly looped the tape around my arm in several locations, and had me flex my limb in many directions, stopping only to write down the numbers.

Her manner was very proper and professional, as if the thing she measured and tested was not a part of me, but rather a separate object to be studied. I couldn't stay so detached. I became aware of a very strange tension that came over me as her fingers lightly brushed against my skin. I suspect I was blushing furiously by the time she finished.

Danjella seemed not to notice anything amiss, but as she took her last numbers, I imagined that she gave my forearm an affectionate squeeze. She spooled the tape measure, closed the notebook, then looked at me with a gentle smile and a glint of wry amusement in her eyes.

"I should like to go for entertainment next Saturday—theater or music hall?"

I took a moment to consider my reply, or I was shocked speechless, you will have to judge.

"Please, is a simple entertainment, no?"

"Uh, theater?" I replied.

She smiled. "Excellent, you may pick me up." Her face turned dark as if she had unpleasant news. "Mrs. Livingstone will be accompanying us. She will be for prosperity? Proclivity? Or some such word."

"Propriety," I supplied, and then bit my tongue when I recalled she did not actually want my assistance.

Instead of reprimanding me, she nodded enthusiastically. "Exactly," she exclaimed, apparently willing to forgive an occasional lapse. "Nicola insisted that she go with us when I told him you wanted to escort me."

She sighed in a strange combination of resignation and amusement. "That woman has the oddest effect on me; I feel like an unruly child and I find myself wishing to do something to shock. But you pick me up, yes?"

I nodded. I think she interpreted it as agreement, but I think I meant it as surrender.

She gave me a playful wave and left me standing there, uncertain of what just happened, but aware that I had a social engagement for the following week.

The summons from the captain came half an hour later. I found the door to Captain Wilson's office closed, which was not his custom. Perhaps this time I was truly in difficult straits. Like a first year at the academy, I took a deep breath, gave three solid knocks to the door, and made myself ready to report formally.

"Come," he replied, in a voice that sounded firm, but not necessarily angry.

I opened the door and he waved me in. I immediately saw why his door was closed; Mr. Cooper-Smythe was sitting in one of the leather chairs smoking a cigar.

The captain crooked his finger for me to approach his desk. As I stepped forward, he scrunched up his face and rubbed the bridge of his nose. "Did you actually threaten him bodily?"

"Yes, that I did, sir," I answered without apology.

He chuckled. "God, I wish I could have seen that. You know he fancies himself a fighter, belongs to some physical culture club in Soho and trains single stick." He referred to a martial sport that is supposed to teach gentleman how to fight with their walking sticks. "He is a very well connected man and he is demanding an apology *and* your immediate relief."

"If I many speak in my defense—"

The captain held up his hand to silence me. "No need, I have apologized to his dumb arse on your behalf, and told him in no uncertain terms that you are not going to be relieved." The captain leaned back in his chair and attempted to rub the tension from his temples. "Additionally, he has been told not to visit the dry dock or work areas without prior notice and my permission."

"Thank you, sir."

He sighed, "Did you look at the changes?"

"Yes sir."

"And what did you think? Would it be sound?"

"I don't know, I haven't run the figures, but Royal Navy specifications are what they are for a purpose. I would not recommend changing without good reason."

"My thoughts as well," he agreed. "But we are falling behind schedule and it would speed things up."

I started to protest and he held up a hand to stop me. "Don't worry; it is just a kind of wishful thinking. I know from experience that when you make that kind of devil deal to cut a corner, it is the men in harm's way most likely to pay the price."

"Thank you again, sir. If you have a moment later there is another matter I think I should discuss with you."

He frowned at my formal tone. "Are there other company men you have made enemies of?"

I eyed Cooper-Smythe. "It is personal, sir."

"Don't mind me." The clandestine agent spoke up and went back to smoking his cigar.

The captain sighed. "If it is too personal for his ears, it is doubtless too personal for mine."

I took in a deep breath, and let it out slowly. "I do not wish to make any more enemies; I fear I have quite enough. Miss Tesla has been suggesting that I take her to the theater."

He looked at the ceiling and laughed. "Is that all?"

"I have a mind to do so."

"Well, good luck to you lad; you will most likely need it. She is a woman who knows her own mind, does not suffer fools at all, and is very single-minded in anything that interests her."

"And Dr. Tesla?" I inquired. "I do not wish ill will."

"At a previous time, I requested that the good doctor take more control of his cousin. He told me he can sort of direct her, much like a man riding a runaway horse can direct, but not truly control."

"Unless you have 'vile intentions'," he said the phrase in a plainly mocking tone, "that I could not credit to be in your character, Tesla will be fine with any friendship with his cousin."

His tone became more serious. "But to real business. I know that you are becoming quite involved with the construction of the new boat, but have you been keeping up with the repairs on the *Ram*?"

"Yes, sir, I looked in on it today. They replaced the pneumatic gun tube with a spare, fabricated a new outer tube hatch, and have nearly gotten the hull back together. She should be ready for trials week after next." I paused for a second. "And of course, they are going to plate her."

"Very good; Tesla told you that, I suppose? We just made that decision this morning. Since we have some time available, I am rearranging the schedule to avoid other delays. We may have to be operational sooner than expected, based on news from our friends at Thirty-nine," he nodded at Cooper-Smythe, referring to the slang term for the intelligence committee based on their office number at the Admiralty.

"Bad news from the German Empire," Cooper-Smythe said. "Kaiser Wilhelm is determined to fortify and expand their possessions in South Africa. Bismarck is trying to draw his attention to domestic affairs, and is pushing his anti-socialist legislation very hard."

Bismarck had succeeded in passing temporary anti-socialist legislation that criminalized trade unions and political associations, but had to be reviewed every two years.

"My informants suggest he may be planning to resort to agent provocateurs to provoke the socialists into violent action, in order to have an excuse for a permanent ban."

He tapped the ash off his cigar. "Which brings us to Kapitän Mueller. The home secretary has asked us to give him his ride in the *Ram*. Your thoughts, commander?"

"I cannot see the harm. He is undoubtedly an astute observer, but the most he could learn from a carefully guided tour and ride is that we use an electric motor. But everyone knows the French and the Americans are working on that. He'd never guess about the battery without being told."

"When is the earliest we could accommodate the naval attaché?"

I rubbed my chin. "We get the *Ram* back Monday a week, two days for test and trials; I would say Wednesday would be the earliest."

"I will arrange an invitation for Wednesday then." Cooper-Smythe nodded to himself, "One suggestion; I understand the Ram is also being fitted with caustic soda filters, to improve the air."

"Yes."

"I would recommend you do not make the filters operational until after the good kapitän takes his jaunt."

The captain and I exchanged glances, and he chuckled a bit. "I think that can be arranged."

The agent responded with a conspiratorial wave of his cigar.

Wilson pulled some paper from a folder on his desk. "So for next week, I have just received approval for our change in the training schedule. We will be setting out on Tuesday for a series of exercises."

"Setting out, sir?"

"Your initial ride in the *Ram* was preparation, but now it is time for a little training on Monday, and for your baptism on Tuesday."

"Baptism?"

He leaned his head back and let out another of his barking laughs. "Full immersion," he announced cryptically.

Chapter Seven

"Full immersion indeed," I muttered.

"Beg pardon?" Mr. Henry Siebe, of Siebe, Gorman and Co., blinked at me.

I was a little grumpy that morning. Perhaps it was anxiety regarding the upcoming exercises, but on Monday I woke a full hour earlier than necessary, my heart pounding and my sheets damp with sweat. By the time I sat up and sorted out my emotions, the foggy tendrils of my dreams had faded in the sunlight which made the heavy curtains glow. I could not remember anything except a feeling that I was still falling into darkness. My feelings of unease had not dissipated before I reported for training at Siebe, Gorman and Company, in Lambeth, a district south of London, roughly a mile southeast of Charing Cross station.

I stood in a reception area of the development building attached to their factory, by a heavy rough oak table. Siebe pulled out an object from a stout wooden box that sat on the surface.

"So it is required that I know how to use this thing?" I asked the two men standing with me.

"The Royal Navy has paid us to start your training," Mr. Siebe replied with emphasis to indicate that it was the navy, not his modest person, that required it. "There are men in your unit who will no doubt work with you once you have the bare essentials. You will need to be able to use the equipment without killing yourself, or looking a fool, when you direct and evaluate the exercises tomorrow."

"I don't understand why I am here, the Royal Navy has been training divers for more than forty years."

"Yes, but the standard school will not train an officer, although I have been given to understand that you have no compunction about being placed under their discipline. Besides, they do not have access to this type of equipment." He rapped the object on the table with his knuckles.

The diving helmet was made of cast bronze, but not nearly as thick as others that I have seen. I lifted it off the table and estimated that it weighed roughly forty pounds. It was fitted as one construction to the metal shoulder piece, or corslet, as it was more properly called.

"I thought a helmet had to weigh sixty pounds," I said to Mr. Siebe.

The previous afternoon I called upon the library of the Royal Institution of Naval Architects and spent a few hours reviewing the mechanical characteristics of diving gear.

Siebe brightened, obviously relieved that I had some knowledge.

"As a rule, yes. That is because there is about a cubic foot of air inside the helm. This helm is a closer fit, with only 1,000 cubic inches of displacement."

I turned it over and examined the oval opening. I would need to turn my head to the side, then direct my cranium through the opening, and rotate my chin forward as the helmet settled on my shoulders. It had one broad oval pane of thick glass for a faceplate and a narrower oval on each side, as well as another oval at the front curve of the top. Each plate of crystal was protected by a piece of bronze, cast as something reminiscent of Scottish knot work, and brazed into place over the ports.

"I have never seen such fine work with a hydrogen blowtorch."

"Acetylene; it is the latest technique," he said.

"And this model does not fasten to the suit?"

He shook his head in regret. "That is its main limitation. The Royal Navy requested a helmet that could be donned quickly and we have yet to find a way to create a seal fast enough for the requirements. Of course, the problem with this helmet is that the deeper you go in the water, the higher the water rises in the helmet, and of course, the danger is you can spill out the air."

"Then what happens?"

"Nothing, as long as you don't panic," replied the other man, an American professional diver named Sam Gross. He shrugged his shoulders. He was a tall man; well over six feet. He had skin like old leather cracking from wear; the cracks in his face showed that he spent most of his time smiling. His hair was close cropped, iron grey with white at the temples, which stood out in stark relief to his skin.

"If you spill the air, you stop breathing and the inside will fill in thirty to forty seconds." He handed me a small pamphlet. "This is nowhere near what you need to know to dive safely, but it's a start. We'll give you some time to study this, and then I will teach you the very basics. It helps that you will use the diving rigs for safety and observation so your training doesn't have to be as rigorous as someone working down there."

I frowned at the pamphlet and nodded.

"After that, we'll do a controlled test dive, and then I will run you through some drills with the bottles."

"Bottles?"

"Emergency protocol," he replied.

I racked my brain. I vaguely remembered someone mentioning bottles. It came to me slowly, and I tapped a finger on the side of my head, as if that could knock the memory loose. Of course, Weber mentioned bottles on the first dive.

"Right," I replied, as the context came back to me.

They left me alone to read the meager pamphlet, then Gross came back and spent another three hours teaching me the basic mechanics of diving. The "lecture" was more a litany of horror stories about people who did not understand Boyle's law and had their lungs shredded or eardrums perforated, or who suffered from the more esoteric after-diving illnesses like the "bends," "chokes," "raptures," and the "staggers."

As dreadfully fascinating as I found the material, the lengthy presentation reminded me how long I had been out of the classroom. I found my mind wandering. I would like to say that I thought about the possible saboteur, or about training in the *Ram*, or about the upcoming exercise, but the plain fact was, I kept thinking about taking Danjella to the theater. Although I imagine that I was quite the rake at school, it was a long time since I enjoyed the genteel company of a lady.

"Commander!" a voice snapped at me.

"Yes?" I jerked up my head and realized that I had gone from woolgathering to nearly napping.

"I think we have covered the basic material," said Gross. "Are you ready for practical application?"

He presented me with an awkward one-piece diving costume made from rubberized canvas that, unlike standard divers' dress, had laces down the arms and legs to pull the outfit tight to the body. He led me to a small room where I stripped off my uniform and donned the ungainly garment. The scent of raw rubber assaulted my nostrils, as well as a variety of other odors about which I did not care to speculate. The clumsy suit in place, I joined Mr. Gross at the training center and we fastened each other's laces.

"Not too tight," he admonished me with a mischievous lilt to his voice, as I tried to knot them with my one hand.

Soon we were standing next to a huge water-filled iron tank, a cylinder ten feet high and ten feet in diameter, with observation ports about midway up through which spectators could comfortably observe. Mr. Siebe stood by a rough wooden table, a twin to the one in the waiting area; he held two of the specialty helmets.

"It is a very advanced design, for a shallow water helmet." Mr. Siebe said, "It is only rated for up to seventy-five feet. We specialize in the deep-water rigs, and we think we can find a way to get this thing to go deeper."

I nodded thoughtfully, but to be honest, seventy-five feet seemed pretty deep to me. I personally did not see an urgent need to go much deeper. I felt a knot in my stomach, my mouth felt unusually dry. I thought about requesting a glass of water.

"If we are ready then?" Siebe clapped his hands and rubbed them together.

Sam and I each lifted one of the specialty diving helmets and carried it to a rail-mounted shelf connected to the top of the tank by a winch. We then added two sets of chest weights as Siebe turned the crank of the windlass that controlled the cable, raising them to the top of the reservoir. The equipment was in position by the time Gross clambered up the ladder in his unwieldy garb. I grabbed the rung to follow and found it difficult to bend my knees in the thick material. Determined to match Gross's ability, I jerked myself up; the suit made tiny squeals of protest as I hauled myself along.

Around the periphery of the uppermost part of the test chamber was a catwalk with a chest-high railing punctuated with access points to the water inside. A flat grey-painted iron ladder extended to a depth of three feet by each gap. There were more winches on the walkway; these were affixed to stands and ran through a sophisticated pulley system mounted in the rafters on the ceiling, next to coils of air lines.

Bright lights shone down on the surface of the water, which reflected a greenish luminosity that gave everything a sickly sheen and cast features into stark relief. The tank created an echo that made all sounds tinny and grating upon the ear. A burly, taciturn man was waiting for us.

"This is Ryder, he will be our safety man today." Gross said.

The powerfully built man nodded grimly.

"Your diving costume, is water proof," Gross reminded me, "but since the helmet is not affixed, water can get through at the neck. Do not be alarmed if water goes into it. The reason we lace it is to eliminate the excess space that water might fill so that it will not drag you to the bottom. But it'll make it god-awful awkward to climb out."

I looked at the water. A chemical smell rose from the surface and faint light marked the observation windows. "Doesn't the complicated lacing of the diving suit defeat the purpose of the quickly donned helm?"

"The diving dress is for a controlled situation, just like the air hoses we will be using today." Gross said. "The concept of the helmet is that, in an emergency, it can be donned over normal clothing. Also the diving dress we have been making for the Admiralty is equipped with compressed air tanks, but for simplicity, we will be using hoses today."

He gestured at the bottom of the tank and from this vantage point; I could barely see that there were pieces of equipment lying all along the bottom, including tool boxes and a huge piece of metal that resembled the bulkhead of a sunken ship."

"The idea is we are going to spend half an hour down there, and you will follow my example and perform several tasks. Monkey see, monkey do; understand?"

I nodded, a knot tightening in my chest.

"What we want to accomplish," he said, "is to get you familiar with the feel and function of the experience. You have to have confidence in the helmet and know when things feel right, and know what to do when things are not so right."

I nodded again.

He affixed a rope to my back. As I glanced up at the pulley in the ceiling, I momentarily pictured myself as a fish on a line, and I chuckled nervously at the thought.

"Excellent. Glad you are in good spirits," Sam said. He demonstrated how to strap on a chest weight and how to attach the air hose to the helmet.

"The hose, and later the tanks, will provide a continuous stream of air, so once you get your helmet on, remember to breathe normally."

With that he took a firm grasp on the heavy helmet and pulled it on over his head.

I lifted mine, mostly by grabbing the corslet with my good hand and using my hook to balance the other side. Turning my head sideways to fit the oval, I lowered the device over my cranium, then rotated my head to rest my jaw just above a sort of pad covered with the same rubberized canvas as my costume. I marveled at the range of vision the multiple ports afforded.

Once in the close confines of the diving apparatus, I could feel the drumming beat of my heart and hear the echo of my breathing, both of which were coming a little fast. *Breathe normally, indeed,* I thought, as I took in copper-flavored breaths laced with an acrid ketone smell. I took stock and felt satisfied that everything was in place before I looked up and could just make out Gross's quizzical expression. He made a "thumbs-up" gesture.

I returned the signal with some enthusiasm.

Gross then waved to Ryder, he opened a valve and air hissed into our helmets. He then leaned over until the metal of the casings touched, and shouted, "I'm going to guide your hook." He took my arm, guiding the appendage until it fit to an indentation over the narrow oval of my left view port.

"Hold that firm there," he instructed. "Now watch me." He moved away from me and walked smartly to the opening in the rail and calmly stepped into the water with both hands clenching the helmet.

Understanding, I held the dome down with the hook, added my good hand to the top and I followed him over the side and into the chill water of the tank. As the cast bronze helmet hit the water, I discovered one of the purposes of the pad beneath my jaw. Fortunately, I did not do myself any injury, and the headpiece settled back on my shoulders as I sank sedately to the bottom.

Gross was waiting for me and gave me an "okay" sign with his thumb and forefinger. Indicating that I should watch him, he bent at the waist until all the air spilled out of his helmet in a rush of bubbles. After a second, he stooped down and struggled to bring the water-laden headpiece back upright.

I counted the seconds and reached forty when the water receded enough to expose his nose and mouth, and the sudden fogging of the faceplate revealed he was breathing.

He pointed at me.

I felt muscles tense and blood beating in my ears, but I clenched my jaw. Then aping his motion, I took in a deep breath and bowed most solemnly. The rush of water was disorienting as the cold liquid spilled over my face. The apparatus suddenly doubled in weight, threatening to pull forward off my head or pull me over, but by anchoring my jaw firmly in the pad, I was able to keep the helmet in place. I stooped low, brought my leg muscles under the sinking helmet; I used my powerful thigh muscles to slowly right myself. Air bubbled into my space, assaulting my ears with a painful change in pressure, which subdued with infinite slowness until it was a dull hissing. The water level receded at a crawl until there was enough air so that my breathing was clear.

I took in a deep breath of welcome air.

Gross held up his thumb and I raised my thumb in an enthusiastic reply, slowed by the clumsy suit and water resistance. I felt silly about being so nervous since the exercise was actually not that difficult.

Then he had me do it again.

And again.

By the time I completed the third repetition, I felt comfortable enough with my equipment to follow him through various tasks. I picked up tools, put them away, swung a hammer, and tried to peen a rivet that was there for that purpose, and generally strained to function as normally as possible under the conditions. Some chemical kept algae from growing in the tank, but in spite of that everything had developed a slimy coating that challenged my grip and left long translucent tendrils floating away from various objects. The anxiety of diving ebbed away, and was rapidly replaced by a sort of mundane tedium. At first I used my imagination to pretend that I was diving on a sunken pirate ship or other ancient wreck, but in the end, I could not escape the fact that I was simply in a shallow tank doing make work. I grew bored and careless.

There was large nut on the bottom of the tank and my task was to stoop down, pick it up, maneuver it to a bolt sticking out at waist level, and then use a spanner to tighten it. When I tried to spin the nut to engage the threads, it proved stubborn and slipped from my fingers. I fumbled to catch it once, which only propelled it further from my grasp, and I extended my reach again as it sank. Without thought, I bent over further to catch it, and the cold water rushed into my helmet.

What was routine when expected became a nightmare when unexpected. I gasped at the shock and my throat spasmed in the water. I coughed, then choked as the weight of the helmet pulled me forward to allow more water to flow in. As my jaw jammed into the padding, I regained enough presence of mind to attempt to right myself. Fortunately, I hadn't spilled all the air and when I finally got my legs under me enough to force the substantial bronze headpiece upright, I could just barely get my mouth above the water. Still choking, I could not get my airway to admit any air. Finally, I drew in air with a harsh wheezing sound, but also inhaled small drops of water bubbling inside my faceplate with it. I gagged and coughed again, and then reflexively wheezed again, which this time brought in just a bit of air that I was able to force past my gagging throat. And with that bit of air in my lungs, I threw up.

Bile spewed from my mouth, filling the helmet with a nauseating stench.

My lungs could not be denied and I reflexively sucked in another breath, aspirating bile that had just come out. My esophagus burned, my entire chest was on fire, my brain screamed for more air, but I forced myself to stop trying to breath. I spat out the foul tasting effluent in my mouth, coughed up as much fluid as I could, and spat it out toward where it floated around my neck. I took another wheezing breath and flailed my arms to go to the surface, but the weights kept me firmly at the bottom.

Another wheezing breath.

After an eternity of thirty seconds, I took a full, deep breath and let it out with an unintentional groan. Pain shot down my left arm and the muscles of my back tightened like violin strings.

I looked over at Gross and he gave me a cheerful, strong "thumbs up." I returned the gesture with a lot less enthusiasm. He raised his fist and made three sharp jerking motions as a signal to Ryder. I felt the rope on my back tighten and I gently rose out of the tank. This time I found it less humorous, but rather a relief to be the fish on the line.

At the top, I grabbed the short ladder and heaved myself up to the railing, dragged my body to the catwalk, and promptly sprawled on the floorboards. Working to get the cumbersome helmet off my head, I threw up again, this time aiming purposely into the bronze headpiece. I heard the voice of the more experienced diver. It seemed to come from far away, but when I looked up, he was standing directly over me.

"You will need to clean your own helmet." His voice was friendly, but without a smidgen of sympathy or concern.

I nodded weakly while I kept my jaw clenched against the pain. I looked up at Ryder; we made eye contact and his head bobbed a "you're welcome" to my silent thanks.

"Everybody does that," Gross informed me. "Generally, smart guys do it only once." He offered me a hand and I let him help me up, then stumbled to the rail and stood there, braced, as I took long slow breaths.

"I've heard people say that drowning is a peaceful death," Gross said, standing beside me on the rail. "I been nigh on about drowning twice in my career, and all I remember is blind panic, thrashing about, coughing, choking on nothing, and puking."

I nodded. If he had told me this an hour ago, I would not have understood.

"You did good for your first time. And you are lucky you made that mistake here. It is harder to recover when you are deeper and not under so much control."

I nodded again. I did not feel lucky, but I knew I was.

"Remember," he chided me, "even in a tank, it's an unforgiving world under the water. Never dive alone and never force any of your men to dive alone."

I nodded again.

"Good," he slapped me on the back. "Now get the puke cleaned out of your hard hat so we can get you back down."

I looked into his smiling face and fought off the urge to hit him with the vomit-filled helmet.

With freshly scrubbed diving gear, we returned to the tank for another round of training, and I did not allow my mind to wander.

As we finished the second session, much of the panic of my accident faded. This time, when I climbed out of the tank onto the catwalk, fighting against the pull of my waterlogged suit, I stood straight, removed the diving helmet, and set it on the bench to be lowered down. Once the helmets were down, Mr. Siebe replaced them with five bottles and sent them back on the lift. The bottles were made of brass, oblong in shape, about two inches in diameter and just over a foot in length. At the top, there was an L-shaped fitting with a lever on the right side that ended in a round tube roughly three-quarters of an inch in diameter. Each bottle had a canvas strap and a padded clamp attached to it by a stout cord.

"These are for you to run the test with." Gross held up the bottle. "The theory is simple; you put your head and left arm through the strap so you do not lose the bottle if you become disoriented. You place the clamp securely over your nose, then grasping the bottle in your left arm; you hold the fitting in your mouth, pull this lever down, and take a breath."

"The bottle is good for two deep breaths. Remember what I taught you about Boyle's law; the air that goes in will have more volume because your body is under pressure, so do not hold your breath, no matter how deep you are, but blow it out all the way to the surface." He took a lung full from the bottle. "See?"

I nodded.

"Now you do it."

I fitted the clamp over my nostrils, clamped the bottle against my body with my forearm, used my right hand to activate the lever, and took a breath. On dry land, the technique was easy.

He reached and took the clamp from my nose with his left hand, and took the bottle from my right. "You think you can do that?"

"Seems straightforward," I replied, trying to sound confident.

"Then go jump in the water and let the weight take you to the bottom. I'm going to wait one minute, and then I will drop a bottle to you. Take one breath of air, count to thirty slowly, and take another, then come to the surface."

I started to unfasten the chest weight we used for the helmet training.

"Leave it on; it will help you stay under for practice and you should be able to swim to the surface if you kick vigorously."

I held up the rope from the pulley on the ceiling.

"That, too."

I nodded, took a deep breath, jumped in the water, and was rapidly drawn into the tank until my feet hit the bottom. I tentatively pushed off, giving a few kicks to assure myself that I could rise when necessary. As I bobbed, the seconds were ticking: one . . . two . . .

I had my eye open to see when the air tank was dropped and the chemical in the water burned, forcing me to blink rapidly: thirty-five . . . Thirty-six . . . Intellectually, I knew I could get air, but an echo of earlier panic reverberated in my head and I fought it: fifty-nine . . . sixty . . .

Was something wrong? I stooped down to kick for the surface: sixty-eight . . . sixty-nine . . . I searched above me for a sign of the air bottle until finally I saw the splash. I caught the sinking bottle with my right hand, and I clumsily draped the canvas strap over my left arm and neck, the wet canvas alternately sticking to my suit or drifting away as I tried to guide it. The nose clip seemed determined to elude me as each time I grasped at it, it skipped away from my fingers. My left arm pressed the bottle against my body as I seized the nose clip cord with my hand and followed it until the errant device was in my fingers. With a twist of my hand, I turned it to clip over my nostrils, blew the rest of the air from my lungs, placed my mouth over the tube and moved the lever down. Unprepared for the force of the discharge, the tube burst from my mouth and air bubbled away uselessly.

My lungs ached, and I could feel my heart pound in my chest, but I was determined to get it right rather than push up the relatively few feet to an abundance of air. I released the lever, pushed the tube back in my mouth, seized it with my teeth, reengaged the valve and was rewarded with a sweet gust of air, which, for all its pleasantness, left a taste of engine oil in my mouth. The valve closed and I counted slowly to thirty before repeating the breath, and finally pushing up to the surface. I thrashed around a bit as my hook did not give me as much resistance in the water. I managed to paddle to the railing and climbed up on the catwalk, where I crumpled against the rail and took in deep breaths.

"Very good." He jerked a thumb toward the tank, "Now back in."

I looked at him, silently asking for a minute to breathe.

"In." He jabbed his thumb, "Now."

I wanted to scream at him, shriek about the pain that racked my body. Instead, with a last gasp of fresh air, I dutifully dropped back into the shallow tank. I was confident that even if I was fatigued, there was no real danger in the practice tank, and the recovery rope was still attached. I counted to sixty again, much slower this time, using the word "Piccadilly" between each number, and the air cylinder came splashing down as I reached fifty-five. Even though it was five seconds earlier than I was expecting it, my lungs were anxious for oxygen and I went through the steps with much more expertise: strap, clip, lever, breathe.

The bottle hissed in its familiar way. I had just enough time to realize the peculiar essence coating my mouth and tongue was nothing like engine oil, but sickeningly sweet and cloying. I had almost identified it when a black spot appeared in front of my eyes, and before I could even marvel at its arrival, it grew until it was my whole field of vision. I sensed that my body was collapsing to the bottom of the tank. I was vaguely aware of choking, and then I was not aware of anything.

The smell of my own bile brought me to my senses. Gross and Ryder stood over me. They must have used the winch to haul me off the bottom, dragging me to the side like some deep-sea game fish.

There was something I wanted to say, and my head rose, my mouth moved, but no sound came out. My throat was still raw and burning from today's second attempt at drowning. The more I tried to push myself up, the more the world spun, and I let my head fall back with an uncomfortable thump.

For a second, I felt I was falling and living smoke attacked me, wrapping around my face, seeking to shove its choking wisps down my throat. I startled, coughed, and recoiled at a sting on my cheeks, finally waking as Sam Gross slapped me again.

"Whoa, partner, what happened down there?"

Everything rushed back with a sense of urgency.

"The bottle," I gasped.

He picked it up, still strapped around my torso. "You want the bottle?"

"It's not right," I gasped. "Air's not right." I weakly pointed at the offending object.

He held the bottle up to his nose and pulled the lever; his head jerked back to get away from the air pouring out as he released the lever. "Jesus, mother of . . ." he exclaimed.

"Smell it?"

"What the hell is in there?"

I shook my head and tried to think. "Don't know, but one gulp of the air from that bottle and I was gone." I looked up at him, then over at Ryder. "Thanks."

More in control of myself, I sat up, but reconsidered as my temples pounded. "Where did those bottles come from?"

Gross replied, "These came from your men. A detail came around to pick up a gross we'd charged for them, and returned a double dozen. These five hadn't been discharged, so we decide to use them."

"Why were they bringing the bottles here? Don't we use our compressors?"

"Well, yes, you do," Ryder said, "but because this is a new technique, it's in the contract for us to test and inspect the cylinders every two months, generally before an exercise. They brought most last week and this last case was the lot."

"Who was on the detail?"

"Sailors," Ryder replied. "They had the right paperwork. There was one wicked-looking guy who appeared to have stepped into the ring one too many times."

"Smith," I said to myself.

The dizziness finally faded and I rose to my feet as Gross steadied me. Together we examined the bottles but only mine had the telltale sickly sweet smell.

A thought came to me and I started to claw at the laces of my costume.

"I fear this time he has been too clever by half."

"Who?" Gross asked.

I did not answer, instead I said, "Please forgive the impropriety, but I think this is most urgent." I pulled at the rubberized garment to yank my arms free, but my hook became firmly entangled. When I contorted to free it, the pain weaving though my muscles peaked, robbing me of the ability to free my arm. The two men came to my assistance, and loosened the jumble, and yanked the suit down to leave me standing there in naught but my skivvies.

I took a step toward the ladder on rubbery legs and Sam Gross grabbed me. "Slow down there; you're gonna need a few minutes."

"No time," I protested, but accepted his help down to the antechamber where my clothes lay. Using all the fortitude I could muster, I pushed myself on to get back to the port. If only a certain set of people had access to the bottles, then our saboteur could be revealed if I could get back before he covered his tracks. Apparently, he expected me to die peacefully—the true cause remaining unknown. Still buttoning my coat, I staggered out into the street in untied shoes and hailed a hansom cab.

"No such luck," Lieutenant Bartley reported.

The minute I reached the facility, I used all the energy I regained during my ride to dash to the captain's office and give him a brief synopsis of what transpired. He sent a runner for Bartley and dispatched him to question the morning detail, while I gave a much more detailed explanation of the day's events. He gave me a rueful smile when I told him about spilling the air out by accident and how it caught me off guard. He became much more serious when I explained about the tampered bottle.

"But how?" he thundered.

"How did he tamper with it, or how did he deliver it?"

"Start with the tampering." Wilson motioned me to hurry.

"That's easy," I said feeling so very tired. "I believe the bottle contained chloroform or possibly ether; both are very volatile substances which are commonly sold as liquids." I shrugged and then winced at the pain in my back.

"We have several air compressors here," I continued. "Someone would just have to take out the paper air filter, soak it in the chemical, then run the compressor and he would have a bottle that would render a man unconscious."

Wilson rubbed his temples. "How was it directed at you?"

"Maybe it wasn't."

The captain's eyes narrowed. "Oh?"

"If the saboteur did not know that all the bottles, even the fully charged ones, were going back to the manufacturer for inspection, he might have been counting on his doctored cylinder to disrupt the entire series of exercises."

"By risking getting the bad bottle?"

"The bottle gave off a distinctive scent and he may have marked it another way, as well."

The captain sat quiet and thoughtful.

Bartley returned to the office with an unsatisfactory report. The four men who delivered the bottles just picked up the racks they were told to, racks that were sitting unattended since Thursday last.

Disappointed, I left the port, with a glance up at Tesla's tower, headed home dejected, exhausted and worried about the next day's exercise.

I let myself into my flat and found Jenkins sitting at the table reading the paper, a mug of beer at his side. He jumped up at my entrance.

"You are quite early, sir."

Waving him back to his seat, I wandered to the sideboard, selected two whiskey glasses and poured both with two fingers of Irish. I took one and handed it to Jenkins.

"Thank yer, sir, but . . ."

I interrupted him. "It's been very bad day and it is too early for me to be drinking alone."

I picked up the other glass, saluted my valet, and gulped the amber liquid. The pleasant fire traced a line down to my stomach and I hoped the numbing effects would soon ease burning muscles.

Jenkins returned the salute and downed his. "Drinking alone was a habit the admiral should have picked up."

"Oh?"

"Yes, he often picked an inopportune time to test his limits."

"Such as?"

"Oh, many times, but the time that comes to mind is at the Naval Ball, the year after his wife died. He had been toasting the queen and got so well toasted he decided to entertain the gathered gentles with a sea chantey that was banned from the fleet long before I was at sea."

"And being banned," I said, "it is sure that everyone knew it." I pinched the bridge of my nose, recalling the only banned chantey I knew. "Not 'The Randy Daughters'?"

Jenkins's face lit up in an evil grin. "The very one." He sang, "The sailor left at home his randy daughters three . . ."

An infamous bit rhyme that was renown for having a bawdy first verse, a profane second verse, and an overwhelmingly obscene third verse.

"How far did he get?"

"Oh, all the way sir," he stated emphatically.

I clenched my eyes shut in sympathy for the admiral's mortification. "And no one thought to stop him?"

His smile broadened, "There was no need. The men present chuckled, knowing the melody, but his words were so slurred by drink the ladies never understood what he was singing."

I laughed at the admiral's plight.

Jenkins made one more remark. "He later claimed to have been singing in Eye-talian."

Chapter Eight

Monday morning found me climbing the ship's ladder on the HMS *Raleigh* enjoying the cool spring air on my face, a welcome relief from the hours I'd spent in the ship's hold since our departure. The cargo space was configured into a classroom and Petty Officer Grant presented diagrams in tedious detail, specifying each man's role and particulars in the drills for the next three days. Finally, I had to excuse myself for fear that the men would catch me falling asleep.

This was the same frigate that Captain Arthur Wilson commanded at the Cape of Good Hope, the ship having just returned as part of the Empire's final strategic withdrawal from Africa. Between ongoing warfare with the native tribes and continuous skirmishes with the Boers, now freshly supplied by Bismarck, Parliament, in its wisdom, decided to completely abandon our holdings. The prevailing political opinion avowed the Boers and natives would grind each other down, and we would return to pick up the pieces. The military opinion was that after our departure, our Empire would not be the one in position to pick up the pieces.

I reached the walkway encircling the bridge to find Wilson himself leaning over the rail, his eyes watching every detail of the ship's handling. I stood beside him at the rail and took in a deep breath, feeling the tang of salt in my lungs. I said as casually as I could, "So, Captain Fawkes still will not let you visit the bridge?"

Captain Wilson accompanied us on the trip, either to ensure that I did not engage in some new non-traditional training, or perhaps out of nostalgia for his old ship. He smiled, a tight humorless expression.

"The good Captain Wilmot Fawkes has sent his compliments, but insists that it would be inconvenient for me to call upon the bridge. They gave my ship to a cocked hat." He scowled out at the sea, it was the first time I had heard him disparage an officer of the old school. He never attended the Naval Academy, though he had left the service briefly to get a degree at Eton.

The waters churned under the power of the ship's steam screw, while her lightly plated iron hull plowed through the channel to the North Sea. In accordance with naval regulations, the ship carried three tall masts complete with spars and rigging, in case it ever was caught short of a coaling station. However, it was the two steam engines that powered the ship; they sent smoke bellowing from the two black smokestacks set between the masts.

"Look there," he jerked his head to the spars. "The blighter has sailors up in the rigging as if he plans to raise sail at any moment."

We were almost to our rendezvous position, just off the coast of East Mersey, across from Point Clear, and I could make out in the distance the crane ship we were to meet. I took the opportunity to change the subject and pointed it out.

"So, here is our destination. I was wondering, what was the dust up with Miss Tesla this morning?" I asked with plainly feigned nonchalance.

He regarded me out of the corner of his eye; his scowl turned to an abashed grin. "So you saw that, did you?"

"Just a bit of it," I admitted. "I heard the tone of your voices and decided to emulate the better part of valor."

He chuckled and raised an eyebrow. "Ran like a dog, did you?"

I nodded. "I will be seeing her socially and I thought absence was the best strategy."

"Well, good for you. I suppose I better tell you before she bends your ear at the theater; she wants to train to serve on the new boat."

"Come again?" I heard the words, but was not sure that I believed him.

"She wants training," he repeated, and then elaborated. "She wants to practice operating and driving the *Ram* so that she might have a berth on the new boat. She was fully prepared to come out for these exercises."

Somewhere deep inside, I was not surprised; nevertheless I felt a powerful sense of denial. "I should have taken her for a suffragette, a position I might well support, but I would not have thought her completely an unnatural woman."

Wilson frowned, clasped his hands together, and leaned further out over the rail.

"I am not so sure, that what we have come to think of as a natural woman is all that in accordance with nature." He stared out at the sea as if looking far beyond the horizon. "In the Sudan, at the battle of El Teb, I attached myself to a battery of the Naval Brigade and mostly through my own stupidity ended up in near hand to hand combat."

I knew much of the story about how he earned the Victoria Cross for valor.

"There were women in the ranks of the Mahdists, carrying water and food, but they picked up swords and came at us as we advanced. I shot, stabbed, and cut my way free." There was a grim determination, and sadness in his tone.

"I did my duty, but there is much to admire in the courage and strength of those women. And if the tales I've heard about Afghanistan are true, our soldiers would rather fight the men than the women."

"Thankfully, we are civilized and we do not ask our women to fight."

"I suspect sometimes," Wilson said thoughtfully, "that what we think of as delicate hothouse flowers, swooning in tight stays, and prattling frivolously at dinner parties, would be able to stand up with as much valor and determination as their uncivilized sisters, if necessary."

"Well, I thank God that it isn't necessary."

"I hope it never will be," he agreed with an impatient nod. He grabbed at his hat as the gesture gave the breeze the opportunity try to snatch it away. "But did you know the Navy has contingency plan for females in case of invasion?"

I looked at him, shocked.

"Yes, a Women's Royal Navy, nicknamed the WRENS. My first reaction was that it was foolish to even consider it, but then I meet a woman like Miss Tesla, whom I believe has the type of fire necessary."

"I, for one, would fight to the death to protect women from such use." I replied instinctively, "Women should not have to suffer that way."

"But what if a woman wishes to seek out the challenge? What if her sense of duty burns as strongly as yours? You know in your heart you deliberately chose this life. What if a woman wants the same choice?"

I started to reply that natural women were not capable of desiring such a choice, but facts and experience forced me to reason with the concept. I believed Danjella to be a natural woman, if a bit forward and brash.

As if reading my thoughts, Wilson continued. "Be warned, I have known Miss Tesla for nearly two years and she is far more determined and capable than anyone I have ever known. She does not argue like a woman; she cuts right to the quick of the matter with logic and a sharp mind." He paused and looked over my shoulder. Whatever point or revelation he was about to make evaporated. "Ah, Lieutenant Graf, how are you this morning?"

Turning, I saw the man for the first time that day as he had avoided the coxswain's class.

He approached and nodded his head to Wilson. "I am well, and looking forward to the drills."

"As much as I hate to sound like a staff wanker," the captain continued, "I need to have a meeting with both of you to schedule a meeting."

"Regarding?" I asked, my eyes narrowing.

"I hope you have both studied the table of organization for the new submersible boat?"

We nodded.

"Each crew will need both a coxswain and boatswain," he pointed out. "We will need to look into promotions. We are going to need at least three new Petty Officers from the ranks, and I need names soon."

"I will have to yield to Lieutenant Graf, although I assume you assigned Seaman Weber to my trial as he was the best engineer."

"That is true," Graf agreed.

"Then, for the record," I said, "I will add that he seems a stable fellow; unless you have some other knowledge."

Graf creased his brow in thought and shook his head.

I addressed the Captain.

"I have faith in the lieutenant's acquaintance with the men, and I will endorse any of his recommendations."

"How generous of you," Graf replied in a flat tone. While I suspected a degree of sarcasm, there was nothing in his face or tone to betray it.

Wilson seemed unaware that anything had passed between me and my subordinate.

"I will need a list for appropriate promotions on Thursday when we return."

"Perhaps," I ventured, "we are not going far enough? What about recruiting chief warrant officers?"

The captain raised his head and laughed, "You do want to go to war with the Navy."

"We still warrant select specialists and I desperately want men with basic technology training, electrical specialists, mechanical technicians, and such to be brought into the unit to serve as the chief of the engine room."

"We can train the men we have to perform in the engine room," Graf said with certainty. "Even they should be able to learn the routine."

"It is not the routine that worries me. It is the unique situations that arise," I said.

"Gentlemen, we will have to table this," Wilson said. He pointedly turned away from us to look out at our home for the next few days.

The HMS *Raleigh* would leave us on the massive crane ship HMS *Creighton*. Once a great sailing ship, her wooden hull was rebuilt to accommodate the great lifting crane used for salvage, repair, or this odd specialty task.

Hanging amidships from the powerful hoist was what appeared to be a rectangular iron box, incongruently fitted with a conning tower that resembled the crown of the HMS *Holland Ram*.

I quietly studied the flat grey of the module, noting the huge tanks that it currently floated on. "So, that is the mockup?"

Graf gave a grunt and nodded. "How do you wish to proceed?"

I outlined the plan I was considering. "We will be doing the shallows this afternoon. I understand it will be roughly twenty-five feet today, so I will go in the first round, leave command of surface operation with you, and put Grant over the divers . . ."

It is one thing to have an intellectual understanding of an exercise and another to be slowly sinking in the North Sea. The interior of the training chamber looked identical to the *Ram*, except that most of the various valves and levers did not move. The two operational valves were located on each bulkhead, just above the hunks of iron standing in for the motor and the air compressor. They were smaller, more recessed than the valves for the ballast tank, and were latched down, requiring deliberate actions to be turned. In addition, they were painted bright red, although now they appeared light grey in the dimming light. The chamber had no electricity, so we sank beneath the waves in oppressive gloom.

When we moored to the crane ship, we were given one last round of instructions, the sailors slipped off their uniform tunics, and I removed my coat to reveal the linen waistcoat, which earned a raised eyebrow from Captain Wilson.

"Submersible uniform," I remarked, and then I made a show of drawing out my watch to consult it. "Can't do without the pockets, I'm afraid."

"I'd heard you've been trotting about the Ironworks in some sort of abbreviated kit." To my surprise, he nodded thoughtfully. "It is not one of your more questionable ideas. I think that we shall make it regulation."

In an even bigger surprise, the rest of the officers nodded agreement, including Graf, although he had one objection.

"There should be some sign of rank."

"Abbreviated shoulder boards," Captain Wilson said decisively.

With that decision made, I followed Seamen Jonas and Smith into the cramped confines of the iron simulation. All of the lectures, diagrams, and practice meant little when I wedged myself through the narrow hatch, ducked into the cold iron shell, and the heavy metal hatch slammed closed.

The box swayed softly in the current, still floating on the two drums, but then swaying increased as the drums filled with water. It had a permanent lead ballast in the bottom plate to keep us generally upright as we rode to the bottom, this time in a shallow spot above a sand bar. The ride was no more unsettling than riding in the actual *Ram*; the truly terrifying part should start once we settled.

We hit bottom much harder than I expected, knocking the breath out of me in a grunt that sounded strangely mechanical as it echoed off the plates. The crew let out a nervous chuckle in the dark. At this depth, some light still seeped in through the six square windows, enough to tease us, but not enough to actually illuminate anything.

"All right lads, please pass out the belts and bottles," I said.

"Aye, aye." Jonas opened the locker and handed out the survival equipment.

I placed the belt around my waist, joined the flat metal hook on the strap to the hook on the other side and pulled the strap tight. I draped the bottle strap around my head and under my left arm, clutching it to my side with my elbow.

Trying to judge the men's level of readiness by peering at them in the gloom, I gave the order, "Stand by to scuttle."

I sensed more than saw the men maneuver around each other to manage the valves that would flood our crew space. If for any reason, the *Ram* were to be trapped underwater, there was only one way out. The hatch was held shut by the weight of the sea water above us and would not open until the pressure inside the boat equaled the weight above and the only way to do that is to flood the craft. Memories of bathing in the cold North Sea, although it was somewhat warmer in the bay, made me long for the diving costume I wore in my first training, ungainly as it was.

"Open scuttling valves."

Instantly, cold water began to pool around my ankles at an alarming rate. I reached across my body and turned the equalization valve that would vent air from the top of the conning tower to allow the water to rise faster to free us. It would take roughly five minutes for the replica to fill completely and that was more than adequate time to contemplate my mortality.

Waiting has a way of making a person feel helpless, as forces beyond our control take their own sweet time to finish before we can do what is needed. But I found my brain straying not only over the forces of physics that currently had us in their grip, but the actions of our saboteur. It was not difficult to imagine that three men trapped underwater in an iron tomb would be a very tempting target. I tried to sit calmly as the water rose above my knees, and the waists of the two men with me. I reached over my head and spun the wheel of the hatch to disengage the lock.

Not wishing the men to think me afraid, I tensed every muscle in my body to prevent shivering from the cold, but as the water reached up to my shoulders, I could not stop my teeth from chattering. Realistically, we were all in equal discomfort and there was no need to hide it. After another minute, the water was sloshing against the plates at the bottom of the conning tower so all three of us crowded our heads in the restricted space, each of us breathing deeply. The air rapidly became stale, my heart beat faster in my chest, and it seemed no matter how much I inhaled, it was never enough.

"Use bottles on my command," I gasped. We all took one last lungful of air from the confines of the tower, then there was no more room to breathe.

As I'd left my watch with Bartley, I started counting in my head—one Piccadilly, two Piccadilly . . . I was surprised by how desperate my body was becoming for air as I was scarcely past thirty-five Piccadilly when a veritable panic inched along my spine; by forty-five, I was sure that I lost count, but I when looked into the faces of my crew for signs of doubt, they seemed unruffled and focused on me.

At fifty-eight, I held up my forefinger, and at sixty, I brought it down with a short chopping motion. The craft filled with bubbles as each man blew out the air held in his lungs and cracked open the valves on the bottles. As I followed suit, a part of me was terrified I would encounter the sickly sweet taste of my last bottle. I was relieved as the taste of machine oil flavored air filled my chest and I was past at least one danger.

I tentatively pushed up on the hatch, not really expecting it to budge, but there was the slightest movement, so I braced my shoulder against the hatch while I used my thigh muscles to shove the access open. The strain burned across my back as the steel hatch moved impossibly slow through the dark water until I could stand entirely upright. With my good hand, I shoved it fully open it until I heard a click as the safety latch engaged.

I opened my eye under water, the salt burning less than the chemical in the practice tank, and in the pale green light, I could make out the forms of four divers watching us, ready in case of emergency. Three of them were hanging suspended in the water from long ropes. Petty Officer Grant himself was standing on the top of the plate that stood in for the hull of the *Ram*, his hands resting on the top of the conning tower. All the divers were wearing a similar costume to the one I trained in, with the distinctive helmet, but instead of an air hose trailing away to the surface, Grant had on his back a tank of compressed air with a smaller spare tank of compressed air sitting on the edge of the conning tower, should one of us need it.

As I dragged myself out of the hatch, I reached around it and engaged my hook in the safety latch so that I might not float immediately away, cleared the access, and floated to one side. With my bulk out of the way, Smith made a smooth exit, took his last draught of air from his bottle and kicked for the surface, a trail of bubbles in his wake as he let the pressure out of his lungs all the way up.

Jonas did not exit as neatly, his hands flailing at the access rim. I reached in, grabbed him by the collar and dragged him out. Once free of the opening, he regained his composure and we took our final bottled breath together. He swam for the surface in a clumsy attempt at a scissors kick as I unhooked myself and followed.

Seconds later, we were at the surface.

I emerged with a whooping laugh, not so much in amusement, but at the sheer joy of being alive. The entire incident was terrifying, and I was exhausted from the effort, my heart still beating a tympani solo in my chest, but it was akin to the fear one feels when being tackled in rugby; a passing fear that exhilarates. Aware that all eyes were on me, I intended to wave away the attention, but as soon as my arm lifted, a cheer went through the assembled crew; many of them waved their hats. A thought shot through my brain: *it was only twenty-five feet.*

I fear I turned quite red as I clumsily paddled to one of the skiffs that were rowing about to pick up escaped sub-mariners. Reaching the boat, I slung my hook over the gunwale to rest for a moment. Before I could make another move, two pairs of strong hands grabbed me under the arms and dragged me bodily into the boat. I lay there on the bottom as my breathing returned to normal and my heartbeat subsided and I laughed in spite of myself.

"Thrilling, isn't it?" I looked up to see that Lieutenant Bartley was on this particular vessel.

"There are no words."

"You better find some." He jerked his thumb toward the crane ship. "The captain wanted to see you as soon you surfaced."

Bartley then ordered the skiff back to the ship and the oarsmen moved with a will.

My clothes were still wet although I managed to wring a goodly amount of saltwater out before I raced up the companionway to the upper deck. Captain Wilson was sitting on a folding chair, watching the drills. At my approach, he produced a towel, threw it at me, and absently tapped the chair next to him.

"You wished to see me, sir?"

He nodded to acknowledge that he heard, but I could see his mind was elsewhere. "I was pleased to see you come out of the water in good spirits."

"It was quite the experience."

"I wanted to talk to you about your predecessor as soon as you'd been through this."

"That would be Commander Waite?"

I sat and used the towel to pat the soggy ends of my dripping cuffs.

"The same," he replied. "I am sure that you have heard how he came to leave the unit."

"Actually, I have not been completely informed." I imagined Wilson had some reason for bringing it up now. "Even Lieutenant Bartley has been uncharacteristically close-mouthed, so I heard only that he had developed a nervous malady."

"That is one way of putting it. You may hear differently, so I will put it to you straight, the commander was the bravest man I ever knew."

"Oh."

"You may hear some people prattle that he left the service in cowardice, but that's a damn lie." He leaned forward, rested his forearms on his knees, and paused to gather his thoughts as he studied the deck.

"Courage comes easily to the ignorant and the stupid; experience and circumstance can make cowards of us all. I have jumped into many dangerous positions mainly through ignorance. If I'd had any knowledge of what I was getting into, I would never have done so." He sighed. "Duty is a more straightforward measure of a man, and to my mind, there is no courage greater than doing your duty even if you are scared witless."

"I must agree with you completely." I looked down at the hook with my one good eye. "Knowing the possible results of my actions aboard the *Indomitable*, I hope that I could do such again, but I will confess I am less than certain."

He clapped me on the knee. "Excellent; I distrust a man who claims never to question himself."

"So, about Commander Waite . . ."

"He was with the team that recovered the *Ram* from the Fenians and towed it to New York. As the only Queen's officer on the spot, it was his duty to train under John Holland so that he could bring the submersible here and teach others, and he did his duty. It wasn't until he was in the damn thing that he discovered a deep aversion for such an enclosed place. I praise his courage because he did what was necessary, even though he was terrified."

I sat in silent commiseration for the man trapped by duty.

Wilson continued, "It embarrassed him that his knees shook violently when he did the scuttling drill, and when he came out of the shallow test, he was visibly shaken. And after the deep test, he needed to spend a few minutes alone to compose himself, but for all that, he did his duty and he did it well. It is a testament to how much the men respected him that no man in this unit ever questioned his courage or spoke about it behind his back."

I felt a great kinship with this man who felt compelled to control his darkest fear in the name of duty. "I can scarce credit that none spoke; I do know sailors."

His head tilted back and he let out a soft chuckle. "Well, for one thing, Georgie Grant would have flayed the first man who did. They'd been together a long time and it was Grant with him against the Fenians."

I pressed the captain since he seemed in a talkative mood. "So what happened to Waite?"

"We discussed replacing him often, for his own sake. But he worked so hard I simply did not have the heart. He was doing a remarkable job, but then there was the accident. Waite, Smith, and Ehrler were diving at operational depth of fifty feet when they hit something very massive, big enough to spring the plates on the port side of the conning tower. The front bow is hardened for ramming, as is the very front of the conning tower, but the original design was relatively weak on the sides, and the damaged plates started to take on water. Whatever the sub hit also damaged the port diving planes, pushing the craft deeper and jamming the controls. The worst-case scenario continued as Waite ordered the crew to blow ballast, but only one side started to empty, and he halted it before they rolled. The boat went down in over a hundred feet of water and he made the only choice, emergency evacuation by scuttling. It is very different when it is real," Wilson concluded. He gave me a meaningful look.

I nodded, having recently confronted the planned versus the emergent.

"He did his duty, upholding the finest tradition. He evacuated his men and preserved the craft for future use, but his nerve, I'm afraid, was shot." Captain Wilson sadly shook his head. "He simply could not go back into the water."

"Could he not be reassigned to a surface ship?"

"He is not well. His family tells me that he has dreams and wakes trembling."

I kept very quiet.

"He is currently in the care of a quality rest home in Essex," he said casually. "They say he is making great progress."

Wilson stood abruptly, brushing his uniform coat. "Again, some say he is a coward, but I cannot fault a man for doing his duty, even if he is damaged." He looked at my hook. "There are many types of wounds. No, he is no coward, just a brave man who pushed himself more than we can understand."

I took the story of Commander Waite with me as I returned to the exercise. By the end of the day, each man had been scuttled at least once, served their time in the diving apparatus suspended above the sea floor, and in the skiffs fishing their shipmates out of the cold channel.

The entirety of the next day was spent moving the crane ship and gear away from the sand bar to a point where the sounding for the bottom was 110 feet. Our men assisted the ship's crew in making fast to the new location and prepping the gantry rigging for the greater depth.

Thursday morning I joined the other officers for a cold breakfast of melon and brown biscuits. We sat on the upper deck as the first rays of dawn turned the low waves to silver, and the cool clear air refreshed me from a night spent in the dank windowless rooms that passed for quarters on the *Creighton*. The creaking of the wooden hull resembled the *Indomitable,* and I woke several times in the night believing, just for an instant, that I was back on the doomed ship.

"You going first?" Bartley asked, interrupting my musing.

I shook my head. "Where's the tea?" I asked and consulted my watch. "I think that morale would be best served by letting the men see me coming up last. The *Raleigh* will pick us up at three, and we must be done by then."

Everyone nodded and we tucked into our meal.

For the deep-water test, no diver would be conveniently by the hatch to assist as the helmets were only rated for seventy-five feet, which meant all of our support divers were hanging twenty-five feet above the mock submersible. While escaping from the iron box was harrowing, diving at this depth is not without its own risk and at a depth of seventy-five feet, the simple task of "watch and wait" can have serious consequences.

The day started poorly. The first trio went down and came up as planned, but Seaman Hays managed to swallow some seawater, which left him in a bit of distress. Treating him stressed our schedule, but it was not a serious delay. The next round, Jonas served as the sub driver and came up wheezing with stiff, painful joints. We hoisted him on board, but he was done for the day.

For my part, I did a long turn in the skiff, encouraging and praising the men, an accolade they truly deserved; their quiet courage filled me with pride. By the time I donned the clumsy diving suit, I judged were running a bit too far behind, so when my shift as safety diver ended, I climbed the ladder up onto the crane ship and immediately changed for the last scuttle mission of the day. I hurried to stay on schedule and get the men back to their barracks before nightfall.

It is surprising how fast the amazing can devolve into the ordinary. Two days ago, just climbing in and closing the hatch was enough to get my blood up, but now the initial prep and ride to the bottom was almost routine. However, there was nothing ordinary about the rest of the experience.

The drop was much longer than before, so to occupy the time, I addressed the young man standing at the engineering position. "Seaman Bell isn't it?"

"Yes sir, they calls me Young Bell."

I recalled his first name was Aloysius, which he disliked, and the crew just called him "young" to differentiate him from Seaman Frank Bell who was a full month older.

"Enjoying the drill?"

"Don' mind the shallows sir, but . . . ." he rubbed his ears, "but the deeps, they's painful."

"And you, Weber?" I addressed the tall sailor who was at the gunnery station today. "You do all right?"

In the growing darkness, I saw him look pointedly at Bell, then up at me. "Beggin' your pardon, sir, I was just hopin' that this trip would be calmer than our last together."

I nodded. "I'll do my best."

We were silent until we hit the bottom, not quite so hard this time. The air was just a bit warm. The humidity condensed on the tiny windows so that even the limited light from them was diminished. I gave the command to distribute the escape supplies and then ordered, "Prepare to scuttle." The two men shifted to the valves.

"Aye, aye." They answered to let me know they were in position, as I could not see in the gloom.

"Open scuttling valves." Once again water flowed in, this time much faster than I could imagine and I certainly never imagined the assault on my ears as the pressure rose. I opened my mouth wide, swallowing huge gulps of air to equalize pressure when the pain in my ears intensified. On the verge of crying out, I was relieved when Young Bell beat me to it.

"It's alright, Bell" I yelled, the sound echoing eerily in the half-filled chamber. The shout achieved some success, and it eased the pain to a level that allowed me to concentrate. The water level was rising so quickly that it gave me less time to contemplate the things that might go wrong, but I also had to work faster to make things right. Before I knew it, I was crouched on the seat and all of us arranged our heads together in the conning tower as we took that last deep breath.

This time, the air in my lungs was not so stale and I found it was easier to hold my breath to the count of sixty as the tiny area filled completely. At my signal, we all brought up our bottles, took in a breath and I pushed on the hatch, relieved as it slowly moved. As I strained, something came upon me— an unusual feeling of calm enveloped me, making me feel much more confident about everything. I felt no pain at all. The sensations that plagued me for the last year receded into an ever-vaguer notion of memory, and even the physical exertion seemed somehow easier. Unlike before, I found myself in no hurry to move, although a small voice deep inside urged me on. I would have rather taken in the view of the divers suspended like angels floating over our heads, than make for the surface.

Grasping the inner handwheel, I floated free of the access, and shook my head as if to clear it; something was affecting my judgment.

As before, I tried to hook myself to the safety latch on the outside of the cover, but missed three times. While I was thus engaged, Weber grabbed the deck ring from below and briskly launched himself from the access port, taking his bottle breath as he ascended. I finally snagged my hook on the exterior handwheel and my body floated to the side, leaving me in no position to assist if necessary, but Bell seemed to be part fish and he, too, gracefully exited the sub.

At this time, I was supposed to do something, but could not remember what. As that thought crossed my mind, my vision narrowed so that the entire periphery vanished. I could only see what lay directly before my one eye, like looking through a tunnel, which finally made me realize what was happening. One of those silly-sounding diving diseases had befallen me. "The raptures" was a condition thought to be caused when "old blood" is pushed from the extremities back into the body under pressure. Identifying the cause of my sensations roused me from my stupor and I fought for control, pushing the stale air from my lungs as I fumbled at the lever to take that last deep gulp of air from the bottle. I attempted to swim upward, but was jerked back by my hook, still engaged in the handwheel. Tugging frantically for a bit, I closed my eye in concentration and thought my way through it, pushing the hook forward to clear the wheel before pulling it back. So simple a task, and so difficult to execute when my treasonous brain refused to work at its best.

Freed, I turned my face to the greenish light filtering from overhead and swam through the expanse to the surface, which was much further away than it seemed. My restricted vision made it seem even more remote, and I had completely emptied my lungs when my face emerged from the water.

This time there was no triumphant laugh or sense of glee; instead my first sound was a choking cough as my first gasp of air included a fine mist of salt spray. The euphoria faded away leaving me with a pounding headache. My arms flailed a bit, then I was aware of the eyes on me, so I attempted to modify my movement to appear I was waving in excitement, although later the other officers told me it looked like I was drowning. In any case, it served, as a cheer went through the men, not as enthusiastic, and a bit more ragged than two days ago, but they were tired, too.

This time I waited for the skiff to approach and allowed myself to be pulled aboard.

I was somewhat recovered by the time the *Raleigh* arrived to transport us back to the port. My uniform was on, but required Jenkins's ministrations. The headache subsided to a dull throb behind my eye sockets, but I had the balance of a drunkard. While my experience underwater may still be lacking, I did have some practice maneuvering while impaired, so eventually I caught up to Captain Wilson and the other officers. Gripping the rail for additional support I joined them outside the bridge of the HMS *Raleigh*. On the quiet voyage back to Leamouth, I contemplated my looming social engagement with Miss Tesla.

Chapter Nine

The cloying sweet smell of laudanum filled my nose and I fought through the numbing haze to find my hands immobile. I tossed my head to dislodge the bandages that covered my eyes, but no light entered my world. Muscles on my back spasmed at my movements and burning pain traveled down my arm to pool just above my wrist. I tried to scream, but my dry mouth and parched throat could make no noise. Suddenly I was released and sat up in bed, cold light edging around my drapes.

Friday morning, I resumed my calisthenics and was surprised to find lieutenants Bartley, Hanley and Bertram at the barracks and kitted up for exercise. As I approached them, I raised a quizzical eyebrow.

"Morning, sir," Bartley called out, evidently speaking for the group. "We made note of how well you did with the drills and our own lack of stamina, and decided to join the formation for a bit, at least until we've built up our wind."

I was about to open my mouth to say something inspirational when the coxswain gave the command to fall in, leaving me just enough time to nod acknowledgement and move into position.

Petty Officer Grant studied the new faces in his ranks for a second and scratched the back of his head. "That's the way of it," he muttered in a stage manner that carried the field. "You let one of them in, and before you know it, the whole bleeding' lot show up."

A good-natured chuckle passed through the group.

"Announcements," he barked. "Training schedule changes; today will be extended hours with a formal evening parade at 1900, full formal kit at the pier."

No one groaned outright, but a definite unease passed through the lines.

"This will be a promotion parade, and many of you will see a rating."

Sullen faces suddenly jerked up and a muttering spread.

"All training canceled for the weekend. Saturday is now listed as a holiday." A whoop started to go up, but Grant quashed it, his powerful voice rising above the murmur. "All right, shut year gobs. Next man I hear gives me fifty press-ups." The noise cut off so quickly the silence echoed.

Grant barely paused before barking commands. "Extend to the left, march!" The formation spread out to double intervals and prepared for exercise.

After cleaning up from my exertions, taking just a few minutes to wolf down a bit of toast with tea and jam, I retreated to my office, promising myself proper eggs and rashers of bacon for the next day. I approached my desk without enthusiasm. The piles of training reports required to be completed by day's end stared at me as I cast about for any duty or service that could delay the inevitable.

A polite knock sounded on my door frame. "Do you have a minute?" Danjella inquired, her voice sounded serious.

"Certainly, what is on your mind?"

She crooked a finger at me and walked away from me, her natural gait imparting a gentle sway to her hips. For a second, I was mesmerized by the corresponding movement of the dark blue business skirts she wore. What is it about being at sea for even just a few days that makes a sailor so susceptible to feminine allure?

I rose and hastened to follow her. As I attempted to catch up to her, she did not say a word, just stayed a few playful steps ahead of me as if daring me to actually break into a run. Eventually, she reached the lift to the electrical laboratory and stood waiting by the control, her face trying to conceal something, but her lips bent at the corners in a mischievous smirk. Once I joined her, she bade me close the double set of doors, and then paused before pushing the handle forward.

I suddenly felt myself in an ethically problematic situation; alone, behind closed doors, with an unattached woman. If I were to invite her to my office and close the doors, I could be charged with conduct unbecoming, but I was uncertain about how social conventions addressed a stopped lift.

Danjella, completely unconcerned about propriety, stood there, one hand on the lever, the other on her hip, with her weight shifted to one side. Her face was cocked with one eyebrow raised, her mouth arranged in an inviting smile.

"Have you secured theater tickets?" She inquired, in a tone a bit more husky than her regular voice.

"I shall have a carriage at your quarters at 1900."

She smiled, and there was a peculiar gleam in her eye, a hint of a blush colored her cheek as she pushed the lever and we ascended to the workshop.

The door opened to reveal her cousin—oblivious to us. Nicola was sitting at a table spectacularly illuminated by the morning sun, wearing goggles of smoked glass and manipulating a device that seemed to shoot lightning bolts at his fingertips. I stared open-mouthed at the apparatus, but Danjella was unimpressed. She tugged at my elbow and bade me turn around.

At her work area, there was a small group of men waiting, a couple of them pacing while the rest fidgeted nervously. John Wells and Elbert Billers stood by a table that was cleared of everything but a pasteboard carton slightly smaller than a hatbox. Two men who worked with the casting molds stood a little behind. I could not recall their names.

There was one other man, at least seventy, but spry and animated, who was consulting a gold pocket watch. The complete stranger wore a charcoal grey frock coat, clutched dove grey gloves in one spotted hand, wore gold-rimmed spectacles on his face and a had monocle pinned to his lapel. His thin white hair was cut close to the scalp, and his heavily lined face was professionally shaved.

Danjella led me straight to this newcomer. "Ian," she started, and I felt a momentary twinge at her familiarity in front of the workers. She continued, "I would like to introduce an old family friend who has consented to help with a project. Commander Ian Rollins, may I present Joerg Gensier. He currently lives here in London, but he is from Switzerland, and was once apprenticed to the Frères Rochat."

My eyebrows arched in surprise. At Edinburgh, we studied their automata, the finest miniaturized mechanisms in the world. I extended my hand and said with awe, "It is an honor, sir."

He took my hand and clasped it warmly with a firm grip that belied his age. "It is I who am honored. My darling Danny has shared your drawings with me."

My head jerked in her direction as a tiny flash of betrayal swept through me, but one look at her told me she meant no malice.

"Joerg has been very helpful to me and my aunt, assisting us to produce our contrivances, so I took the liberty to show him your work."

Joerg Gensier spoke up, his voice serious. "I must congratulate you on a remarkable design. The control escarpment wheel is unique, it gives a mechanical advantage that is beyond anything on the market. I was wondering how you intended to patent it."

"I hadn't thought about it; I'm not sure it is worth the effort."

"I have thought about it," Danjella said. "That is why I have invited Joerg here today. He deals with several Swiss companies and has a . . . proposal? Proposition? Some word like that."

"What we would like to do," Jeorg said, "is arrange the patents and build the prototypes for your use in exchange for a percentage of the licensing fees, say 30 percent?" He gave a playful flinch under Danjella's glare. "I meant 20 percent, of course."

My head swiveled from one to another in complete confusion. "I do not know; I am afraid I do not have much of a head for commerce."

"We could just buy the rights completely," he offered. Danjella glared at him again.

I stared at her face, seeing an almost imperceptible nod and made a decision. "Twenty sounds fair, I suppose," I said slowly, watching her eyes the entire time.

"Excellent," he exclaimed, rubbing his hand together. "I shall bring papers to your office this week and you may have your solicitor review them."

I am sure Jenkins knows a solicitor, I mused, *possibly even a reputable one.*

Jeorg bowed to Danjella, "And now, I believe Danny has something to show you."

Danjella smiled, gathered her skirts, and slipped past me to join the men from the factory. She crooked a finger at me to join them at the table.

I approached slowly.

"I took another liberty," Danjella said. "I told the men that today was your birthday."

I rocked back on my heels as I realized she was correct. With everything happening so fast it had quite slipped my mind.

"I understand the accident in the *Indomitable* occurred just three days before your last birthday."

The thought of my waking dream caused a cold shiver to travel up my spine, and a warning spark down my arm.

"We decided that with a little extra work, we could give you something positive to mark the occasion." She laid her hands on the pasteboard box and without further ceremony, she lifted it up to reveal a device that was a symphony in brass and bronze. It was nothing like what I was designing, but I instantly understood what she meant by an intermediate step.

She held up the thing in her left hand and made a sweeping gesture with her right. "These men rushed through the mold making and casting so that I could put this together for you."

I turned toward the men with gratitude in my eye and they replied with shy smiles and shuffling feet. I opened my mouth to speak, but each phrase I considered sounded insufficient to my mind, leaving me to stand there with my mouth gaping.

Their reticent demeanor gave way to good-natured chuckles as they saw my reaction.

Danjella saved me by offering the device to me.

In my abbreviated sub-mariner kit, there were no coat sleeves to be concerned with, so I rolled back the shirt sleeve, and fumbled at the laces of my hook in a daze. As the tool fell away, I felt only a twinge of discomfiture as it was hard to feel shame in the company of such generosity.

Holding the straps out of the way, she slid the mechanism on to my naked forearm. Eight inches of carefully formed bronze plate lined with soft leather fit with extraordinary comfort on my skin. Once it was completely on, I could feel the ivory inlay pieces pressing against the pronators and supinators, so that they could react to the change of muscle. The assembly was secured by a thick leather strap that separated into three strips. The straps were fastened by corresponding small buckles. Danjella fitted a cloth strap across my chest and a leather piece over my shoulder. It was attached to a brass cable inset in the device. Another strap fastened just above my elbow and attached to the second cable.

Instead of a hook or the apparatus I designed, the machine had two sets of pincers, projecting about three inches, with about a half inch of space between them. I used a combination of turning my wrist, flexing my arm and shrugging my shoulder to make the pincers open and close. I tried making them move, and they opened and closed at random as I tried to coordinate my motions.

Danjella smiled. "You will need to practice. The movement to make the lower pincers open and close are what you will need to operate the fingers later, and the upper emulates? Isolates? Some word like that, the thumb." She took my elbow in her other hand and guided me through the motion.

I moved away from her, nodded dumbly and shifted again, which closed both pinchers, bringing a muted cheer from the assembly.

She touched a nub on the plate by the upper pincer. "This catch has strong spring behind it. Press it and you can twist the entire assembly and remove the pincer apparatus. When the spring-wound construction is completed, it will fit on the base the same way."

I finally found my voice I said, "I do not know what to say."

"I think the standard phrase is 'thank you.'" She looked up at the others. "Is that not right?"

They laughed in a friendly way.

"Yes," I replied, "thank you' is correct." I tried to flex the pincers closed and they moved slightly. "But I fear it is inadequate. I do most seriously thank you. You have gone to such great effort, this was not necessary.

"Nonsense," Danjella replied in a very practical tone. "You cannot drive the *Ram* with one hand. It was strictly necessary."

I lowered my arms and bowed my head to acknowledge her point.

I stood there and accepted the well wishes of all, and shook each man's hand to ensure they understood the true depth of my gratitude, but finally I was able to escape back to my office and the burden of Admiralty reports.

I honestly tried to keep my mind on the papers in front of me, but how was I supposed to know how many tons of coal the *Raleigh* burned on the trip, or how to assess the total lost man-hours due to Jonas being ill?

I managed to complete most of the bloody forms, but found I had to stop periodically and marvel at the apparatus that replaced my hand. I sat opening and closing it, picking up various objects, tossing them in the air, and straining to catch them. I had to look at the apparatus to grasp anything, as I could not feel when I clutched something. After some practice, I began to gauge my grip by how tight the shoulder cable felt, but it was still an awkward guess.

Thus I was chucking a paperweight from hand to pincer when there was knock on the open door and a voice called out, "The captain sends his compliments." The young man in a port messenger's blue jacket was clearly in a hurry, and without pausing, delivered his breathless message. "He requests you visit his office at your earliest convenience."

I smiled at the euphemism: "leisure" meant sometime today, "convenience" meant in a few minutes, while "earliest convenience" meant now. I stood up, walked to the coat rack to retrieve my formal coat, then thought better of it. The captain approved my waistcoat as regulation, so I tugged at the front to straighten it and went to report.

Ensign Robeson, the captain's aide, sat at a desk just outside Wilson's office door and he waved me right in without knocking. The captain looked up at me, discreetly removed a tiny pair of spectacles, slid them into an inner pocket of his uniform coat, then closed his eyes, and rubbed his temples for a moment.

"We have guests on the way." His eyes opened and he frowned at me, "What the devil is that thing?"

I tugged at the waistcoat, "Sorry sir, I will fetch my coat."

"Not talking about the bloody waistcoat, that's fine." He pointed at my left arm. "I want to know about your new . . . appendage."

"Oh." I raised the apparatus and worked the pincers. "A project I am working on with Miss Tesla."

His eyes glinted with amusement. "So you have more than one project with Miss Tesla?" He was interrupted by a loud knock on the open doorframe. A tall, older man stood stiffly. He wore the well-worn uniform of an able seaman and had his sailor tam tucked under his arm. An air of human labor and coal smoke surrounded him.

"Come," the captain ordered. The man stepped into the office, closed the door behind him, and saluted the captain, his manner just a bit slow as if he had to think out each movement.

Standing to his side, I saw only a narrow view of his face. His slack jaw was indifferently shaved, his eyes dull and uncurious. He was obviously not the sharpest sailor I'd seen, which was probably the reason he reached such an age without promotion.

The captain returned the salute and froze halfway before slamming his hand down on the desk. "Oh good God, what do you want?"

The seaman smiled slightly, his face sharpened, and his eyes took on new life.

"Mr. Cooper-Smythe, I must avow you make a most convincing slackard," Wilson said.

Cooper-Smythe acknowledged the compliment with slight bow of his head. He wore no stage make-up or false beard, although he had trimmed back the severe muttonchops, but the way he held his face was an extraordinary disguise. I needed to look at him at least twice to penetrate it.

"Do you intend to tell me the meaning of this pantomime?" the captain inquired. "And how did you get past Robeson?"

Cooper-Smythe's lips twitched into a wolfish grin. "He was momentarily called away on an urgent matter."

Unbidden, he crossed to a chair and took a seat, removed a cheap tin cigar case from within his tunic and, opening it, offered us each one. I declined as I now had a distaste for willingly inhaling smoke.

"I've been seeing to a bit of business on the docks," he announced. "A man was caught stealing supplies."

"A dock thief?" Wilson asked with mock incredulity. "I am glad that the admiralty is on top of the situation, it's not like there is anything more important."

"We do not care about the theft," the clandestine agent said patiently, "but the bugger has turned informant, identifying the people he is selling to, and furthermore, admitting to selling more than pilfered tools and supplies." He lit his cigar.

Wilson drummed his finger on the desk as Cooper-Smythe worked to get the tobacco started. "Yes?" he finally prompted.

"Information on the *Ram*. Maintenance, training schedule, crew, everything and anything."

The Captain considered this intelligence. "So, we know who our saboteur is?"

"Not directly," Cooper-Smythe admitted, "but we know there are at least six men involved, although our wharf rat knows only one by name and another by sight, and claims they all take orders from a man they call, 'The Priest'."

"And you trust this man?"

"Good god, no. But I do trust that he is willing to sell out his customers to avoid gaol."

He puffed on the cigar and the acrid fumes of very cheap tobacco emanated from its tip. Apparently, he went to great detail in his disguise.

"Are clergy involved in the gangs?" I asked.

"I doubt the fellow is a real priest," Cooper-Smythe replied patiently. "But enough of that for now, I am also here out of curiosity about your next guest."

"Oh?"

"The Admiralty is sending over an American as an unofficial representative of his country, and we are asked to show him every consideration."

He extracted a telegram form his sailor's tunic, "The Department of the Navy would consider it a great gesture of goodwill to provide their representatives a tour of the submarine," he looked over the paper at me. "Their word for a submersible boat."

"They didn't seem so keen on the thing when it was in New York," Wilson said.

"Perhaps they have heard about the electric engine, or, more likely, they are concerned by the interest in submersibles by France, Germany,

Russia, and Turkey," I said.

"Do not forget Japan," Cooper-Smythe added. "They are modernizing so quickly they may out-innovate the Empire if we are not careful. But more to our point, one of the dockworkers under suspicion is an American. A representative of American interests and one from the Kaiser show up at the same time." He took another puff of the cigar and muttered, more to himself, "I should like to know how much information the Americans are sharing with the German Empire." He raised his sharp eyes to us, "That relationship has gotten far too cozy for my taste, and in case of hostilities, our shipping could be squeezed from both ends."

"I thought since that bit about us burning their capital, we'd worked things out," I said. "Now, what do we know about this visitor?"

"Not much." He dismissively flicked the ash off the end of his cigar. "As far as I can tell he is what the French would call a poseur; he styles himself as a cowboy and talks about his ranch but he has an address in New York City, is well connected there and with the American Naval Department. I am told he is a stout fellow, sort of a squinty, four eyed specimen. Married a London social type last December and has just returned from a bridal tour of the continent."

"A bridal tour?" Wilson asked, with a trace of amusement. Although such trips were de rigeuer for the social class, they were considered an effete affectation by most men.

"What type of cowboy marries a London socialite?" I asked.

"What type of cowboy is named 'Theodore'?" snorted Cooper-Smythe.

I was suddenly reminded of a classmate in primary school with that name. He was a portly, asthmatic boy.

"We can accommodate him the same day as the German, provided he'll fit through the hatch." I pictured him as my old schoolmate grown up.

"He may be a buffoon, but my people are wary of his associate. that is the man we should keep an eye on," Cooper-Smythe warned. "America is a bit late getting into the Great Game, but it is showing some talent."

Wilson saw the confused look on my face. "That is how these skulldugerous types refer to intelligence activities."

"Is that a word?" Cooper-Smythe asked as he ground out his cigar and stood.

"As always, it has been a pleasure." He methodically patted his uniform to ensure that everything was back in its place. "I must be off before your cowboy arrives."

He faced Wilson, rubbed his temples for a moment, shifted his neck a bit as if loosening muscles, then relaxed his jawline, and the fire faded from his eyes. He shifted his weight back on his hips, which gave him a clumsy, unbalanced stance and then made a rigid salute that looked to be the result of years of practice from a man who would need years to learn how to salute.

Wilson responded with a halfhearted wave as the unkempt sailor turned on his heel and stepped out, leaving the door open.

The captain closed his eyes and pinched the bridge of his nose. "That was interesting," he said, then looked at me and frowned. "While we have a moment; are you ready for the promotion parade tonight?"

"Yes sir, are the promotions in order?"

"I have the authority to make the awards; it's the damnable paperwork that will have to catch up. After the stress of this week, the coxswain wants to give the men a break, so we suspended training this afternoon for the men to prepare for the formal parade, and then we will give them the rest of the weekend off. We will make petty officers of Weber, Frank Bell, and Jonas. In addition, every ordinary will be reclassified as able, and each able rating will receive an upgrade."

"That is very generous."

"I just hope they will be sober by Monday," he muttered, then looked back up at me. "We will be needing new volunteers, and it would not be amiss if sailors get the notion rank comes quickly under the waves. The only advancement left to be approved is promoting Graf to commander, I haven't the authority for that and we must wait for the wheels of the Admiralty to turn. Have you two divvied up your crews yet?"

"No, sir," I replied lightly. "I figure when the time comes, we'll do it like a pickup rugby game. I'll choose one, he'll . . ."

"Commander," he interrupted.

"No sir, we are discussing it and have a tentative list drawn up, balancing out the relative strengths and weaknesses of the crews."

"Better answer." He thought a moment, "Of course if your first one is true, I do not want to know about it."

Robeson knocked on the door. "Your visitors from the Admiralty are here."

"Show them in."

The first man who entered was a clerk from the Admiralty whom I knew slightly, but the second was obviously our New York cowboy. At first glance, I quickly changed my estimation of him. He fit the description exactly, but there was a shrewd intelligence behind the glass of his spectacles and his stout frame was not soft, but ran more to muscle. He moved with a great deal of animation, as if eternally in a hurry, and even his moustache seemed to be bristling with energy. On the rugby field, his sort would be the blindsider I would watch for.

The third man was more of an enigma; a tall, well-groomed man wearing a tan frock coat with a velvet collar. He held a brown bowler casually at his side in his left hand. His waistcoat was of Chinese silk brocade with a black on black design, and every bit of his kit looked fit for a gentleman. His eyes were hard, his face chiseled, wind-burned, and while his hands were clean, they were also hard and calloused. From his droopy mustache to his western riding boots, he looked more like a true cowboy.

The clerk indicated our official guest. "Captain Wilson, may I present Mr. Theodore Roosevelt."

Roosevelt stepped forward, extended one hand as he casually dropped a John Bull-style top hat on the desk with the other. "Pleased to meet you sir, pleased," he affirmed.

Wilson stood and put out his hand. Roosevelt seized it with some eagerness and gave his arm three vigorous pumps in the American fashion. Released, Wilson discreetly flexed his digits. The captain then gestured to me.

"This is Commander Rollins; the skipper of the HMS *Holland Ram*. Anything regarding the vessel is his decision."

"Bully," Roosevelt exclaimed and bounded up to present me with his bone-crushing greeting. "Good to meet you, sir." He looked me up and down, his gaze never wavering as he noted my injuries. "Stouthearted fellow, I'll warrant."

I stood speechless. The man was a dynamo, a force of nature. I have to admit that he left me bereft of metaphor; suffice to say, he was slightly larger than life.

"Let me introduce my assistant." He made a sweeping motion toward the man in the fancy vest, "Mr. Adam Greer."

The laconic man frowned, more in concentration than displeasure, regarded each of us in turn as if assessing danger, and nodded his head. "Howdy."

I suppressed a laugh. Aside from the fine clothes, the man seemed to have stepped from the pages of a penny dreadful.

"I understand," Roosevelt continued, barely pausing for breath, "that you've been informed of the reason for my visit."
"We were just discussing it," Wilson said.

"I hear tell," Roosevelt said, "that you purloined a clever craft from a band of Irish hooligans." He glanced sideways at Mr. Greer as if expecting him to say something, but the man remained silent.

"We made no secret of our interest in the craft, and exported it in compliance with applicable laws and treaties," the captain said.

Roosevelt made a sharp laughing sound that was half a snort. "Of course you did, my friends in the Department of the Navy were shortsighted, but they are coming along, beginning to see the light and are now in talks with Holland to build something. They asked me, since I was in the vicinity, to drop by take and look at Holland's product and request a practical demonstration."

I looked the man over. Far from having to cram him down the hatch and listen to him complain the entire time, as I imagined, it seemed that he would not have any antipathy for the close quarters, or a fear of being under water. My only concern now was how much those astute eyes would learn, but I said aloud, "I have no objection."

"Bully!" He exclaimed and pumped his two clenched fists.

"Excellent," Wilson said, "we can offer you a ride in the submersible next Wednesday, the same day, in fact, that we will be hosting the German naval attaché."

"Bully," Roosevelt repeated with an enthusiastic grin that did not reach his eyes. I saw a glimpse of some misgivings there.

Greer remained stoic, but I caught him gazing very intently at Wilson as if trying to divine something from his manner.

Roosevelt clapped his hands, holding them together, and shaking them. "Then it is agreed. We will waste no more of your time then. Adam?"

"One more thing," I said, "be prepared to strip down to your shirtsleeves."

His discerning gaze flickered over me and then he nodded. "Certainly."

Roosevelt retrieved his short John Bull topper, and waved it at each of us. "Gentlemen, it has been a pleasure and an honor." With that, he rushed out the door with his assistant in tow.

They did not make it far when the familiar voice of Petty Officer Grant carried from the antechamber. "Mr. Greer, it is funny seeing you here after so long. How have you been?"

Curious, I followed our departing guest into the antechamber and stood by the door.

"George," Greer replied, with a smile that mixed pleasure with some chagrin. "I be fine. And yourself?"

"Ah," Roosevelt said, "You're old friends!"

"We've met," Grant replied. He smiled but his eyes were wary. "Are you still working for the Pinkertons?" he asked Greer.

"Detective work is a young man's game," he drawled. "I stopped that some time ago. I'm here as an assistant to Mr. Roosevelt. Uh, TD, this is George Grant. He was there when we confronted the Fenians."

"Good man," Roosevelt exclaimed. He offered Grant one of his bone bruising grips.

"I'd heard that all of the original men left," Greer remarked.

"All but me, sir," Grant said, "and two of the marines are still here as guards."

"I see," he nodded.

Roosevelt waved his hat at the door. "We have places to be; it was good to meet you, petty officer."

Greer and Grant shook hands cordially, and Greer left behind Roosevelt.

Once our visitors were out of earshot, the coxswain turned to me. "Greer there is a good man when you are in a tight spot, but his presence here is a bit suspicious."

"Agreed."

"Grant!" Wilson called from the office, "You have those papers for the promotions?"

Chapter Ten

"Good God, Jenkins, are you mad? I can't afford this." I waved my arms at the ostentatious landau-style carriage. "Take it back this instant!"

I knew the command was hopeless when I checked my pocket watch; even if I called for a common cab, I would not be on time to collect Danjella and her companion.

I still had a bit of my back pay and had decided to use some of it to make my evening out with Danjella pleasant, so I gave Jenkins a strict budget, sent him off to hire a horse and carriage for the evening, and agreed to trust to his judgment. I was expecting something along the lines of a growler, or a brougham— a comfortable conveyance that could accommodate Danjella and me, along with the inevitable Mrs. Livingstone.

Pleasant, but not expensive. This carriage reeked of expense.

He returned just about an hour after I gave him the funds, driving the coach himself. The landau was not enclosed but rather a convertible, with its rich leather roof folded into an elegant mound marked by the distinctive "landau bar" supports. It was pulled by a matched pair of greys, both of which—even with my sailor's knowledge of horseflesh— were obviously well-gaited and carefully groomed animals. The paneling was of imported mahogany with a deep, rich gleam that only hours of hand rubbing can produce. Its thick-lensed side lamps were intricately cast in gleaming brass, matching all the fittings from the door handles to the top rail. A night's rental of such a vehicle could easily set me back a month's pay.

"Not t' worry, guvn'r," he replied, his natural accent more pronounced as he caught his breath from the effort of driving the team. "It's within the budget yer set."

"The deuce you say."

"I do say," he replied, his face a mask of wounded virtue. He removed the low cloth cap he wore, and wiped the sweat from his brow. "I figure, this bein' the first time you been out with a Lady since you been out of 'ospital, you should shine up a bit, if yer follow."

"Fine thought, but I can't afford . . ."

"All taken care of, it is." He waved a placating hand. "I called in a long-ago marker from me old brother-in-law, 'e rents 'em out, 'e does."

He set the brake and tied off the reins before carefully climbing from the driver's seat.

I watched him dismount and eyed him with some suspicion. "I was quite unaware that you were ever married."

"Oh, not me, guv." He waved his hands. "Lord no." He turned back and retrieved a pasteboard package from the floor of the driver's box. "I'm talking about me little sis's husband."

"And he owes you . . .?"

"Seems there was an incident where he tried to, shall we say, negotiate the virtue of an actress."

"Oh?" I arched an eyebrow at him.

He laughed. "Young Sophie took 'im for 10 shillings, and left 'im high and dry, and then came round and told me all about it, as a lesson to 'im." He lowered his voice and continued in a mutter, "As if the likes of 'im would get Young Sophie for ten shillings."

"And Young Sophie knows you how?" I asked.

"She bein' the daughter of Old Sophie," he said offhandedly, "a particular friend o' mine, at one time." His voice turned a bit wistful, and then he shook his head and firmly patted the landau's solid frame. "So's anyways it bein' yers for the night."

"Wait a minute. Are you saying you kept such an indiscretion from your own sister?"

"Oh, lord love you, no, told 'er first up, and she figured it would be better to watch me make 'im twitch than for her to scream at 'im." He chuckled. "Besides she were more upset that 'e wasted the ten shillings. To this day, if she wants to make him sweat, she just starts a sentence with 'my brother told me something very interesting . . .'"

I held up my arm. "I understand. What is in the box?"

"This?" He held up the package for my inspection, and then removed the cover to reveal a coachman's top hat.

"And when did you become a coachman?"

"A valet needs to be a man of many talents. Many's the time I ferried the admiral to an' fro. I remember the night 'e 'ad to attend some duke's party; 'ired a coach and four with a liveried driver an all, but the bugger showed up reeling with drink."

"So you drove?"

"Not only that, but the admiral stripped him bare and trussed him up, and left him lying on the floorboards. Made me put on the bugger's livery."

He looked down at the hat, his eyes shining. "Drove many times, but I ne'er had a proper topper." He sighed, lost in thought for a second. "Many talents," he repeated. "And speakin' o' talents, what is that thing around your neck?"

I raised a hand to my throat. "A tie," I answered.

"Could'a fooled me." he replied contemptuously.

I was wearing my newly tailored dress uniform, very pleased by the improved fit. As it was an evening affair of some formality, I donned a black tie. I had practiced enough with my daily four-in-hand to tie a smart knot with one hand, but the bow tie was trickier to accurately balance. I had finally given up and left it leaning lamely to port.

Jenkins removed the traveling coat he'd been wearing to reveal his finest waistcoat, pushed back his sleeves, stepped up to me, and deftly jerked the tie, causing the knot to collapse.

"Many's the time I had to tie a bow for the admiral. After 1800 he was generally a mite too unsteady to do it properly."

His hand rapidly reformed the bow, tugging the ends precisely into place.

"He particularly thanked me after an argument at the officers' mess turned into a bit o' a brawl. When the matter was settled, his coat required extensive mending and the buttons were off his shirt, but his tie was just as smart as when he started."

He brushed my shoulders, inspected the rest of my attire, nodded sharply, then retrieved his good long coat from the driver's, and stowed the cloth cap and traveler. He threw me a self-satisfied glance and ceremoniously donned the topper. Without another word, he opened the carriage's half-door and bid me enter.

I climbed on board with a sense that tonight's events were sailing beyond my control and the best I could do was hang on and hope to see the destination.

Danjella looked properly impressed with the coach I hired. I preened just a tad when I saw her eyes widen at the elegant transport. I expected to submit to the ritual of sending her my card when we arrived, but she was waiting for us at the stoop, and strode from the row house as soon as the carriage came to a halt, with Mrs. Livingstone a black tide in pursuit.

I scrambled out the door and barely hit the ground with enough time to make a proper bow, a gesture that might have been smarter if I had not stumbled, forgetting that the blasted folding stair was . . . well, folded. Even so I managed to keep my feet and make an inviting gesture toward the landau before I kicked the miscreant step into place.

Danjella reached the curb and stopped to greet me with a smile, then gathered her skirts to make an elegant curtsey.

"I doubt even the fairies conjured up such a coach for Aschenputtel." She used the Eastern European variant of the name.

"I do not think they dressed Cinderella so finely either."

Her gown was a very deep violet with a smart bustle, and I was momentarily disappointed to discover she was wearing a more fashionable, tightly laced and intricately boned corset. She stood close to me, with the indomitable Mrs. Livingstone looming and I held out my hand to assist her into the flashy carriage. Looking down to ensure she trod correctly on the folding step, I noticed that the corset pushed up some of her attributes provocatively and the swell of her feminine charms could be dimly seen through her lace décolletage. I felt honor-bound to avert my gaze. She gave my hand an affectionate squeeze, and I returned the gesture with a genteel nod as I guided her into her seat.

Mrs. Livingstone was clad in a slightly more elegant set of widow's weeds, with a neat flat hat adorned with black ribbons. She sniffed disapproval as I offered to assist her. She did not properly take my hand, but rather used it to push herself up quickly as if it sustained touch would contaminate her. Determined not to enjoy the evening, she immediately began to vocalize a list of things that earned her displeasure starting with my appearance. My lack of proper grooming appalled her, although I was shaved blue, suitably bathed, with a fresh haircut and well-trimmed nails. She did not much like the landau and by the time we traveled a mile, she suggested the elegant carriage was below the standards of a lady, far too gaudy for a gentleman, and that I was a wastrel for spending money on it.

We were making smart time as the horse's rhythmic gait gave us a very smooth ride. I noticed that Mrs. Livingstone was glaring over my shoulder. Her nose wrinkled in distaste as her eyes narrowed in concentration.

"From whence did you hire that driver?"

I blinked and thought, *Did she really say whence?* Then I caught up to the content of her sentence.

"He is filling in for the driver. He is actually my valet, Mr. Jenkins."

At the sound of his name, Jenkins looked over his shoulder and tipped his fine topper.

"That man, is actually your manservant?"

"Indeed he is." I said, with a certain degree of fatalism.

"Well, I just saw him slip something out of his coat, and drink from it. I suspect spirits." She pressed her lips together and clasped her hands in her lap.

I sighed and turned around in my seat.

"Jenkins," I called with disapproval in my voice. "Hand it over."

At first he pretended not to know what I was talking about, but as he looked back at me to protest his innocence, he saw the look in my eye, and reached into his breast pocket to produce a pewter hip flask. I took it from him and turned back around. I opened the cap and sniffed at the contents.

"Yes," I said, holding the flask at arm's length to study it, "it is indeed spirits."

"I never . . . ." Mrs. Livingstone started to censure me, but Danjella leaned forward in her seat and snatched the flask away.

She flipped back the cap, sniffed daintily at the contents, and took a strong draught. She looked up at me, smiled and winked, coughed delicately, and then made a most unladylike display of wiping her lips with the back of her hand.

"I believe that Ian is correct, it is spirits. And very good spirits, if I may say so."

"Oh?" I took the flask back and took a small sip, noting the fine taste of well-aged Irish whiskey. "I fear I pay the man too well."

I handed the spirits back to Jenkins, who in turn opened the flask and drained it.

Mrs. Livingstone's forehead creased in a fierce scowl, and her frosty eyes flickered at each of us, although Jenkins got far more than his share.

"I do hope the theater is more entertaining."

"So, what are we to see?" Danjella asked, leaning forward with excitement.

"*The Mikado*, an operetta by Gilbert and Sullivan," I replied.

Danjella's eyes widened in pleasure, and even Mrs. Livingstone seemed to unbend at my mention of the very popular show. Danjella asserted that I take her theater, but left the actual choice of entertainment up to me. I spent time reading the papers to select the best show. "*The Mikado,*" received consistently fine reviews, and it was fortunate that I could acquire tickets as it opened only three months earlier. Until recently, tickets had to be purchased several weeks in advance, or from a third party at an exorbitant markup. However, the rush recently dwindled, making tonight one of the first nights that men of modest means could attend.

Even though the show was popular, it was the theater itself I longed to see. The Savoy is a marvel of modern technology; the first public building lit entirely by electric light. The inventor of the light bulb, or at least the British patent holder, Mr. Joseph Swan, donated hundreds of his handmade bulbs to brighten the stage and the rest of the famous building.

The day was unseasonably warm, but a steady wind picked up as evening deepened and Jenkins deftly guided the pair of greys through the increasing press of traffic. From the landau we could see the setting sun threatened by dark clouds on the horizon as Jenkins pulled to the curb a small distance from the theater of light.

The street swirled with uniforms; it seemed that every officer above the junior grades had an inclination to go the theater, as the price was reasonable. A marine major and an elegant lady I took to be his wife pulled up alongside us in a sensible brougham driven by a young lad not over fourteen, although he handled the single horse with care that spoke of experience. As they caught sight of us, the major waved in greeting and the lady nodded stiffly, seeming a trifle distressed by my ruined face. An empty hansom steered around, probably having already delivered its fare. The wheels clattered on the paving stones, the noise bouncing around the inside of the landau. The driver had his face averted, studying the traffic to move to the middle lane, but he glanced back at us. In that quick movement, I thought his face familiar, but before I could place it, he was swallowed up in traffic.

Jenkins set the brake, tied the reins and jumped down from the coach seat with more agility than one would suspect; but despite his years and atrocious personal habits, he managed to be quite spry. Although I suspected that the small tipple he'd enjoyed provided some of the lubrication for his joints.

He adroitly kicked the folding step into place, opened the half-door of the landau, and assisted the ladies as they gingerly stepped down to the pavement. Mrs. Livingstone went first and she gave Jenkins a good hard stare as he extended his hand, but she took it more willingly than mine, although as soon as her feet touched the cobble pavement she snatched it back.

To my surprise, Jenkins colored a bit; even the tips of his ears reddened.

He assisted Danjella who expressed her gratitude for the minor service with a small curtsey and a smile, which he returned before leaving me to dismount on my own. It was an acknowledgement of my self-reliance, for which I was grateful.

Mrs. Livingstone pulled Danjella from the street to the sidewalk, and began fussing over her dress, tugging and brushing at real and imagined travel wrinkles.

Alone for a fleeting instant, I placed my good hand on Jenkins's shoulder. "Sorry to drain your flask."

"Not to bother, sir. I 'as another." He looked after the two women still sorting out the dresses after their bustles had been squashed in the landau. "'At is a fine figure of a proper woman."

I opened my mouth to reprimand him for speaking such about the woman I was escorting for the evening. Then I followed his gaze and realized that it was fixed not on Danjella, but on her severe companion.

Chuckling, I shook my head. "That fine proper woman would make your Methodist look like a libertine."

"Well sir, a proper woman 'elps a man curb 'is . . ." he stopped and frowned in concentration, then carefully enunciated, "his lesser self."

I pondered that bit of romantic philosophy as I joined the ladies and we made our way through the growing throng toward the Savoy. Danjella was thrilled by the spectacle of all the carriages arriving, unloading clusters of people. My navy blue finery looked positively dowdy contrasted with soldiers and marines in scarlet, dripping with gold braid. It seemed to me even the bottle green and black of a colonel in the Rifle Brigade looked far more dashing.

In the press, Danjella took it upon herself to take my arm, placing her hand on the inside of my elbow where it felt unreasonably warm. Mrs. Livingstone, with the instincts of a mother bear, glared at us and marched right on Danjella's heels.

The lobby was dotted with dozens of Swan electric lights, but even it couldn't rival the setting sun behind us. I blinked at the transition. The Savoy is sumptuously decorated and received many fine notices on its decor, but as my eyes adjusted the detail seemed indistinct, as if I were peering at it through gauze.

An usher took my ticket and seated us in the first balcony of the left side; these had been the finest seats I could afford. The chairs were upholstered in dark blue velvet, and the sides and backs were made of dark polished wood with gilded highlights. While they were expensive looking, my back did not find them comfortable. The rest of the theater was just as opulent, the proscenium arch so huge the rigging of a battleship could have fit under it, and the cost of the miles of velvet curtains that covered the stage would have paid my salary for a year.

The house lights dimmed and the footlights brightened, as the stage manager stepped out to welcome us. He was dressed in white tie and tails, and should have been delighted to see the full house but he tugged at his collar and shuffled from foot to foot while the audience quieted.

"There are some announcements before tonight's performance. We are greatly honored to see many of Her Majesty's officer's in attendance tonight . . ." he faltered. "When you leave here tonight, the newsies will be screaming in the streets, so I would like to take this opportunity to inform you. We have received news that Kaiser Wilhelm of Germany has been shot."

A collective gasp came from the crowd and several men jumped to their feet.

"The only thing we know at this time is that the would-be assassin was killed at the scene, and the Kaiser is in the care of his physician." He let his words sink in and a murmur filled the hall. After a full minute, he raised his hands and the room quieted.

"I hope that you may set aside your shock and concern, and enjoy tonight's presentation of *The Mikado*." With that, he bowed and the theater plunged into darkness, the only illumination coming from the orchestra pit, and the only sound the conductor's baton as it beat out a time on the podium, and soon we were enveloped in the opening music.

The first act was quite clever and many times I needed to check myself to avoid laughing like some braying animal. Strange strangling noises came from Mrs. Livingstone as if she were trying to avoid any sound of humor escaping her throat, while Danjella did not feel the need for such modest constraint. Her musical laugh sounded almost continuously until the curtains closed for intermission.

I rose and gave a small bow to the two women. "If you like, I will procure some refreshment."

Mrs. Livingstone made a show of smoothing out her skirts. "A tonic water would not be amiss."

Danjella stood and performed a slight, if somewhat unladylike stretch, which captured not only my attention, but that of a few other officers seated in our section.

"If I may accompany you? My legs would like to take a stroke? Strode? Some word like that."

Mrs. Livingstone started to lever her sturdy form out of the chair, but Danjella waved her back. "Please, keep yourself comfortable. Surely I should be fine to accompany Ian to the lobby?"

Mrs. Livingstone's perpetual frown deepened, but she did not rise and I led us out through the small door at the end of the balcony to the lobby.

We hesitated too long and the queue stretched out the length of the hall. We had nearly maneuvered to take our place in the back, when a lieutenant stepped on the hem of a lady's gown. The woman yelped, creating a knot of interest and separating me from Danjella. I was working my way back to her when an unfamiliar voice with a thick German accent called out, "*Fregattenkapitän* Rollins."

At the sound of my name I turned to see if it was possible he meant me, and he did. A broad fellow resplendent in the dress mess uniform of a *Kaiserliche Marine* captain, or more properly *Kapitän*, was barreling down at me, his hand outstretched in greeting. He addressed me again, this time in English, "Commander Rollins." He seized my hand, "Please to let me introduce myself, I am Kapitän Gottfried Mueller."

He gestured over my shoulder to a man just catching up with him. I turned and saw the man I knew to be Mr. Cooper-Smythe approaching. The kapitän continued his introduction, "My English friend here is Sir Reginald Ross."

I tried to keep the stunned expression off my face as Cooper-Smythe extended his hand, holding it at a strange downward angle. "Reggie Ross," he introduced himself with a great beaming smile that never touched his eyes. He gave my hand a thorough vigorous shake and clapped me on the shoulder.

"Capital to meet you! Capital!"

I cast around for Danjella, then took control of my voice before replying.

"Pleased to make your acquaintance, Sir Reginald." My voice lacked conviction.

He made a fist and punched me on the arm in very good humor. "Reggie, Reggie; you must call me Reggie."

"Nice to meet you. . . Reggie." I tried to throw more sincerity into my words.

"When our distinguished visitor saw you, he wanted to meet you," he cried.

I looked back and discovered that the refreshment line had moved, but I still could not catch sight of Danjella.

"You are the commander of the *unterzeeboot, ja*?" Mueller asked.

"Yes, I have that distinction."

"Capital!" Reggie bellowed again, eliciting some interest from the crowd.

"The kapitän is the naval attaché to the embassy here. He is Kaiser Wilhelm's man in London."

"I am so sorry to hear about the attempt on the Kaiser's life," I said, happy to say something in true sincerity.

The kapitän's face clouded. "I received a cable before I left the embassy, but I cannot rush to his side." He shrugged in a most un-Prussian manner. "All that I can do is wait for news."

He glanced down and was the first person to look unabashedly at my apparatus, "May I see?"

I lifted up my pincers for examination; others took the opportunity to openly stare.

Mueller whipped out a monocle, screwed it into place, then grasped the apparatus, and turned it back and forth, carefully inspecting its function.

"Ach, this is amazing. Could you?" He mimed opening and closing the pincers, and I complied to his evident glee.

"So, so clever, *nein*?"

Danjella interrupted. "It is Commander Rollin's own design," she stated. She had arrived from my blind side and carried a small tray with two glasses of red wine and one of bubbly tonic water.

"Ah," the German officer exclaimed. He removed the monocle with a flourish and presented her with a stiff Prussian bow, accompanied by an audible click of his heels. His eyes widened noticeably when he perceived just how much was revealed through the lace panel of her décolletage.

Danjella responded with a petite curtsey.

"And this charming lady is?" He kept her eyes on her though he clearly addressed me.

She replied quickly, without allowing me to provide a polite introduction.

"I am Danjella, a secretary for the Thames Ironworks."

He smiled at her, but seemed to mentally dismiss her. He said to me, "That is where you are keeping the unterzeeboot."

"Yes, the deuced thing seems to demand constant maintenance."

"*Ja*, but it will be ready for our visit on Wednesday?"

"At this time, I believe it will be."

"Visit?" Reggie asked Mueller. "You didn't say anything about a visit."

I was amazed that Cooper-Smythe made so convincing a dandy and addressed him as formally as possible.

"Yes, the kapitän will call on us along with an American representative this Wednesday for a tour, and possibly a short voyage." Kapitän Mueller's lip twitched at the news of another visitor, generating doubt in the theory of American/German collusion. I saw a frown flicker across Reggie's face indicating he was reaching the same conclusion, but his face betrayed nothing more.

Reggie clapped his hand together several times, nodding toward Danjella and me and exclaimed, "Well, well, well. Isn't this a nice group?" he spread his hands. "You should join us for a late supper after the show."

Reggie offered his continuously beaming smile, and a nearly imperceptible shake of his head.

"I'm so sorry, but Danjella has a curfew," I said , striving to sound sincere. I caught her eye as I suspected she would make an immediate denial.

But either she also noted Reggie's demeanor, or had her own reasons, for she nodded and pressed a maidenly hand to her chest.

"I must be home at an early hour; another time perhaps?"

"Of course," the kapitän replied with a smile.

The lights flickered and I expressed my regrets. "We must return to our seats."

I held up my hand and pincers to take the tray, but Danjella politely waved me away.

"My apologies for the distraction," I said as I dropped my arms. "I will reimburse you for the refreshment."

She shook her head decisively. "Will not be necessary, as I am employed and have my own money."

"Employed, as a secretary?"

She shrugged. "Captain Arthur insists that my exact role in the project should remain confidential. He is trying to keep civilian involvement, how you say? Out of limelight? He is concerned that it might undermine credibility of the project."

It suddenly occurred to me that I didn't really know what her exact role was, other than serving as Tesla's assistant.

We took our refreshment, and sat through the second part of the play. It was entertaining, but I found my attention wandering to the persona of Reggie Ross and its purpose. I could still hear the rather strange way he had of repeating the name.

The play finished and I was hoping to get out of the theater in a timely manner, preferably without any more awkward encounters.

No such luck.

Chapter Eleven

The stage company finished their final bows and the applause echoed in the great hall while resplendent men and women rose in ovation. Danjella stood, bobbing slightly as she clapped her hands in giddy excitement; I stood beside her, politely clapping my hand against my wrist as Mrs. Livingstone sat in sullen resentment. The commotion died down and we resumed our seats to make polite chitchat about the play as we waited for the throng to thin out.

Mrs. Livingstone leaned forward between Danjella and I and said, "That Mikado chap, should have just had them all beheaded and been done with it.

Danjella rolled her eyes and tapped her foot until the doorway was about clear. Her pronouncement effectively ended conversation before it began, and the throng thinned and we headed to the lobby, Mrs. Livingstone interposing herself between Danjella and me in case our bodies might touch in the crowd.

We shuffled to the lobby in single file. Normally I would have let the ladies go first, but in the shifting crowd I took the lead like an icebreaker clearing an arctic channel for a supply convoy. I established a rhythm of taking two steps forward and pausing, and started to make headway. I turned to check on my companions. At that moment, there was a disruption, some shoving, and a man bumped into me. He wore an elegant frock coat with a velvet collar that appeared too warm for the spring night. He was of solid build and seemed quite fit, and carried a very utilitarian walking stick. He quickly stepped back and nodded. "Sorry about that sir, lost my footing."

"Not a bit," I replied. I looked around and realized that I had become separated from my convoy.

He smiled, a genial light in his eyes revealing the good nature of a man who is self-assured.

"Excellent," he said, and made to turn away when a familiar voice spoke out.

"John?" the slightly petulant baritone called out. "Where have you got to?"

The speech was maddeningly familiar, with no pleasant associations. Even though I could not immediately place it, instinct made me turn away, but not in time.

"Oh, good God, John," the newcomer continued, having evidently recognized me. "That is that bogus engineer I was telling you about."

Identifying the voice, I slowly turned and smiled with my lips as my eyes narrowed.

"Mr. Wilkins of the Thames company, I believe?'' I said.

He stared at me with a malignant grin and lifted the walking stick he held in his right hand. A mob of people streamed by us and, though I wanted to survey the room for Danjella, I kept my gaze leveled at him.

He raised the walking stick further and rested it on his shoulder.

"I have been hoping to see you when you could not in call a squad of armed men."

John spoke up, his voice incredulous.

"What are you doing?" He demanded, aware of the people who had paused to look at us, "You do not mean to be threatening this man, do you? He looked at the pincers of my left hand, and laid a firm hand on Wilkins's shoulder.

"Pardon my companion here," he said in an even tone. "He has had a bit to drink."

Wilkins glared at the other man, misunderstanding his motives. "Do not take pity on this ruffian, he has already accosted me once, and before I could give him his comeuppance, he sicced a brace of marines on me."

"Well," John replied. "He hasn't got any marines here. What just say we leave him to an evening in peace? I would say he is hardly dangerous at the moment."

"I disagree," I said hotly, unmindful of the place or circumstance. My more evolved self realized that John was trying to avoid a confrontation, but his casual condescension sparked something in me. "I think I am more than a match for Mr. Wilkins, and if he wants to start something, I will have a mind to finish it."

John kept his hand on Wilkins's shoulder, but held the other up in a conciliatory gesture and spoke with grave sincerity. "I mean no disrespect; you are obviously a man of courage and honor, so bravely wounded in Her Majesty's service. Please, let me invite you for a drink; we can settle this matter more cordially."

Before I could reply, another familiar voice called out. "You are quite wrong, you know," the latest voice said with aristocratic disdain. "He was not injured in action, but rather through his own stupidity and he should have been sacked from the service."

My night just got better and better as Captain William Clarke, late of the HMS *Indomitable*, stepped forward in his mess uniform, his gilded buttons glowing in the pale electric light and his cocked hat held stiffly under his arm.

"You are acquainted with this lout?" Wilkins inquired.

He looked down his nose and raised one supercilious eyebrow.

"The idiot sunk my ship and had me beached."

 The crowd completely thinned out, leaving just a few curious onlookers. I finally spotted Danjella and Mrs. Livingstone standing much further back along the wall. Mrs. Livingstone was trying to maneuver Danjella even further away from the confrontation, and while Danjella was not trying to approach, she resisted being led away. She seemed content with watching, and appeared to be waiting for something.

"Gentlemen," John spoke up sharply. "I understand that both of you have cause for enmity with this person, but for god's sake man, you should not be threatening a cripple with bodily harm." He placed a restraining hand on Wilkins's arm.

I could not brook his condescension. Again, I knew in my heart the man actually meant well, but to be dismissed as a rotted derelict was intolerable. There was heat in my face and blood pounded in my ears as I focused on the young dandy. I set my feet and made ready to show him just how crippled I was.

"Ian," Danjella called out in a perfectly timed, pleasant voice. "There you are. She strode purposefully to my side, placed her hand in the crook of my elbow, and regarded the men.

"Is there some . . ." she paused to regard each man in turn, "difficulty?"

Clarke's lip twitched in repressed scorn, as if he were too well-bred to allow himself a complete sneer. He turned away.

Wilkins's manner changed abruptly at Danjella's approach and he bowed deeply.

"Miss Tesla, I did not realize you were visiting the theater."

Danjella looked at him with blank eyes. "I am sorry. Am I supposed to know you?"

He drew himself up and said, "Timothy Wilkins, with the Thames Iron and Boatworks. We have had several meetings."

"Have we?" Her brow furrowed and she stared at him intently. "I do not recall. You must not be very, enlightening? Edifying? Some such word."

John stifled a laugh.

"Miss Tesla," Wilkins began again, but she raised her hand and interrupted him.

"Ian, Commander Rollins here, has been so kind as to escort me to the theater. I hope there is no unpleasantness." Her gaze flickered back and forth between the two men.

Wilkins' eyes bugged out.

"Miss Tesla," his voice hardened, but then he gentled his tone as if speaking to a precocious but unruly child. "You are foreign to these parts, you need to know that you debase yourself to be in the company of such a man." He waved his stick at me.

"Really?" she replied with an icy gleam in her eyes and a smile that chilled my blood.

"My mistake then, as I thought that to debase myself; I would have to be seen with a swaggering dandy possessing the brain of mule, a face that resembles the further end of a mule, the manners of a particularly dull villager, and the smell . . . of a *bordello*." She stepped closer to me and made a point of further entwining her arm with mine.

Wilkins purpled, his mouth agape.

John interrupted with a slight grin. "Tim, old boy, you do tend to use *a bit* of cologne."

Wilkins looked daggers at his companion, then, as he was not so well bred as Captain Clarke, openly sneered at me.

"Miss Tesla," he addressed her. "It is my concerned hope that one day you will tire of playing with broken toys."

And with what he assumed to be a clever retort, he spun on his heel and stormed away, following the same path as Captain Clarke.

"He's not really such a bad fellow," John said after a pause.

"I wouldn't know," I replied coolly.

"I hope that we have not caused distress? Disregard? Some word like that, with your friend, Mr . . .?" She smiled at him with genuine concern.

"Bellows, John Bellows." He reached into his breast pocket, retrieved a card and presented it to me.

Danjella craned her neck to look at it. "You are an instructor in physical culture?"

"Yes, ma'am, I teach single stick to gentlemen. It is a martial sport—"

"I've heard of it." I interrupted sharply. The man was making an effort, but I still chafed under his earlier remarks. I looked at Danjella, intending to drag her over to Mrs. Livingstone, but she looked back at me with such disappointment I was instantly crestfallen. The man sighed.

"Well, I see I've made a hash of it." He spread his hands out.

With Danjella still looking at me, I turned back to Mr. Bellows and forced a smile.

"No sir, I am making a hash of it." I extended a hand. "Ian Rollins, and this is Danjella Tesla." I gestured to where our chaperone was dawdling by a potted plant, "Her companion is Mrs. Livingstone."

At the mention of her name, Mrs. Livingstone began to approach.

Bellows made a sharp direct bow of his head to each of the ladies, although he did not click his heels like the *kapitän*.

"It is a pleasure." The smile he bestowed on Danjella was sincere.

Danjella gazed back at him with a glint of approval in her eyes. I thought it looked quite unbecoming on her.

John was not quite as tall as me. He was trim at the waist; but had a depth of chest to testify to his habit of physical culture, though he was not thickly muscled. The brown bowler he carried was just few shades darker than his hair, and his piercing blue eyes were set above chiseled cheekbones and a rugged jaw. Actually, a most unremarkable man—I could not see what Danjella was looking at.

He pointed at the card still in my hand, but addressed Danjella. "That has the address of my studio, if you would like to stop by, I will be happy to spot either of you some lessons."

"Thank you," I suspected that while the instructor may welcome me, his students may not be so pleased.

He bowed again to Danjella, to the newly arrived Mrs. Livingstone, and with a wave of his hat, took his leave.

"What a nice man," Danjella said.

"A physical culture instructor?" Mrs. Livingstone snapped. "He's little more than a thug."

I somehow felt compelled to defend him from the judgmental Mrs. Livingstone, but found myself unwilling to flatter him in Danjella's presence.

"I suppose," I said grudgingly, "he is a decent sort of fellow. Few men have been so thoroughly damned with faint praise.

Danjella released my arm to step in front of me. She looked directly at my eye, regarded me with sort of sad pout, and patted me on the shoulder.

"Oh, Ian, he is pretty to look at, very handsome, very rutted? Rubbed? Some word like that. However, when you get to know me better, you will know that I like to shop, and I enjoy looking at pretty things. But," she reached out a gentle hand and smoothed my lapel, "there are very few things special enough, intricate enough, interesting enough, that I stop to actually examine. And even fewer that I would consider taking home."

"Ahem!" Mrs. Livingstone cleared her throat and pointedly crossed her arms.

Danjella rolled her eyes and made a frustrated hissing sound in her throat. She took me by the left wrist, just above the cuff for the pincers, and moved my arm out far enough to entwine her arm and rest her hand on my forearm.

I escorted the ladies out of the nearly deserted theater and into the street. There was a distinct chill in the air, with a salt tang on the breeze that stirred up the dust on the streets into small swirling eddies.

Evidently, Jenkins was watching for us, for when we emerged by one of the ornate gaslights that ringed the square, he called out, waved his hat, and drove the landau over to greet us. His weather eye was as sharp as mine and he raised the top of the carriage. I watched his approach and stared at the conveyance, trying to find some excuse to prolong the evening, perhaps taking the ladies for tea or some late evening sweet, but there were no respectable places that allowed women at that hour. Regretfully, I patted Danjella's hand to let go of my arm and I was vividly aware of the empty space as she stepped aside. It was as if when we were together, a mild electric current traveled through us, giving me energy and light, but once the circuit broke everything darkened.

I assisted Mrs. Livingstone into the carriage, then Danjella, and was about to pull myself in when a small figure dashed out of the gloom.

"Commander Rollins!" a young tenor voice cried out, somewhat out of breath.

I turned, half expecting some new verbal assault. A young man of twelve to fourteen years dressed in basic trousers and a plain blue tunic, rushed up, stopped, and saluted. I recognized him as one of the runners from the port, so I gravely returned the gesture, touching my hand to the brim of my service cap.

"Hello, young man," I said. I had absolutely no clue what his name was.

He did not enlighten me, instead he drew his breath and started speaking.

"I'm sorry, I thought I'd missed you, and was headed back to the port when I saw you come out." He worked the words out between gasps: he had been running hard.

"You were looking for me?'

"Captain Wilson told me where to find you." He pulled in a deep breath and let it out slowly, then stood straight, his manner now very formal.

"Captain Wilson sends his regards and hopes you have had a pleasant evening. Unfortunately, he requires your presence, as well as the presence of Miss Tesla, at the tower. There is a lightning storm approaching."

I looked at him blankly.

"Ian," Danjella called out. "I have to get to the tower to charge electrolyte."

I looked up to the night sky and felt the freshening breeze on my cheeks as flashes of light illuminated the ash grey clouds on the horizon. I clenched my jaw. I had wished to find an excuse to prolong the evening, but . . .

"All right," I said, taking control of my emotions. I called to Jenkins, "Take us to the port, if you please."

"Ian!"

I looked up, puzzled.

"I need to change." She plucked at the front of her lovely, but cumbersome gown.

I nodded, casting my glance at the young messenger, then at the carriage, and then I surveyed the square.

"Jenkins," I said, "please take the ladies to their flat and wait for Miss Tesla, and then bring her to the port. I will go with the boy."

The boy nodded in excitement. "We can run there in under an hour."

I looked at his eager face. "A hansom will have us there in twenty minutes."

His shoulders sagged. "Yes, sir."

"Jenkins, go now."

"Very good," he said.

"Ian," Danjella called out. She extended her right hand over the half-door of the landau. I reached for it, grabbed her by the fingers, and in an impulse went to kiss it, or at least the air above it.

At the last second, fingers made strong from endless hours manipulating small gears, forcing them into place, and making small bits of metal bend to her will, seized my hand and pulled with astounding strength. My head jerked up in sheer astonishment just in time for my lips to meet hers. If there had been gentle electricity moving between us earlier, at that moment, I was thunderstruck.

Even as the carriage jerked us apart I could taste something sweet and faintly salty on my lips. Upon reflection, I think she meant for her lips to merely touch my brow, but suddenly raising my head changed her plans.

I did not complain.

My scattered thoughts were interrupted by an overly dramatic attempt at a discreet cough, followed by an impatient tenor voice.

"If you are quite finished, sir," the runner said, standing with his hands behind his back and rocking on his heels.

I looked him in the eye. "Quite."

He responded with a raised eyebrow, and I turned to hail a hansom.

Chapter Twelve

From the urgency of the orders, I expected to see the port humming with activity, but instead the hansom delivered us to the gate of a quiet and mostly deserted facility. The only stirrings of action were around the enclosed ship works as the night crew worked riveting together the steel plates of the hull. We dismounted and I peered through the gloom in an attempt to spot any movement by the pier or the buildings as we approached the gate.

The marine guard saluted me, but gave us a grim inspection as he reviewed the very short access list. He pursed his lips and pointed at me. "You can go in." He pointed at the messenger and said, "but not you."

Puzzled at the deserted nature of the yard, I started up the path to the foundry works. Suddenly, lights blazed from the top of Tesla's tower laboratory, illuminating the lattice structure as if it were the lighthouse it resembled. The brightness revealed shadows moving inside and more people on the roof. I increased my pace to a trot, reached the lift and rode it to the laboratory. As I pushed open the lift cage, I found Captain Wilson standing before one of the great windows, his hands behind his back as he stared into the murky night made moonless by low hanging clouds and fog rolling in from the North Sea. His uniform was just as crisp and ready as any normal workday. The only change in his appearance was the unlit briarwood pipe clenched in his teeth. Thumps, thuds, and stamping noises came from overhead, announcing an elevated level of activity on the roof.

Tesla himself was working at some apparatus; obviously in haste to make it ready. I nodded to him, joined Wilson at the window, and stared out across the port waiting to be acknowledged.

"Big storm?" I finally asked.

"Not really," he replied in a low tone, speaking around the pipe stem. "Telegraph reported it formed rather quickly off the coast of Ireland and blew our way. Not much rain, but a deuced amount of lightning."

He took the pipe out of his mouth and considered it. "Tesla was ready to send out a summons for his cousin and the engineers to charge the vats of electrolyte, but I intercepted him and sent for the officers instead."

"Because?"

"Your fault, don't you know?" He gave a barking laugh. "I agree with your notion that the officers need to be trained on all functions, so here you are."

"And everyone else?"

He pointed up. "We are quite at a standstill until Miss Tesla arrives. I was rather hoping you would deliver her."

"She is on her way in a carriage of my employ, after a quick rush home as her clothing was not suitable for work. If I may ask, sir, just what exactly is her function here tonight?"

Captain Wilson tore his gaze from the window and smiled at me, a small twinkle in his eye.

"So," he said after a minute, "how did you like the theater?"

I shrugged. "The evening was intriguing, on many levels, but not very informative about the Japans, I think."

Wilson snorted. "One does not go to the Savoy for accurate information."

"I ran into Mr. Cooper-Smythe," I ventured.

The captain frowned in thought. "Now, he can tell you about the Japans; he spent six years there."

"Really?"

"Yes, he was assigned to the naval garrison at Hong Kong when two sailors from the Sloop *Icarus* were murdered in *Nagasaki*. Several factions tried to use the incident for advantage; Cooper-Smythe was dispatched to discern the facts."

"Did he?"

"Much to the displeasure of the ruling shogunate, but it did result in proper reparations to the victims' families. So, was he enjoying the theater?"

"I do not know precisely, but he was with the German naval attaché, Gottfried Mueller."

He pinched the bridge of his nose and sighed.

"That is . . . interesting, and not the good kind of interesting."

"Yes," I agreed. "He made a point to introduce himself as Sir Reginald Ross."

"Ah no, not Reggie Ross," he said, mimicking the eccentric intonation Cooper-Smythe had used.

"You are aware of this stratagem?"

"Oh yes. Sir Reginald is a distant relation of our skulking friend, and Cooper-Smythe uses that identity when he means to incite something. The real Sir Reginald is reclusive, and sticks to the family home in Northumberland. I understand he is amused by his relation's antics in his name." He studied me with his sharp eyes. "I do hope you did not give too much away."

"I was too shocked by Cooper-Smythe's behavior, and I was at quite a loss. I fear I spent most of the evening with a stunned look on my face. It was an intriguing night." I smiled in spite of myself.

At that moment, Tesla dropped a spanner and stood up, placed his hands in the small of his back, and straightened kinked muscles.

"The integrator is ready." He waved at us. His suit was rumpled, and he had removed his bow tie, leaving the collar open. His thick black hair was disheveled, giving him a nearly feral appearance. Even his mustache was unruly, missing its customary sheen of pomade. "Tesla needs you to open the panels," he said.

I raised a quizzical eyebrow at Captain Wilson who shook his head and just hurried to the back wall, gesturing for me to follow. On my previous visits, the back of the tower laboratory seemed to be a solid partition made of walnut finished paneling, but Wilson indicated a series of hidden catches set into a chair rail along the wall. Together we pulled down the panels to reveal a series of porcelain vats interconnected with glass pipes.

Tesla rubbed his hands together and studied them with a critical eye.

"We will energize vat one and three tonight, and if we have time we will add to vat two," he announced.

A rattling noise arose as two men clambered down from the roof on a set of metal stairs bolted to the outside of the building. The door to the tower balcony opened as lieutenants Hanley and Bartley, both wearing mackintosh coats, came in out of the growing wind.

Bartley grinned at me.

"Commander Rollins, glad to see you could join us. You need to get to the roof." He pointed up in excitement. "My God, it's incredible."

"How so?"

"You have got to see it to believe it. I just constructed a miniature air ship." His eyes shone with a sense of pride. He turned from me to Dr. Tesla. "We can see the lightning bolts in the distance, not just the flashes. Are we ready to start?"

Tesla waved both his hands in the air, and then went back to examining the electrolyte vats.

Wilson thoughtfully eyed the pipe in his hand.

"Before Miss Tesla arrives, there are things you all need to be aware of, right, doctor?"

Tesla glanced up at the sound of his title, but otherwise ignored us, and continued with whatever he was looking at.

"Well, she better hurry," Bartley remarked. "The storm is upon us. If she doesn't get here soon she'll have to learn the system with the next storm."

"No," Wilson corrected, "if *she* does not arrive in time, I'm afraid *we* may have to learn the system in the next storm." He looked up at the ceiling as if trying to peer through it. "Is Bertram still up there?"

"He was right behind us," Hanley said as footsteps clanged down the wrought iron stairs and Bertram slipped in from the wind, seeming to swim in an oversized mackintosh.

"Glad you could join us," Wilson said with a smile. His gaze flicked across each of us. "This charging system was designed by Dr. Tesla, but designing the full-scale components, detailing procedures, that is what Miss Tesla does. I understand you assembled one of the collector ships on the roof?"

"Yes, it isn't difficult but the result —" Bartley said.

"Yes, yes," Wilson interrupted. "Dr. Tesla designed the system to draw lightning to his devices, but it was Miss Tesla who designed the frames, the gasbags, and the braided copper cable we are using. She is more than Tesla's assistant; she is the person who translates his theories and scale models into full scale." He regarded us very seriously as he tapped the small briarwood pipe against the side of his leg. "This is confidential; Miss Tesla is the linchpin of the program. Not only is she the one person with the most practical knowledge of the charging system, the battery works, and the electric motors, but she was the chief designer on the team that modified the plans we acquired from John Holland." He looked at us and frowned. "Does anyone know where to find Lieutenant Graf? I have a runner out looking for him."

"He will not find him," I said. "I am sorry; I granted him leave for the weekend and he took his family grouse shooting."

"No," Wilson said, "my fault. I played this one too close to the vest. Spring is the best time for electrical storms, and I should have let you know to keep personnel close." He looked at Bertram. "As I was saying, Miss Tesla is the expert on all of the equipment and procedures you will need to know."

Lightning flashed so close it brightened the interior like the muzzle flash from heaven's main guns, followed by a crash of thunder that shook the tower and momentarily deafened us. When my senses returned, I heard a whirring noise as the lift rose from the ground. The door opened to reveal Danjella, kitted up for work in a dark blue divided skirt and lady's waistcoat, a tan oilskin coat over her arm. Goggles with smoked lenses were pushed up on her forehead, pinning back her thick hair, and in her hand she carried heavy leather gloves lined in India rubber. She inspected our gathering and frowned.

"Why are you down here?" she asked rhetorically, then made a sweeping gesture toward the stairs. "To the roof! We haven't a moment to spare." As we started to comply, she yelled, "Stop!" She pointed to me, and drew her finger to a rack of Macintosh raincoats.

I grabbed one and wrestled it on over my pincers as I headed up to the roof.

At the top of the stairs, I saw Bartley's miniature airship moored tightly to the tower roof. It was fully a dozen feet long by six in diameter and constructed of a lattice-work cage of what appeared to be brass or bronze. Four large fins of the same material gave it directionality. This assembly was filled with a stout leather envelope cut as a green split, like the heat-resistant apron of a blacksmith, and sewn into an elongated cylinder. Inside, no doubt, it was filled with a bladder of helium. Next to the assembled unit, lay a collection of the lattice pieces, copper rods and a folded leather envelope.

"Good," Danjella exclaimed as she emerged, "you have already one constructed." She was not wearing a heavy mac, but rather her much lighter oilskin coat, cut in the manner of a floor-length French riding coat. It was very form-fitting at the waist and flared out at the hips to wide skirts split for riding. The tan garment was double breasted with a short mantle at the shoulders, and a high turned-up collar. Her goggles were the only thing holding her long hair in place, and loose curls whipped around her in the rising wind. She stooped down to inspect the airship and the shifting winds blew her hair up, revealing the pale nape of her neck. A shiver went through me, evidently caused by the cold wind catching the hem of my mac.

Danjella assessed the assembled craft. "Good work. It looks like you got it solid," she looked around the group. "Who?"

Lieutenant Bertram held up a finger, and pointed it between himself and Bartley.

"Good," she turned to me. "You and Hand? Hame?"

"Hanley," the lieutenant said.

"Yes, thank you," she nodded. "You two can put the other together." She waved her hands to indicate we should begin.

I eyed the components dubiously.

"Not as hard as it looks," Bartley spoke up. "It's sort of obvious."

Comparing the assembled craft to the components before me I quickly saw what he meant. The pieces were directional so the frame only went together one way, with clever springs built into the struts to keep them together. With the storm bearing down on us, I picked up the first pieces to fit together, paused, feeling the weight, or rather lack of weight in my hand.

"That's not brass, is it?"

"No, that would be too heavy. Is plated aluminium."

I gaped at the riches laid before me. Aluminium was more costly than silver, and I had only seen small pieces of it worked into jewelry. I could retire on the material from the contraptions we were about to launch. I said something under my breath about using much cheaper silver, and Danjella laughed.

"Do not go out and invest money in stocks of aluminium," she advised with a grin. "The price has dropped remarkably and it will soon be as cheap as dirt. My cousin worked with Paul Héroult in Paris and he has developed a new way to produce it. We are one of his first customers, but soon you will see aluminum replace tin as the base metal of choice. I would bet all my money within few years they make your ships of this."

"Are you that sure?"

"Indomitably? Indolently?" She stared at me and I remained quiet.

She stamped her foot. "This time I would like some help, am I thinking of a real word?"

"Indubitably," I replied.

Her eyes narrowed and she looked at me suspiciously. "Is that a real word?"

"Indubitably," I replied. "It means beyond any doubt."

She glared at me, still suspecting I was playing a trick on her.

A flash of light interrupted our discussion. Hanley and I hurriedly returned to our task connecting the sections together, and made ready to situate the leather bag with the bladder inside.

As we finished, Danjella and Lieutenant Bertram pushed a portable winch assembly to us, its skids squealing as it crossed the roof. Danjella hooked the winch to the solid frame, and placed a brace against it to serve as an anchor. When it was firmly moored to the ground, she moved a hose from a tank of helium to inflate the bladder. The leather envelope expanded, and I could see it was kept from direct contact with the frame by clever coils of wire that served as spacers and heat sinks. Even so, the split hide was visibly scorched from previous use.

Once the second balloon was inflated, Danjella straightened up, smiled, and hastily returned to the first, holding up a finger to judge the direction of the wind. The approaching storm made it difficult to gauge direction as the winds swirled around us, but eventually she nodded in satisfaction, and pulled the smoked glass goggles over her eyes. She carefully grabbed the large locking lever in both hands, squeezed the handle release, and then jerked it hard, freeing the balloon to float from its anchor.

At first, the ungainly object strayed more east than up, but after traveling horizontally for several feet, it began to gain altitude. Danjella climbed up on top of the winch, slowly playing out the line while guiding it from the reel with her heavy gloves like a big ungainly kite. She watched intently through her darkened lenses, tugging on the line to steer the thing in some way that only she could see.

Lightning cracked across the sky, but did not strike the balloon. Even so, Danjella's hair, which was flying haphazardly in the wind, now stood straight from her head like a dark brown cloud. A crackling laugh escaped her lips. I watched as she played out over fifty feet of cable, made note of the height and movement of the balloon, then stopped the line as she assessed the airship. It stopped rising and the line began to sag under its own weight.

"This you must learn to judge," she yelled against the wind as she drew some line back in. "The point of vexation—where to add more cable will lower the conductor with the added weight. It is different all the time; you must learnt to see." She stared up at the cable, hauling on it with both hands to test the strain, and, seeming satisfied, released it. Hands on her hips, she gazed at the ship as if she suspected it would either fall or slip away the minute she let it out of her sight.

Finally, she raised her goggles, leapt nimbly from the winch and dashed for the second assembly, raising a finger to the wind again. With waving hands and a few shouted words, she directed us to move the second airship several feet away. Hanley and I each grabbed a cable. I clutched my line to my good hand and wrapped it through my pincer.

I heard Danjella shout a warning as the wind gusted, and the airship shifted over Hanley with surprising force.

"Hold it!" he yelled to me and I threw my weight against the ship as she listed toward the east side of the tower, dragging Hanley and me with her. As I wrestled with it, the wind changed direction, and the cumbersome device moved back to the correct position. I freed my pincers from the line.

Danjella studied the angles for a moment, tested the air one more time, replaced her goggles, and released the lever. As with the first, she clambered up on top and adroitly played out the cable until she determined the right amount.

A large wet drop smacked me between the eyes. I looked up and its brother splashed on my brow, followed by its cousins, in-laws, tribe, village.

In seconds, my hair was drenched and water ran down the back of my mac, chilling me. Danjella's hair turned black as a raven's wing and was plastered to her head, but she was still smiling. She used one hand to wipe the spray from her lenses as she tugged incessantly at the tow cable. She threw her entire weight against it, though her effort did not travel more than a few feet up the line.

Lightning ripped the sky, followed by an explosive assault upon our ears, but still our apparatus floated peacefully. The air around Danjella fairly tingled; wisps of her hair danced around in the charged atmosphere. Her eyes met mine and I saw an expression of pure joy. Though I returned a pensive smile, I could not duplicate her elation as I have spent too much time in storms at sea, rocking in dank misery contemplating all the extra work necessary when the squall finally passed.

But in Danjella's eyes I saw an elemental, ferocious spirit reveling in the violent glory of the gale, and her mania touched a nerve in my body. I felt dread in the cold rain on my cheeks, as if something very cold brushed against my heart. In Danjella's eyes I saw the same hint of the hidden conflagration that marked each year of my mother's descent into hysteria. For a moment, I saw a woman on the edge of madness.

I always expected to marry one day. I frequently imagined my wife to be a strong woman, accustomed to long periods of separation as I deployed with the fleet. She would be a solid woman, capable with finances, steady and sober in temperament, a proper lady in all ways, a suitable officer's wife, and above all, emotionally stable. Sane.

Before me was a fundamental force of nature. Trying to tie her to home and hearth would be like trying to turn a tiger into a house pet. Watching her steer an airship meant to channel lightning, I knew I desired her. I could even love such a woman, but could I ever marry one? What kind of life could I offer her? Would I be able to trust her, or would

I spend all our time looking for a sign of an imminent breakdown? With this knowledge chilling my heart, I realized to continue to consort with her would be selfish and useless.

She looked down at me, her face animated by the fierce joy of the storm, but she must have noticed something in my expression. A questioning frown creased her brow, and I tore my eyes from the rain-lashed oilskin that clung so tightly to her curves and stared instead at the rain. Had I not looked up at precisely that moment, I might have missed it. One second the airship was dancing in the wind, the next an arc of electricity enveloped it, and I suddenly understood the utility of the smoked lenses Miss Tesla wore. The light exploded with a flash brighter than any photographer's powder, so bright that even as I closed my eyes I could see the brilliance through my lids, and when it abruptly died, the greenish afterimage remained in front of me. I knew I would not be able to see the power traveling down the cable, yet I looked as if I expected it to burn like quick match.

Amid this intensity, Danjella blithely hopped from the perch and waved her arms for us to follow inside. Once in the laboratory, she grabbed a towel which hung by the door and wiped her face.

"With luck, we'll get at least one more strike, but now here is where the action is," she said as she waved to the vats of electrolyte, where a blue sheen glowed around the ports and lugs.

For the next hour, we handled porcelain pumps and glass tubing, pumping the gritty slurry from one vat to another, balancing the load and forming the whole mess into fully charged batteries. It was just after midnight when I straightened from tightening the port on a battery to see everyone standing about.

With that part of the exercise completed, we ran back out into the dwindling storm and retrieved the balloon airships. They came apart readily and were quickly stowed.

Back down from the roof, I recovered my uniform coat and Danjella exchanged her oilskin for her cloth coat, handing it to me to hold for her, which I did with tense fingers. I then accompanied her down to the gate to find the hired carriage still waiting. Jenkins had found some shelter and had endeavored to stay dry. I escorted her to the landau, assisted her up, and then closed the door.

"Ian," she called out, "Come on, get in. Do not be silly."

I shook my head as my shoulders sagged.

"It would not be proper, and there are enough people about that tongues would wag." I looked at the fine carriage, thought of how pleasant her company was, then squared my shoulders in resolve. "Jenkins, take her home."

"Aye sir," he answered in a tone tinged with disapproval. "I'll be dropping the carriage off, too."

As I nodded acknowledgement, Danjella called out, "Ian, have I said something to offend?" Her voice sounded small and hurt.

A large part of me wanted to vault into the carriage, and the rigid controlled, portion of my soul wanted to explain, to give voice to the doubts which stirred in my breast. Neither option was acceptable. I looked at her, so tired and so content from her day that I could not say anything to dampen her spirit, so I forced a wan smile.

"No, I am tired, you are tired, and if we are going to work together, discretion must be our friend. Go with Jenkins."

I watched the horse trot away, and felt my heart sink like it was made of lead. It was nearly a mile down the road before I found a cab for hire, although in my mood I could have walked the entire distance and not felt any more miserable. I arrived home to a cold, empty flat. Without bothering to remove my coat, I sat in one of the comfortable wing chairs by the sideboard, and poured myself a double measure of whiskey.

By the time Jenkins returned, I had helped myself to a second double measure, or perhaps it was a third; my mind was fuzzy on that point.

My heart was heavy and blackness filled my sight. I was being an idiot, of course, as I had not actually formed an understanding, let alone a relationship, with that remarkable, but impossible woman. It was good fortune I came to my senses before I misled her and allowed my stupid selfishness to hurt her. I should be happy I avoided all that heartache.

Jenkins regarded me silently, approaching my chair. "Let me help yer, sir."

I stood, but the carpet must have shifted as my foot turned aside, so I took a half step to stabilize my stance.

Jenkins helped steady me as the carpet slipped again. He deftly eased me out of my coat and back into the chair.

"Yer doin' a'right?" he inquired, his tired voice thick with his accent.

I nodded, and lifted my glass, which was empty. I reached for the decanter but it was empty too, and I asked Jenkins, "Did you empty that?"

"No, sir." His voice was cool and part of me realized my words may have sounded like an accusation, which I did not mean.
"Do we have more?"

"Yes sir, we do," he admitted. "If I may be so bold, I'm not generally one to say a man 'as 'ad enough, but might yer want ter sleep a bit before yer 'ave more?"

I glared at him as sleep beckoned to me, just as attractive as Danjella beckoning to me from the carriage, but I resisted just as strongly. "Bring it to me." I demanded.

Jenkins sighed, strode to our small pantry to retrieve a bottle of Irish whiskey and frowning, poured me a glass. I drank it greedily, not even tasting the liquid, simply craving the numbness.

Sunday morning, I awoke in the same chair, alone. My lips tasted of salt while my face was stiff as if sea spray had dried there, and I chalked it up to the rain blowing in off the port the night before. My throat was as dry as the plains of the Sahara, and a drum throbbed inside my head, as my stomach roiled at any tiny movement. I took in deep breaths to try to stabilize my condition; I realized I must have caught some ailment standing out in the rain and wind, so I took to my bed for the rest of the day.

Chapter Thirteen

Monday morning I was well enough to attend calisthenics and was gladdened to see my officers, except Lieutenant Graf, were still game to work out with the men. After the morning's exertions, I refreshed my kit and cleaned up. I made my way to the shipyard to speak with the foreman in charge of the *Ram* hull repair, who confirmed it fit for launch. Per my instructions, Lieutenant Graf arranged for a noon parade at the pier for the men to witness the recommissioning, followed by depth trials.

With those tasks completed, I made my way to the second floor of the administration building and reported to Captain Wilson.

He regarded the schedule I handed him.

"This is pretty tight, do you think your crew can get all this done this week?"

"Yes, sir," I replied without hesitation. "They are good men and well rested."

"Including dealing with our visitors on Wednesday?"

"Yes, sir. We are going to remove the *Ram* from dry dock at a noon parade." I paused. "I would appreciate it if you could attend."

He pushed out his lower lip in concentration. "I will take it under advisement."

He looked up at me with a gleam in his eye. "Meanwhile, Miss Tesla has been looking for you. She seems to think you may be avoiding her."

I took a deep breath, swallowed, and nodded. "I may be, sir."

He let out his breath in an exasperated sigh, raised his hands to his temples and rubbed them, "Is there something I should be aware of?"

"No sir, I can handle it."

My tone seemed to concern him and he leaned forward in his chair to rest his elbows, then steepled his fingers, and placed them over his lips. He regarded me for a tick, then spoke gravely, "I warned you she is not one to trifle with."

"No sir, that is, I will not be trifling with her."

He frowned, looking as if he wanted to say something, but thought better of it. "I will leave it to you then, but remember, I will not allow personal considerations to disrupt good order and discipline."

Upon quitting Wilson's office, I headed to the larger dry dock facility to look in at progress on the new boat. The outer hull riveting was nearly complete, and the final plates were laid out by the great hatches in the front where the torpedoes would be loaded.

Stretched out on a series of trestle tables were the two prismatic devices to be mounted in the conning tower. The first was a telescope, thirty feet long, based on an instrument the French developed for their submersible. It used prisms and mirrors to allow observation above the waves. Ours was so much larger it needed to be commissioned in several pieces from a firm in Switzerland. The intricate pieces were finally assembled and I examined the instrument carefully, eager to try it out. The other, much smaller device, was designed to allow the conning officer to read the compass, which is housed in a sealed wooden box outside the steel hull, so its magnetic lines would not be influenced.

Under the shift foreman's attentive eyes, I climbed the scaffolding to the top of the conning tower and clambered through a wide circular hatch to the bridge. I planted my feet on the stout wooden deck, still not sure using oak was a good idea, but I had to admit there was a singular feeling to having the sturdy planks beneath my feet. The control center was spare—a half installed Chadburn ship's telegraph stood in the center back, just six feet behind the opening for the prismatic telescope.

The bridge was not quite a perfect circle, twelve feet in diameter. The conning tower itself was teardrop shaped, and lay lengthwise along the top of the hull proper, the "point" at the back housed a small gasoline dynamo for charging electrolyte. Two pipes would stick up from there, an intake and exhaust, allowing us to run the dynamo when the craft was submerged as deep as twenty feet. At the front of the bridge two large gaping holes marked the locations where two observation ports would be located. Eventually the openings would be filled with inch-thick quartz glass and equipped with watertight steel hatches that slid on rails and could quickly seal the ports during action.

To the left of the ports, was the first officer's station, and its Chadburn appeared to be working. The station also already had its speaking tube in place, with the whistle cover installed. This device was cleverly designed to route commands either to the engine room, the planesmen, or the torpedo room. I stood at the working station for a few minutes, practicing with the telegraph, then tried my hand at the speaking tube, first blowing through it to activate the whistle and then yelling commands. I was startled when a voice snapped back, "Who the bugger is this?"

I paused, bit my lips, then replied firmly,

"This is Commander Rollins," I said calmly. "Who might you be?"

I heard sharp intake of breath. "Beggin' yer pardon, sir. Didn't know you was aboard. This is Petty Officer Grant. I thought you was some yard dog screwin, er . . . foolin' around."

"It's all right; I didn't know you were aboard either." I should have;

Lieutenant Graf forwarded me a schedule of the familiarization visits the men were engaged in.

I thought about joining them in the engine room, but decided I would be interfering, so I finished my quick examination of the bridge and returned to my office. I intended to approach Danjella before lunch, but she had other plans.

Five minutes after I removed my coat and sat at my desk, she knocked on the open doorframe.

"Ian, do you have a minute?" She smiled cautiously.

I frowned. It would be cowardly to plead I was too busy, but cowardice was suddenly very attractive. I took a deep breath to steady my nerves and discovered that emotions that had been so clear before grew impossibly muddled. However, as I gazed into her eyes, I resolved to face the situation squarely. "I have a few minutes, Miss Tesla."

The world became so very still that I imagined I could hear the riveting gang from the dry dock as she regarded me for a moment, her eyes flashing confusion at first, but her jaw set in a hard line.

She spoke quietly, "Commander Rollins, I wished to inform you the foundry has done quite well fabricating your design, and I am prepared to begin the final assembly."

It was not what I expected to hear. "Thank you, I. . . I can see to that."

"Really?" she replied, her voice incredulous. "When? Next week? Month? Year? This is not kindness I am suggesting, but a matter of operational practicality. You need to be as operational as you can be."

I was taken aback by the way she referred to me like a machine, one of her contraptions, but I conceded. "Alright, how long until—"

"Friday," she interrupted, her tone frosty. She glanced at the floor, then back up at me, her hand resting on the doorframe,

"I had also meant to request you accompany me to a lecture at Cambridge on Thursday, but I sense you would be too busy."

"I am afraid you are correct," I said, avoiding her direct gaze.

"True," she said. "Once again you are afraid."

Through the anger, I detected a note of sorrow as silence hung between us. She took a deep breath, steadied her shoulders, raised her jaw defiantly and fixed her eyes on me. "Tell me, have I offended you?"

The die was cast. "No," I admitted shaking my head, in part to gather my thoughts. "You are an amazing person, but I have taken a lot of time to think, and you should not see me socially. You should seek out someone more supportive of your work. You should not even think you need to settle for a relationship with a navy officer, a position fraught with duty and responsibility to hearth and home."

As I spoke, her face assumed neutral lines, but her eyes glimmered with hurt. They rapidly hardened, though, and by the time I finished speaking they were fixed in anger.

I continued, "What you should—"

"I have a very good mind of what I should do," she snapped,

slapping her hand on the doorframe.

"Again you are correct," she clenched her jaw and nodded in a determined manner. "I should not see you again, but not for the reason you imagine." Her eyes took an odd shine.

"Since you have seen fit to define our relationship, made a decision to end it, claiming to be for my benefit, and, then tell me what I should be doing . . . To do all this, without ever bothering to ask my opinion, thought, or plan, tells me something about you."

Her grasp of English was suddenly flawless as she had no trouble finding the right words or tone to thoroughly skewer me.

The chill of her last words struck me. I tried to speak in my defense, but my mind could not frame the necessary words.

"I thought you to be intricate, but you are simple, bordering on the dull," she said.

I stood to defend myself, but she raised a hand.

"Please," she said and shook her head, "you have said quite enough." A slight smile twitched the corners of her lips, but did not convey any genuine mirth or ease.

"Rest assured," she forced her voice into a sweet tone. "I will not let my romantic disappointments prevent me from doing my duty. Your device will be finished; the systems for the new boat will be completed on time. Good day, Commander Rollins." She turned on her heel, started to walk away, but stopped, still facing away from me.

"Just a suggestion," she said, her voice unaccountably kind and just a little sad, "if you ever meet a woman who you respect, be sure you ask her opinion before you go making all the decisions, or telling her what she *should* do." She strode away out of sight.

I stared after her, certain I completely mishandled the situation, but could not fathom how or what to do about it, so I stayed in my office until time for the noon parade.

I met my officers out front of the foundry and we walked *en masse* to the small dry dock. The men were standing in formed rows facing the water when I arrived at the pier, and I marched up to take my place in the formation. Petty Officer Grant saluted: I returned the gesture and directed, "Fall in."

"Aye, sir," he responded, crisply turned on his heel, and marched to a position behind the ranks. I took command of the parade and turned to direct the men's attention to the small dry dock harboring the *Ram*. It was flooded in the morning and yard workers still scurried around the *Ram* to secure lines to stanchions, as the work crew finished removing the dock's riverside wall. Since the craft's ballast tanks were empty, it rode high in the water, lifting off of the poles that supported it during the dry operations. A steam tug stood by to tow the craft out once the final barrier was removed.

This was the first time I'd seen the vessel since its plating and the fresh coating shone like bright brass; the diving planes and rudder were painted a severe flat black. The sheen gave it a futuristic appearance, startlingly close to an image I saw in *The Strand* not long ago, where artists depicted their imaginings of the twenty-first century. I could almost see the gentleman from the drawing jauntily tipping his top hat as he emerged from the hatch.

We stood in silence as mooring lines were run to the sub and at an order from the maintenance chief, the rest of the barrier was removed. A cheer rose from the men and I turned to see Petty Officer Grant trying to restore order, but I shook my head to stop him. I heard not just cheers, but the sound of a deep-seated morale that the unit would need to do the mission before us. The tug towed the boat from its temporary berth back to its accustomed slip at the pier where the overly buoyant vessel rocked in the gentle swell of the tide.

"Coxswain, take a party to secure the *Ram*," I ordered in a loud voice.

He selected a detail and they ran to their duty.

"Lieutenant Graf, proceed with the diver-assisted depth trials to 150 feet."

We were going to stress the boat to three times operational depth. That should boost crew confidence in the device.

"Let me know when you are finished," I said to the lieutenant in a quieter voice. "I'd like to spend some time working with the controls. I mean to drive the sub this week."

"Driving shouldn't be too difficult," Graf said. "It is not complicated, as long as you have a good engineer who can trim the ballast, otherwise the damned boat handles like a pregnant cow. A particularly stupid, pregnant cow."

I nodded, figuring I could take some time after hours, if necessary. "Very well, let me know if there is any problem which will make the craft unavailable to our visitors."

"Yes, sir," he acknowledged. He then paused and bit his lower lip. His waxed mustache flicked from side to side, accentuating the motion of his upper lip as he seemed to wrestle with something.

"About the visitors," he said carefully, "I would like to request to be excused that day."

I raised a questioning eyebrow.

"Mueller is a distant relation," he explained with a sigh. "I would rather not have to deal with him."

"I appreciate that, as I would rather not have to deal with him either, but, I believe I will need you, and your knowledge."

He looked at me coolly, but I'd already dealt with a far colder stare that day.

"Yes, sir," he said, his pursed lips drawing the mustache tight to his mouth. The lieutenant saluted, turned on his heel, and took two men with him to the steam tug.

As predicted, the ambitious testing schedule went well over hours, and so I stayed late in my office that evening, until I was certain everyone else in the administration area had left, especially the Teslas, not that I was avoiding anyone. Of course, there were still crews working in the foundry. The forges took a long time to heat up, so they were kept running around the clock as the massive rollers created the steel plates necessary to complete the new boat. There were crew at the construction site itself, too, where workmen continued to rivet the enormous plates together.

I finished my overdue paperwork, leaned back, and fished my watch from my waistcoat pocket. It was late enough to go about my business undisturbed, so I left my office, surprised by how dark it was. The setting sun was obscured by low clouds as an early fog rolled in from the North Sea. The wind turned so the grey mist was tinged with coal ash from the city, and the familiar reek of sulfur filled my lungs as I made my way home.

Jenkins was waiting for me with a plate of cheeses laid next to a waiting tea cup and wine glass. My attention focused on the clenched pain in my back and I eschewed all. I walked directly to the whiskey decanter and poured a double helping.

Jenkins pursed his lips but said nothing.

I settled in the leather wing chair and held the glass in my hand, examining it. On a whim, I used my hand to fit the glass into one set of pincers, and tried to drink, spilling it down my chin.

"I would suggest, sir . . ." Jenkins voice betrayed exasperation, and he pronounced each word with care, ". . . that if you mean to slop it about, you might want to remove your coat first."

Feeling contrary, I lifted the glass and took another draught, this time with more success.

My valet drew a long suffering sigh. "Might I be excused then?"

I did not bother to answer, just saluted him with the glass and watched him withdraw. A moment later I felt the alcohol flush my face as the clenched pain in my back eased, and I reached for the empty decanter, and frowned at it. I walked over to the cupboard and was unable to find another bottle. I thought about ringing for Jenkins, but as the pain was pushed aside, decided I did not want to put up with his attitude, so I went to bed for a very long night.

The relief did not last long. The lack of strong drink left me vulnerable to the night, as I woke several times gasping for air in my dreams of smoke and flame somehow transformed into black water and foundering decks, giving me a glimpse of the terrors my predecessor found under the sea.

Chapter Fourteen

The day began with a grey fog, not so much in the streets, but in my brain. I rose earlier than intended, but spent more time with my morning ablutions. Since I started doing calisthenics with the men, Jenkins had made a point of having a pot of very strong tea ready for me to imbibe as I perused the papers. Today, instead of his solemn morning manner, he whistled merrily as he set the pot down, his lightheartedness accentuating my ill manner.

"Have you seen the morning paper, sir?"

"Of course not, you ninny, you're still holding it." I snapped, in no mood for his levity.

He did not take umbrage at my mood and handed the paper to me with a flourish, folded to display the front page headline: "Captain 'Claw' helms Britain's new sub."

My eyebrows arched as I stared at the offending article, attributed to B. Monroe. I read the text aloud.

"Captain Ian Rollins, called 'Claw' by his men . . ."

I stopped reading. "This is rubbish. How can they print this bloody crap?"

"The drawing hardly looks like you," Jenkins remarked, with an ill-disguised smirk.

"That's probably a good thing," I sighed.

The story was flanked by two pictures, the first a drawing of the HMS *Holland Ram* that made it look like something directly out of Jules Verne. It had been rendered to look about twice as large as reality, with wings and a barbed, pointed spire of a nose. The second was a drawing of me, with a slightly more rugged face adorned by more pronounced scars, and an overlarge eye patch which covered nearly half my face. I was holding up my pincers as if looking at them and the artist made the humble brackets look more like sharpened scythes.

I leaned back in my chair and buried my face in the palm of my right hand.

"This is not going to be good." I sighed as I pushed the hand over my brow, running my tired fingers through my short hair. Considering the picture again, I glanced up at Jenkins who was still enjoying the morning too much.

"You've been down to the port often enough; the men do not call me 'Claw' do they?"

"Oh, good God, no, sir," he answered firmly. "They calls you 'Stumpy.'"

Fearing problems from the unwanted publicity, I had given up my morning exercise and went directly to headquarters, where Captain Wilson awaited me, having already seen the morning editions. He greeted me far more calmly than I expected and seemed very philosophical about the whole thing.

"Newspapers feel the need to tell a tale, and they are best at tales of heroes and villains." Captain Wilson said while I poured myself a cup of tea. "Today, they cast you as a hero."

"I simply cannot believe that little bugger wrote such tripe about me and my men. Why now?" I groused. "The navy's had the bloody thing for nearly two years. Hell, the papers have *already* written articles about it with nowhere near this interest."

Wilson replied thoughtfully, "Yesterday's launch brought us more attention than we imagined. Previously, we possessed a grey little boat sinking quietly in the Thames, but yesterday we launched a golden submersible and people took note. The public's imagination has been captured and, unfortunately, our time of lying low has come to an end."

He took a heavy envelope decorated with an elaborate seal from his desk, opened it where the wax was previously broken and spilled the contents before me. The document was printed on hefty parchment and likewise decorated with a substantial seal.

"This is the christening order for the new boat. Apparently, the Admiralty disregarded every suggestion for the name."

"And they choose what? Not the *Nautilus*."

He shook his head. "I am just glad they decided against HMS *Smart Whale*, which several clerks wanted to call it. No, they went with Her Majesty's Submersible. . ." he paused for effect, ". . . *Thunderbolt*."

I poked out my lower lip in consideration and thought about harvesting lightning from the sky.

"I like it."

"Good." He frowned and regarded his teacup. "If launching a small golden boat elicited this much attention, imagine what will happen the end of next week when we launch the *Thunderbolt*."

"I am trying to not think about it." I took a sip of the tepid Darjeeling tea left in my cup.

"No, I am afraid after this, we will have to go completely public, including a formal launch ceremony with the press and all."

He set down his tea, stood, and walked to the window.

"Have you looked outside yet?" he asked.

I opened my mouth to reply when the office door opened and Mr. Cooper-Smythe slipped in, wearing a morning coat and the same florid bow tie from the theater, and carrying a delicate walking stick. I took my cue from the neckwear.

"Reggie Ross, as I live and breathe."

His sharp eyes gleamed with intelligence for a second and then his face shifted into an appalling grin as he bowed.

"Capital to see you again commander, capital."

Wilson rubbed the bridge of his nose, screwing his eyes tightly closed.

"To what do we owe the honor of this visit, Sir Reginald?"

Cooper-Smythe addressed his current persona in third person. "Reggie is here to see the new submersible the papers are all in a lather about. Its debut is now the social event of the week."

"Splendid," I muttered.

"Also, our suspects on the docks have bolted. They have been tipped off and took off."

"Bad news for your boys," Wilson said, "but good riddance."

"I just hope it's not like an iceberg, and we just lopped off the top we could see." Cooper-Smythe smiled. "I would like to hang around, but there are too many opportunities in a crowd like the one forming." He lifted the knob of his cane to his brow and saluted. "*Bon voyage*," he said and slipped out.

I let Captain Wilson collect his thoughts for a moment while he stared out the window. The rising sun had not yet completed the task of burning away the thick fog and soot from the night before and smoky tendrils still lingered along the bank.

A bank lined with people.

"What do they think they are going to see?" I asked rhetorically. The morning article listed what channel of the river was reserved for our use this morning, effectively announcing our schedule and route.

"I expect they think they will see your craft fly across the water and dive like pelican. How is the boat? Is she sound for trial?" Wilson asked.

"Aye, sir," I replied, with a proud smile. "Did two unmanned test dives yesterday and Lieutenant Graf and his people got her down to 150 feet and recovered her. No leak or deformity."

He thought it over. "Excellent. You have a trial crew in mind for this morning?"

"For the first trip, I intend to finish the ride I started weeks ago."

"Of course."

"And for the second, I'll let Lieutenant Graf select the crew, but I will pilot the craft."

He chuckled, "You think you are ready? The whole world will be watching."

At eight bells, fourteen of the men were lined up at parade in front of the pier. The sun burned off all of the remaining mist and the *Ram* gleamed in the morning sun. Most of the hull was developing a rich bronze patina from being immersed in seawater, but the conning tower was still bright gold.

The gathering crowd along the river was progressively taking on a carnival air. Bartley peered through the conning binoculars.

"I'll be damned, they're coming with picnic lunches and vendors are moving through the crowd selling sweets and sausages. It looks more like a holiday than a work day along the Thames."

I turned to Lieutenant Graf. "Bartley will be driving, as before, but I understand Weber is not available."

Graf nodded with minimal sharp movements. "He is with my crew on the new boat."

"The HMS *Thunderbolt*," I reminded him.

His lip twitched in irritation; the new name did not sit so well with him. I suspected he preferred *Smart Whale*, or *Swordfish*.

Graf continued, "I would recommend Smith as engineer."

I glanced at the men, "Forgive me, lieutenant, remind me which one is Smith."

"The man on the end over there." He flicked his chin toward the entire formation, but I instantly remembered which one Smith was. Standing almost half a head taller than me, with a thick build, a chest like a barrel, and big bony hands with scarred knuckles.

"Smith looks a fright." Bartley said. "But trust me; he is possibly just about our best engineer, and a well-disciplined sailor."

I frowned and looked at my shoes for a second. I knew better than to judge a seaman by his looks, but it was hard to credit much sense behind that battered skull. However, I nodded, bowing to Bartley's more intimate knowledge of the men.

"All right, Smith will go as engineer," I said.

"Smith," Graf called out, his voice cracking like a whip.

The large man looked up and lumbered our way. As he drew closer, I could see scars around his left eye, an eye which constantly stared off to the side. He had dark circles and a permanently pinched brow. I recognized the symptoms of strain from constantly focusing one eye.

He saluted.

I returned the gesture and made a show of looking him up and down. "Seaman Smith, I am told you have performed remarkably well as the boat engineer."

His stoic face did not hint at his thoughts, but he nodded slightly. "I tries sir."

"You box much?"

He poked out his lower lip and shook his head slowly. "Not nae more, sir." I caught just a hint of a Scots accent.

"Used to be squadron champion, until the last match." He shrugged.

I nodded with more sympathy than he could guess.

"Make ready for departure," I ordered.

Smith saluted and headed for the boat to mount the gangplank and check the moorings.

"Commander Rollins." Bartley waved to me, indicating I should join him at the front of the pier. I had taken a step in his direction when I heard the sound of raised voices on the breeze. About fifty yards away at the main gate, a carriage pulled up and a man in a checked jacket was angrily waving a bowler hat at the marines. I turned away to let the marines deal with it.

"Yes, lieutenant?" I asked as I joined Bartley.

"This morning I did a quick pass through the boat."

"And?"

"Everything is fine, but I would like to point out that it is difficult for me to make any further inquiries while trying to keep my intention secret from Lieutenant Graf. He is my superior after all." Bartley shrugged. "The time has come to enlist his aid."

I frowned in thought. I hadn't warmed to my executive officer, but I did trust him.

"We will talk with him this afternoon," I replied a bit testily. The commotion at the gate was growing louder and it was getting on my nerves. Looking up at the hullabaloo by the fence, I caught the eye of one of the guards and waved for him to report to me.

The red-jacketed marine corporal ran down to my location, arriving red-faced at the dock. At first I thought his flushed face was from the sudden exertion, but as he started to speak, I detected a fair bit of wrath as well.

"There is a man at the gate what wants to photograph the submersible," he announced angrily. "I told the man to piss off." He caught himself and made a correction. "Ah, I meant I told him to leave."

"Plain speech is fine with me, corporal. You may tell him the officer in charge told him to piss off."

The corporal smiled and shook his head. "I'll tell the bugger, but he's intent on making an unholy row. Permission to detain him?"

I looked at the crowd on the opposite bank. The papers printed most of what there was to know, but as yet we had not taken out an advertisement.

"Very well." I sighed, not sure how much of my frustration was due to the situation and how much was the lack of charity I felt for journalists. "Sit on him if need be."

The marine started to salute when I reconsidered.

"Hold on," I instructed. The artist's depiction ran through my head, could photographs be any worse? I took out my pocket watch and looked at the time; the left channel of this section of the river was restricted for our use until two in the afternoon. I turned a weather eye to the sky.

"Corporal, if you would send a runner to Captain Wilson, who should be in his office at this hour, I would be greatly obliged."

"Aye, sir. Message sir?" he replied.

"Please give the captain my compliments, inform him of the photographer, and ask him if he has a moment to join us."

The corporal ran back to the gate and dispatched a private to run past the foundry to the administration building. I gestured for Lieutenant Graf to accompany me and we walked over to the main gate, but I froze at a new sight approaching in the distance. The lieutenant's lip twisted in reflex.

At the turn-off from the main road I spotted the official coach of the ambassador of the German Empire. It had the imperial arms painted on the door in bright colors with liveried coachmen and footmen, and was pulled by a team of four matched greys. It was flanked by two outriders in the full uniform of Royal Saxon Hussars, their tall bearskin hats bearing the matte silver *totenkopf*, or death's-head insignia. They wore their flashy black pelisses as half capes, the gold frogging shining in the morning sun as the material waved in the breeze. The horsemen trotted along with their sabers drawn, the tips resting on their shoulders.

I sighed and glanced at my watch; at that pace they should be here in about fifteen minutes. I turned my attention back to the current commotion. The corporal stood with his face set in resignation as the man in the checkered coat lectured in loud tones about the rights of the press. I motioned for Lieutenant Graf to follow me, and we walked up to the gate with all the enthusiasm of men approaching a firing squad. As I arrived, the animated newspaperman addressed me.

"See here, admiral —" he began. I held up my hand for silence, which he ignored so I spoke over him.

"Who are you?" I demanded in my most forceful command voice.

He rocked back a bit, but barely paused. "Like I was telling this boy here," he puffed himself up a bit, "I'm Barney Monroe, from the *Times*."

My lips moved in a malicious smile. "The very villain himself."

He looked at me with some confusion. I lifted my left hand and extended the pincers out to him.

The gesture did not stem the tide of words pouring out, "Now see here Admiral–"

I snapped the pincers closed with such force they made a loud snap. "You know who I am. Please address me as Commander Rollins."

We stared at each other in silence until our tableau was interrupted by a loud clatter as an older man clumsily exited the carriage. He carried a large camera mounted on a tripod, which he braced over his shoulder, holding it steady with both hands as he practically tumbled out of the wagon.

Monroe continued, "That is Petey, my photographer."

Petey recovered his balance and tipped his cap to reveal a bald head with iron-grey fringe on the sides.

"We're here to take some pictures of the submersible," he explained in a calmer tone.

"I am afraid we are about to embark on an exercise." I stood formally, putting my hand and pincers behind my back. "Perhaps you could make an appointment with the Admiralty."

I do not know what use I thought I could accomplish by talking to the man for I was certain he would be unbearable once he spotted the German coach and four.

"Every time I try to get out here to get a picture, my sources in the yard tell me the bloody thing is either being repaired or painted or some such. But I heard from several sources that it is sailing today, and I'm a mind to get a picture and a story."

"So, who are these sources?"

He tapped his forefinger to the side of his noise. "Nah, can't be naming names, but I got eyes and ears all over the yard."

I frowned and nodded in thought. I looked toward the path to the administration building to see the private returning with a bemused Captain Wilson moving at a pace faster than "with alacrity," but just shy of "undue haste."

Addressing Lieutenant Graf, the marines, and the newspapermen I muttered, "Wait here." I turned away and marched to meet the captain roughly thirty feet from the gate.

He smiled tightly and made a show of glancing over my shoulder.

"So you have encountered one of the more obnoxious members of an obnoxious bunch. What do you intend?"

"We have more trouble coming down the road." I informed him of the German coach.

He took a deep breath in through his nose, raised his chin and rocked gently on his heels, hands clasped behind his back. "No chance he confused the day?"

I shook my head.

"What do you want to do about the press?"

"Well, once the Germans arrive, there is no way to send him away; besides, the weasel claims to have eyes all over the dock. I would like to know how much he knows. I figure if we let him near the *Ram*, he will push for more. If he knows about the *Thunderbolt*, he will want the story and he will push. By learning what he wants to know, we can determine what he does know."

"I think you have overthought this, and you haven't had much experience with the press. It's more likely you will tell him far more than you meant, learn nothing, and the story he prints will be complete fantasy anyway."

I mulled his words over.

"But," Wilson said, "go ahead and let the bugger in. There is no use in keeping him out now."

I waved to the gate to allow the men in, and I started walking up to the dock. Mr. Monroe scrambled to catch up to me.

"So anyway admiral—" he started again.

"Commander," I corrected through clenched teeth.

He grinned. "Well, of course, Commander Claw, isn't it?"

"Rollins," I corrected. "If you must refer to me, I would appreciate it if you would use my name, not the ridiculous moniker you created."

His grin did not flicker.

"Of course. You mind answering a few questions?" he asked, as he scampered along with me.

"Yes, I do mind."

He nodded as if he seemed to think I had agreed.

"How far can she go underwater?"

"Far enough."

"How fast can she go?"

"Fast enough."

We reached the pier and stopped to look at my command. The men seemed amused by all the attention.

"Well, you can at least tell me where she came from," Monroe said, "All I know is she was built in America."

I thought about it and decided there was no harm in telling him about John Holland and the Fenian Brotherhood.

When I finished, he slapped his knee. "Nicked it from the Irish, did you? Bravo."

"Not me personally."

He squinted at the dock. "Bit small, isn't it?"

"Thirty feet long, six wide. Fits three comfortably." I exaggerated, but he had stopped listening, his head turned to the gate where he finally took note of the new arrivals.

I followed his gaze. The approaching coach slowed down to a stately pace, and was arriving with all the pomp it could manage. The cavalry men drew up to attention, and the footmen leapt from their post and opened the door. I was afraid the ambassador himself would step out, but it was only Kapitän Mueller and his aide, dismounting.

"What do the bloody krauts want?" Monroe said more to himself than to me.

"*They* are invited," I said, with far more authority than I had.

The Monroe chap seemed to forget completely about me as he strode away, catching his photographer and dragging him to the Germans.

Lieutenant Graf stormed up to me, his eyes hard and his scar livid in the morning sun.

"I hope you know what you are doing." He practically snarled, and seem to think the whole mess was somehow my idea.

The German delegation posed for photos, then made their way through the gates and down to the wharf, with Mr. Monroe yapping at their heels. Graf and I stood together, with fixed smiles that bore no trace of sincerity.

As the German attaché and aide neared I found myself squaring my shoulders and straightening my posture in an attempt to match their Prussian bearing. I made a distinct effort to improve the sincerity of my smile and nodded to Kapitän Mueller.

"We were expecting you tomorrow."

He was dressed in a uniform that was just slightly subdued from the mess dress he wore at the theater. The high collar of the black tunic was covered in gold braid, matching the braid on his epaulettes and the aiguillette on his shoulder. Overall though, the clean lines of his uniform served as a field to display the cluster of medals that fought for room on his chest. A very modern, brilliantly white, peaked cap topped the outfit. It clashed jarringly with the antique appearance of his accompanying hussars.

"*Ja, ja,*" he agreed with a smile. "I look forward to our official visit, but when I read the papers this morning, I had to come out and see for myself."

"Not much to see, just a standard trial," I said indifferently. "But if you would like to stay, you are welcome."

I turned to Lieutenant Graf, whose fake smile did not diminish, "I believe you are acquainted with my trusted executive officer."

Mueller gave Graf a sharp nod accompanied by a heel click; the lieutenant returned the nod, sans heel click. The men regarded each other with fixed smiles and narrowed eyes.

Looking at them together, I saw a family resemblance.

"Nice to see you again, Hienrich." The kapitän greeted his cousin in a bland tone.

"The feeling is mutual," Graf replied, matching the tenor.

I clapped my exec on the back in a gesture designed to convey my full confidence.

"Please keep our guest company and answer any questions he has," I instructed, knowing full well Lieutenant Graf would know which questions to avoid.

I stepped away from them as yet another pair of carriages pulled up. One was a modest brougham with two men, and I immediately recognized the forceful demeanor of the American Roosevelt and his "assistant" Adam Greer. The other carriage was a richly decorated hansom and from it stepped a man with fussy movements and a particularly florid bow tie.

The three men greeted each other and I could imagine 'Reggie Ross' introducing himself, and wondered if the adopted persona would pass muster with the sharp-eyed Pinkerton.

"In for a penny," I said aloud, to no one in particular.

The marine at the gate looked overwhelmed and waved at me for attention. In return, I made a broad sweeping circle with my hand to instruct him to let everyone in.

"Commander," the newspaperman Monroe called to me from the dock. I turned to face him.

Petey's camera was set up, but the photographer was shaking his head, looking forlorn.

I sighed and walked down to them. "What's the matter?"

"Scale," Petey said. "Bloody thing looks like a toy. I'll be needin' someone to stand on her, or climb in the hatch to make it look real."

"Ah," Monroe, exclaimed with exaggerated excitement. He took me by the arm and waved theatrically out to the boat. "Commander this is your chance to be in the papers."

"No, thank you." I replied coolly. Looking up I saw my other officers watching. "Lt Graf?"

He interrupted his stilted conversation and looked stricken, as if he were suddenly overcome with both dysentery and fever. I realized I'd asked too much of him already.

I turned to Lieutenant Bartley, who waved his hand in a negative motion. "If my father saw my face in the papers, he would disown me, and I am quite counting on the inheritance. It's bad enough I am working with the submersible, but to be publicly linked to it, in the press . . ." He shook his head.

I took a deep breath; some duties always fell to the commander.

"I will do it." I strolled down, crossed the gangplank, and stood on the gently bobbing conning tower.

"Could yer look a little less like you bit a lemon?" Petey called. "Think of something cheery."

I tried not to glare at him, but turned in profile, gazing out over the waves.

"Now," Petey said, "Could yer get in the hatch?"

Reluctantly, I opened the hatch and eased myself into the narrow opening. My uniform coat rode up, sliding against the hatch rim. I stood with my arms at my sides on the commander's chair with my chest and head out of the hatch.

"That'll do, but can you bring your hands out? It will help with scale."

I grimaced, but complied and rested my pincers on the deck.

"It will be just a minute." Petey ducked under the camera's hood. He fiddled with the bellows to get the focus right, and then held up the squeeze bulb, clasping it firmly to trip the shutter.

"Got it, Mr. Monroe," he called out.

I looked at the two men, trying to imagine how I appeared in the shot, and then looked back to where my exec was trying to herd the visitors. Reggie Ross was giving the glad hand to all and sundry, while the Americans were chatting warmly with the Germans. I was tempted to stay right where I was and just call for the rest of the crew, but not wanting to ruin my uniform coat, I levered myself out and made my way up to the knot of guests. As I passed the camera, I addressed the newspaperman without stopping. "Anything else, Mr. Monroe?"

"That'll do then. I have enough for the article." He chased after me and stuck out his hand. I shook it without warmth and continued. Reaching the gaggle of tourists, I took the time to shake each proffered hand from men whose smiles seemed even less genuine than mine, excepting Mr. Greer, as the detective seemed sincerely amused by the gathering. Finally, I broke from the group, retrieved Lieutenant Bartley, and we made our way back to the dock and the men.

By the pier, we ignored the uninvited and stripped out of our uniform jackets. Lieutenant Bartley revealed his new waistcoat, and I nodded approvingly.

He smiled back at me roguishly. "I can't do without the pockets." He mimicked me surprisingly well. The men suppressed snickers, and then Bartley pulled out a pocket watch and consulted it.

I shook my head.

We entered the cramped space of the *Ram*, I was fore again in the gunners position. Smith crammed his massive frame into the engineer position, looking almost pinched between the electric motor and the air compressor. Lieutenant Bartley settled himself in the commander's seat, the large binoculars hanging around his neck, and gave the orders for departure.

The actual trip was anticlimactic. We traveled a quarter-mile awash, then submerged for another five miles, keeping us underwater for about an hour before we surfaced to refresh our air, and then returned by the same route. The *Ram* was equipped with sufficient air for the entire trip, but the CO_2 built up quickly because the alkali filters were not installed yet.

I memorized the operational instructions for the boat and spent time in the commander's seat but I still watched carefully how Smith and Bartley operated the pumps and valves as the boat sailed. I felt a little apprehensive throughout the trip, but the operation was a complete success, and we finished the exercise in a little more than two hours.

At that point, I had high hopes the rest of the day would go smoothly. Unfortunately, there was no wood to knock on in the iron boat.

Chapter Fifteen

Captain Wilson shrugged, opened his watch, and squinted at the small numbers. "You do not want to be late for your first command."

Earlier, the submersible returned from its first trip to applause and shouts that echoed across the Thames, the crowd treating the surfacing boat like the climax of some conjurer's trick; it had vanished into the water and reappeared just over two hours later.

Our German and American delegations stood by and greeted Lieutenant Bartley and I with great enthusiasm, ignoring our wilted uniforms and sweat-stained shirts. I left Bartley to speak with them as he seemed in high spirits and was always ready to spin a tale. I instructed the petty officer to take charge of the men and secure them a somewhat early luncheon. I used the pretense of submitting an after-action report to the captain to escape to the privacy of his office and comfort myself with a cup of tea.

I checked the time as well, hesitantly set down my cup, stood, and picked up my hat. I tried to stifle a grin beginning to take hold of my features.

"Something amusing, commander?" The captain inquired, smiling to himself.

"No sir," I answered slowly. "It's just I feel an unnatural excitement at the idea I am finally going to drive the boat myself."

He chuckled, "Well, commander, *bon voyage*."

Upon my return to the pier, I was gratified to see that our guests had departed, or at least most of them. Approaching the dock, I spotted Mr. Adam Greer propped up on an empty stanchion, still loitering about. He was idly scratching his droopy mustache while his sharp eyes studied the *Ram*. I looked up at the gate and noticed the brougham he'd arrived in was still there, along with the hansom which delivered Reggie Ross.

The men I sent for food had returned, and had been joined by Lieutenant Graf and the men he'd chosen for training that morning, so the entire ship's company was milling about as I drew near. Lieutenant Graf caught sight of me and started to instruct Petty Officer Grant to call the men to attention, but I waved him off. Holding up my fist in a gesture meaning to hold fast, I then extended my forefinger and pointed to Greer.

Both my executive officer and the coxswain understood that I was going to speak to the American first.

Greer was still keenly scrutinizing the lines of the submersible, seemingly unaware of my approach.

"What can I do for you?" I asked.

If I startled him, he gave no sign, just idly shook his head.

"Don't rightly know if you can do anything for me, just hanging around, if'n you don't mind"

"I do not mind a bit," I said with more enthusiasm than I felt. "Is Mr. Roosevelt about?"

His eyes narrowed and his jaw worked side to side with his mustache swaying along.

"He accepted an invitation to lunch with the German." He looked at me sideways. "That Reggie Ross character insinuated himself along."

"Ah, Sir Reginald," I said, suddenly aware my tone and face were probably conveying too much information. I struggled to control my features and reflected I was not cut out for subterfuge.

Greer seemed not to notice, his attention still on the boat. "That is one strange duck if you ask me."

"Oh?" I tried to sound diffident.

He looked at me, frowning as if deciding what he should say, if anything. Apparently, he made up his mind and continued.

"I like to think I can get a pretty good bead on a man." He thoughtfully scratched the side of his neck just above his starched collar. "First, I like to look at how a man presents himself, see if'n he acts the straight shooter, or keeps it close."

"And Sir Reginald, is he a straight shooter?"

"Not hardly," he snorted. "The man smiles too quick and his eyes don't mean it. Reminds me of a confidence trickster I know out in Jersey."

I nodded as if weighing his words. "Well, I shall be very careful then if he tries to talk me into any investment."

But then Greer's shrewd eyes narrowed at me. "See, I thought you were a straight shooter but just then your eyes did not match your smile. If I was a betting man, I'd bet you already know quite a bit about that Reggie feller." His eyes softened. "Well, maybe there is a difference with the way you limeys smile."

I was taken aback. An awkward silence hung between us that I did not know how to terminate, and I fear my fidgeting expressed volumes about Reggie Ross.

"I have to get on with the day's training," I said after a few seconds, my voice sounding hollow to my own ears.

"Like what you done with the underwater boat, looks nice; all painted up."

I nodded. It did look more impressive with the plating.

Greer glanced at me and nodded, "Good luck."

I thanked him and walked a few paces, stared down the gentle sloping path to the river's edge at Grant until I caught his eye, and then nodded sharply.

He returned the signal, and in turn called the men to form parade. Lieutenant Graf strode to the front to assume command. I waited for the men to assemble before starting my march to the formation, pacing with measured strides right up to Lieutenant Graf, who offered me a stiff salute. His face was pinched in a frown that was not quite disapproval, but still almost taunting me to say or do . . . something. I returned the salute, relieving him, and taking command of the formation. He turned smartly, and with parade-ground precision marched to his place at the rear, but as he stepped away, I noticed for the first time a wooden plaque lying on the ground.

Mounted on it was the preserved claw from some large bird of prey. My face and bearing must have betrayed more astonishment than I realized as I heard a veritable chorus of suppressed chuckles. I snapped my head up and glared at the men, working hard to keep the smile off my own face. I pretended I had not seen the item and, in doing so, dared them to do anything to call it to my attention. Under my glare, the men stood still and so I feigned ignorance of the significance of the subdued smirks on their faces.

"Good Day," I said. "Lieutenant Bartley and Seaman Grayson, you are with me. Coxswain, send the rest of the men to their duties." According to procedure, I should have chosen anyone other than Bartley since he had just been down, but I wanted someone I could trust on board for my first trip as pilot.

As the men broke formation and headed for their daily assignments, Lieutenant Bartley, Grayson and I stripped off our uniform outer layers. From my coat, I drew a length of brass pipe, exactly one and a quarter inches in diameter and ten inches long, with knurled grooves cut into the entire length of it. Bartley raised a quizzical eyebrow, but remained mute, while Grayson frowned as I tucked it under my left arm. Grayson was by nature a frowner, and I have it on good authority he is a natural pessimist who can find the dark cloud in any sunny situation. He is on record as saying he knew from the second he entered the navy he was destined to drown. I asked him, if he was so certain of drowning, why had he volunteered for submersible service. His reply was that he figured if the boat started underwater, the whole sinking and dying thing would be over quickly.

Lieutenant Graf set down the case he'd been carrying since morning, opened it and handed me the set of Italian Porro-prism binoculars, which I dutifully hung around my neck, surprised by the exhilaration inherent in the physical symbol of command. Bartley eased out onto the gangplank and descended into the dark hatch of the sub, and Grayson silently followed. I was the last one to board; the boat bobbed from the crew's movements as I carefully crossed the gangplank. I did not tarry on the flat top, but quickly sat, hung my legs into the dark and levered myself into the boat, where I crouched on the seat. Two sailors released the mooring lines while I settled in my seat, pulled the hatch closed, and dogged it down. I paused a moment, allowing my eyes to adjust to the slightly shimmering greenish light that glimmered through the tiny glass windows.

I then removed the piece of brass pipe from under my arm, used my right hand to hold it in place above the dive plane lever, and then forcefully shoved it down, using hand and pincers to press it over the control. I'd lined the tube with India rubber so it would fit snugly to the cast iron handle. Placing my pincers on it experimentally, I squeezed the adapter and felt a solid grip on the control.

Realizing what I'd accomplished, Bartley gave me a thumbs-up sign, then jerked the same thumb toward the fuse locker and armament rack before giving me another thumbs-up. I'd asked him to triple-check the locker and the dummy rounds we carried. This trial was supposed to be very simple, a repeat of the morning course with one addition; we were to dry fire the Zelinsky compressed air-gun to test the repairs.

With our added weight, the boat was properly awash, and my function was to work with Grayson to keep it that way, relying on the planes to maneuver the neutrally buoyant craft. My right hand gripped the rudder and I made cautious movements to get the feel of the helm, and at the same time, I continued to use my pincers to tug on the diving planes. Satisfied everything was in my grip, I gave my first command.

"Bring up power, if you please."

"Aye, aye," Able Seaman Grayson replied when he engaged the switch, the cool pale glow from the windows was replaced by the warm light of Swan lamps.

The electric motor began to hum and a chill ran down my spine. In my mouth, I tasted the metallic copper tang of excitement tinged with anxiety.

"Reverse one-eighth."

"Aye, aye." Grayson checked the motor and then heaved on the lever that engaged the great differential gear under my seat, and I felt the clutch assembly take hold. Immediately, the craft lurched and I felt the river current fighting the diving plane as the motor ramped up to the ordered speed. The boat pitched and yawed like a longboat fighting through heavy surf as I fought to hold it steady. *How the devil did Bartley manage to make it look so easy?*

I looked up at him, and noticed he and Grayson anticipated the *Ram's* motion and were quite solidly braced. Grunting with effort, I put my shoulder into the task of moving the rudder control all the way to starboard as the boat ever so slowly came about. The nose finally pointed the right direction and I checked the course setting on the compass viewer.

"All stop," I commanded.

The viewer was added during the recent repairs and was similar to the device just installed on the HMS *Thunderbolt*. Because of the iron bulk of the craft, the magnetic compass was located in a box mounted just in front of the conning tower, and was visible to the pilot through a small mirror set in front of the driver. The only instruments I possessed were the compass viewer, a simple bob to mark the angle of descent, and a modified version of a Bushnell depth gauge (a reinforced glass tube vented to the outside which used a floating brass ball to indicate exterior pressure).

"Ahead, half speed." I ordered, not as confidently as the first orders, and I saw the crew brace again. The boat pitched forward, and then continued to buck; moving forward in fits as I grappled with the diving planes. In all my practice, the levers had been hard to move, but now with water sweeping through the planes, I fought to keep them steady. Any untoward motion caused the nose to rise or dip violently. I could see both men were watching me stoically and their calm manner assured me they fully expected this to happen. When we came up to speed, I could feel the controls become more responsive, but we still listed to port a bit.

"Grayson, please trim the ballast," I directed. The seaman relaxed a death grip on a support and turned the ballast control wheels. Nothing seemed to change immediately, but he continued to work, and after a few minutes I had a better feel for the planes. We continued in silence along the approved course, but I kept it at half speed all the way to the dive phase and even then was reluctant to accelerate.

"Prepare to dive."

Both men tightened their grip on support structures more firmly than I thought strictly necessary, and I pushed forward on the dive planes. The craft bucked like it was hit, and I was almost thrown from my seat, dazed when my forehead hit the edge of the conning tower right below the compass viewer. With my pincers, I wrestled with the control lever and the deck dipped and rose under my seat. By gripping the lever as tightly as my pincers were capable, I managed to smooth out the descent after a minute. I caught my breath and checked the depth gauge, shocked to see the craft was down barely twenty feet of the fifty I intended. Sighing, I kept the pressure on the control lever and checked the bob, equally surprised to see I barely pushed the sub into a fifteen-degree descent. I decided to leave well enough alone and waited, our descent to operational depth taking much longer than under Bartley's skilled hands.

Eventually, the slow- moving gauge revealed the depth desired. I leveled off very smoothly and checked my compass, using small movements of the rudder to adjust course.

"Grayson, please bring the motor to three-quarter power." I wasn't sure I trusted myself at full power and I became aware of Bartley looking at me.

"How was that?" I asked.

He shrugged and gave tight smile, "Fair to middling, sir."

"Really?" I replied dumbfounded. "I thought it was bloody awful."

Both men smiled.

I shook my head, "I have no idea how you keep the motion so smooth."

Grayson said, "Sir, the lieutenant is the best driver in the command."

I nodded, "So I've heard."

A few minutes passed and I noticed even with the planes level, we were rising slightly, so I instructed Grayson to adjust ballast again. He turned the wheels one at a time trying to maintain trim, carefully bracing himself as if concerned a small shift in balance might make me overreact. I checked my watch and almost thirty minutes of the first leg of our journey was still ahead of us. The air was already getting close. I became aware that I was sweating profusely. I saw that the unwholesome air was having the same effect on the crew. As our exhalations fouled the atmosphere, the lingering stink of the boat filled my nostrils with the heavy oppressive oil stench and the sickly sweet odor of grimy men. I checked my watch again, less than two minutes had passed. I resolved to have a proper ship's chronometer installed.

The thick air discouraged conversation and we saved our breath until finally I felt very lightheaded and reckoned we reached our objective.

"Make ready to surface." The crew seemed awfully relieved and I pulled back on the control lever with my pincers, keeping my motions and the movement of the sub much smoother this time. I risked the sharper angle for ascent, and a few minutes later, we broke the surface. "All stop," I ordered.

Grayson pulled on the gear handle. The differential noise faded, and the only sound was the quiet hum of the electric motor. Without forward momentum, we began to sink.

"Adjust ballast."

Grayson turned the wheel and with a hissing whine, compressed air flowed into the ballast chambers until the boat was awash with the entire conning tower above surface. I secured the controls and crouched in my seat to undog the hatch. Sweet air washed into the craft. My clammy shirt stuck to my body as I rose and stood on the chair, surveying the river. I raised the conning binoculars to my eyes and mentally reviewed the procedure to dry fire the main gun.

Due to my decision to travel at reduced speed, our position was well over half a mile from where we were supposed to surface. I noticed something moving in the water. I flipped up the siting stand and mounted the binoculars, intending to practice aiming at the object, but then realized it was moving directly toward us. I squinted into one side of the field glasses, and stared at a steam launch, not quite a mile away, bearing down at us at breakneck speed. If I had surfaced anywhere near the correct spot, the speedy boat would be almost upon us.

"What the devil?" I exclaimed, studying the craft. "There is a bloody newspaperman in a steam launch bearing down on us."

"How do you know he is a newspaper man?" Bartley asked.

"He's got a damned cameraman in the bow taking pictures."

The lieutenant gave me a queer look. "That's not possible."

It struck me. Camera and subject needed to hold very still for the total exposure, and any picture taken from a moving boat would be nothing but a blur.

I stood back up and looked again to see the damnable boat still coming on full speed. Now I could make out four men on the launch, one of them at the back where he seemed to working hard to haul on something with a windlass. I got the impression they were towing something.

I watched them come on. There was no doubt they saw us and their course was completely intentional. Surely they couldn't be intending to run right into us? The *Holland Ram* was designed with a reinforced bow which could be used as a weapon; and the entire conning tower had been strengthened since Commander Waite's collision. If the wooden steam launch collided with us, it would likely be the worse off.

As the thought flickered through my brain, the launch suddenly swerved and I reacted violently as I recognized the maneuver. I yanked the binocular stand down into the boat and ducked back in, my head glancing off the bracket. I called out orders even before sealing the hatch.

"Flood all ballast tanks, ahead one-quarter." I fought to keep my voice calm. "Torpedo in the water."

Bartley's eyes bugged out in disbelief. Grayson turned white, but increased motor power with one hand while engaging the gear with the other. I sealed the hatch and grabbed the levers, hoping for some movement to give me diving control. I ordered quarter speed because if I attempted faster from a dead stop the propeller would spin too fast, causing the water to wash away from it, the cavitation resulting in no movement at all. As it was, there was still no perceptible motion although both Bartley and Grayson were spinning ballast wheels, making the boat rock, but I feared we were not sinking fast enough.

Water lapped over the forward window and I could feel minute thrust, so I yelled, "Brace yourselves," and pushed the lever forward just as I saw the wake of the approaching object.

There was a scraping noise along the top of the conning tower, then silence. I felt enough forward motion to increase the downward angle, and by the time I checked the depth gauge we'd reached thirty feet. I was thinking I'd been mistaken in the launch's intention when the blast rocked us violently. Grayson smacked his head on a valve and sat down hard.

Bartley looked at me. "What the devil was that?"

"The damn steam launch was towing a Harvey torpedo," I sputtered at him. A Harvey torpedo was actually a type of directed mine, not a self-propelled warhead like the new Whitehead torpedoes. The type of armament was old-fashioned, simple, and inexpensive to manufacture, but reliable in the hands of a skilled operator. The Harvey was towed behind a fast boat, which cuts sharply as a windlass operator reeled in and released the mine like a skater "cracks the whip."

Bartley stared back, his eyes wide and a curse on his lips as if the attempt was directed at him personally.

"Blow ballast," I ordered. "Ahead full speed, prepare to surface." They surely did not have another torpedo and I wanted to try to catch them.

Grayson pulled himself to his feet, weaving just a bit, but grabbed the throttle and brought the craft up to speed. Lieutenant Bartley started to assist with the ballast wheels, but I stopped him.

"Stand fast," I ordered. "Mount a fuse set on the first projectile."

Realizing my intent, he objected. "But they're inert."

"Our assailant doesn't know that, and with luck, we'll scare him as much as he scared us."

He nodded and pulled out a detonator set.

We broke the surface riding higher than we should and the top of the large propeller was fanning the air. I whipped my head around, scanning the waterline for the hostile launch while Grayson worked at the ballast trying to correct our buoyancy.

"Leave it," I ordered.

He looked puzzled, but I did not have time to elaborate. I spotted the launch running straight away from us, along the same route it had approached, and I adjusted course for pursuit. With the propeller outside its optimum depth, we were only making twelve knots, and our opponent was pulling away at nearly twenty.

"Tube clear?" I asked.

"Aye, aye," Bartley replied, his voice picking up enthusiasm.

"Load projectile," I ordered. The two men lifted all six feet of the dummy round and steered it into the firing chamber as I opened the hatch and raised the binoculars back to their siting position. Since I had only one eye, I needed to switch back and forth between the eyepieces to correct for the built-in parallax. The weapon was designed for hitting a ship broadside below the waterline and shooting at the stern was a low percentage shot in the best of times. With them speeding away it was going to be especially difficult. However, in my research, I saw where the gun's effective range could be increased by shooting above the water and allowing the round to skim the surface to its target. The tradeoff was less accuracy, but I wanted the thing to at least go far enough to get their attention.

"Flood tube," I called out.

"Flooded and outdoor open," Bartley replied.

Normally I would have stern words for anyone who anticipated firing commands, but under the circumstances, I just nodded. I checked the siting and made a small adjustment with the rudder.

"Fire!" I snapped.

The boat shuddered and this time a jet of water and compressed air shot from the front of the sub as the projectile lanced through the air, traveling nearly a hundred yards in the time it took for the whoosh of the expelled gasses to fade from my hearing. The white dart skipped along the surface for another 500 yards.

"All stop! I ordered, as there was no use in our pursuit.

The launch saw it coming. Through the binoculars, I could see the torpedo man gesticulating wildly, knowing what was coming after them. The pilot made an error, cutting to starboard so sharply he turned his broadside to the weapon, but I judged his speed to be enough and the projectile would still pass several yards astern. They declined to continue their flight on the river and I watched them steer for a construction dock set up just beyond the site for the Woolwich Ferry. I continued to watch them scramble for the shore. At this distance, they were just moving figures, dressed as common river men. They could be from dozens of construction or shipping ports along the banks and they would soon fade into the hundreds of workers the length of the port.

I balled my right hand into a fist and my pincers snapped shut in frustration. I had no semaphore mast, no heliograph, no way to signal what had happened. I could see people on shore who had witnessed the incident. They were pointing, waving, and milling about, but no one was pursuing. The salt breeze blew in my face as the *Ram* shed the last of its momentum and began to rock in the gentle swell of the tide.

"Grayson, please give me quarter speed, and trim the ballast, if you please."

A tug had been sent out to keep the channel clear for the exercise, and it was now steaming toward us in all haste, but even they didn't seem to understand what had occurred. She was making good speed toward us and I turned to meet her, hoping to use her semaphore mast to relay a message.

"Well, we have recovered the steam launch," Mr. Cooper-Smythe announced as he joined us in Captain Wilson's office. Gone was any trace of the supercilious Reggie Ross.

I sat in one of the Queen Anne chairs by the fireplace, sipping at a very strong cup of tea. Wilson had offered a tot of rum to steady my nerves, but they were plenty steady and I was determined to remain focused.

Before I could ask a question, he continued. "The boat was stolen during a luncheon break; the crew had nipped out for a beer and the attack occurred before the owner knew it was missing."

"We will need to investigate the owner and the work they were doing."

"You think it wasn't really stolen?" Cooper-Smythe's eyes narrowed in suspicion.

"No, but the thieves knew exactly what they were stealing, they didn't just happen to grab the first unattended boat they saw."

Cooper-Smythe chewed over the thought. "Good point," he acknowledged. "However, the thieves took the time to paint 'Clan Na Gael' on the bow."

"Irish rebels?" I replied in disbelief. "In league with the Germans?"

"It wouldn't be the first time," Cooper-Smythe replied through clenched teeth. He rubbed his right temple as if the thought were giving him a headache. "Or they may be in competition, or the phrase was meant to throw us off. And where did they get a Harvey torpedo?"

"I don't think it was a Harvey, not an actual one, just a gunpowder bomb rigged up. It could be done very quickly and cheaply. No, the real question is where did they get a torpedo man?" I looked Cooper-Smythe in the eye, and then over to Captain Wilson, who remained silently seated at his desk.

"That's the skill," I pointed out.

Wilson stroked his beard and addressed the agent. "I think you need to involve more of your friends at thirty-nine."

"This will take top priority; we're even bringing in Scotland Yard." The disdain in his voice demonstrated his reluctance to involve the civilian police.

"Did Reggie learn much from his our guests?"

"Roosevelt is polite to the waiters, and Mueller is cheap."

"Anything more relevant?" Wilson asked, his tone a little sharper.

"Nothing good. Mueller hinted Bismarck is out of favor, indicating the Young Willie is considering re-energizing expansionist policy."

"What about Frederick?" Wilson asked.

"Too sick, he's letting his son hold the reigns."

"Sir, I've been thinking . . ." I said.

"Too late for that now; I'm keeping you as commander," Wilson quipped.

"No, I was thinking these incidents demonstrate we need some way to communicate at a distance. We need to mount at least a heliograph and a signal lamp."

"Good God," Wilson exclaimed, "Where would you put a signal lamp on the *Ram*? And if you could, the damn thing would betray your position. The only advantage a submersible has is stealth, and you propose lighting it up?"

"I don't know, but this is the second time I have had vital information I could only pass along as fast as the boat could carry me." I frowned and looked at my pincers. "Perhaps Tesla has an idea."

Tesla did not have an idea. Cooper-Smythe excused himself and Wilson accompanied me to the doctor's laboratory. He was in fine form, and when he caught sight of Captain Wilson he slipped into full bombast.

"Ridiculous," he announced waving his hand as if trying to shoo away such a silly thought. "A lamp bright enough would drain the battery faster than the motor." He shook his head, "Wasted, wasted, wasted."

The most common available signal lamp was based on an arc light, where the operator fed rods of carbon into its mirrored chamber until a sustained electrical spark jumped between them. The light was intense and carried for miles, but the apparatus was difficult to use, inefficient and bulky.

"Told you." Wilson said.

Tesla glared at him, his brow creased and he paused, annoyed he might inadvertently agree with Wilson's opinion. He stepped back to his desk and sat down, his hand straying toward a silver sphere humming on his desk. When his hand approached, lightning shot out and touched his fingertips.

"Interesting toy, no?"

"Interesting, yes," I replied.

He looked up and seemed startled to see Wilson still standing there. He made a dismissive gesture with his hand. "Go 'way. Tesla will think about this."

Wilson nodded and left.

I'd noticed upon entering that Danjella was not about, and as Tesla sat thinking, I wandered over to her work area. The desk had an unfamiliar cluttered appearance and something lay in the center covered with a piece of white cloth, like a specimen of sculpture being prepped for a formal unveiling. I examined the outline, resisting the urge to reveal the device.

"Is this . . .?" I asked vaguely.

"Yes," Nicola replied, his voice sounding slightly peeved. "He has finished it. Tesla is embarrassed . . ." he looked at the lift door as if as assuring himself that Wilson had departed, "that he, I, could not come up with a workable idea for your eye."

"For my eye?" I replied in amazement.

"To do something." He stated impatiently as he made lighting shoot to his fingers, "Maybe shoot electricity, or send messages, but the only thing I can do with something that size, was make it light up."

"Light up?"

He waved his hand. "Like an electric torch, for maybe an hour," he shrugged indifferently.

"I'll take it."

He looked at me as if I were not very intelligent.

"I'll take it," I repeated.

"For why? There is no utility."

"Utility?" I exclaimed, "It could provide me an emergency light in a submersible I could keep with me at all times. I'll take it."

He sighed and his shoulders slumped. "I will look into it."

I longed to look under the material, but propriety stayed my hand. "She said it would not be finished until Friday."

Nicola chose his words carefully. "I do not know what transpired with you, but I see outcome." He traced a pattern on his desk with his finger. "Danjella, when he is happy, is very creative, but when she is angry is very productive. Obsession is how she treats frustration and disappointment."

I flinched. "So, she has finished; she's gone to rest?"

Tesla frowned. "She will rest when she is ready. You do not know where he go?"

I shook my head.

"Your man, Jenks? He took her and Mrs. Livingstone to a meeting at the officers' mess."

"Why? Women aren't allowed in the mess."

"No? But Jenks—" he started to answer.

"Jenkins," I corrected and he ignored me.

"And the Captain Wilson, she talked to them about a *soiree*? Reception? Some formal thing to celebrate the new boat, something with family and associates."

"A Guest Night?" I suggested, "Or a Dining Out?" Not as old a tradition as the Dining In which was generally a raucous affair with much camaraderie and something I sort of missed since becoming a technical officer.

"Some such," Tesla replied. "Danny started working on it two weeks ago. You man Jenkins," he said the name slowly, "knows people and such."

Jenkins was a former ship's steward and valet to the admiral, saying he knew some people was an understatement.

"How long ago did they leave?"

"Hour ago, I think be back soon."

I looked wistfully at the covered device and left Tesla tinkering with his lightning toy. I headed back to the Captain's office to discuss an idea I had about the attack.

I arrived just as one of the port runners burst in. He did not stop or salute, he just blurted, "The American is at the gate, and he's got a dead man and a madwoman with him."

Chapter Sixteen

There was no one dead, or even insane, but it was easy to see how the young man came to that conclusion. I heard the wailing as soon as I exited the building, running with urgent steps to the gate until my breath came in short gasps and my heart pounded like the two-stroke thrum of a steam engine.

At the gate, Adam Greer was in his carriage surrounded by marine guards, workmen, and other curious eyes. The high-pitched wail which assaulted my ears emanated from Mrs. Livingstone, who huddled over the limp form of my valet, Jenkins. Her eyes were wild, she was missing her hat, her hair was disheveled; she was the very picture of madness.

Jenkins's fringe of white hair was matted with blood and more gore soaked his shirt and sack suit. The jacket sleeve was neatly sliced open, revealing an arm tightly bound in a bloody rag that used to be his neck scarf. From the amount of blood alone, I would have thought him dead, but as Mrs. Livingstone wailed again, rocking him slightly, I could see him flinch.

"Calm down," I shouted to no avail. The only person who seemed to pay any attention was the American Greer, and since he was already calm, he merely shrugged.

I turned to one of the marines. "Send a runner for the ambulance." The port kept a cart on duty to deliver injured workers who were beyond the utility of the port aid station to London Hospital.

Jenkins stirred and his features twisted in pain as he defiantly shook his head, "No," he managed to say past a swollen lip. "Don't send me to the bleedin' slaughterhouse."

"Don't be a ninny, Jenkins," I snapped at him. "You need proper care."

"Not goin' ta get that at the bleedin' 'ospital," he gasped.

I curled my lip in a mixture of distaste and dilemma. I was fortunate enough after my accident to be treated at St. Bart's, where I was cared for by nurses trained at Florence Nightingale's school of nursing at St. Thomas's. The women who took care of me received their training from the hands that treated the most grievous injuries during the Crimean war. In comparison, the charity hospital of London was a pit full of the effluvia of the destitute sick and dying, and was ill-suited for a speedy recovery. If he were still actively serving in the navy there might have been some alternative, but as a private hospital was beyond his purse and mine, I could not see any other option.

"I can care for him," Mrs. Livingstone offered, her high-pitched voice still loud, "He fought so brave; like a tiger, he was." She squeezed his hand.

Torn between interrogating them to determine what had happened to Danjella and the need to establish the extent of my man's injuries, I choose the latter. I pushed my way up to the front and clambered into the brougham to kneel beside him. Evaluating his visible injuries, I prized open the least swollen eye and he looked back at me, cringing in pain, but his pupil was reactive and not over large. "Anything broken?" I inquired.

"Maybe a rib, but prolly just bruised, like as not." He licked his swollen lip and blood oozed from the split. "Me 'eads clear, and me teeth are solid." His jaw moved as he probed them with his tongue to be certain, "I been stomped worse trying ta get the admiral out of a knocking-shop."

Mrs. Livingstone scrunched up her face in confusion.

"Er, that is, I mean t' say, a tea room, in Singapore."

I relaxed a bit. If the old rascal was telling admiral stories his head couldn't be cracked too badly. The thing that worried me most was the jagged wound across his scalp, as if his head were laid open by a vicious clubbing. The wound had supplied the mass of blood caked on his face and soaking his shirt. The bleeding had mostly stopped and straw-colored serum seeped from the gash. It would require mending, but he did not seem to be in immediate danger of bleeding to death from that injury. I turned my attention to the arm and the makeshift bandage.

I tapped on Mrs. Livingstone's arm. Danjella's companion eased away from the injured man to give me room for a quick examination. She pushed herself up enough to sit on the seat, gathering her customary black skirts under her. The movement called attention to the smears of dried blood and road dust which covered her attire.

I took gentle hold of Jenkins's wrist and turned the limb to see more clearly. "What happened here?"

"That brigand, sliced it open with a knife," she declared indignantly.

"Straight razor," Jenkins mumbled. "It's a right good gash, but I can wiggle me fingers, so's it's not too deep."

"What happened?" I demanded as I looked at Greer.

He stuck out his lower lip and shook his head. "Don't rightly know, I think they got their wagon hijacked down the road a piece."

"Hijacked?" I retorted incredulously. "In broad daylight? On the Dock Road?"

"They was waitin' fer us." Jenkins coughed few times, and then used his less injured hand to wipe his mouth. Even that extremity was turning black and blue, the imprint of a boot heel clearly visible across the back of his hand. His little finger was obviously broken. I took a clean handkerchief from my coat pocket and bound the fractured digit to its neighbor.

Mrs. Livingstone bent over his head and used a fine lace hanky to wipe the blood and sweat from Jenkins's eyes.

I looked up at her to get her attention, "Can you tell me what happened?"

She sniffled and looked like she was about to wail again.

"Mrs. Livingstone." I interrupted her more sharply than I intended, but I was out of patience. I continued without raising my voice, but put all the intensity of command training into the next question. "Where is Danjella?"

That caught her attention and she sort of deflated. Instead of a piercing wail, quiet tears spilled down her cheeks and she replied in a small voice, "They took her."

"Who took her?" I insisted. "Where?"

She looked at me, her mouth gaping but no words came out and I realized browbeating her was not going to get me anywhere, so I modified my speech, trying to be more sympathetic. "How did they take her?" I asked more gently.

She swallowed. "We were coming back from a meeting with the master steward at the officers' mess in the growler that Mr. Jenkins here was kind enough to hire for us. Miss Tesla was not in a particularly good mood, and I ended up doing most of the planning for the dinner and Mr. Jenkins was a huge help." Large tears brimmed in her eyes and she held up her hanky to stem them, then noticed the bloody lace and thought better of it.

"I was so mean to him," she sobbed. "He was trying to help." She paused to take a deep breath to compose herself. "Anyway, we were coming back down Dock Road and there was a man walking along carrying a fold out guide. He looked quite the gentleman, fine-looking, a trifle underdressed without a proper coat, just a brocade waistcoat and bowler hat. He waved to the driver."

"And the driver stopped?"

"Oh, no." She shook her head and more tears spilled. "He sort of waved back and made to continue, but the man shouted a question as we passed."

"What question?"

"I couldn't make it out. I just heard the first part, 'Where is . . .'" She held up the back of her wrist to her nose, trying to discretely wipe it. "The driver slowed and yelled something back over his shoulder. Then two men seemed to appear out of nowhere and ran up to the other side of the carriage, both carrying cudgels. The driver tried to snap the reins, but the first man fairly flew into the driver box and snatched them from him. They scuffled, and the brigand jerked on the brake and then tossed the driver out onto the road. The other ruffian, he was a bit bigger and slower; well, he jumped right into the carriage with us. That's when Mr.

Jenkins here gave him what for." She tenderly stroked Jenkins's brow.

I blinked. "Jenkins?"

"Oh, yes," she insisted, as she made a fist with her right hand and mimed an awkward swing, admiration shining in her eyes. "He laid into that big fellow good, hitting him at least four or five good times in the face."

"Two," Jenkins said through cracked lips.

"Then what?"

"Then the man in the bowler walked right up, as bold as brass, and with an impudent grin on his face, opened the door and climbed in. He was waving a huge knife, practically a sword, just in the air, back and forth."

"Straight razor," Jenkins corrected.

"And then, as cool as you please, sliced down poor Mr. Jenkins's arm. I never saw so much blood," she said in a small voice. Her head drooped forward and she fell silent, gently sniffing.

I made an impatient gesture, like waving her on, but struggled to keep my voice composed, "And then?"

Mrs. Livingstone's head jerked up suddenly, her voice angry and indignant. "And then the cheeky bastard tipped his hat, and told me to get out of the carriage or he'd slice off two pounds." Self-consciously, she tugged at her dress in a hopeless attempt to straighten it, and her voice became defensive. "I got out, of course thinking they were just going to send Danjella and poor Mr. Jenkins out after me, but then the man with the bowler held the knife at Danjella's throat while the other man started just beating on poor Mr. Jenkins with his cudgel and kicking him. Finally, he tossed him out onto the road and they drove away."

I looked up at Greer. "How did you find them?"

He scratched at the side of his mustache. "I'd been dawdling around since that little incident out on the river, but things seemed to calm right on down, and I figured I'd head back to the hotel."

"Where are you staying?" I asked.

"Mr. Roosevelt and his bride hired rooms at the Langham, 1c Portland Place, Regent Street. I got a bed at the servant's quarters. Anyways, I was just about a couple a hundred yards down the way, when I hear this woman a wailing. Found and the pair of them on the side of the road."

"Did you see the carriage?"

"Nope, not hide nor hair."

The port ambulance pulled up. It was a modified wagonette or omnibus painted white some years ago, and periodically touched up so it developed a mottled, leprous appearance. It had a low covered driver's box in the front with an enclosed compartment behind containing two long benches for the wounded to lie on. The ungainly thing was pulled by an aging draft horse, and the cart, as well as the animal, looked to be built for slow steady transport, rather than speed. The wagon orderly stepped out and ambled up, not seeming to be in any great hurry.

"What's the fuss about?" he called out before catching sight of Jenkins. He regarded the injured man with an experienced eye. "Something fall on him?"

When no one responded, he scratched his head as his face screwed up in concentration. "He don't look like a yardie."

I observed Jenkins and then allowed my eyes to swing toward the dingy white closed wagon with rusty bloodstains that served as the best transport available for gravely wounded men. In my mind's eye, I envisioned the overcrowded wards in London Hospital, and the overpowering smell of puss and gangrene. I trained my eye on Mrs. Livingstone, and she met my gaze, her eyes pleading.

"You think you can care for him?"

"I've had some nurse training," she declared, and then indicated the improvised dressing on his arm. "I did that."

I nodded to myself, made a decision, and addressed the orderly. "Can you take this man to my rooms at 22 Connaught Square?"

The man groaned and made a pathetic face. "Sir, there be rules, forms, paperwork . . ." he raised his hands and shook his head in despair.

I reached into my uniform coat, extracted a thin wallet, and removed a banknote.

He frowned and looked at Jenkins. "I dunno," he said as he shook his head but his eyes never moved from the money. "We're only supposed to run to London Hospital."

I extracted another note.

His eyes flickered from side to side. He spoke conspiratorially, and with some hesitation. "It'd be the same for the driver."

I stared at him hard, but then handed him four notes. He pocketed three and walked to the driver's box at the front of the ambulance.

I took the rest of the banknotes and passed them to Mrs. Livingstone.

"My Landlady knows a consulting doctor about a block over; have him come over and suture Jenkins's wounds."

She took the money and nodded.

A second later, the orderly waved for us and stood waiting.

Apparently, my money was enough to get them to transport Jenkins, but not enough for them to carry him on a stretcher. I stood up, straightened my back, stooped on Jenkins's right side while Greer scrambled from the driver's box to get the other side. Together, we got my valet to a half-standing crouch where he got his feet under him and managed to fight his way to a full standing posture. We guided him off the brougham and got him settled on one of the benches in the rear of the other wagon. I assisted Mrs. Livingstone into the cramped compartment and watched as the ambulance plodded off.

Greer removed his hat and brushed back his shaggy mane before speaking. "So," he said, seeming unruffled by the events, "who is Danjella?"

I was caught off guard, having forgotten he did not know, but instead of replying honestly, I recalled the story she told. "She is a secretary here at the boatworks."

"Particular friend of yours?"

"I respect her."

He chewed on that for a moment. "You know of any reason someone would want to harm her?" he ventured.

"No," I said abruptly, not sure if it was actually a lie or not. "But she does have access to a lot of confidential material."

"You thinkin' she was grabbed for what she might know?"

"Possible."

"Seems a might extreme for intelligence work," he said.

I narrowed my eyes at his turn of phrase.

"Maybe you all do things a mite different over here, but in New York that kinda thing smacks of something personal. Was she involved with any gang folk?"

"Street ruffians?" I replied, incredulous.

"Yeah, puts me in mind of the Whyos." He scratched his ear.

"The what's?"

"Whyos," he said. "Irish immigrant gang that likes to cut people up."

I chewed on the information, "We have reason to believe the attack on the submersible was the work of Irish Nationalists."

"Now Whyos and them like that, as a rule ain't exactly friendly with the politicos or the nationalists. Hell, the gangs mostly prey on the other Irish. Anything for a dime, and if they get to bust a few heads, so much the better."

I turned to one of the marines. "Has anyone alerted the authorities?"

"We sent a runner to the port provost's office and another to the constabulary."

The port provost was new to the position; as his predecessor had retired after years of honorable service. This new fellow was a florid-faced man, just a few inches shy of being as wide as he was tall, and given to picking his teeth when he talked to you. His main function was to use the men assigned to him to prevent theft and graft on the docks, but it was widely rumored he was more inclined to keep it to a tolerable level, as long as he got his share.

The local constables were slightly better, but they were more used to taking reports of theft, and breaking up the occasional workingman's brawl and were not used to doing a lot of investigating. I looked around trying to decide what to do. Of course, this was going to have to be kicked up to Scotland Yard, but how quickly?

I looked at the marines, and identified the corporal in charge. "Send a runner to Captain Wilson and let him know what has transpired. When the authorities arrive, please escort them directly to the captain's office."

"Yes, sir, and wouldn't you rather report to the captain?"

"Later." I turned to Greer. "Can you show me where this occurred?"

He nodded and climbed back into the driver's box and I followed, squeezing in beside him since the bench had just enough room for us both. Releasing the brake, he gave a flick of the reins and the horse took a few steps before breaking into a fast trot.

The port road was a water-bound macadam construction consisting of a thick layer of hand broke aggregate stone covered by a layer of more finely crushed rock that was bound by a slurry of stone dust and water when it was laid. As a result, on a warm dry afternoon, anything moving on the road raised a cloud of thick grey dust. As Greer indicated, the spot was not too far away and it was a good spot for a well-planned ambush. There was a copse of trees at a curve in the road not directly visible from any of the port buildings. We stopped and I disembarked to inspect the area, finally locating bloodstains that marked the place where Mrs. Livingstone tended to Jenkins. I picked up Mrs. Livingstone's ruined hat from the road. "Nothing much to look at here," I said.

"Nope," Greer agreed.

"They must have gone back toward town."

"Yep," Greer agreed.

I looked up at the former detective, suspecting he was making a joke at my expense, but realized he already considered everything I was thinking and was just waiting for me to catch up. "Then we should look, there?" I pointed down the rough track.

"Good a place as any," he replied.

I climbed back up and we set out. Five minutes later, we met the port omnibus. Greer took off his hat to flag down the driver and asked if he had seen anything suspicious. He directed us to an abandoned carriage another half mile down the road. When we arrived, we found an open top growler with the traces cut; and the driver was trying to rig the straps to get the thing moving again.

"You okay?" Greer called.

His head jerked up nervously. He was a skinny man with brown hair going grey, a little over five feet tall, and looked as if he had done work as a jockey. He certainly seemed to know how to handle the horse.

"We're fine," he said.

"Do you know what happened to your passengers?" Greer asked.

The man was visibly dazed and he shook his head. "I don't want any trouble."

Greer nodded. "Not inclined to give you any, but we'd be much obliged if'n you'd come along and tell us what you know."

He slumped as if giving in to inevitable unpleasantness.

Greer alighted from the bench, helped the man secure the damaged leatherwork, and then bade him follow us back.

Even with our short excursion, we arrived back before any of the authorities. I left Mr. Greer and the driver at the gate to wait for the constables. I made my way up to Captain Wilson's office where he was in consultation with Mr. Cooper-Smythe. The agent was pacing in front of the window with an unlit cigar clamped in his mouth. Before I could address my commander, he bellowed, "What the devil is going on?"

I looked at Wilson who merely shrugged and bade me answer Cooper-Smythe's question.

I made a full report about the carriage hijacking, Danjella's disappearance, and even included Greer's commentary about the New York 'whosis.'"

"Whyos," Cooper-Smythe corrected me, "I've heard of them."

I looked up, but he waved away my interest. "Not on this side of the ocean, but I wouldn't be surprised if we aren't looking for the same ilk. Razor boys are common in the penny mobs, and they make good muscle for hire."

"Uh, during my, um, less fortunate days, I saw a lot of street toughs," I said. "They preferred to squeeze doxies and roll drunks for money and saved the really vicious stuff for their rival gangs. I just don't see them out here hijacking."

Cooper-Smythe rubbed his thumb against his fingers. "They will pretty much do anything, if there is enough money involved."

There was a knock at the door and Copper-Smith looked at me in surprise.

"That would be the constable and the port provost."

"That's pretty useless," Cooper-Smythe remarked quietly. "I've already sent a runner to the yard and the Admiralty."

"We'll still need to make a report." I thought for a second. "Also Mr. Adam Greer is probably out there."

There was a more insistent knock.

Cooper-Smythe stopped pacing, his lip twisted in a sneer. He took the cigar out of his mouth and pocketed it, without returning it to a case. He patted his other pockets as if hoping to find something. He turned to Wilson and then to me. "Nothing to be done for it, let them in."

As I opened the door I hear the high prattling voice of Reggie Ross behind me.

"Wretched business Arthur, wretched, wretched, indeed," he declared.

Our visitors filed into the office, led by the Provost Walter Hammond. He had his helmet tucked under his left arm and bowed his bulk slightly toward the captain.

"Evenin,' sir," he said in a breathless tenor. "I hears you 'ad some trouble." His aitches were not consistent, but spread randomly through his speech.

"Wretched business," Reggie repeated, and shook his head to demonstrate reluctance. "I must go, Arthur, but please keep me apprised." He reached across the desk and grasped Wilson's hand and shook it. He then turned to the rest of us, his arm held straight in front of him and his hand canted at an awkward angle. He moved through the knot of visitors, shaking each man's hand as if he were the principal in a receiving line at a formal dinner. He greeted Greer with a broad smile which again did not touch his eyes. "Capital to see you again, old man."

Greer took his hand and returned an equally broad smile which was just as sincere.

Reggie practically trotted away and I watched him disappear through the outer office.

When I turned back, I noticed the provost idly wiping his hand on his uniform tunic. He saw me take notice, nodded, and then faced Captain Wilson. He absentmindedly brought his thumbnail up to his mouth and made a 'tsking' sound as he scraped at something on his tooth.

The constable stepped forward to take charge, and removed a small notebook from his breast pocket, extracted a pencil and licked the tip. "What's all this then?" he inquired.

Greer gave him a concise and professional description of the events. The constable asked to see Mrs. Livingstone and I informed him where she and Jenkins had gone. He frowned and rocked on his heels as if I were deliberately making more work for him.

Greer introduced the driver, but he offered no additional detail because he had not lingered to observe the beating. He stated that when they threw him out of the carriage, he decided to run for help, unaware that there wasn't anyone for more than a mile in the direction he headed.

The constable addressed Captain Wilson. "Does this Miss Tesla, who you say is missing, have a particular man friend?"

"No," I replied. "She does not."

The constable regarded me with narrowed eyes. "Well, you seem very sure," he replied in a knowing voice, "but you might not know what she is up about. These foreigners get up to some slippery business when they are away from home. She's Serbian, you say? Very little self-control; probably got involved with some unsavory chap. Odds are that's the man we're looking for."

"I accompanied Miss Tesla to the theater last week. She lives with a female companion hired by her cousin to protect her propriety. I assure you she is properly chaperoned."

"Male cousin?"

"Yes, Nicola Tesla."

The constable made a thoughtful face and then spoke with a hint of distaste. "Lot of them foreigners get up to some slippery ways with their 'cousins'," I could hear the quotation marks in his voice.

Irritated, Wilson said, "Dr. Tesla has been here all day."

"Right then." He consulted his notebook. "Well I should call around in the morning and talk to Mrs. Livingstone."

"So, is that all you are going to do tonight?" I asked.

The constable looked at me and blinked. "Why bless you no, sir. I shall write an account being sure to make a note of all the particulars. Then, if the woman hasn't returned by morning, we'll make inquiries."

"A woman has been abducted in broad daylight, and a man is

injured."

"Well, so you say, sir, but once we have a complete report, we will move it up the line, so to speak, and someone from the yard will want to speak to you tomorrow." He consulted his notebook again. "If there is gang activity, it will be a mite tricky."

"Provost," I addressed the other man. "Has there been any gang activity at the port?"

The portly port provost snorted. "Sorry, sir, but you might as well 'ave asked is there shipping going on at the port."

"I'll take that as a yes," Captain Wilson said.

"Any gangs use razors?" I asked.

"Just about all of them 'as got at least one razor boy," the provost responded.

"Any of them with Irish background?"

"Funny you should mention that," the constable replied thoughtfully. "Most of our Irish troubles has been from the Nationalists. Lately, the bomb throwers been quiet, but we been having some troubles with the Glasgow mob, and they do like their razors."

"Isn't Glasgow in Scotland?" Greer asked.

"So it is," The constable said. "But a bunch of the Paddies moved there after they lost their potatoes and their yahoo offspring have taken up some violent ways. O'er the last year they been sending boys down to stake out part of London, hanging out at the Dead Duck, or was it a Red Lion? I'll send a man round to the metropolitan to see if they heard anything." He consulted his notebook one last time. "I think I have all I need, I'll just get back to the station and start things moving." He tipped his helmet, turned, and left.

The port provost spoke up. "I will start some inquiries, but my jurisdiction is very limited and it seems they have already gone beyond it." He nodded to Captain Wilson and left.

"Those two idiots . . ." I began.

"Commander, control yourself," Wilson said. "You are turning purple."

I clenched my teeth.

"We've already sent a runner to Thirty-nine and the Yard. They will get to work on the situation. In the meantime you should go back to your quarters, but stand by and I'll send a message if anything happens."

I walked out of the building with Greer on my heels. The afternoon deepened into twilight and the sun cast long shadows. I kept moving at a swift pace, nervous energy quickening my stride, and we approached the gate where carriages and cabs convened. I noted a hansom parked away from the actual gate so it took advantage of the shade. The driver was huddled on the low bench, his face turned away, but even so he seemed way too familiar, and something about his manner aroused my suspicion. As I stepped through the gate, I turned and ran at him.

He hesitated a moment as he spotted me, then realizing I was going after him, he fumbled for the reins, causing his hat to tip back. I saw he was unquestionably the driver I'd spotted following Danjella on at least two occasions, and the same man I had spotted at the theater.

He managed to release the brake, but by then I had my foot on the driver's step. I seized the top of the cab with my good hand, and used the other to tangle into the reins and snatch them out of his grip.

Without control of the horses, he reset the brake. I hauled myself up to the driver's box, seized him by the lapels, and brandished my pincers in front of his face. He writhed in an attempt to get away, but I yanked him to me bodily.

"Where is she?" I demanded.

"I don't know," he replied angrily.

"You've been following her."

"Well, of course I was following her, you idiot," he replied indignantly. "Been following her for the better part of a year. I'm her minder . . . from the admiralty. 'Spose to keep her safe."

I lowered my pincers but did not release the young man. "Good job."

"Not my fault," he replied huffily. "She knows she's 'spose to stay put during work hours. Never took off like that afore."

I pushed him away and climbed back down. Greer was standing there; he had seen the exchange.

"What?" I demanded.

He shook his head. "Must be some kind of, what was it you said she did? Secretary? To be needin' a bodyguard."

"Like I said, she has access."

He nodded. "Well, partner, you better come with me," he said, as he turned toward his brougham.

"Why?"

Greer turned back to me. "You have that look about you of a man what's about to do something stupid. Can't rightly tell if it's going to be jackass stupid, or prodigiously stupid." He shrugged and fixed me in his sight. "Either way, I kinda want to be along."

Chapter Seventeen

"And you think you can talk me out of stupidity?' I asked.

He chuckled. "Nope, I'm coming along. See, I know a good many fellers what achieved something phenomenal by setting out to do something prodigiously stupid." He smiled and there was a mischievous gleam in his eye. "And if it turns out to be jackass stupid . . ."

"Yes?" I waved for him to continue.

"Well, then that's just fun to watch." He patted me on the back and turned me to the brougham. We both climbed onto the broad bench in the driver's box. Greer took the reins and off we went. "Got to get this rig back to the Langham afore it gets too late, then where you want to go?"

"We can't wait for the constable to write up a report," I groused.

"The good captain seems to be callin' in a higher authority."

"It will take some doing to get the Yard to take this seriously. They have no concept of what's at stake." I let out a disgusted breath, and searched the Dock Road for some sign or clue in the deepening twilight, which grew darker as thick grey clouds gathered.

"Look for the boyfriend, indeed," I sniffed.

We rode in silence for a second and then Greer spoke earnestly. "Just what is at stake?"

I stopped my inspection of the gravel surface and studied the former Pinkerton. "Are you just an assistant to Roosevelt?"

"I'm being paid to assist him," he replied, carefully parsing his words.

"You want me to be straight with you, you be straight with me. Who pays you?"

"It ain't been no secret, so surely you know I'm being paid through the embassy."

"Which department?" I countered.

His head bobbled a bit and he almost snorted. "Office of Naval intelligence," he replied. He looked at me sideways. "Come on, you aren't going to try and tell me you didn't know TD was looking at the boat for the navy."

"And your job?"

"I saw the thing when your men picked it up, and was a mite curious. By the time we towed it to New York harbor and got it to one of your ships, I saw quite a bit of her. The navy wanted me to see if I could tell what changes you made."

I thought the revelation over in silence.

Greer briefly left me to my internal reverie, then suddenly asked, "So, aside from the plain fact you've taken a shine to this Tesla woman, what is the deal?"

"She has in-depth knowledge of several confidential projects associated with the submersible program; highly detailed and practical information. I believe some foreign governments would go to great lengths to obtain what she knows."

He let out a low whistle. "You seem stuck on that idea. Have you considered they might want what you know? That they intend to use her as leverage for actual plans, drawings?"

I mulled that over.

"Tell me," he asked, "this woman, she the feisty kind?"

I suddenly saw her dripping wet, her face challenging the fierce storm, and I smiled. "You could say that." He didn't immediately respond.

"So," he said a few minutes later, with extra emphasis to make a point, "just where are we headed?"

"The constable mentioned the 'Dead Duck'."

"He also mentioned a 'Red Lion,'" he pointed out.

"Yes, but there are a thousand pubs called the Red Lion in the United Kingdom, although only twenty or so here in London. But in the city, there is only one place called the Dead Duck. It's actually a pub in Whitechapel properly called The Wounded Swan, and many Irish immigrants gather there."

"You been there?"

"No, but I'm familiar with a sailor's pub on the same block." I was grateful he could not see my face directly. "I intend to go and have a look, and see what I can see."

Greer shook his head as if he were bouncing the idea around to see if he liked the feel of it. "Ya know," he said, "I been in a few saloons like you're talking about and people who ask too many questions don't stay healthy."

"I plan on keeping my mouth shut and ears sharp until I know what's about. In fact, it'll be best if you do all the talking. My accent may not be welcome, but they might be amused by a visit from an American cousin."

"Well, we'll drop this off then." He indicated the brougham, and then frowned in thought, "Doubt we could drive a carriage where we're goin' anyways."

I nodded even though he was facing straight ahead and could not see. You don't take a wagon or a horse to that part of town without a guard.

At the Langham carriage house, I found myself pacing with short jerky steps as I waited for Greer to go through the formalities of returning our livery. The groom and stable master took their sweet time with every detail, but eventually provided a hansom and driver for us.

By the time we left, the shadows of twilight were gone, replaced by a dense cloud cover and a thickening gloom that had the lamplighters scurrying on their rounds. They did not reach my neighborhood before our arrival and the cabman was forced to drive slowly, picking his way by the flickering coach lights mounted on either side.

I gave him a few coins to wait while we entered my chambers to find both Mrs. Livingstone and Mrs. Hawn scurrying around. Both widows fretted over the wounded Jenkins who was ensconsed in his pantry off the common room. Mrs. Livingstone loitered at my side as I took a moment to look in on my valet. He gave me a weak smile, his arm and brow neatly bound with clean bandages.

"Did the doctor do a good job on the sutures?" I inquired.

Jenkins seemed unusually quiet and Mrs. Livingstone shuffled her feet.

"You did get the doctor?"

"No, sir," Jenkins finally spoke up, his words coming slow through his swollen lip. "I didn't want no sawbones ta be cutting on me." He paused for breath, but still managed to get his words in before I could object. "I sent for an old shipmate of mine, a sail maker. 'e's sewn me up a time or two. 'ell, he sewed up the admiral after the, uh, incident in Singapore."

I kept quiet, but gave him a stern look, and then shared that look with Mrs. Livingstone. Mrs. Hawn shooed us from the bedside. "I've invited Gertrude to stay with me," my landlady informed me, although it took a second for me to realize that "Gertrude" referred to Mrs. Livingstone.

I left the pair to minister to the injured valet, stepped back into the common room, and crossed to the heavy wardrobe. From a drawer in the back, I unfolded my rather disreputable pea coat, which still held traces of tobacco smoke and coal ash. Jenkins had laundered the woolen coat and watch cap, but found them too fouled for gentle use and wished to discard them. I objected and we compromised by storing them in the back of the wooden clothes locker. I selected my most threadbare shirt, nodded to Greer, and slipped into my chambers to change.

Returning to the common area I was surprised to see the American had changed as well. It seems his clothes were reversible and his brocaded waistcoat had become dark brown wool, shiny with wear along the edges. His gentleman's frock coat went from a fine charcoal grey with a velvet collar to a coarse black wool with mended elbows, and his shirt collar was open with no tie at all. In addition, his entire manner had changed, harder with a no-nonsense air of competency. I sensed I was seeing the real Pinkerton detective as he shed the thin veneer of being Mr. Roosevelt's assistant.

In his right hand, he held a bowler, a well-made chocolate brown item with a silk hatband. He then set it on the table. "Mind if I just leave my derby here for a bit?"

I blinked, realized he meant the hat and nodded.

He produced a flat workingman's cap from a hidden pocket and slipped it on; the headgear suited his rougher comportment and costume but changed his manner so that he seemed less affable and somehow more ill-disposed.

I took out a small key from my pocket, used it to open a sliding compartment in the wardrobe, and took out the Webley Mk1 revolver I'd purchased to replace my Enfield Mk 1. I looked at the detective, "Are you armed?" I asked, trying to think where I might procure another firearm.

Greer calmly reached into his coat and produced a prodigious revolver with a barrel over seven inches. He did not brandish it, but held it by the cylinder as if offering me handle. "Colt .45 Cavalry Standard," he replied offhandedly, "I feel undressed without it."

I looked at the oversized weapon, and then back at my relatively small, but deadly accurate pistol. "Looks heavy," I observed with a trace of self-assuredness, "I can't image you can hit anything at much of a distance."

He grinned. "This here hogleg'll take the legs off a tick at a far piece."

I blinked at him, and realized he thought he was still speaking English. But to me it seemed he'd slipped into some red-Indian dialect.

"All right," I replied once I worked out the gist of his meaning, "but where we're going, do not draw unless there is no alternative, and you will need to be ready to shoot immediately."

"People that nervous about guns?"

"No, guns are that valuable. Toughs travel in groups of about six. If they see you have a gun and think there is good chance of getting it from you, they will be on you. A gunshot will have villains and bobbies congregating around you. A woman in Whitechapel can scream bloody murder all night long and no one will turn a hair, but one gunshot brings everybody running."

"I understand. Don't draw unless you shoot, and if you shoot, vamoose."

I narrowed my eyes, suspicious he was now using Americanisms to poke fun at me.

Back outside, the cabman was visibly uneasy at our change of appearance, and was even more upset when I gave him our destination, even though it was nearly half a mile from our true endpoint. There were cabs and even private coaches prowling the neighborhood, but all were crewed by at least two attendants and each carried a stout club, or had one stashed under the seat. Our cabbie demanded his fare up front and ran us down St. Boltoph's Street and as far down Whitechapel Road as he dared. He barely paused long enough for us to exit before he turned the cab and quickly trotted back the way he came.

We stepped out into a damp spring night in the East End of London. The evening was warmer than I'd expected and the fog had fully rolled in, adding to the dingy grey haze of coal ash which settled on this part of the city. Greer seemed game to follow me through the dim streets north toward the infamous Nichol Rookery, but we wouldn't be so injudicious as to enter that pit, rather keeping to the southern edge. It was a Tuesday night, and there were fewer wagons and no carriages at all heading through the streets, but as we turned the corner just off Osborne Street we spotted an enclosed wagon. Its white paint seemed to grow dingy from the heavy air. A burly man in a short white coat sat in the driver's box.

I felt a shiver and fought the urge to cross the street, but settled for averting my eye and hurried past.

"What in tarnation was that about," Greer asked as he lengthened his stride to keep up.

I slowed, realizing just how poorly I'd reacted to the sudden encounter. "That wagon is from St. Mary of Bethlehem Hospital, called Bedlam for short. It's a home for the unfortunates."

"You mean like a poorhouse?"

"No, I mean like a madhouse."

"Oh, a looney bin."

I looked at him, grateful for the darkness which hid the flush in my face, but he seemed to sense my expression.

"Don't mean no disrespect or nothin' like that."

There was a family association I did not want to go into, but I felt I could not just leave it. "There are people who lose sight of the truths in this world, and become confused; thinking all of creation is against them. They are not moral deviants or cowards," I said hotly, "but they are ill and they rave because they do not understand people are trying to help them. They are incapable of understanding, and they need to be restrained for their own good."

"Easy there, boy, didn't mean to ruffle your feathers."

"Sorry," I muttered without sincerity. I'd not paid conscious attention to our path as my feet knew the way along this part of the rabbit warren of alleys and side streets, but if I wandered too far afield it could take days to find my way back out. The city commissioners had installed gaslights in the streets, but they did little to relieve the overall gloom, rather they created small islands where doxies bartered with their clients, or were relieved of their money by pimps and 'protectors,' or where small groups of young toughs passed bottles or scuffled.

Greer wiped his nose and mouth, obviously ill at ease with the consistency of the air which clung to the skin, adding texture to the eternal stink of vomit and urine in the rookery streets.

"You stay long enough, you get used to it." I said.

"I ain't stayin' that long."

"People who live here don't trust air they can't chew." I tucked my pincers into my left pocket and let my arm relax and my shoulders slump. I needed to be the desperate sailor who craved a drink and a place to be alone in a crowd. Greer followed me through the shadows and back to another street where the lamps barely illuminated oppressive gloom until we reached the open door of The Fouled Anchor. Standing just outside the cone of diffused light radiating from the pub's open door, I pointed down the street to The Wounded Swan, denoted by a dingy swan- shaped sign with an arrow through the arching neck.

Greer looked around and scratched his ear. "You got a plan?"

I shrugged. "Go in, nurse a tin cup of gin and listen to see if anybody's bragging, complaining or talking about a big score. Then we will try to determine who might be the best one to ask a few questions."

"You think that'll do any good?"

"It's doing something. You got a better idea?"

"Don't know enough about these parts." He looked over his shoulder and made a sort of show of taking the lay of the land, "Back home, I'd prefer to go in with a local and a third man watching our backs. Then the local points out the most likely bad actor, and we'd separate that particular galoot from his friends and do a little persuading."

"So, you just go and beat it out of them."

"Ain't generally necessary. See once we're alone most of these guys will sell their mother for pint of whiskey. The trouble is getting them to talk about what you want, and not just name names to settle old scores."

I motioned him to follow me into the pub. We sauntered up to the bar doing our best to look like a pair of workers looking for a cheap drink and anonymity.

Behind the bar stood a weasel of a man, no more than five and a half feet tall with sharp rodent features accentuated by crooked front teeth.

"Gin," Greer ordered. "Two."

I dropped sixpence on the bar.

The publican regarded us for a moment, his beady eyes shifting over our unfamiliar features, unnaturally wary of our presence, but he poured our drinks, and we shuffled to an empty table in the corner. Business seemed uncommonly slow and the place was just over half filled, but it was still a bit early and I expected the pub would be overfull by last call, which on a weeknight would be 2130.

We sat and sipped at the gin, conversing in low tones while trying to quietly evaluate the patrons. He asked me about the attack on the *Ram* and I answered him in the most oblique terms, instead changing the subject to the *Indomitable* and life as a navy officer. He spun some yarns about chasing down criminals for the Pinkerton Agency. I was still too tense about Danjella to actually warm to the man, but I felt he was solid and I could trust him.

After a while, we dropped into a companionable silence, each with our own thoughts, although the nervous energy which permeated my spirit kept me drumming my fingers on the table. I did not want to display my pocket watch, but estimated it would be half an hour to last orders, although the pub would stay open for another hour after that. Disappointed our trip had been for naught, I was about to recommend we leave when the Pinkerton's eyes narrowed and his lips twitched into a crooked grin.

"Did you say," he asked with exaggerated care, "that one of the suspicious dockworkers was an American?"

"Yes."

"That ginger feller carryin' the newsboy cap over there look familiar?" he placed his left hand on the back of his neck and rotated his head as if loosening tired muscles, but the motion managed to indicate a particular patron.

I assumed the newsboy cap referred to the eight panel flat cap he clutched nervously. The man was tall, with short bristly red hair, in a rumpled sack suit with an ill-fitting jacket and no tie. He seemed to be agitated and his eyes kept flickering to the door, as if he were either expecting someone, or afraid of someone.

Close examination was difficult as I worked to avoid attention, but his features seemed somewhat familiar. I finally shrugged and replied, "He looks like a dockworker, just like every other dockworker."

Greer drew his lips back making a sharp 'tsk' sound. "I don't think I ever heard his name, but he speaks with a Brooklyn accent and was one of Fenians what stole the *Ram*."

Looking at the man again, all I could say was that he might look sort of familiar.

Greer stood.

"What are you going to do?"

"See if he's who I think. Why don't you mosey on over to the door, in case he goes rabbit."

I nodded, after working out what he meant.

The Pinkerton sauntered over to the bar, turned his back to it and leaned to the rear, propping himself on the counter with both elbows, the picture of nonthreatening innocence. He addressed the ginger fellow, exaggerating his American accent. "Long time no see."

The man turned to him, frowned, started to say something, and reconsidered. He looked at the exit, then back at Greer, whose face suddenly developed a very wicked grin. Recognition blazed in the Fenian's eyes, and he bolted for the door, running right at me, oblivious of my presence.

I yanked my pincers from the shelter of my left pocket, opened them wide while stepping into his path, and brandished the extended grippers in front of his face. He tried to backpedal, staggering somewhat as I shoved the apparatus forward, grasping around the front of his neck. His feet went out from under him and I followed him to the ground, where he hit the wooden floor with a thump loud enough to quiet the entire pub. I stayed there with my pincers at his throat keeping him under control as the room stayed deathly silent. I could feel the intense gaze of the regulars and the quiet buzz of energy that goes through a crowd just before violence.

"That boy with anybody here?" Greer demanded, his voice loud, but calm, as he stilled leaned casually on the bar.

Two men stepped forward, and two more stood up from a table.

The man under me tried to twist free and I squeezed the grippers into the side of his neck and shook my head in warning.

"Don't know what he is to you," Greer continued, "but our beef goes back to America. And truth be told, our current dispute has to do with a woman. Now, I have nothing agin you, and I'd like you all to just stay out of it." He stood up straight and shrugged, not in indecision, but like a fighter loosening up before a match. "But if you feel you got to step in, well," he paused, and I think I was the only one who saw his hand moving in position to retrieve his revolver, "let's be about it then."

The men at the table exchanged glances with the other two and sat down. One of the others drifted over to Greer, who acted unconcerned. They talked in low tones and Greer nodded amiably, as did the other who walked away.

Greer straightened his coat, resettled his cap on his head, and walked past me out the door.

I jerked the ginger fellow to his feet, amazed at how persuasive the steel pincers on his throat were, and marched him backwards out into the street.

The dark night had become gloomier as the oppressive weight of the fog settled, and a cold misty drizzle fell from the sky, not nearly substantial enough to be called rain, but enough to dampen our coats.

Greer struck off at a quick pace. I grabbed my prisoner by the arm and twisted it behind him, relieving the pressure on his throat just long enough to resettle the grippers on the back of his neck, with the cold edges digging in just at his jugular. I gave him a slight squeeze with the pincers and pushed forward, frog marching him behind Greer.

He led me on a bit, stopping to look at alleyways and passages between the row houses, finally settling on a space between two crumbling overcrowded buildings. The opening was barely three feet wide and through it we could see a glow of a gaslight on the next block, but there was also a spot about twenty feet in where a pool of light shone from a second-story window. Greer strode down the passage and waited for me at the illuminated spot, where he bade me release the man.

As soon as I did, the man swung at the Pinkerton. Greer anticipated the movement, stepped into the blow, blocking it with his left forearm, while simultaneously jabbing a vicious right into the man's solar plexus. He then grabbed him by the collar and sat him down hard on the cold bricks of the passage.

The man gasped for breath and we stood there for a minute just letting him get his wind back. Finally, he took a lung full of air and declared in the expected Brooklyn accent, "I got nuttin' to say to you."

"We could make this right peaceable," Greer responded, almost lazily.

"Screw you."

"Pity," Greer said. "Cause right now the expectation that you have something to say is the only thing holdin' back my companion, The Claw." He winked at me but his voice dripped menace.

I sneered and clicked my pincers.

"The only thing," Greer repeated theatrically, "that keeps him from ripping out your throat, or other delicate parts."

"You wouldn't."

"We ain't been properly introduced. My name is Greer, and I'm looking for a Lady. Now you tell me your name and where to find her."

"Wait, this is about a woman?" His head jerked up at the detective, then back to me. "You want a woman, there's a pimp on the corner, he'll fetch a lady for you."

"Okay," Greer looked up at me. "Claw, take out his eye." He paused to look at me. "You can have it if you like."

"Wait, what?"

"Where is the lady?" Greer continued.

"What lady?" the man demanded. "I thought you was picking on me for bombing the damn boat."

Greer nodded. "I know you attacked the boat, but you see, I don't rightly care see'n how you missed it. But my friend here will tear little bits off you until you tell us where to find the lady."

There was a disturbance in the gloom at the end of the alley and a man abruptly stumbled out of the dark. I dodged aside as he lost his footing and sprawled face first into the paving bricks at Greer's feet.

He was a man of medium height with light brown hair and a workman's grey shirt with a pair of oft-mended trousers and an unbuttoned waistcoat. Unintelligible noises came from his mouth, bloody from its contact with the ground. He'd landed that way because his hands were clenched into fists held up near his ears. They were secured there by a blue cord wrapped around his throat, secured by an ornate knot at the base of his neck. The cord was knotted in such a way that if he were to struggle, it would choke him.

"He followed you out of the pub," a gruff voice called out of the dark. An eight-inch long leather tube filled with sand sailed out of the dark to land at my feet. "That was his only weapon."

I nudged the sap with my toe, then picked it up and slipped it into my pocket.

Greer nodded. "Much obliged, Mr. Ross, or is it Sir Reggie?"

Cooper-Smythe stepped out of the shadows dressed much the way I'd first met him, formal coat and all, although he was bareheaded. "Ross will do for now."

"You're pretty slick, but your driver isn't. Saw you following us at the Langham, and then again at the commander's place. Glad you had our backs." He shook the collar of the ginger chap he was still holding, "You think you can secure this here fellow, like you done that guy? And we'll just take them on in."

"Aren't we going to question them?" I insisted.

Greer shook his head, his upper lip moving back and forth in thought, causing the mustache to sway. "I'm pert sure they don't know nothin' 'bout what we want. But they know about the bomb, so we'll turn them over the people that want that information." He smiled at the newcomer. "I suspect Ross here knows who that would be."

Cooper-Smythe nodded. He approached, produced a hemp cord dyed indigo blue, and secured our original prisoner faster than a bobby could've locked him in a set of darbies.

"Neat trick," Greer observed.

Cooper-Smythe just grunted an acknowledgement, and then he and Greer dragged the two men to their feet. He pushed the ginger chap to me. "Grab the cord firmly here," he instructed, "use it like a horse leader, but do not tug on it, unless he tries to get away, then give one good jerk and you'll strangle him. Come along." He turned to leave.

My captive gulped at Cooper-Smythe's offhanded description and I grabbed the cord as instructed, following the clandestine agent out of the passage, our footsteps splashing as the thickening drizzle began to puddle. We made our way through the gloom for about a quarter mile west up Whitechapel Road, about half the way to the London Hospital that Jenkins begged to avoid. The people living in the area exhibited no interest in a group of men leading bound prisoners through the night. No, not just no interest, but a willful avoidance of interest. Those who accidently spied us or passed near us quickly turned away into the darkness.

A gunshot rang out, unnaturally loud in the dank thick air. I flinched, before noting it was some distance away. Greer and Cooper-Smythe did not.

"Thought you said guns were scarce around these parts," Greer said.

"It's none of our concern," Cooper-Smythe retorted, in a tone that was just above a whisper.

Just ahead, off the side of the road was the outline of an enclosed growler which Cooper-Smythe signaled with a whistle and the driver opened bull's-eye coach lanterns in response. We approached. Up close I recognized the driver as Danjella's minder. Our eyes met and he gave me a nod of recognition that established he bore no ill will from our last encounter.

Cooper-Smythe recovered his topper from the interior. We put our two prisoners inside the carriage, seated across from each other with their heads bent down to almost touching, while Greer and I sat across from each other next to them. Cooper-Smythe climbed up to join his companion in the driver's box and we set off with a jerk as the horse pulled the wagon back onto the road, driving west down Whitechapel

Road, heading toward the Admiralty and the city center at a leisurely pace.

Greer was facing forward and his eyes took on a thoughtful expression, which developed into a concerned crease in his forehead. The edges of his mustache drooped as he frowned in thought and peered ahead out the side window at something beyond. I followed his gaze, turning to look over my shoulder, which took some stretching to get my right eye around, until I detected another cart moving toward us in the other lane at a brisk trot. The white vehicle passed us as it went on its way, its dim coach lights casting a wan glow barely sufficient to read the black lettering on the side.

"That Bedlam place you mentioned, where is it?" Greer asked.

"St.George's Field, Southwark," I replied.

"Okay." He continued with a touch of impatience. "Where's that?'

"'Bout a mile west, other side of the river."

"Nearest bridge, also west?" he prompted, craning his head around to catch sight of it through the small oval back window.

"South actually, Tower Bridge, but he'd more likely use the Iron Bridge at Southwark."

"That wagon from Bedlam was headin' east, making good time," he said.

"Probably heading up to London Hospital for a pickup," I said, unable to fathom his interest.

"Likely," he admitted. He pointed to the sliding door behind my head. "Signal up front."

I tapped the panel and it slid open.

"If you'd be so kind to indulge me," he called to Mr. Cooper-Smythe, "I'd be obliged if you could turn this thing around so I could have a look-see at that wagon what just passed, see if'n it turns toward the hospital up there."

Cooper-Smythe saluted with his forefinger in acknowledgement and closed the trap.

The carriage tilted and swayed as the driver brought it around in a tight turn and I needed to brace myself from falling on the prisoners. They were unprepared for the changes and struggled as they shifted, inadvertently pulling on their restraints, thrashing about, seeking air. Greer and I quickly steadied our charges, and as the cords went slack, they calmed down.

The horse picked up speed as it discarded its leisurely ways and moved into an easy trot, and then to an even brisker gait, and we started to cover territory.

"What are we doing?" I asked Greer.

"Seems to me, if you had woman and you need to restrain her, say she was the feisty kind that would yell and kick and scream . . ."

"Not to mention bite and claw," I added, imagining Danjella.

"Not to mention," he repeated, "then you couldn't do much better than moving her in a wagon from a madhouse."

I puffed out a frustrated breath, "That is really reaching. I can think of a hundred reasons for that wagon to be going out this way."

"Name one," he challenged.

"Well, there uh . . ."

"Now it's got be a legitimate reason."

The trap slid open, and Cooper-Smythe leaned over to look in. "They went past the hospital without even slowing down."

Chapter Eighteen

Greer leaned forward to say something, but Cooper-Smythe snapped the panel shut as the carriage slewed to a stop, the steel-rimmed wheels grinding on the road's crushed rock. Caught off-guard and unrestrained, the two of us slid toward the prisoners. I caught the inner door handle with my pincers and managed to grab one of the captives to keep him from falling over and asphyxiating himself, while Greer succeeded in bracing himself and controlling his man.

The carriage door flew open and Cooper-Smythe barked at us, "Get them out." He waved for us to exit with his right hand and held his left arm crooked up at his side like a maître d' at a fine restaurant, but instead of a towel draped over his forearm, there was a long section of the now familiar blue cord. The rope was artfully arrayed so each loop on his sleeve was of equal measurement and no part of the cord covered another.

I hopped out and turned around to lead my detainee out by his cord, guiding his feet so he would not stumble. Greer did the same with the other. As soon as the second bound man had his feet firmly on the ground, Cooper-Smythe moved in, deftly taking control of both men with his right hand, and without causing any undue discomfort, transferred them a short distance off the side of the road. There he forced them to kneel side by side. His practiced hands swiftly wrapped the cord around the two men even quicker than before, until the prisoners were secured together.

As Cooper-Smythe finished, Greer spoke, his usually slow manner of talking dragging down to a lazy drawl. "You know, at a rodeo, after you roped the steer you have to stand clear and raise your hands so they know when to stop the timer."

"I do not need a timer," Cooper-Smythe replied, equally unhurried and with a trace of amusement. "That binding takes me twenty three seconds." He dusted off his hands and looked at us. "Can either of you drive?"

"After a fashion," I said.

"I can drive a cart," Greer said.

"Moore," Cooper-Smythe called to the driver, "get down here." He continued giving directions as the man scampered from his perch.

"Watch these two," he jerked his head at the captives and then looked at Greer, "Well, what are you waiting for?"

Greer grimaced and scratched behind his ear, looking as if he were about to say something, but realized we were in a hurry. He turned and swiftly ascended to the driver's box, scooting over to the far side to make room for Cooper-Smythe, who followed without a pause. Not wanting to be left out, I followed him just as closely, which led to more shifting in seats to accommodate a third on the bench. Greer dropped the brake, snapped the reins, and we were off before I could wriggle into the small space allowed.

"How's your night vision?" Cooper-Smythe asked both of us. He did not wait for an answer, but leaned back and reached behind Greer's head to lower the lever controlling the aperture of the driver's bull's-eye lantern. "Rollins, get the other one," he directed.

I made an awkward attempt to lean forward enough to get my right hand on the lever just above my right shoulder, then thought better of it and twisted in my seat to use the pincers to close the lever.

"Ya want me to try and catch 'em in the dark?" Greer asked, squinting into the blackness ahead, his eyes sheltered from the interminable drizzle by the short bill of his cap.

With my one eye, I could not tell if there was road or cliff or trees ahead, but Greer kept us going at a fast walk.

"You need to speed up," Cooper-Smythe pointed out patiently. "We need to get close enough to see where they are going."

Greer mulled this over; evidently weighing the danger of driving in blackout conditions against losing our quarry. He shrugged and, as he evidently considered himself a good driver with superior night vision, deliberately brought the middle-aged gelding up to a gentle trot for some minutes to gauge the road before easing the horse into a light canter to make up distance.

We rode in silence for some minutes as each seemed reluctant to interfere with Greer's concentration. He finally broke the silence, addressing Cooper-Smythe, his voice still slow and composed. "Pretty fancy rope work," he remarked, still leaning forward and straining to see through the murky drizzle. "Those some of them sailor's knots I hear about?"

"Not in any navy I'm familiar with," I replied.

I could feel Cooper-Smythe shift in his seat, deciding whether or not to bother with an answer. "It's called hojojutsu," he finally replied. "A system of securing prisoners used by the Japanese before they started using handcuffs." He paused as if considering how much explanation to provide. "But the older police in Nagasaki still prefer to use the cords."

I gave a tiny nod and filed away the information as I tried to peer into the shadows on of top shadows that lay ahead. The knitted watch cap on my head did not have a brim or visor, and the thickening drizzle ran down my face, requiring me to constantly wipe my eye clear. I tried to search the sides of the road, afraid the wagon we pursued had turned to some side road or drive. For all I could see, this section of the thoroughfare did not have any place where a wagon could conveniently turn off; as the rough stone road was flanked by a narrow shoulder of packed earth and drainage ditches. As I peered through the gloom I feared we were wasting time.

We continued quietly for a few more minutes straining our ears in the darkness, where the nasty weather transmitted sounds in a most curious manner. Most of the world's noises were strangely muffled, as if wrapped in cotton wool, while a select few noises like the clank of metal on metal or the jingle of the horse's bridle seemed preternaturally piercing.

The road curved ahead in a cut between various small rolling hills northeast of the city. For a second, a dark moving shape was silhouetted against a sky whose charcoal grey clouds were barely a shade lighter than the deep shadows. We cleared the curve and twinkling lights on the front sides of our objective became apparent.

Greer eased up on the horses and we continued to creep up on the other carriage, closing the distance between us now at a much slower, quieter pace.

"I can't even tell if it's the same one," I hissed.

"I can tell," Cooper-Smythe replied calmly under his breath.

"That be the one," Greer added, his voice also pitched low.

"Where do you think they're going?" I asked.

Greer mulled the question over, then replied, "Spose' you're right and they took her for intelligence."

Cooper-Smythe pursed his lips and turned toward me just enough to regard me with a cool glare out of the corner of his eye.

"They want to get her out of the country quick-like. There any place where smugglers are known to be?" Greer asked.

I snorted.

"Not this way," Cooper-Smythe replied. "The great smuggling bands are way south, Kent and Sussex."

"They wouldn't go that way," I pointed out. "The smugglers are very active down there, but they don't take well to outsiders. They have a very carefully planned operation, because the coastal patrol is pretty good about keeping the most egregious at check. If they want to move her with smugglers, they'd definitely have to go north of Chichester. Maybe Maldon."

"Maldon," Cooper-Smythe repeated, chewing it over. "It would be a hard road to Heybridge Basin. Maybe three hours, and they'd probably lose us around Romford; the road splits a couple times."

Greer pulled his lips back and made that 'tsk' noise again. "We'll have to stop them and find out what they got." He leaned over to Cooper-Smythe. "You heeled?"

Cooper-Smythe regarded Greer quizzically.

"He wants to know if you're armed," I translated, feeling I was getting a grip on the Americanisms.

"Always." Cooper-Smythe replied his voice grave.

Greer nodded in satisfaction, "Whatcha carrying?"

"A sharp wit."

Greer made the "tsk" noise yet again.

We continued on and I began to fidget in the cold air. "We have to know if we are chasing will- o'-the-wisps."

The other two exchanged glances. "We'll need to make a move soon." Cooper-Smythe agreed.

Greer peered ahead, studying the bobbing lights in the distance, and brought the horse back up to a brisk trot, closing the distance.

I grasped at the seat, and leaned out, about to demand what he had in mind when Cooper-Smythe spoke.

"What are you doing," he asked in a voice which sounded merely curious and not as concerned as mine would have been.

"We'll need to stop for a second," Greer replied, "and I don't want to lose sight of them while we do what's needed."

"What do you have in mind?" Cooper-Smythe asked, a note of anticipation in his voice.

The two men put their heads together and I heard Greer murmur something which earned a grimace and a rueful chuckle from Cooper-Smythe. "That is the only play. I grant you."

Greer pulled up the horse, and Cooper-Smythe fairly shoved me off the seat. "Down inside we go."

My right leg was numb from pressing against the armrest. I stumbled climbing off the bench and took two steps on the rain-slicked rocks to recover my balance.

Cooper-Smythe dismounted without concern, threw open the carriage door and bade me enter. "On the floor," he demanded.

"What?" I asked as he stepped up, grabbed the sleeve of my coat and fairly tossed me into the compartment, so that I ended up on all fours on the floor space.

Cooper-Smythe explained as he ascended behind me. "Greer can just about pass for a coachman, while I am a gentleman. You look quite the ruffian, I must say, and that character in the upcoming drama must be kept from view for now."

I dutifully sank to the floor where the clandestine agent immediately covered me with a musty travel rug. The brougham lurched back into motion and I snatched the heavy wool from my face to see Cooper-Smythe slide all the way across the back bench to sit on the left side. From the joggling lights visible in the window, I realized Greer had opened the lanterns and we were now very visible, the carriage of a country gentleman heading back home from the city.

Cooper-Smythe regained his top hat and lounged comfortably on the bench seat, his boots up on the bench across, while his features took on the ingratiating smirk of Reggie Ross.

"We'll pass them on the right, so you stay down," he instructed. The brougham picked up speed, and I heard a protesting whinny from the horse. Cooper-Smythe sat upright and peered out the side window, his breath fogging the glass. With a grunt of impatience, he slid open the window to get a better view. The drizzle trickled in on the floor of the small compartment and dampened my cover. At the higher speed, the leaf springs failed to smooth out the ride, and I found myself being jolted as the wheels bumped along the rough road.

Oblivious to any discomfort on my part, Cooper-Smythe extracted a hip flask from inside his coat. He flipped back the top and took a mouthful, rinsed it about, then spat it out the window, and dribbled some on his clothes.

The overpowering scent of cheap gin filled the compartment. Common pub owners preferred to serve gin because the strong smell of juniper berries masked most adulteration, and the patrons of such public houses didn't care as long as it got them drunk. But the smell had a tendency to linger, which seemed to be the desired effect.

Cooper-Smythe checked to see how close we were to the wagon and then lounged drunkenly; putting his boots back up on the opposite bench, seemingly unmindful of the lightly falling drops of rain that now dampened his trousers.

"Here we go, lad," Cooper-Smythe said under his breath. I was not certain if he was addressing me or himself, but he immediately let out a high-pitched laugh so irritating I gritted my teeth and refrained from covering my ears. He sat back up straight in his seat, although he weaved doing so, and began clapping his hands in loud measured thwacks as we passed the wagon. He called "Capital! Capital!" as if in approval, then took his hat off and waved it out the window. He sang a ditty that was a perennial favorite in the music halls. "For to see mad Tom o' Bedlam, ten-thousand miles I'd travel," he bellowed in a drunken slur. He pulled the hat in and stuck his head out into thick mist, "Mad Maudlin goes on dirty toes, for to save her soles from gravel, And still I sing, bonny boys, bonny mad boys . . ." his song petered out as we passed out of earshot.

I started to inquire how the men on the wagon responded to his antics, but Cooper-Smythe waved me quiet. He shifted his body around to stare out the back window at the wagon, confident the men following could not see him.

"They are not being very attentive," he said at last, dragging the heavy woolen rug off me and indicating the seat opposite. "The wet is making them huddle in the driver's box. The driver gave me an Irish salute," he added and grinned, referring to the rude two fingered gesture. "He seems in a rather foul temper. I hope our American can find a suitable spot quickly."

"Suitable for what?" I demanded.

He reached across to give me an amiable punch on the shoulder. "Why, for you to rob the coach, of course." He outlined the plan.

"Why must I be the brigand?"

He glared at me as if I were being particularly thick, "Because you look the part. Besides, it might not even be necessary. Once they stop the coach, we will attempt to talk with them, but if that fails, you will step out of the shadows with a gun and we'll take charge." He slid open a compartment under the seat, rummaged about, finally brandished a heavy canvass satchel and bade me extend my left arm. "Hold still, that damn device of yours is too recognizable." He contrived to wrap the handle straps around my pincers, arranging them so I might grasp the bag while completely hiding my apparatus.

I looked out the window for the first time since concealing myself on the floorboards. The drizzle continued, but the fog showing in the lantern light was thin and wispy. Even the cloud cover thinned during our progress and a hint of moonlight reflected off the clouds, turning the near-black sky light enough to see the shapes of trees. As the road dipped lower and the small rise around us leveled out, I smelled the stink of algae that clings to ponds and small lakes in the spring, stronger than just the odor of the slurry at the bottom of the ditches.

The road was narrower at this point and it was evident we were entering a stretch which was not well maintained. As we drove around another curve, I could see the road itself was deeply rutted and the shoulders crumbled into the ditches. In a few places, the ditches themselves dissolved into lengths of marshy fields just beyond the road, the water level unusually high due to the heavy spring rains.

A few minutes later, Greer seemed to have picked his spot where a small copse of trees hid us from our followers. The carriage skidded sideways, effectively blocking most of the road. Cooper-Smythe opened the door and assisted me out before I was quite ready but I alighted without incident. He jumped out behind me, rubbing his hands together in anticipation, or perhaps just from the cold. He left his topper in the carriage again and smiled as he surveyed the spot. "Not bad, not bad at all," he muttered.

We were situated just around an especially sharp bend in the road where the following wagon would not likely see our blockade until they were almost upon us. Looking back, the road to my right seemed fairly worn. The shoulder sloped gently into the ditch, where the ground rose sharply on the far side to the concealing trees, no doubt bordering some small bit of farmland or pasture. To my left, the road was in disrepair, and large chunks of the shoulder had washed into the ditch. Beyond was a berm meant to separate the drainage from the soft wetland beyond.

"Pay attention. I am going to play sick like this," Cooper-Smythe bent over and mimed heaving his innards out like a man who had imbibed too well. "If you see me pull my hair thus," he grabbed his hair with both hands and looked like a man most distraught, "show up with your revolver immediately, understand?"

"Yes," I assured him,

"Well, don't just stand there, make for some cover," he said and pointed at the thicket of trees.

I set off at a trot, intending to jump the ditch, but on my approach realized I could not see well enough to pick out a place to land. I stepped down, made a short leap over the mud and muck at the bottom, only to have my left foot sink up to the ankle in the soft side opposite. I clambered up into the shadows, trying to keep my gun out of the mud, dragging my muddy foot, and studying the area so my return trip might be easier.

All I could do at that point was catch my breath and wait, one hand bound in the satchel, the other holding the pistol at my side. It did not take long before I heard the crunch of steel-rimmed wheels on uneven ground followed by the gleaming coach lights wavering down the left side of the road. Greer placed the carriage perfectly and the Bedlam coach coming around the bend barely had time to stop.

Caught in the coach lights, Cooper-Smythe braced himself on the side of the brougham and began retching, adding wet disgusting coughs, which sounded like he was violently expelling his overindulgence. I figured as soon as my companions were spotted, either the Bedlam wagon would stop to offer assistance, which I considered unlikely, or they would swear at the obstruction and demand it moved.

The oncoming driver had a completely different idea. As soon as he spotted the impasse, he whipped his horse, cruelly pulling the animal it into a sharp right turn while setting the brake. The wheels kicked up loose stones as the cart skidded into a turn, and it became apparent the driver was not going to stop, but rather flee.

This time I did fling myself across the ditch, landing on the shoulder on all fours, my canvas entwined pincers catching on the stones. I scrambled to my feet and charged the driver's box, waving the pistol in the air so the villains could not help but see it.

I started to bring my gun to bear on them when I saw the attendant without the reins lean toward me in his seat with both hands coming up. Too late, I realized he was not surrendering and he shot something which hit me in the face.

There was no the report of a gun, but for a moment, I was certain I'd been shot. The projectile hit me square on the heavy leather patch over the socket of my left eye, and if I had not already lost that organ, that would have been the end of it. I staggered back, my feet flew out from under me, and I landed hard on the rough macadam. The entire front of my skull was momentarily numb from the impact. As that faded, there was still no pain, but a pounding pressure built all along the left hemisphere of my face, letting me know I was still alive, and identifying the parts which would soon be throbbing.

The Bedlam cart was completing its turn and I realized I needed to act, so I struggled to stand, managing to push myself upright into a wobbly stagger. The wagon succeeded in its effort to turn all the way around and the bulk of the cart box protected the two men from any shot by Greer.

The driver was shouting at the horse while the man who perhaps shot me had swung out of the seat stall that was sunk into the front of the wagon. He had one leg anchored on the floorboard with the other hanging in space. He clutched the mounting rail and for a moment I got a clearer view of his weapon. His left hand stretched out in front of him, connected to his right which did double duty holding the object with thumb and forefinger while the rest of the fingers maintained his grasp on the rail.

A shot rang out and a chunk of wood exploded not two inches from the attendant's grip, compelling him to release the rail and tumble from the wagon. I spun to see Greer balanced on the carriage, his Colt .45 pointed at the fleeing wagon.

I realized the driver was about to get away with whatever he may have. I steadied myself, trying to assess the actual damage to determine if I could engage in pursuit. I was astounded to find I was not that badly impaired. My nose was most likely broken again (well actually for the third time) but while I was a little dizzy, my head seemed remarkably clear. I dashed toward the retreating cart, stuffing the gun in my pocket to free my hand as my pincers were still tangled in the satchel straps.

Speed was not my forte, I preferred using my brain and muscle power. The cart was accelerating and I sprinted to catch it, my legs burning with the long strides needed to cover ground, but the speeding vehicle stayed just outside my reach. There was a narrow backboard, maybe eight inches wide, sticking out from the bottom of the wagon deck just above the running gear, about three feet off the ground. I leapt forward and seized the backboard with both arms, one hand grasping the far end, both elbows resting on the narrow ledge, while my legs dangled uselessly and my shoes dragged on the sharp rocks.

The driver must have seen me or felt me climb on, as he immediately instigated a series of fishtail maneuvers to shake me off. Luckily, the first jerking turn coincided with my effort to raise my legs and the jolt, as the wagon jerked to one side, gave me enough momentum to pull myself up on the backboard, though the corresponding jerk in the opposite direction nearly sent me hurtling into the ditch. I grabbed the massive rear door handle to prevent another maneuver from dislodging me, and I took a moment to catch my breath. From this precarious spot, I inspected my ruined footwear and rested my feet on the ledge.

The door handles I clung to were overlarge and secured with a hinged bar held in place by a padlock. If I possessed any doubts about what might be in the wagon, they were dispelled by a series of thumps accompanied by shrill noises I could easily believe emanated from a captive person. A woman in fact, or a very young tenor.

Bringing my pincers to my mouth, I used my teeth to free myself from the stupid satchel and with a toss of my head flicked it into the road. The driver abandoned his wild maneuvers allowing me to seize both door handles and struggle to my feet.

I reached up with my right hand and found I could grasp one baggage rail on the roof of the wagon, so I hooked my pincers on the other rail and pulled myself up. The locking bar was just below waist height, protruding enough to allow my feet purchase.

Aside from the bumps in the rutted road, the progress of the speeding wagon was relatively steady, so I hooked my elbows over the baggage rail and lifted my left foot up to the roof. I had only to lever my torso up into position to achieve the roof, when the driver attempted another sharp turn, causing the wheels to slide out of control. The maneuver was poorly judged and the careening wheels slid beyond the crumbling shoulder on the left side.

For a split second, the slightly smaller front wheel hung out in space, only a few inches from the security of the roadway. I thought the wagon would recover, but the back wheel also sailed further into space. The wagon twisted, the left front wheel now digging into the gooey mud as the back end canted up and started to go over. Shutting out fears, pain, and even the screaming of the poor horse as it was brutally dragged by the shafts which bound it; I fought to throw myself off the overturning cart onto the unforgiving crushed-stone road. I instinctively tried to break my fall with my hand and pincers, the force of the fall twisting and mangling the apparatus as the skin was stripped from my hand. The wagon continued to tip over the ditch, smashed through the berm on the far side, and came to rest in a stinking marshland. It had rolled about three-quarters of the way onto its roof, its four wheels lazily turning in the air as it began to sink.

I gasped to regain my breath and huddled in a fetal position where I fervently wished to remain, but I knew I needed to get up.

"Ya bloody bastard!" A voice bellowed above me in a mixture of Irish and cockney accent, "I'm a goin' to kill ya!"

I looked up to see the relatively undamaged driver standing over me, his stout cudgel raised.

Chapter Nineteen

The club came down hard. I weakly thrust my left arm up at the two-foot long, thick, blackthorn stick which ended in a rounded ball. I got my arm up just enough to blunt the savage blow, but the cudgel still clouted me on the top of my head, and I lay there stunned. My mind was incapable of comprehension, for an instant unable to grasp the reality of the entire situation, or the level of danger I was in. I should have curled up, protected my head, made some defensive, or at the very least, offensive move, but I could only gape at my attacker and straighten up, attempting to rise.

The driver laughed at my disorientation, and at that moment I should have received the ultimate beating. I sensed him raise the cudgel as he took the measure of my unprotected cranium, started the swing which would break my skull and dash my brains into the gravel road, when the air was split by the flat crack of a pistol shot. He hesitated, startled.

A second shot followed, the man flinched, and I shook my head to rouse from my stupor. Some animal instinct took hold of me, and I scuttled away toward the ditch like some drunken crab. My attacker took one step toward me before hesitating again. I reached the shelter of the gully and rolled into the sodden slurry of mud, rocks, and rotted . . . something, as bobbing lights announced the arrival of my companions.

The driver fled into the dark.

I took deep gasping breaths to calm my thumping heart and ease the anxiety in my head. I desperately strained to make sense of what was transpiring. At that instant, the carriage accident and the explosion on the *Indomitable* were conflated in my head. I somewhat fathomed where I was, but the exact sequence of events was as elusive as the cause of the powerful apprehension that seized me. I recognized the metallic taste of fear in my mouth. My heart pounded faster and faster, despite my efforts to calm it, as if I were already in a fight, if only I could remember who or what I needed to fight.

Trust my body to remember before I did. With no deliberate notion, I scrambled out of the ditch, across the road, and slid shin deep into a low-lying, flooded field. The white wagon from Bedlam was a dark blot a few paces beyond. Slogging through the swampy mess, I fought my way to the padlocked door of the overturned wreck and clawed at the locking bar with my lacerated right hand while trying to use my broken pincers to pry something loose. The dread rising in my chest would not allow me to work in cool logical steps. Everything before me was a mangled mess and my panic rose. I lifted my left hand, the damned thing was little better than a club now. Abruptly mindful of the heft of the ruined apparatus on my arm, the brass and steel pieces weighing over two pounds, perhaps a club was what I needed. I hauled back my arm and slung the device at the wooden panels, treating it more like a hammer than a sophisticated replacement for my hand. I smashed repeatedly into the brittle pine boards until they cracked. Again and again, chunks of wood flew as the ruined apparatus battered the door. I was unmindful of the additional damage to the device, or the jolting force on my own arm as I kept up the frenzied assault. Finally, a hole appeared, completely blocked by cotton wool and heavy canvas.

Taking in great gasps of air, I stared at the obstruction, unable to focus or understand. The realization dawned on me that the inside of the wagon was padded. Layers of stuffing and cloth stood between me and the interior. I stabilized my breathing, taking in air in quick gulps, but letting it out slowly until my mind cleared enough for reason to take hold of at least a corner of my brain. The hole was in close proximity to the locking bar, so I attacked the lock, rather than the door. With a cry of anger and frustration, I hammered at the bracket supporting the locking bar, and with a few blows, the mechanism collapsed. I grabbed the handle and heaved, sending electric shocks of agony through my shoulder, but I ignored them as the door moved slowly in the muddy water.

I stepped inside, bringing my foot over the transom to land on the roof. The wagon had settled an additional six inches in the mud, and the water lapped at my knees. In the blackness, I heard someone thrashing about and saw a figure seated in water up to its shoulders, the person struggled against some binding force while making muffled sputtering sounds. I grabbed the figure and could feel features covered with a heavy bag of sailcloth; further inspection revealed that below the water the wretch was tightly wrapped in a madcoat or straitjacket with its arms wrapped around itself and firmly secured. I confirmed it was a woman when she tried to kick at me with both legs and I encountered voluminous skirts covering her limbs which were bound together by thick leather straps around the knees and ankles. Taking a firm grip on the collar of the restraining jacket, while the woman thrashed and twisted with even more fury, I yelled, "Danjella!" My voice literally rang in the small compartment, "For God's sake let me rescue you!"

The thrashing stopped.

I heaved her over my shoulder, the extra weight of her soaked garments making me stagger a step before I could steady myself against a padded wall. She hung further rearwards than I intended, her hips almost past my shoulder and her head fairly banging against my tailbone, but I took a firm grip around her knees and stepped out of the door, wincing when I heard her head collide with the door frame. I stepped back and exited more carefully.

The other two men had arrived and I was astonished how much the feeble glow from the two carriage lanterns illuminated the area. I called out as I tottered forward with the valuable bundle on my shoulder. I picked my way into the ditch and eager hands reached down from the far side to pull the burden from me, then more hands reached out. Greer grabbed me by the forearms and dragged me up to the road, where I staggered and sat down, right next to where they laid the woman.

Cooper-Smythe cut the drawstring holding the bag over her face and drew it off, revealing the prisoner was indeed Danjella, instead of some other random madwoman. Another leather strap was affixed round her head as a gag, situated so the stiff belt bit cruelly into the edges of her mouth. Cooper-Smythe gently uncinched the buckle. Danjella shook the strap from her head, spat in a most unladylike manner, gasped for breath, and began sobbing. Not a great wailing cry, but rather tears that streamed down her cheeks while she made a quiet choking sound that, I must admit in confidence, wrenched at my soul.

Too exhausted to do naught but sit, I watched as the two other men gently rolled her over to undo the confining canvas jacket and unfasten the straps on her legs. Released, she still lay as she'd been positioned, her limbs stiff and numb from confinement. She was unable to do little more than weep.

Sympathetic tears welled up in my eye, but as I let my head drop to my chest, a peaceful warmth spread through my body and I slumped full length to the ground. Cool mud oozed against my cheek and I may have heard Danjella crying, "Ian!" just before a comforting darkness covered me.

Waking was not peaceful. I became aware of a rhythmic jolt sending dull daggers to a spot at the top of my head as fiery echoes of pain rolled down my arm. I felt immediately ill and could taste bile in my mouth, though I could not remember retching. Every muscle ached and my left arm was a special area of pain that screamed for attention. Additionally, I seemed to have done something to my ankle.

I groaned involuntarily at another bump. That was followed by a gentle sway and a crunch of stone and I realized I was lying on the back bench of a carriage, my legs propped up on a travel box of some kind with my feet practically out the window. I opened my bleary eye and recognized the inside of Cooper-Smythe's brougham, but now a single candle in a hurricane lamp illuminated the interior. There were three men bound and arranged in a cramped heap on the floor. Danjella was huddled in the opposite corner of the compartment, her eyes shining large in the dark, and her chin was set in a most determined angle. Mr. Cooper-Smythe sat beside her, his arms crossed in front of his chest and his attentive gaze locked the prisoners.

"Where?" I gasped out.

Danjella's eyes immediately flicked over to me, filled with concern, but as soon as they met my gaze, they darted back away and she even turned her face.

"You are in our coach," Cooper-Smythe replied. "We are on our way to the admiralty. I sent young Moore ahead so there will be adequate medical care awaiting."

I turned to Danjella. "Are you hurt?"

She looked up, startled. "The care is for you, you, you—" She had something to say but her English failed her so she took a breath. "You may be too thick to realize it, but you are injured, and you look a fright."

I tried to nod, but the pain arched through my head and dissuaded me from trying again. So I relaxed as best I could into my corner, allowing myself to fall into a light doze in spite of the ache.

Someone loaded me out of the carriage and onto a stretcher, tossed me to a brusque naval surgeon whom I did not know, and he examined my injuries with a forcible competency. He expressed concern about the blow to my head, but even as he bandaged my hand, he was dismissive of the rest of my injuries, judging them to be superficial. I did not have the strength to beg to differ. I recalled a quip common in the service, "A minor injury is what happens to someone else."

"How bad is it?"

"You seem to have been lucky. The skull isn't cracked, your eye seems responsive. Pity you've already lost the other one." He made it sound like that was just plain carelessness on my part. "I'd have liked to compare pupil reaction."

He offered me a draught for the pain, which I drank eagerly, my stomach roiling at the familiar taste of laudanum mixed with spirits. I found myself sometime later with a ridiculous head bandage, my left arm in a sling, my right hand swathed in clean cotton bindings, and a pocket watch which must have stopped as it read one o'clock. I shook the bloody thing (quite literally bloody; I would have to thoroughly clean it) and held it to my ear. It was dark outside, so it could not be afternoon. Had I been out all the next day?

No such luck.

After being prodded by the surgeon, I was moved to an austere sitting room with aged curtains and block furnishings. I was left to myself for several minutes until Captain Arthur Wilson opened the door and stepped in.

"Good God, sir," I exclaimed. "What day is it?"

"Wednesday morning," he replied with a sigh of resignation.

I could scarce credit it.

"It seems you've had an exciting night of it." He crossed to a simple wooden chair. "I don't know if I should congratulate you, or discipline you."

"If it is discipline, I beg you convene a firing squad at your earliest convenience."

My reply caught him off-guard. He raised his head and released a sharp bark of a laugh.

"Glad you can jest," he said. "God, you look a fright. How do you feel?"

I took stock, which I'd actually been trying to do for some minutes. My pains were dulled by the mild opiate, but unfortunately, my ability to assess my injuries was also impaired. I replied slowly, "I think I am well. My vision is clear, although the light hurts my eye." I blinked several times, and then held out my left arm. They removed the surviving pieces of the pincers device when the surgeon examined my arm. "I realize the device is destroyed, but if possible, I'd like to get the cuff back. Lacing it on will ease the stump. I may have to dig out the hook again."

Wilson chewed at the edge of his moustache, scratched at his temple, and regarded me. "We should pick it up as we go to our next consultation. The worthies are about to meet to get a statement from Miss Tesla. Do you feel well enough to attend?"

"You are going to interrogate her? Tonight?" I objected, "Hasn't she been through enough?"

Wilson shook his head with genuine regret. "This can't be helped. There are other events unfolding and what she can, or cannot tell us, will be a factor in the next proceedings."

"What about the prisoners?"

"The men from Thirty-nine are taking their statements and they are being modestly helpful."

"Seriously? They are willing to talk?"

"Once it was pointed out that they are guilty of treason, and subject to immediate execution, they started communicating. It is amazing how the presence of a rope can focus the mind, you might be interested to know the driver who got away and our guests used to be attendants at Bedlam, until they got sacked for mistreating the inmates. That's how they came to steal the wagon."

I grimaced. I was familiar with the treatment of people in such a place, and I could not envision what would constitute mistreatment.

"The other two," he continued, "were less impressed with the threat of execution and deny knowing anything about the abduction, but freely admit to being Irish Nationalists and trying to sink your boat with the Harvey torpedo."

"I tend to believe them."

He stood, placed his hands in the small of his back, arched his spine, and stretched backwards. His body, too, was paying the toll for a long day. He shook himself and extended a hand to help me up. I grasped it as firmly as I could with my bandaged hand, and dragged myself to a standing position as the ground momentarily swayed beneath my feet like the deck of a schooner in a hurricane. My sailor's senses soon adapted, and I lurched after the admiral who slackened his customary brisk stride, allowing me to keep up. We stopped briefly by the office where I was treated and retrieved my cuff, which I clumsily strapped on as we walked.

Together we approached a door guarded by a uniformed adjutant. He ushered us into a small windowless office on the first floor of the Ripley building where four people sat waiting around an intimate conference table. Messer's Cooper-Smythe and Greer sat quietly, the British clandestine agent with his hands folded on the table, the picture of attentiveness, while Greer lounged in his chair with his eyes half-closed.

Danjella Tesla was politely listening to an older man of deceptively frail appearance as he gravely explained some point to her in an overloud voice. His wrinkled bald head had a wreath of thinning white hair that simply served to accentuate the age spots. Sir Hastings Reginald Yelverton was in declining health, and needed to have conversation constantly repeated. People whispered that he was well past his service years, but the eyes of the First Naval Lord burned with a clear intelligence.

Without pausing his conversation, he swept his sharp eyes over me, and I could see him evaluate everything about my aspect—clothing, appearance, stature, and injuries. He absently nodded with a sort of approval and his eyes returned to Danjella, who seemed to be listening with half interest. Her jaw was still set in its determined line, but her shoulders were slumped with fatigue. Like Cooper-Smythe, her hands were clasped on the table and Sir Hastings patted them as he finished his statement. He then addressed us, "Do not stand on formality, please be seated."

We took the two remaining chairs and I gestured for Greer to move over a bit so I could have room to maneuver. Mr. Cooper-Smythe started, "Miss Tesla, can you tell us—"

"One moment," Danjella interjected, her accent unusually thick. She turned her gaze to me. "Jenkins and Mrs. Livingstone, are they . . .?"

"They are well," I replied. "They are both at my quarters where Mrs. Livingstone is staying a few days with my landlady to care for Mr. Jenkins."

"That's all right," Cooper-Smithe said. "We have collected a some things for Miss Tesla and she will be staying under Admiralty security for a few days." He must have reacted to something in my face as he said, "No, she will not be locked up, but she will be escorted everywhere until we have eliminated the threats facing us." He turned to Danjella. "Perhaps you can enlighten us about what transpired."

Danjella brought her clasped hands up to her mouth which was pursed in concentration, "I was ambuscaded."

"Excuse me?" Greer said.

Danjella frowned in embarrassment. "Is English word, yes? Something like that."

"It is English," the first lord said, "just not common."

I leaned over to Greer. "Bushwacked," I translated for the American and he rewarded me with an amused glance.

"Commander Rollins," Sir Hasting said sharply.

"Sir," Captain Wilson spoke up in my behalf. "They treated him with laudanum and he is a bit . . . relaxed, but I am sure he can pull himself together."

Danjella looked at me, as if noticing my injuries all over again, but her eyes flickered away when she saw that I noticed. She then resumed her narrative, "Then, they threw that damned bag over my head. I managed to kick someone, but the man with the razor told me to stop. He said they wanted me alive, but that didn't mean he could not cut off my nose if I did not cooperate. He then said he'd start cutting off my fingers." Her eyes dropped as if she were ashamed of succumbing to threats. "I stopped struggling. They moved me to another wagon and bound me in that awful thing."

"Straitjacket," I supplied.

"Yes, yes," Danjella nodded. "They started to argue. They were set to collect a sum of money if they drove me to meet a boat somewhere. Ipswich?" Danjella looked at Wilson. "Is that a place?"

"Yes, it is," Sir Hastings assured her.

"But the man with the razor—they called him tenor. Like a singer I think."

"Tenner," Cooper-Smythe corrected. "The local constabulary has identified him as a resident thug called 'Ten-bob,' or 'Tenner' Bill Compton. That is his price for killing people."

The table sat silent.

Danjella continued, "He said there was more money if they did it up right. I was shut up, driven somewhere, and then I was dragged out of the wagon to some place that smelled of cabbage and . . ." she crinkled her nose and her forehead wrinkled as she tried to find a polite word. She settled on "dung."

"What happened then?" Sir Hastings asked, his voice kindly, but insistent.

"They kept me there some time." Her voice and face spoke of indignities she did not actually specify. "Always with bag over my head. Finally the man they called 'the German priest' arrived."

Copper-Smythe and I both sat up a little straighter in our seats. "Did they say anything else about him?"

She shook her head, "Calling him 'the German priest' was all they said about him, but Tenner told them the man wanted me so bad he'd pay quite well."

"Did you get to see or hear the priest?" Cooper-Smythe asked.

"I am getting to that," Danjella replied, moderately exasperated. "When the Priest arrived he seemed quite genial, and spoke with a peculiar accent."

"German?" I ventured ironically.

"Yes," she replied. Her exasperation more evident this time, "But odd, maybe an unusual dialect."

"Mueller," I said.

Cooper-Smythe shook his head. "Mueller's Prussian. You don't get a more standard German accent than that. Also I can't imagine he'd be involved. As naval attaché he is definitely gathering intelligence, but not as a spy, more like Mr. Greer, no offense meant."

"None taken," Greer replied amicably.

Cooper-Smythe persisted. "For him to be directly involved with actual espionage would be unthinkable. He would not risk being declared *persona non-grata*." He looked back at Danjella expectantly.

She cleared her throat. "So the Tenner person said he wanted triple what he'd already received. And then there was a gunshot." She paused. "And then the priest very politely asked if anyone else objected to the deal. The other man pathetically protested he had not received any money at all.

"The priest said he was agreeable to make a deal, but he would not tolerate being cheated. They were already bundling me back to the wagon when he told the man he would give him and his partner five pounds to take me to Ipswich, and they would get five more once I was delivered."

"Delivered where?" Cooper-Smythe asked.

"They did not say, at least when I could hear. But I was back in the wagon, and next thing I knew, the wagon is flipped, and Commander Ian is yelling at me."

Sir Hastings spoke; his tone was more matter-of-fact than polite. "We are most pleased to have you back." He drew out his pocket watch. "Admiralty business in the dead of night during peacetime is a very rare occurrence, but tonight we have to make decisions that will affect the next few days' events, and Royal Navy policy for years. Please let in our other visitor." He said to the adjutant, who opened the door.

"I believe most of you know Mr. Wilkins from the Thames ironworks."

The business agent beamed at us. His smile flickered when he spotted me, and then turned briefly into a sneer. "I am happy to be of service." He bowed his head in feigned humility.

Sir Hastings invited Wilkins into the room in a voice more of resignation than welcome. There were no more chairs, so the man stood just behind me as the first lord pressed on.

"This man has offered us several plans to modify the design of the HMS *Thunderbolt*, to speed up production. I believe, Captain Wilson, you have perused his suggestions?"

Wilson rubbed his jowl and said, "Some."

"Do they have merit?" Sir Hastings asked.

"The plans I have seen have only the merits of lower cost and time."

"Are they detrimental?" He insisted.

Wilson paused in concentration. "That is a hard question. For a warship, we strive for multiple redundancies. We make each part to withstand three times the stresses we expect."

"I do agree with you." Sir Hastings withdrew a folded paper from his breast pocket and produced a set of reading glasses. "Permit me to read an extract of an official missive sent by the Office of the Crown Prince of the German Empire Wilhelm, and received by Her Majesty Victoria, yesterday morning. The letter emphasizes that Germany expects to extend its holdings in South Africa along with its Dutch 'cousins.' For the purpose of peaceful security, the Germans will establish a fleet presence off the Cape of Good Hope, and will regulate military transport in the region. They request no Royal Navy ship attempt to pass through the Cape without prior notification, and that, in the interests of peace, Germany will provide an escort to guide the ship through."

There was a stirring of disbelief regarding the sweeping demands, but Sir Hastings waved for our attention. "As the German Empire has shouldered the expense of keeping this area peaceful, such escort will require a payment to the German government, depending on the tonnage of the escorted ships. And finally, all commercial ships not bearing the German Imperial flag will be charged a similar fee for passage."

"That is outrageous," said Wilkins. "Why the queen should call him on his impudence."

"She will," Sir Hastings said grimly. "But Wilhelm would never send this . . . offensive letter unless he thought he could support it. Our analysts say the result of a conflict in the Cape at this time is too close to call, but no analysis takes into account the *Thunderbolt*." He looked around the room. "Wilhelm wants war with England—he is making no secret of that, but if we can convince the Crown Prince that adventurism in the Cape is not presently in his best interests, we can buy time to meet him on better terms. Mr. Wilkins here has presented a plan to launch the *Thunderbolt* by Friday."

"That is reckless," Captain Wilson thundered, as he jumped to his feet in shock.

Cooper-Smythe and Danjella joined him. For my part, I nodded gravely in support.

"Please be seated," Sir Hastings said. "I do not like it either, and I like the rest of the accelerated plan even less. We will conduct immediate depth testing, even before the motors are fully operational. As soon as they are working, the boat will have one week for a shakedown cruise before being deployed."

"A week?" Wilson boomed, making sure he was loud enough that Sir Hastings had no trouble hearing exactly how he felt. "For an experimental boat, with an inexperienced crew?" He leaned across the table and knocked on it. "I know you are against the very concept of submersible warfare, and I thank you for having have been willing to give the project a fair trial, but now you are setting it up to fail."

"The crew will train as they sail to the Cape," the first lord replied just as forcefully. "I want the boat ready to deploy to the Cape in ten days."

The entire table, except Mr. Greer, looked at him as if he were mad. Greer's expression wavered between concern and confusion.

In the silence, Captain Wilson's voice sounded slow and sad. "Hastings, you win. You will have my resignation within the hour . . ."

The first lord's fist hammered a crashing blow to the tabletop. "Dammit, Artie, there is no time for posturing, you have a duty and I have a duty. Tomorrow," he hesitated and corrected himself, "today, Wilhelm's man in London is expecting to go for a ride in your little toy, you are going to also give him and the American a tour of the new boat."

A glint of comprehension gleamed in Greer's eye.

"You will pointedly mention its advanced design and superior capabilities, and then invite him to the launch on Friday. I will ensure everyone knows it is to be deployed to the Cape. We need to get Willie to realize there is currently no defense against this craft, so he will rethink this course, or we will be at war by Christmas, and very likely invaded by Boxing Day."

There was dead silence around the table, broken as Greer spoke up. "Your lordship I'm sort of wonderin,' why am I at this meeting? You have to reckon that I'm going to report on it to my people; I don't have any discretion in that."

"Absolutely," Hastings agreed. "I want every word spoken here transmitted to American ears."

Greer nodded.

"Excepting our American friend," Hastings said, "everyone at this table should meet with Mr. Wilkins and he will give you a briefing on his proposed shortcuts." He took a deep breath as if he found the next words difficult to say. "I want you to give every support to his proposals, and you will need to justify to me, in writing, any objections."

"We will meet in in my office at 0600," Captain Wilson said. "The commander will have to forgo his morning exercise."

"I am afraid that I do not customarily rise before eight AM," Wilkins responded.

"You are not under my authority," Wilson replied, "and so you may rise when you please, but all the decisions will be made at the meeting which begins at six."

Sir Hastings interrupted, "Gentlemen, please work out your differences." He turned to the American, "Mr. Greer, it has been a pleasure meeting you. Please give my best to Theodore and his new bride." As everyone stood to leave he addressed Captain Wilson. "Artie, please stay a minute."

As we stepped out of the office, a young woman fell in step with Danjella, her chaperone from the Admiralty. Wilkins stomped off in a huff while Greer patted me roughly on the shoulder, his eyes glinting with amusement as I winced.

"Have to admit, that was entertaining." He held out his hand and I shook it. He turned to the man next to me and offered him his hand. "Pleasure to work with your Mr. Ross."

"Cooper-Smythe," he replied as they shook hands.

"And you darlin'," he addressed Miss Tesla. "I still don't know exactly why you are so important, but I can see why the commander here was so put out. I'm glad we found you."

She extended her hand and he took it with a courtly nod of his head. He excused himself and set off down the hall. Cooper-Smythe turned to leave as the young woman from the Admiralty was trying to guide Danjella the opposite way. Danjella stepped past her minder and caught at my sleeve.

"I understand that I have much to thank you for, Commander Ian." Her address let me know that if I weren't restored in her affections, I was at least no longer in her bad graces.

"I did what I had to do," I replied stoically. The laudanum numbed both my emotional and physical pain.

"I am still appreciative, but I would like to request another small service."

My ears perked up and strange feeling warmed my chest. "Anything."

Her eyes narrowed and she was suddenly self-conscious. "That man we met at the theater, the physical culture instructor? Do you still have his card?"

"I can get it," I replied more coolly than I intended.

She laid a hand on my left arm. "He trains people to fight. I will not be used in such a way again, I must be able to fight." She took a firmer hold on my sleeve and raised my arm to examine the mangled remains of my pincers. "Come to my workstation tomorrow and we will install the new device, if we can." She turned my arm to and fro, studying the damage with a practiced eye. "It seems to me you are hard on nice things."

With that, she said a polite good evening and allowed the young woman to lead her off.

"I am going to my office. Is there someone around that I can send to my quarters for a uniform and clean linen?" I asked.

Cooper-Smythe nodded. "That can be arranged."

"Good, I still have a saboteur to catch."

"Well, here," Cooper-Smythe said and produced a device from under his coat. It was a Y-shaped piece of carved wood with two heavy red bands and a leather patch affixed. "I thought you'd want to see this."

"What the devil is that?"

"They are calling it a 'slingshot.' The young hooligans are using them to run the constables ragged." He stretched it out to demonstrate how it worked. "The young devils cut the inner layer out of the pneumatic wheels you see on fancier carriages and motorcars, and make them into these weapons. The man we grabbed from the cart was using this one to nick at animals. He had a pile of stones and a pocket full of lead balls."

The door opened and Wilson came out, his service hat clenched under his arm, and his eyes flickering with an angry fire. "Commander, glad you are still here."

"I was just heading for the shipyard."

"Excellent, you can ride with me." He walked right past me assuming I would follow, and this time he made no allowances for my condition. "There is much work to be done tonight. We have been ordered to prepare an explosive surprise for our visiting dignitaries."

Chapter Twenty

New pain is the worst. My head hurts nearly constant, varying by degrees from a mild ache to a throbbing around my missing eye, and of course the "hysterical pain" in my arm has been my constant companion since the explosion. However, but until last night, my ankle had been in pretty good shape, even through my rugby career. It was that particular pain of which I was acutely aware of as I lay on a folding camp bed Captain Wilson had sent to my office, delivered with orders for me to have at least two hours of sleep.

The sharp rap at my door startled me, followed by a young voice. "Commander, it is the time you specified."

Until that moment, I was not aware I had slept at all, but I sat up abruptly with a gasp, a vague feeling of unease, and a half-recollected vision of unending streams of salt water flooding my room. I reached to my desk and checked my pocket watch—0500 precisely.

"Good lad," I replied loud enough for my voice to carry through the heavy door, and with what I hoped was a confident tone. "Now, fetch me two runners and return in fifteen minutes."

I hastily donned my shirt and trousers, and scurried down the hall to the washroom to make myself presentable. In the mirror, I studied the absurd bandage covering my head like some Hindu turban. The thing was still mostly white. I gingerly touched it and determined the wound had stopped seeping, although the cloth was stuck to the skin by dried serum and blood. With the judicious use of warm water, I could prize the bandage off. The unwrapping was successful, no wounds reopened. I noticed with a certain amount of humor the surgeon had carelessly shaved a portion of my scalp to fully inspect the wound, giving me the appearance of a poorly tonsured monk.

My ministrations were uncomfortable, but when complete, it seemed I could do without the dressing, but the ridiculous appearance left me resolved to wear my service cap all day. The bandage on my hand, however, revealed too much dried blood accented by fresh red streaks to remove it. I committed to get it changed before greeting our visitors.

By the time I returned to my office, someone had removed the camp bed and the two messengers I requested were waiting. I sat at my desk and hastily scribbled a note, folded it into quarters, and handed it to the first. "Take this note to Barney Monroe at the *Times*, give it to no one else."

"Fleet Street?" he asked, his voice cracked, causing him to wince with adolescent awkwardness, but when I nodded, he saluted and left.

I turned to the other boy, still too young to worry about his voice changing. "Now you," I directed, "go to the men's barracks and instruct the coxswain to cancel the morning exercises. Inform him I want a parade at the pier by 0630. Can you remember that?"

The youngster nodded, his eyes wide. He seemed to be both apprehensive and excited to be giving orders to a petty officer.

"Then off you go," I said, smiling as he saluted and scurried on his way.

Thirty minutes later, I sat before Captain Wilson's desk with the rest of the officers rounded up for the early morning meeting, thankful for the pot of strong tea and plate of scones served by Robeson, the captain's aide. Robeson finished pouring and departed as the captain tapped his finger on the desk impatiently.

"There needs to be several changes to today's plans," he said, addressing me. "I need you to get technicians down to the *Ram* to install alkali scrubbers. See if they have some of that lemon oil to make the damn thing smell a little a little less like a, a . . ." he faltered for a description, but simply gave up and continued, "The strategic situation compels us to impress them with the capabilities of the craft. We have invited our visitors for a luncheon, but what they do not know yet is that we are going to give them a tour of the *Thunderbolt* and invite them to the launch on Friday."

"Friday?" Graf exclaimed, the rest of the officers reflected his shock.

The captain gave a quick sketch of the rapidly evolving political situation. "Our mission is to convince them that our submersible fleet," he smiled sardonically at the word, "is a credible deterrent to any plan for an open water blockade."

"The commander and I will formally greet our guests, but as he has managed to mangle himself again, Lieutenant Bartley will take our first visitor, the naval attaché Mueller, for a short voyage. Pick your engineer."

Bartley looked at me as if seeking my approval. "I'd like to use Smith, if you don't mind."

I looked at him sideways; his choice seemed an odd one. I had expected him to prefer Weber, but then I suspected he anticipated Lieutenant Graf would be assigned as the following escort, and wanted to leave the new petty officer available for his use. "That is acceptable," I replied.

"Lieutenant Graf—" Wilson started, but was interrupted by a sharp knock on the door.

"Come!" he replied gruffly.

Robeson stuck his head in the door. "Mr. Wilkins from the Thames Company is here for your appointment."

The captain consulted his watch. The civilian was on time, but Wilson smiled wolfishly. "Tell him it will be just a few minutes."

"Very good," Robeson replied before he closed the door.

"As I was saying, Graf will be responsible for dealing with our American visitors."

Graf nodded vigorously. He was grateful to avoid dealing with family complications.

"If it is agreeable to the Commander, I'll take Weber with me."

I nodded.

"That being settled, everyone but Rollins and Graf get going. We have four hours to make a very solid impression on our guests. The rest of us will have to evaluate Wilkins's proposals."

The other officers left and Robeson ushered Wilkins in the office. He made no attempt to hide his displeasure at being required to appear at the early hour, nor his annoyance at being told to wait, even for a few minutes. Without preamble, he extracted a set of blueprints from a leather tube and spread them on the desk. He indicated five sections where the work was still unfinished, and made suggestions I would normally find hasty, if not downright dodgy. But, truthfully, none of his proposals were directly hazardous. I nodded resigned agreement until he made his last recommendation—to launch the boat with the diving planes and the rudder installed.

"Are you serious?" I objected. The projections were most vulnerable to the sideways plunge from the dry dock. Even though that particular channel had been dredged to accommodate ships with a deep draft, the sideways procedure was always used for a Thames launch.

He pursed his lips and nodded, not quite as confidently as before. "I will admit it is a bit of a risk, but it will save two days of divers fitting them on afterwards."

"And if they are fouled or damaged in the descent?"

"The odds are, if anything is damaged at all it would be the two port diving planes, and it would be much faster to replace or repair them than install all four planes as well the rudder."

I was forced to give grudging approval to his logic.

I looked at the rest of his plans, then gathered them up to take to John Fells at the ironworks after the meeting.

Captain Wilson abruptly dismissed Wilkins, who scowled, retrieved his walking stick and top hat and departed. Assuming we were all dismissed, I started to follow Graf out the door, but Captain Wilson gestured for me to stay and waved Lieutenant Graf on his way.

"One moment," I told Wilson, then addressed my subordinate. "I've ordered the men to parade at the pier at 0630. If you could please take command and instruct the men not involved with the tuppence dance for the worthies to spend the day drilling on torpedo procedure, particularly using the loading hatches and slings."

Graf's upper lip twitched, accented by the tips of his deftly waxed mustache, although I could not determine if his reaction was from irritation or confusion. "As you command," he replied with a sharp nod of his head and left, closing the door behind him.

Wilson gestured for me to take one of the seats by the fireplace, picked up two cups of tea and joined me in that somewhat less formal setting. "That is an interesting tonsorial style you have acquired," he smiled grimly.

I remained silent, too tired to make a witty reply.

"Bothering you much?"

I shook my head.

He pushed one of the cups at me. "Have you given thought about how to proceed with the plan I outlined last night?"

"I was hoping you would have reconsidered," I replied firmly. "I cannot imagine how to get approval from the harbor master to shoot a whitehead torpedo in the Thames, let alone one with an active warhead."

The plan Wilson relayed to me in the wee hours of the morning was to invite our guests to see the launch, and celebrate the successful inauguration of our newest class of boat. But then while the band played, two steam tugs would position the craft, load and fire two torpedoes from a submerged attitude at a prepared target, and then follow with a third fully armed torpedo.

In the Thames.

It would be a bold and overwhelming demonstration. I could not imagine how to accomplish it. The mere suggestion to the harbor master would give him apoplexy, and rightly so. The only sane part of the plan was that we would target a salvage hulk that had been grounded on a sandbar for some time, and which was already a navigation hazard.

"We may forgo the active warhead if it becomes the sticking point. But the sub needs to fire at least three torpedoes to prove reloading capability." He sipped at his cup. It was an indication of how tired he was that he leaned back and actually slouched in the delicate Queen Anne chair. "Four countries, including the damn Germans, are racing to build a submersible that can actually fire an effective torpedo. The Americans are considered to be the closest to accomplishing that."

"You're referring to the *Nordenfeldt*." I replied, naming the boat which had successfully demonstrated its ability to fire one torpedo from an exterior tube.

"Yes, and the report described the craft as so dangerous and erratic to operate, it was more threatening to the crew and friendly ships than it was to the enemy. Before the Queen sends her official response to Wilhelm's 'proposal,' we need to convince the Germans that our craft can fire two at a time, and successfully reload. If we can do that, it that would completely change the dynamic."

"Well, I'm glad you did not announce your thought to Wilkins as he'd want to launch the damn thing loaded with torpedoes."

Wilson rolled his eyes. "Your men will be practicing with the loading hatches. I want the bloody things on board and ready to fire by the time our guests have a celebratory tot of champagne and some *hors d'oeuvres*."

The captain bade me finish my tea before sending me off. I left the office attempting to walk normally despite the pain in my ankle, while trying to wrap my mind around all the bureaucratic hurdles I was about to fight through, and the reams of thrice-dammed paperwork.

In the hallway, another of the young port runners waited. He needed to call my name twice before I discerned his presence. "Yes?" I finally replied testily, and instantly felt remorse for my discourtesy.

The young boy saluted. "Miss Tesla sends her compliments, sir, and would like you to visit the laboratory at your earliest convenience."

I consulted my watch. I had at least half an hour before I could meet with the foremen about the change in plans, so I handed the boy a coin for his service, as well as to assuage my guilt, before heading to the tower lift. In variance of custom, I put on my peaked service cap.

Danjella appeared to have been there for hours. Ample evidence of her industry spilled over her desk as she worked to find ways to expedite the electrical system installation. Her esteemed cousin, Dr. Tesla, was not in evidence, but the matron from the Admiralty sat nearby watching with eagle eyes.

"Commander Ian," Danjella greeted me with a polite, if tightly controlled smile. "It is good to see you about. You are well?"

"I'm fine," I responded, with a smile that even I didn't believe.

"Good. You did look a fight? Freight? Some word like that, last night. May I see the arm?"

I offered the appendage and she glowered at the remaining pieces of the apparatus, studying the fragments far more carefully than she had the night before. With sad resolve, she shook her head and picked at bits of metal. "You have ripped out control cables," she said. "I shall have to replace them before anything else can be done. Can you leave this here?"

I nodded; my old hook was down in the office. I hesitated just a moment, then simply turned my back, removed my uniform coat, and opened my shirt just enough to unfasten the chest and arm strap before hastily wriggling the cuff from my stump. Even after the conflict in our relationship, and despite my exhaustion, the action brought an involuntary tinge of red to my cheeks. I recovered and placed the remains of the twisted apparatus on her desk. She produced a powerful magnifier to study the thing.

I shuffled my feet, trying to decide if I should wait for her to mention it, but instead took the initiative. I removed a calling card from the case in my breast pocket and laid it on her desk.

Her eyes widened slightly as she recognized the name of John Bellows, the instructor in physical culture. "I did not think you would take me for serious," she said, looking at me over the magnifier poised delicately in her hand.

I smiled ruefully. "I have learned that I should always take you seriously." Our eyes met for a moment and she looked away abruptly; this time her cheeks colored a bit.

"Thank you," she said, her voice quiet and her eyes still avoiding mine. "I will make some attempt to contact him today." She looked at the pieces on her desk, and worked hard to keep her voice composed. "I thank you very much for all your assistance."

"You're welcome," I said. Then I nodded and turned to leave, noticing the queer look which Danjella's minder from the Admiralty bestowed upon me. In some ways, it reminded me of the way the American Greer looked at me last night. I nodded to the unfamiliar woman before heading back to my office.

Alone, I went through the tedious ritual of lacing on the hook. The pain in my arm increased, perhaps from the night's exertions, or from positioning the leather cuff of my hook. The line of pain extended down from my shoulder, making my elbow feel like it was burning and brought the plain, unadorned sense of agony to my forearm. At one time, these spasms were positional; I could hold my arm close and find some relief, but now, I had no recourse but to wait them out. There were moments I feared I'd involuntarily cry out, but the feeling slowly subsided to the familiar background ache.

I was still clutching my painful forearm with my wounded hand when I was interrupted by the arrival of Mr. Barney Monroe, accompanied by his photographer, Petey. The pair obtained entrance by brandishing the note I'd sent, but the marine guard looked dubious as he delivered them to my office. Mr. Monroe looking exceedingly pleased with himself, and apparently expected me to pour out state secrets for immediate publication.

Instead, I glared at them from my desk. "Being that it appears you can write, I expected you could also read."

"Your note said you wanted to alert the press to an important event, so I came . . ."

"Noon," I announced over him. "The note said for you to come at noon. That is," I consulted my watch, "nearly four hours from now."

"Well, there are lots of things going on around our beat," Monroe replied testily. "So I figured we'd just pop by and you could tell us your little bit, and we'd be off."

I frowned. "This is not a 'tidbit,' and I intend to allow pictures, provided you come back at *noon*."

Monroe casually dropped into a leather chair across from me and rested his tan bowler on his knee. "Well then, I figure we'll just hang about 'til we see what all the fuss is about."

"Fair enough," I snapped, then addressed the marine standing by the door. "Take these two to a windowless room and keep them there under guard until I send for them."

Monroe jumped to his feet, "You can't . . ."

I ignored his outburst and continued to address the marine. "If they give you any trouble, I authorize you to put them in shackles. If they still give you trouble, escort them off the premises." I allowed myself a tight smile. "You needn't remove the shackles. I am certain I can find a reasonable reporter who wants to break a big story."

The two men left sullenly with the guard.

The rest of our visitors were appropriately punctual for their 1000 appointment. They arrived with much the same level of ceremony as the day before, with Kapitän Mueller riding in his coach with four matched greys, and an escort of mounted dragoons, whereas Mr. Roosevelt showed up five minutes later in the same growler carriage he had arrived in the day before, driven by Mr. Greer.

The men stood at attention as Captain Wilson made a speech, informed them of the schedule, and introduced Lieutenant Bartley, who would take the good Kapitän out for his tour. I fidgeted internally, standing at the command position in front of my sailors as the visitors passed quickly in review. One thing I felt relieved about was that the prankster with the preserved claw had not repeated his jest and the plaque was not in evidence.

The morning sun struck at the back of my neck and the heat, combined with nervous impatience, made sweat trickle down my back as I ached to get the men back to their drills.

After too much talk and more than enough ceremony, the men not directly involved were finally released. I stepped forward with my junior officers to make my proper apologies to our guests. I exchanged a formal salute with the German naval attaché, which he followed with a stiff bow and a sharp click of his heels. The curt bow of his head called my attention to the Iron Cross around his neck. The medal had been altered since our last encounter and now bore a white escutcheon with a plain black cross in the center. Out of the corner of my eye, I noticed Lieutenant Graf also taking note, but his eyes grew hard and his nose wrinkled at the sight.

Kapitän Mueller straightened, looked at my hook and freshly bandaged hand. "You will not be piloting the craft yourself today?"

"No, I was involved in a carriage accident last night," I explained. "The damn thing rolled over. But, rest assured you will be in the hands of my two best officers." I patted Lieutenant Bartley on the shoulder, turned to Roosevelt, and gestured to my other officer, "Lieutenant Graf will be commanding your trip."

Graf bowed with as much precision as his distant cousin, but refrained from the heel click.

"And when you finish," I said. "I would like for you to join me for luncheon followed by a personal tour of our full facilities."

The kapitän raised an eyebrow in surprised interest, but Roosevelt just smiled. I bade them a temporary farewell, retreated, and left orders to alert me to the end of the second voyage.

The port runner notified me just in time for me to don my uniform coat and make my way to the pier as Lieutenant Graf exited from the conning tower, looking remarkably fresh for having completed a submerged trip. He had adopted the abbreviated waistcoat uniform, though his shirt sleeves were wilted, his hair damp with sweat, and his artfully waxed mustache hung limply by the corners of his mouth. However, he was smiling and abnormally cheerful. He saluted properly as he disembarked, followed by Petty Officer Weber and our visitor, Mr. Roosevelt, who crossed the gangplank to the main pier, bounded right up to me and, ignoring the bandage on my hand, seized it with painful enthusiasm.

"Amazing!" he announced, his spectacles still fogged from the close environment. "Amazing!" he repeated, as he pumped my hand, congratulating me as if it were all my own idea. "This device of yours is astonishing! I am truly impressed with her, not to mention the fortitude of the men who sail in her. I am not easily impressed," he assured me in a more confidential tone. Despite the thick sheen of sweat on his face, he was positively beaming with delight.

I thanked him and, gesturing for Mr. Greer to accompany us, I guided them both up to the conference room where Captain Wilson had arranged a light luncheon of cold chicken, salad, and a few bottles of wine. After the meal, cigars were produced and the meeting took on an amicable air of informality.

Captain Wilson shattered the calm by abruptly standing. He said in a serious voice, "I am glad you are impressed with our little boat, but now that you are here, I would like to take you on a tour to show you the full extent of our current project." He gestured to the door. "If you please?"

I slipped out of the room first to find a runner, sent him to escort the reporter and photographer to the large dry dock, and then rejoined the group as we approached the large building. Mr. Roosevelt stopped at the sign announcing the construction of the submersible tender, and he immediately grasped the utility of such a purpose built craft.

"But does that also not make the boat vulnerable?" Kapitän Mueller said dryly. "If the submersible is completely dependent upon this adjutant ship, then as soon as it is hunted down and destroyed, the small boat will be useless." The two men discussed the pros and cons of this type of warfare as we entered the main building and they followed me down the short hall. I unceremoniously opened the inner door to allow them their first glimpse of the HMS *Thunderbolt*.

The work crews had been relieved for the duration of the tour, leaving only a few men inside the craft working on essential systems. The cavernous hall was as quiet as it ever had been. Roosevelt's eyes widened behind his glasses. "My God," he exclaimed in a voice no louder than usual, but thick with intensity.

"I did not think you British had the stomach for total war," Mueller said stiffly, his mouth in a firm line. "This is the weapon of an assassin," he said, a touch of envy and accusation in his voice. "It is the tool of an aggressive nation that desires to strike his enemy without warning or declaration."

"Ridiculous," Captain Wilson replied, impatiently waving away the allegation. "This is a powerful tool to defend our harbors or open sea routes, if necessary, from enemy blockade or unreasonable restriction."

Mueller's lower lip jutted out in a most un-Prussian glower of concentration as he stared at the boat.

But even as his eyes narrowed in consideration, I could not help but feel certain he already knew about the boat and was at least peripherally involved in the accidents which had plagued the *Ram* project, but which had so far spared the *Thunderbolt*. It was possible he simply hadn't been able to get any of his men close enough to do anything.

"Commander Rollins," Captain Wilson instructed, "please show our guests your new vessel."

I shepherded our visitors up to the scaffolding and across the narrow bridge to the top of the conning tower. We passed through one of the six gates in the waist-high bronze rail that now encircled the teardrop-shaped structure, which was fourteen feet wide and nearly eighteen feet long. The steel plates that formed the top of the tower were covered by a layer of creosote-treated pinewood. The covering served to provide traction for people to walk on and work as the boat sailed awash to take on air or run the gasoline dynamo.

Two ventilation pipes projected from the dynamo compartment; they were extended to their full elevation of twenty feet and ended in hooks that contained a check valve to seal them when submerged. Likewise, the newly installed prismatic telescope jutted up just a few feet shorter than the vents, and was situated five feet from the front. This was the first time I had seen it fully assembled, and stopped to admire its clean lines. Unlike the ventilation pipes, the telescope was not retractable because no one had devised a reliable method to prevent leaks.

The primary access was a hatchway located at the very fore. To simplify design, all hatches and watertight doors were designed to be identical; round and two and a half feet in diameter. The cover was locked open and I led the way. I gripped the bronze rail with my hand and hook, while I stepped into the familiar entrance, and my foot easily found the first rung on the entry ladder. At the bottom, I carefully stepped to the side, avoiding the yawning access to another hatch directly below, which led to the torpedo room and forward diving plane controls. A similar hatch at the rear gave access to the crew's quarters, as well as the engine room and rear diving planes. Kapitän Mueller and Mr. Roosevelt followed my example, and boarded without difficulty.

Once they settled themselves, I gave them a few minutes to stare at the bridge. The interior of the conning tower was roughly thirteen feet in diameter. It was currently illuminated by the dual oval observation windows, nearly two feet in width and eighteen inches high. They were constructed of inch-thick quartz glass riveted into perfectly machined plates to allow no leaks, a design tested to a depth of 300 feet. Additionally, a porthole cover on sliding rails was positioned by each aperture, so that they could be completely sealed. The deck itself was treated oak, firm and somehow reassuring under my feet. The visitors made no attempt to disguise how intently they surveyed the control room. While most of the boat was austere, with pipes and valves jutting from the walls, and machinery placed to optimize space and utility. The conning tower, like the crew's quarters below, was designed to appear comfortable. Removable wooden panels with polished brass light fixtures covered the fittings that lined the bulkheads. Built-in cupboards contained the instruments of navigation, and fold-down tables held the charts. The area looked tidy; almost homey, in a giant steel-cylinder kind of way.

Roosevelt smiled with open admiration and amazement. "Your boat, sir, is a marvel, beyond anything I ever expected to see in my lifetime."

Mueller's face stayed impassive, save for his keen eyes which darted around the chamber and took in every detail. "Most interesting, but do you not find the decoration diminishes the utility?" He waved his hand vaguely at the walls.

"Not at all," I replied with a slight smile. I made a point of looking around the room and nodding my approval, and that is when I saw it.

I fought to keep the smile on my lips, but longed to grimace and bury my face into my palm. I thought the self-appointed wit with his claw plaque had abandoned his jest, but instead he escalated. On the left side, at eye level was the bronzed commissioning plate giving the name of the vessel, and directly below that was the offending plaque. The mounted claw was now gilded with a brass plate of its own: "Commander Ian 'Claw' Rollins, Royal Navy."

Mueller seemed about to say something when I interrupted him. "Over here is the Captain's seat." I indicated a stout wooden chair with the barest leather padding. Breaking centuries of tradition where naval officers stand watch, I'd insisted on seats for the planesmen and myself. I stepped around the prismatic telescope, took two long strides and sat down, placing my right hand on the Chadburn telegraph. "I can command the boat myself, using this, and the speaking tube," I pointed to the device suspended from the upper hull by a retractable cord. I pointed to similar equipment at a station to the left of the view ports. "Or leave it to my first officer."

Kapitän Mueller nodded thoughtfully and stepped over to the forward hatch, peering into the dimly lit void. "And the rest of the boat?"

"I am sorry I cannot presently show you more." That was a both direct and an indirect lie. I was not sorry, and despite my implication, I never intended to allow Herr Kapitän a more detailed view. "We're in the final stages of construction, moving men and equipment through the vessel, and things are not properly braced. So it is not safe to wander through the compartments."

Mueller closed his eyes for a second, and I could see him actively listening to the sounds of hurried activity emanating from the hatch. "There does seem to be quite a flurry of effort."

I stood and took a deep breath. "That is because they are preparing to launch the boat on Friday at noon."

Both men looked completely stunned. Mueller recovered first. "That is impossible," he said.

I kept my face impassive as I enjoyed the expressions of shock and dismay which crossed the faces of our visitors. No matter how much they knew before, it was obvious they had no idea the submersible device was anywhere close to completion. I did not bother to mention the accelerated nature of our timetable. Instead I merely bowed, and said, "On behalf of her Majesty's navy, I would like to extend invitations to the naval attaché of the German empire, as well as our American friends, to join us for the christening ceremony. I think we should have some other interesting surprises to show you." I did not tell them how various bureaucrats were scrambling throughout the port authority to acquire permission to practice fire whitehead torpedoes in the Thames.

"Bully!" Roosevelt exclaimed, clasping his hands together and rubbing them with enthusiasm.

Chapter Twenty-one

Captain Wilson leaned back in his office chair, rubbed his temples, and shook his head slowly, "I certainly hope the Admiralty knows what it's doing."

"It would be the first time," Cooper-Smythe retorted. However, a glimmer of humor sparked in his eye as he sat rolling an unlit cigar between his palms.

I shook my head as well. "They seem to think that the deterrent effect of the weapon is more likely to resolve the current conflict than continued secrecy. Do you think the demonstration is going to have the intended effect?"

"Apparently even First Lord Sir Hastings Reginald Yelverton has to fight for permission to launch a torpedo in the Thames." Captain Wilson leaned forward and fixed his sharp eyes on me. "Do ensure that any demonstration is impressive enough to serve as a deterrent."

I nodded even as my brain raced to imagine a way to make it happen.

The pain was shooting through my back as I left the captain and I wanted to hide in my office to brace my arm until it subsided enough that I could ignore it. However, with a quick glance at my pocket watch, I realized that if I waited longer Danjella may leave for her temporary lodgings before I could see if she'd been able to do anything about my apparatus.

I strode stiffly toward the laboratory lift, keeping my arm slightly crooked to ease my discomfort. I arrived at the workroom to find Dr. Tesla sitting, studying a page covered in unfathomable mathematics. He was tugging the hair at his temples, his teeth bared as his eyes scanned the page over and over again as if expecting it to change. Wishing to ease his distress, I had approached to inquire what evoked such consternation when Danjella called out in a quiet but urgent tone from her work bench.

"Leave him," she advised.

He said something incomprehensible in a low snarling tone, his musing having reverted to Serbian. He seemed completely oblivious to my presence, so I decided discretion was best and left him to his conundrum. I walked over to his cousin, feeling more anxious with each step, nodding at the woman from the Admiralty. The woman nodded back and resumed perusing an issue of the *The Strand* magazine.

"He is about to do something brilliant," Danjella informed me quietly, waving vaguely at her cousin. She was attired the way I'd first met her, with a leather apron covering her utilitarian dress and smoked glass goggles covering much of her face, a spirit torch burning before her as she soldered some mechanism together. She paused and pushed the lenses up on her forehead. "When he gets this way he can be vehicle? Vehement? Some such word like that means angry, if you interrupt. But he will be calm soon. He knows he is right, but will obsess until he proves it."

"Then what happens?"

She shrugged. "Something spectacular." She sighed gently and cast her eyes to the ground. "Generally good."

Unsure how to respond, I went right to the point. "How is the apparatus?"

She took a deep, patient breath and twisted her lips in disapproval. "If you come back in the morning and give me about an hour of your time, I think we can get this worked out."

I shook my head in consternation; there were so many details and last-minute items that I could not imagine where I would find the time.

She put her soldering aside and lifted familiar assemblies. "I have almost rebuilt the casing where you ripped cabling out of the cuff," she indicated an incredibly fine line of welded metal that had been replated. "But I still need to straighten the gearing interface." She indicated a brass spur gear on her desk. "This gear is the same size as one you destroy, but I will need to file notches on the interior to match the control spline." She picked up a jeweler's loupe and examined the piece. "I've also taken liberty to order several sets of repair parts, since I strongly suspect that this is going to be recurring problem."

"Do I owe you any money for the parts?"

She looked up at me with a tight smile. "That is not going to be a concern, your gear design is more popular than we imagined. You should have all the parts you need and tidy sum in addition."

I nodded awkwardly, unsure how to continue the conversation, or even how to adroitly excuse myself. I noticed an elegant walking stick propped up on the side of the desk. It was slim with an octagonal shaft topped by a sturdy brass knob on one end, and thick leather tip on the other.

"So, Mr. Bellows has agreed to take you on as a student?"

"Yes," she replied. "He has scheduled private lessons in evening hours, between beginner and advance class. I convinced him of my need, but he is dubious . . . Yes, right word . . . that I can develop proficiency, but thinks that I may be able to learn basics." She lifted the cane, and waved it as if testing its balance. "John has graciously loaned this walking stick to start practice, wants me to make a habit of carrying and feeling comfortable with it."

"May I?" She reversed her hold to offer me the pommel. Grasping it, I discovered the stick to be deceptively heavy, its stylish form disguising a dangerous heft and a comfortable balance. "Is it loaded?" I asked, referring to the practice of hollowing out a wooden truncheon or club, and filling with lead shot.

She smiled. "No need; this is a made of something he called *Lignum vitae*."

I nodded. Lignum vitae is a tropical hardwood much prized by the navy for making bearings and other items that receive a lot of wear; and the incredibly dense wood lasts a long time. It is so dense it does not float, and is better than ivory for durability and strength, while its mass makes it excellent for a weapon.

"So this is going to be your protection?"

"Like I said, John was a dear and loaned this to me. We have a luncheon tomorrow. He wants to discuss a more efficient way to teach me self-defense."

I bet he does. I felt a spasm of irritation at the knowledge that she was going to be lunching with the man two days in a row. I surreptitiously took a deep breath in through my nose and reminded myself that I had made a very reasonable and intellectual decision to curtail our relationship, and so I should be happy that she was spending time with someone who might be more appropriate. I congratulated myself on my reasoning and sound decision, but the twinge in my stomach that echoed in my chest was not convinced.

"Well," she sighed, "back to work." She screwed the jeweler's loupe into her eye, picked up a scratch awl, marked the tiny gear, removed the loupe, and pulled down the goggles. It took me a second to realize I had been summarily dismissed.

I fidgeted for a minute, trying to decide if I should say something, perhaps object to her manner, but decided against it. The minder looked up from her magazine and made a slight clicking sound with her tongue, shook her head, and went back to reading.

I walked away.

My mind was reeled with emotion, but I firmly turned my thoughts back to naval problems as I stepped out of the lift and crossed the corridor to exit the building. My gait was uneven as I was still favoring my injured ankle. In addition, my posture was stiff as a spasm flared and I held my arm slightly out from my body to ease the shooting pain. I paused to let the feeling subside when an unexpected slap on the shoulder caused me to wince, which led to a more powerful spasm sin my arm. I kept from crying out only by clenching my jaw and biting the insides of my cheeks. I spun to my left to see Cooper-Smythe standing beside me. I'd been unaware that he had been waiting for me to leave the building and he seemed quite taken aback by my reaction to his friendly attempt to get my attention. "Problem?" he inquired.

"It's nothing," I replied curtly, unable to hide the pain in my voice. "My back is sore."

His eyes narrowed at something in my tone. "From jumping off the carriage?"

"Of course," I replied defensively.

He cocked his mouth to one side and his eyes examined my face carefully. "You are a bad liar, and I do not understand why you need to lie."

"It is nothing," I repeated. He continued to stare at me, his gaze hardening until I felt myself squirm inwardly. "I seem to be more susceptible to back and shoulder pain since the incident on the *Indomitable*." I tried to explain with half-truths.

"Have the doctors identified the reason for your, susceptibility?"

"They have put forth some ideas," I said too harshly.

"You are lying again."

"No," I insisted. "They have given me their *opinions*."

He continued to glare at me.

"They have determined that the pain is …imaginary."

Cooper-Smythe snorted. "That's absurd. You are not some hysterical old woman moaning about fancied aches and pains. Follow me, I know an expert in pain."

"Where are we off to?"

"Limehouse," he replied.

The yard was abuzz with activity. We found ourselves swimming against the tide of workers arriving for night work; two extra crews of men would be laboring through the night to prepare for the launch. As we threaded our way through the throng toward the main gate, we came across lieutenants Bartley and Bertram also straining for the exit. When they saw me, they stopped and saluted, becoming obstacles for the flow. I motioned them aside.

"We've just come from the *Thunderbolt,* sir." Bartley informed me. "We were going to go over some details of the power plant operation, but there is a crew in the engine room, and one working on the energizing chambers."

"Very well. I applaud your dedication but it is getting late and we have a very long day ahead of us, and very possibly a long weekend. I recommend you both go home and get some rest." I noticed both men taking surreptitious glances at my companion.

In response, Cooper-Smythe stepped forward and held out his hand, the arm straight but the wrist at the odd angle that I had come to recognize. Reggie Ross, he announced with that vacuous smile on his face. "Old friend of the commander's father, don't you know," he said, by way of explaining his presence. He swiftly shook hands with both officers.

"Yes," I responded dryly, hoping the lieutenants would not notice the note of resignation in my voice. "Sir Reginald is taking me to Limehouse for dinner." Limehouse was primarily known for its large Oriental population, and as a consequence, it contained a few well-known exotic restaurants.

"There is excellent food at Limehouse," Bartley agreed, "I am particularly fond of a very good curry place."

"I say, have you served in Injah." Cooper-Smythe pronounced the name of the country like the colonials of the last century.

"Six years," Bartley said with a cheerful nod.

He stuck out his hand to Bartley again. "Ah, I can always spot an old Injah hand."

Bartley politely accepted his grip, "And you?"

Cooper-Smythe clutched an astonished hand to his chest. "What me?" He lied with a touch of incredulity in his voice. "No, no, good sir. My father and grandfather both spent some time, so that I wouldn't have to."

"Well," I stepped back into the conversation, "I think we need to be on our way." I waved the lieutenants toward the gate. "Go get some rest."

The two men joined us as we exited past the marine guard where we all caught the Port Road tram to The East India Dock Road. Cooper-Smythe and I exited the tram and he flagged down a hackney to haul us the short distance to Limehouse.

He dismissed the hired coach when we reached Commercial Road, and then led me through a small maze of buildings as the sun slowly set over the rooftops. Few people were about on the dirty narrow streets. The smell of foreign cooking and strange pungent spices filled the air. I suspected there were more people about, but that they were actively avoiding the two strange Englishmen prowling through the streets, one in military uniform, to boot.

At last we reached the end of one particular building, and Cooper-Smythe confidently stepped into the stairwell leading to a basement entrance. I paused and looked, my head whipping back and forth as if I were concerned someone would see me. Cooper-Smythe gestured impatiently, and I apprehensively joined him at the bottom of the stairs. As he knocked on the door, I placed a concerned hand on his shoulder. "You are not taking me into an opium den, are you?" I inquired only half in jest.

He looked at me quizzically with one eyebrow raised and his lips twisted in a slightly mischievous grin. "Of course, I am not taking you to an opium den. Good god man, how embarrassing that would be." He turned back to knock on the door again. "You wouldn't know how to behave."

Before I could retort, the door was opened by a young Chinaman, who bowed to us. He wore a grey smock with a medium length queue braided down his back. He did not say a word, but recognizing Cooper-Smythe, nodded, turned, and walked away, plainly expecting us to follow him into the dimly lit basement hallway. The short passage opened into a large room filled with bundles of herbs hanging from the ceiling, and baskets of more dried aromatic plants arranged in rows. Before us there was a counter. Behind the counter were rows of shelves filled with glass jars labeled in Chinese characters. An older Chinese man whose wispy beard and mustache had faded to a dingy, tobacco-stained white also stood behind the counter. His hair still had some black woven into the grey queue that spilled out beneath his low, round brimless hat. His eyes crinkled and his lips drew wide revealing brownish teeth, as he smiled at Cooper-Smythe. "How may I be of service?" He asked in a quiet, thickly accented voice.

"I am bringing my friend to see the lady from Yokohama."

I turned to him, startled. I started to make an inquiry as this was clearly a Chinese shop and I knew that Yokohama was in Japan.

The proprietor said something in Chinese to the young man who led us in, who in turn bowed and left by a side door. Within a minute a young girl emerged. The child wore a grey smock, but with big wide sleeves, and a square hat over long unbraided hair that was gathered in a loose knot at the nape of her neck. Upon seeing Cooper-Smythe, she smiled, but then quickly quashed the enthusiasm and bowed with dignity while addressing us. "I am pleased to see you again, Cooper-san." The young voice betrayed no accent.

Cooper-Smythe return the bow and his face formed the most honest smile I'd seen from him. "It is good to see you, Mi-chan. Please inform your mother that I have a patient for her."

The child bowed gravely and backed out of the room, bowing again at the door before turning away from us. Cooper-Smythe gently pushed me, indicating I should follow and we stepped into another dimly lit hallway with four doors that led in different directions. We ignored them, and arrived at a portal at the very end. Mi-chan pushed open a door that was lacquered black with fine gold, silver, and crimson patterns of vines, leaves, and flowers. Warm Jasmine-scented air spilled out of the room and the child moved confidently in the darkness. She deftly lit two candles, then wordlessly motioned for us to enter. We stepped up from the laid bricks of the hallway to a hardwood floor finished with oil and rubbed to a deep luster. She then bade us sit, indicating two low canvas-covered benches sitting parallel in the surprisingly spacious room. Only two other pieces of furniture were in the room—a short stool with wide ornately carved legs and one other item that was also some sort of stool. It had a triangular seat, and at the point of the triangle, a single wooden post stood up so that it came to just above waist high. The post was topped by a padded rail almost two feet across.

In the center of the far wall sat a bronze brazier with a water-filled bowl containing flowers and herbs that kept the room temperate and perfumed with a pleasant, if exotic, scent. Folding paper screens covered the side walls; they were framed with the same black lacquer finish as the entrance. Two thick woven straw mats sat on the floor in front of the brazier.

I sat on the proffered bench. Cooper-Smythe removed his coat, and hung it with his hat on the edge of the screen along the right wall, before slipping past me to kneel on the mat, resting back on his feet and looking most comfortable.

The decorations and design of the room were similar to Chinese rooms I'd seen, but contained several subtle differences. "Japanese?" I inquired.

Cooper-Smythe explained, "The lady we are about to see is a Japanese doctor, a specialist. Some years ago, the emperor of Japan sent a group of scholars to attend Cambridge and King's College. One of these academic envoys was an older man who brought with him several attendants, including his doctor. Unfortunately, the elder scholar died and his family did not wish to pay for his attendants to return home. Most of the domestic help were forced to find menial jobs, but Emiko Hiromatsu is a specialist, and the Chinese community is familiar with her style of medicine. It took a year for her to establish a practice but, now she is well trusted."

"A heathen woman doctor?" I exclaimed, "Is this some kind of pagan priestess who is going to dance across the floor and chase off evil spirits?"

Cooper-Smythe frowned at me, his eyes half closing as if he were considering the best way to communicate with an imbecile. "No, she is going to stick pins in you like a voodoo doll," he replied in a sincere tone meant to reassure me.

I was not reassured.

He was saved from having to explain further when the door opened again and the Mi-chan entered, followed by a most exotic and elegant lady. She wore multiple layers of floor length silk robes that were dark and marked by unusual embroidery in strategic locations on the cloth. These wraps were held modestly closed by a wide red sash intricately bound about her waist, emphasizing her thin frame. She moved in short mincing steps that gave her the appearance of gliding across the floor, but even her bowed head and submissive posture could not hide her confident nature. Her features seemed frozen, but projected a certain knowing look that could not be hidden by her carefully applied makeup. Her face had been artificially whitened, but not to the point of the porcelain Gilbert and Sullivan caricature. Her lips were painted to a small red bow, and her eyes shaded in a lighter shade of red. Her long hair was artfully piled on top of her head and held in place by elegant combs.

She said something in Japanese while staring straight ahead, her expressionless eyes not settling on either one of us. Mi-chan replied in the same language and the lady doctor nodded patiently while the child gave a complete report.

"Ian, this talented healer is Emiko Hiromatsu," Cooper-Smythe said. He then addressed the doctor in Japanese. His words sounded more coarse and guttural, but the lady's manner took on a note of genuine pleasure at the sound of his voice. She bowed deeply in his direction. He returned the bow from the kneeling position, actually touching his forehead to the mat, and continued speaking. I could not understand the language, except when he said my name. The doctor made a small shift and turned her body in my direction, her eyes still looking past me.

I realized she had not blinked since she entered the room, nor had she looked about. I waved my hand before her face, and realized that she was blind.

"I can feel breeze when you do that," she said, her voice making English sound musical. "Is rude." She turned toward the child. "You met my daughter, Michiko; she assist me." She spoke to the girl in Japanese; she bowed and left the room.

"Ian-san," the lady said in a very high, sweet voice, "Please remove jacket an' shirt, also hook thing."

I hesitated for a minute. Cooper-Smythe made a rolling gesture with his hand as if telling me to get on with it, so I complied, still feeling very awkward undressing in front of the blind woman.

She moved very securely through the spacious room and indicated by swooshing motions that I should sit on the strange triangle-shaped chair facing the padded rail so that my arms drooped over it. With strong, sure fingers she began to prod, probing the muscles of my back, and after a few seconds, she made an intonation conveying across the language barrier a sense of certitude. "You pain, start here?" She placed her finger upon a sore spot just to the left of my spine and near the top of my shoulder blade. "An' continue this way?" She firmly traced her finger in a circuitous route under my shoulder blade, back up to the underside of my shoulder, and then down along the bottom of my left arm over the elbow, stopping midway down my left forearm. The firm pressure left a fiery trail as she exactly tracked the path of the hysterical pain that had plagued me for the last year. I nodded, then realized how stupid that was, but before I could speak, she continued, having sensed my nod.

"This spleen meridian. You *qui*, or energy, trapped here, an' here." she touched the top of my shoulder blade by the collar bone and my elbow.

She sniffed delicately at the top of my head, and her hand gently brushed the wound. "This clean?"

"Yes."

"Head hurt?"

"A little."

"We do some for that."

Mi-chan entered the room, carrying a glass box which she placed on one of the low upholstered benches, then stepped back.

The woman doctor held her hands out to her sides and the girl produced a cloth belt she used to tie her mother's wide flowing sleeves back, revealing pale, well-toned arms. Without looking toward the box or fumbling for it, the Japanese doctor deftly picked up a long slender needle.

"Please, face forward," she directed, "you feel pinch." I felt a very tiny pinprick by my shoulder. She repeated the warning several more times so that within a minute she placed fifteen needles in my back and shoulder, as well as three at the base of my neck. She stepped around the stool to where my right hand was hanging from the padded rail. Her fingers carefully explored the back of my hand before placing a needle in the center, just back from the knuckles and I cried out, more from shock than the pain. All the other needle placements had been unremarkable, but that small puncture sent an electric pain shooting up my arm, across my shoulders, and down to the opposite wrist. I bit my lip to keep from crying out again as she gently twisted the needle, causing waves of agony to shoot through my body.

"Is uncomfortable?" she asked.

"Yes," I managed to reply, without adding an involuntary yelp.

"Good," she replied. "Will be better soon. How you arm feel?"

I concentrated on my left arm. "It feels tired, heavy, it . . ." I had difficulty describing the feeling.

"Good."

I was aware her daughter was now doing something with the needles in my back and arm. I looked over my shoulder to see her forming little bits of what looked like dough, roughly the size of a pea, and placing the small round balls on the needles.

"I have other duties," the doctor said. She bowed, and walking with her curious gliding gait, left the room.

Cooper-Smythe stood. "I'll be right back," he said, and quietly followed her through the lacquered door.

When the child finished adding the bits to the needles, she picked up a candle and lit them. My head jerked up in alarm, but she shook her head with firm dignity. "Do not move, stay very still so the moxa can work."

"The what?"

She sighed in frustration, "Just sit still," she replied, rolling her eyes at my ignorance.

"Okay." I felt I should express my gratitude. "Thank you, Mi-chan."

The child froze and I sensed that I had somehow affronted her, perhaps it was inappropriate to thank her?

"I do not know you," she said in a low voice with imperial dignity. "If you must address me, you call me Michiko-san." Without waiting for me to apologize, she gathered up the glass box and left me alone. The air filled with the strange scent of the herbs burning on the needles.

Very soon I noticed something odd— the pain in my back and arm was gone. For a second, I feared I was paralyzed, but calmed down when I discovered that I could wiggle my fingers and move my left arm, which still felt unnaturally heavy. With the ache gone, I felt myself sink into the chair as a drowsy haze settled on me. My mind began to wander, fixating on the implications of my treatment. If the pain was real enough to be treated, then I was not a hysteric, and not in danger of going mad.

It may seem strange that such a small thing could cause me to reevaluate my life. Almost every decision I made since the *Indomitable* event was shaded by the fear that I may be judged mad, or may in fact, be mad. One bitter thought burst through, *Could this medicine have helped my mother?* Surely though, she suffered from far more than mere physical pain.

The warmth and pleasant atmosphere helped me quash that train of reason. My lack of sleep and late hours caught up with me, and I began to doze.

I was roused from a pleasant stupor when the doctor returned with the child and Cooper-Smythe. The elegant lady glided up to me and began quickly removing the needles, dropping them into the glass box her daughter held. "This no heal, not so fast. You come back two times next week; we will work from there."

"Yes," I said, then paused and clenched my teeth, having already made a faux pas addressing the child, I settled on, "Yes, doctor."

The child bowed and left the room.

"How you feel?" the doctor asked.

I straightened up in the chair and was tentatively stretching my shoulders, when the door burst open and three men pushed their way into the room. One man stopped slightly in front of the others. All of them were Chinese, but very similarly dressed in London fashion, their bare heads revealing hair cut short without the traditional queue. Their frock coats and striped trousers could have come from Saville Row and they wore waistcoats of Chinese silk brocade decorated with small golden dragons on a black background.

Cooper-Smythe stood and looked ready to object to the disturbance, but the last of the men to enter dragged Mi-chan in with him, holding his hands firmly around her neck. She struggled and said something harsh under her breath.

The doctor's head shot up, and cocked to one side. From the practiced look of exasperation on her face, she seemed to know exactly who the intruders were.

"You have no right. Leave."

"I am sorry to intrude," the man in front said. "But we have business." The apparent leader was distinguished by a gold watch chain across his waistcoat. His tone was very polite, even deferential."

"I no do wrong," the doctor said.

"Not you," the man drew a short-handled hatchet from under his frock coat. "This man," he said as he thrust the blade in my direction.

"Why is the tong threatening an officer in Her Majesty's navy?" Cooper-Smythe demanded. "I was under the impression that you were more of a local security force."

"We protect local businesses and we protect our own," the leader replied, "But we have agreements with others and we have been asked to collect a debt."

"A debt?" I asked as my mind raced. It was true that during the last year I had run up several arrears, but I had diligently paid them off after receiving my back pay. "I owe no one."

The man nodded sadly. "So often such debts seem to slip the mind. We are here to remind you." He used his free hand to reach into an inside pocket and retrieve a folded paper, apparently a bookmaker's marker. "If you choose, you may pay us 100 pounds now or we break one leg." He brandished the hatchet in his hand, turning the point upward so the dull end was positioned like a hammer.

Cooper-Smythe looked at me.

"We will be civilized," the man said with a smile. "You may choose; left or right?" he stepped forward lightly striking his left palm with the dull side of the small axe, his facial expression neutral.

"Why you insult me?" Emiko Hiromatsu exploded. "You should wait 'til he leave. Why insult me? Why hurt my child?"

Her blind eyes seemed to bore in on the leader, "How you leg? You walk? You owe me." She adjusted her direction to address one of the others. "You sister, how her hand?" She raised her chin. "How you come here like this?"

"Shut up woman," the leader snapped.

At that moment, Mi-chan spun on her captor, wildly wind-milling her arms. Surprised, he released his powerful grip on her throat to try to grasp at her flailing arms. The youngster yelled out one word in Japanese, and instantly Dr. Hiromatsu and Cooper-Smythe each knocked over one of the candles, pitching us into deep shadow, the only illumination came through the door from a lantern down the hallway.

The Chinaman attempting to subdue the struggling girl yelped in pain, and bent over as the child struck him, slipped from his grasp, and escaped out the door, slamming it behind her.

I head the locked door rattle as someone strained to open it, and now the six of us were sealed together in the pitch black room.

Chapter Twenty-two

Suddenly sounds echoed through the humid air as everyone seemed to be in motion. The leader called out orders in Chinese. I reached toward the bench for my hook, the only thing I had to use as a weapon. I managed to brush it with my fingers, but only knocked it further away, and it fell to the floor with a loud clunk. My efforts were interrupted by a large crash as one of the folding screens was knocked over, and someone yelped in pain.

Sliding off the stool, I made a sort of controlled fall to the floor, and landed awkwardly on my hip. A slight man ran into me, fell across my back, stumbled into one of the leather benches, and tumbled into a hard landing. The next attack could be more effective and I frantically explored the ground around me until my fingers closed on the cool iron of my hook. I didn't bother to put it in place, but rather brandished it like a knife as I jumped up to join the fray.

Straightaway, a stick or club hit me along the shoulder, and I instantly crouched back down to the floor to avoid the attacker. A silken robe brushed by me. Someone cried out in pain and I heard a very firm thwack of something solid smacking someone. Simultaneously, there was a piteous groan and an awkward thump, like someone dropping a rolled carpet from a second-story window. Abruptly the only noise was someone scrambling away. Then everything became very quiet.

Minutes passed as we all stayed silent, struggling to quiet our breathing, afraid that the slightest noise would bring unwanted attention. The humid air became quite thick from all the people in the room. As sweat trickled down my body I deliberated how long this impasse could continue.

In the quiet, the new rattling noise from the door seemed unnaturally loud. I fixed my eye in that direction and took a firm grip on my makeshift weapon. I reckoned it could equal one of their hatchets if I had the initiative. Sharp intakes of breath and shuffling sounds indicated that I was not the only person preparing to strike a target as soon as the open door provided light.

The lacquered wooden panel swung in on well-oiled hinges, and at the first glimmer, I jumped to my feet to behold a startling tableau. Cooper-Smythe sat on one of the benches with a cigar in hand, looking as he were preparing to light it. The leader of the three intruders sat not a yard away from me, cross-legged on the floor, cradling his head in his hands as blood seeped through his fingers. The other two stood with their backs against the wall, trying desperately to fade into the structure. Standing tall and firm, Dr. Emiko Hiromatsu, brandished a four-foot long staff that apparently came from a series brackets on the left wall, revealed when the folding screen was knocked over. There was another of the short sticks, as well as two longer staves, and two six-foot long bladed staffs still mounted. The good doctor had selected the least lethal tool.

Her features were calm, almost serene as she stood in a ready position, prepared to attack the next thing that made noise. Her attention was focused on the now open doorway. Mi-chan opened the door, but moved out of the way to admit an elderly Chinaman. Like the three intruders, he was dressed in London fashion and wore a bowler hat with an almost perfectly flat brim. His beard and mustache were thin, wispy and completely white, as was his short hair.

The two young men who pressed themselves against the wall tried to become even more inconspicuous. The leader, still cradling his head, craned his neck around to see what was happening. When he saw the old man, he gave an audible groan, visibly paled and clambered drunkenly to his feet.

The old man addressed the leader in a quiet puzzled voice with a mild Chinese accent, "George, what are you doing?"

The doctor relaxed her stance.

"I . . . I . . ." George stuttered as blood bubbled out his nose. "I bought this man's debt."

"From whom?" the old man demanded. His voice was soft but backed by a tone that would not be denied.

"The priest," George replied defensively.

The old man turned his head to the side in puzzlement, his voice taking on an incredulous hiss, "When did you start buying the priest's accounts? You cannot trust the German." He regarded me carefully, then raised one hoary eyebrow, and glared at the young man. "Why was I not informed?"

"I bought it myself," he burbled, "it was my private business." He tried to sound bold, but merely managed to sound defensive. He lowered his eyes to the floor.

The old man frowned and pursed his lips. He then turned his head deliberately to the left, then to the right, to fix his gaze on each of the other two men. His expression indicated that he was aware of their presence, but heretofore considered them beneath his notice. "Leave," he commanded.

The two men scrambled to exit the room and collided at the doorway, but they did not pause. Both bodies squeezed through; their running feet echoed down the corridor.

The old man looked at George. "You used two of my men."

"They work for me," George snapped, managing to sound defiant this time.

"Because I tell them to," the old man countered with forced patience. "You do not have private business that I do not know about." He glanced around the room. "Why have you insulted our friend?"

George fidgeted, "The Priest said the Britisher would fight. I thought to catch him when he was vulnerable."

"How much was the debt?"

"Fifty pounds," the young man replied quietly.

"For fifty pounds, you insulted our friend, involved the navy?" He looked at the man and shook his head in disbelief. "Give me the marker and your wallet."

George complied. The old man roughly pushed him out of the way and stepped forward to offer the marker to me. Despite the fact that the man had demanded one hundred pounds, the marker was clearly for fifty, and was signed by a close approximation of my actual signature. The old man then produced a wad of banknotes from the wallet and placed them at the end of one of the leather benches.

"I hope this will conclude our business," the old man said. His manner and tone indicated he was speaking to me as well as to the doctor. He turned to George. "Apologize to our friend."

George turned towards the doctor and bowed very low. "I am sorry to have offended you and your guests."

The old man seized the young man by the ear and jerked his head up. "Now, you go with me and we will discuss your 'private business.'" He casually dragged the young man out the door.

Cooper-Smythe finally lit his cigar.

The lady doctor held her short staff lightly at her side, turned in my general direction, and bowed. "Please to dress, and come back next week."

"How much do I owe—"

"The fee," she interrupted, "has been paid." She let her hand drop to the leather couch. Her fingers traced a path on the upholstery until they encountered the money, then the bills disappeared into her robe.

She bowed one more time and left.

Cooper-Smythe took a long pull on the cigar. "I had hoped when the lights went out, you'd be smart enough to hit the floor and stay out of her way." He waved his cheroot at the darkening bruise across my shoulder.

I didn't bother to respond. I got dressed while he gathered up his coat and hat, and we headed out.

By the time I arrived home, my back and arm were showing signs of reverting to a more uncomfortable state, but I was so exhausted I simply wanted to collapse into bed. First I was obligated to look in on Jenkins, who was not only improving, but seemed to be thriving on the attentions of Mrs. Livingstone. Despite my fatigue, I was drawn into a tediously polite conversation with the woman. After accepting a cold supper from Mrs. Hawn, I managed to extricate myself and finally flop into bed, expecting a quick and restful slumber.

That did not happen. Every dark memory from the previous year revisited me, and rest was held at bay by the flood of thoughts. Sleep finally fell upon me, but instead of comfort, I witnessed men drowning in dark water pouring through the burning boiler room of the *Indomitable*, smoke so thick I found myself choking. I woke in panic, drawing in a deep gasp of air as I sat upright in my bed with my heart pounding in my chest and bile in my throat. I drew wheezing breaths until I could swallow; the bile burned the back of my esophagus. This had happened a few times during the last year and was always frightening, but at least this time, I could lie right back down without my back spasming from my sudden rousing. However, my mind still found no rest. Lighting a taper, I saw it was not yet five in the morning, and I rose to pace back and forth across my chamber.

I was concerned about disturbing the rest of the household, especially Jenkins and the ill effect my own restlessness would have upon the injured valet. So, I quietly gathered my things, cleaned up as best I could, and headed off to my office, the only place where I felt I could accomplish anything. It was a very dark, but unusually clear, morning, and too early for tram or trolley service. It took me nearly half an hour to hail a hansom to take me across the Iron Bridge, its burnished struts reflecting the pale glow of the recently lit gaslights. We then proceeded out to the Port Road.

In my office, I actually sneered at the confounded pile of paperwork accumulating like barnacles. They all required my signature and authorization if we were to launch the *Thunderbolt* on Friday morning. Indeed, like barnacles, the accumulation of paperwork at any one site slowed down everything, so for an hour I plowed through.

Infrequent sounds of activity gradually increased until the bustling sound of regular activity echoed through the building. So I left my office to see if the Teslas had arrived. Up in the laboratory, I discovered Dr. Tesla seemed to have come to some solution about whatever problem caused such consternation, and now he sat frantically scribbling on a pad of paper as if he could not get the knowledge out of his head quickly enough.

Danjella waved me away from him as she covered her work with a white linen cloth.

"We are ready to fit your device for a test," she said with a smile. She had that gleam in her eye I'd noticed on our first meeting, but I attributed it to excitement for the new apparatus.

"You worked through the night?" I exclaimed. I was interrupted by a low snoring sound. I looked past Danjella to see her admiralty minder asleep on a pallet put together from the foul weather coats and towels, and what looked like a boiler insulation sheet. Her red hair had escaped its prim bun and fanned out around her face.

Danjella held a finger to her lips and spoke just above a whisper. "Please let Miss Raymond sleep. Robin has been such a dear and very patient with my habits." She twirled a finger at my hook. "Now, let's get that thing off."

I did as requested, still feeling shy about displaying my stump to her.

She handed me the repaired cuff assembly, and I stood there dumbly for a minute until I realized she was waiting for me to put it on. She must have understood my reluctance, so, with a sly smile she turned her chair around and averted her gaze. I also turned about, quickly enough to expose my left arm. By now, the familiar straps fastened easily around my torso and shoulder, so I quickly recovered my clothing, then rotated to face Danjella's desk.

"All right," I said.

Danjella spun her chair back, the sly smile still on her lips, and I found myself wishing to know the cause of her amusement. She screwed a jeweler's loupe into her eye and reached out for the cuff, studying it carefully as she turned it to and fro.

"I think repairs will hold … until next time you feel urge to hit something." She tugged on the control cables. "I must apologize," she said without emotion. Her hands moved from the cuff to remove the loupe and whisk away the white linen cloth. "You are clever, despite what I may say in anger."

I barely heard her voice, frozen by the sight before me. It was simply the most well-constructed instrument I'd ever seen in my life; my sketches and scrawling made into beautiful working form. The mechanism was designed, perhaps by a sense of vanity, to resemble as far as possible a human hand, albeit one of plated steel. The tiny plates I had designed were open at the base of the fingers to reveal intricate gears, which would allow them to open and close. The backplate was also open to reveal four separate spring-wound motors—two controlling the operation of the fingers, and two more just to control the thumb.

I placed a tentative finger on the thumb. "May I?"

"Of course."

I lifted and examined it carefully, noting minute changes in my design. She had fixed miniature clips on the fingertips in order to better secure the fitted leather pads impregnated with India rubber to provide grip. She also added a stud that provided a quick way to replace the tight springs that pulled the hand open. I nervously fitted the creation to the locking mechanism on the cuff, and connected the control wires.

Danjella tapped a metal object on her desk that appeared to be a watch fob, then offered it to me. It was the winding key to the spring motors, made ornate with scrollwork. There were four little winding studs on the hand that energized the motor. Minute tabs folded flat along the body of the hand could also be flipped up to wind them, but the key would make the job far easier. I quickly wound the studs to their full tightness, and began maneuvering the straps and control wires to open and close the hand, much like I had controlled the pincers. It moved beautifully, although I found coordinating the thumb tricky.

I must have cried out in wonder as Miss Raymond suddenly awoke and glared at me through bleary eyes.

Danjella offered me a small screwdriver. I took it from her with my "new" hand (it was my hand; I designed it), closing the fingers around the wooden handle until they automatically stopped as they met resistance. Then, using her improvement, I closed the hand incrementally, gripping the tool tighter, trying to visually determine when I had it in a firm grip. I judged I needed one more increment, and the wooden handle cracked with a sharp pop, startling me.

"I owe you another screw driver," I said hastily. I released the tool and it clattered to the floor.

"Do not concern yourself," Danjella said. She chuckled ruefully and reached out to stroke my mechanical hand as if it were flesh. The surprising intimacy of her gesture caused a wave of emotion to rise in my chest, but I was confident she was just admiring her own craftsmanship. I used the device to take her hand, closed the fingers, allowed them to stop as they again met resistance, and then made certain to not move them further.

I thought I saw a shine in her eyes as I took her hand, and I quickly released it. I focused my attention back on my hand, noting the tiny cutouts by the winding studs that indicated how much tension was left. I started to open and close my hand rapidly, gratified to see how little energy was used each time.

"All springs will need to be changed often. You will soon get a feel for when it is necessary."

I closed the cover plates to keep as much dust and dirt out of the well-oiled mechanism as possible, and studied it closely. There were still several features I needed to work with, including the pads pressing against my pronator and supinator muscles, which would allow me to release and flex the wrist.

Danjella yawned in a most unfeminine manner, her mouth gaping open with her hands stretching up above her head. As I was reminded how much I found her lightly bound form attractive, and recalling my new attitude, I decided I had some serious thinking to do. I forced my eyes back on the hand.

"Go play with your new toy," Danjella said, still yawning as she shooed me away. She turned her attention to Miss Raymond. "I think I need some food and a nap before my luncheon assignation? Appointment? Some word like that." I must have imagined a look in her eyes that implied she knew exactly what each of the words meant and was tweaking me.

I thanked her again and turned to leave.

"Commander, come here," Nicola called across the room.

Nicola had finished his frantic writing, and was now motioning me over.

"May I help you?"

"*Neh*," he said and waved me on until I stood by his desk.

"I like you look at something." He opened a small wooden box and turned it so I could see the contents. Ten glass orbs, arranged from smallest to largest, filled the box.

My shoulders slumped.

"These are—"

"I know what they are," I said. "I looked into getting a glass eye, and even went through the sizing procedure." I didn't intend to say more, but he stared at me in such eloquent silence I felt compelled to explain myself. "I didn't go through with it, partly for the expense, but also because it seemed, I don't know, dishonest? I would look like I had two eyes, but I don't."

"No dishonesty here," he replied with a half grin. "Will be a light, at least; something useful."

I nodded and pointed to the globe marked #4.

I promptly forgot about the glass eye and rushed down to the dry dock. I had to work my way through the *Thunderbolt*, testing how well I could control all onboard systems with my new appendage. I was able to do that for almost an hour before a runner appeared with another list of urgent paperwork that I needed to generate, authenticate, or triplicate.

After a few hours at my desk, I became acutely aware of how early my day began, and a growing twinge in my stomach reminded me that I missed breakfast. It was a bit early for luncheon, but I rationalized my need for energy and decided, against habit, to take a meal at the officer's mess.

This time my shirt was crisp and my coat sharp, and I was appearing in public for the first time with my new apparatus. Several people noted my entrance, and cast curious glances at me. However, no one approached me as I made my way through the field of brilliantly starched table cloths. My goal was a small table near the kitchen where I could have a quick meal, but before I could make it that far, I heard Lieutenant Bartley.

"Commander Rollins, sir," he called out, standing on tiptoe with his head inclined. He motioned me over.

I do prefer eating with genial company, so I changed tack and made my way toward him. As I neared the table, I slowed down and my smile faded. Bartley's table partner was eating soup, pointedly ignoring my approach. His deep-set eyes seemed unnaturally focused on the table in front of him, and his thin mouth was twisted in displeasure as if the soup tasted bad.

Bartley indicated a seat for me before resuming his own. "Commander, you know Lieutenant Gaither, of course."

"Of course."

The Thunderbolt Affair

The former fifth officer of the *Indomitable* looked at me, acknowledging my presence with a twitch of an eyebrow.

"I've been telling him about life among the submersibles." Bartley frowned a bit. "Terry here isn't really keen on the idea."

"Waste of time and money on a weapon that should be condemned by any civilized navy," Gaither said in his quiet, raspy voice. "At least, 'ceptin Bartley, they haven't wasted any good men or officers."

I did not take the bait, but sat quietly as the steward brought my water and took my order.

Gaither, for his part, was not inclined to linger. He wiped his lips with the napkin, expressed a friendly farewell to Bartley, retrieved his hat and left, all the while making a show of ignoring me.

"Been friends long?" I inquired.

"Not really close, mind you, but we served in India before his illness." He squirmed a bit in his chair. "I'm sorry if that was unpleasant. He's generally quiet but I have never before seen him be intentionally rude. I waved you over because, although he definitely disapproves of the submersibles, he did have a lot of interesting questions and thoughts. I invited him to the launch tomorrow."

I nodded.

"Sir, is that the device I've heard so much about?" he asked shyly.

I placed my left hand on the table, surprised I actually thought of it as my left hand. "You've heard about it?"

"From the foundry boys. They've been speculating how it would work once Miss Tesla specified the gears."

I held it up and displayed the workings for Bartley before working the fingers, opening and closing them, and finished with an awkward thumbs-up.

Bartley acknowledged his approval by drumming his knuckles lightly on the table. I noticed a few speculative glances. Most serving officers knew someone who could benefit from such a device, if it were successful.

We finished the meal with a few pleasantries, but Gaither's manner had placed a pall over the repast.

I returned to the Ironworks in a pensive mood. Gaither, the *Indomitable* and the mounds of paperwork awaiting me kept my thoughts jumbled and distracted. I absently returned the marine's salute at the gate. Miss Raymond, Danjella's minder, seemed to be keeping him company. Her presence did not seem out of place until, out of the corner of my eye, I caught an elegant carriage pulling up to the gate. A gentleman swiftly alighted and turned to assist his companion. The man was John Bellows, the physical culture instructor from the theater. He stood smiling as Danjella grasped his hand and used it to steady herself as she disembarked the coach. The pair of them had been unescorted.

I turned away sharply to give them their privacy. I imagined they had much to discuss as this was the second day in a row they'd shared luncheon together, in addition to seeing one another at her lessons in the evening.

I was walking toward my office building when I heard brisk, delicate footsteps approaching from behind. Bending over papers all morning had aggravated my arm and put a kink in my back. Unable to simply turn my head, I was obliged to rotate my frame around to see Danjella approach.

"Ian," she said, advancing at a quick pace with Miss Raymond dutifully behind her. Danjella wore one of her utilitarian work dresses, but had accessorized the deep maroon garment with a smart hat with a demi veil and a cameo on a velvet ribbon around her neck. She carried no bag, but instead held the handle of a flat wooden case approximately two feet square but no more than two inches thick. A brass plaque on the front advertised the Reilly Company. She smiled politely and continued more formally as if she regretted her casual greeting. "Commander, how is your hand working?"

I smiled and held it up, making opening and closing gestures at her. "Far better than I expected. You do impressive work," I said.

She smiled briefly and pride shone in her eyes, but then she lowered her gaze, trying unsuccessfully to portray humility. I did not understand why she tried to appear modest; she was a talented craftsman and a brilliant inventor.

"How was your day?" I inquired politely.

"It could turn out to be very profitable. John is such a dear and he is introduced me to some people. They have offered me a lot of business if I can improve some devices they make."

"Oh?"

"Yes, I hope you don't mind. I showed them some pieces and mechanisms you designed for your new hand. You see, John showed me some of their products and I saw immediately how they could be improved. I promise you, if I use any of your designs or gearing, I will ensure you receive complete royalties." She paused and indicated the case. "They have been so kind as to give me one of the devices they manufacture, and I am going to spend some time the next few days prototyping the improvements."

"You will be there for the *Thunderbolt* launch tomorrow, correct?"

"I would not miss it, but have to start thinking about how I am going to make a living." Her voice suddenly became quite serious. "I work under my cousin's contract, technically through the Thames Ironworks, and the contract will close soon after the submersible launches. So far, the Admiralty has not contracted to build any more submersibles. I need to find some work before I find myself out in street."

"And Nicola?"

She waved her hand airily. "My good cousin has been ready to move for some weeks. He's actually been finding the time he takes solving small problems with the submersible to be interfering with his newest work. He's corresponding with George Westinghouse in United

States. Nicola has been drawing sketches …" she paused, her face screwed up in concentration. "Have you heard of Niagara Falls in New York?"

I nodded.

"He wants to turn them into an electrical generating system using an alternating current system he has developed."

I suddenly felt unaccountably forlorn. Somehow I assumed Danjella would be part of the project for some time.

"I'm sure," I ventured, "there is much work for you with the Admiralty, if you wished to stay."

She looked at me sadly, and then looked out over the shipyard and piers. "I do not think the Admiralty is interested in continuing … affliction? affiliation? Some word like that." She sighed, still looking away from me. "Projects end. You must move forward, or move on."

I nodded. Miss Raymond glared at me as though she wanted to kick me.

Danjella returned my nod with a sharp one of her own, and continued on with bold strides as if she suddenly wanted to put distance between us.

I withdrew to my office where a near unending stream of paperwork, technicians, and other annoyances kept me until well after any decent hour. It was after ten when I was finally able to leave. As I passed the lift, I was struck by an outlandish fancy. If Danjella was still at her laboratory, maybe I could apologize, explain myself; perhaps even convince her to stay. My reason told me such a thought was irrational, but as I walked toward the exit, the desire to go and talk to her grew. If her laboratory had been illuminated, I do not know what I might have done, but I was saved from making a fool of myself by her absence, and I continued on home.

Chapter Twenty-three

I would like to go on record that at no time did I think it was a good idea to load torpedoes on a newly launched boat of any sort and fire them in the Thames. I never met anyone who admitted the notion was their brainchild.

The water in the Thames was remarkably smooth. A low, ocean-going barge coated in standard navy grey paint lay anchored not four yards from the *Thunderbolt*. A crane ship, with its derrick painted a jolly safety yellow, lifted Whitehead torpedoes from its deck. They'd been rushed from the Royal Laboratories in Woolwich for the event. Even under time pressure, the deadly missiles were meticulously moved one at a time. The crane operator slung the first two weapons over easily enough. I was very proud of the well-drilled men who received them in the open loading hatch and guided them to the waiting tubes.

The trouble started as the third swung up off the deck, hanging awkwardly in its frame. As it crossed the water to the front of the *Thunderbolt,* it tilted precariously forward, threatening to slide out of its canvas support. The crane operator sped up the derrick arm, intending to get it to the boat before it got loose, but overcompensated. He brought the boom so far that it led the cargo, giving the incoming explosive a great deal of momentum.

I called to the men to get out of the way. The four strong men instinctively sought to grab the load to guide it, but the inertia knocked two men sprawling. Seaman Stewart was bashed the worst. The impact sent him over the rail and he fell from the loading catwalk to the steel deck of the torpedo room, fifteen feet down. I rushed to the railing, but before I could even shout an inquiry, he waved that he was fine, although he was not getting up quickly. The remaining men waited a few minutes and watched as the last fish hung on the end of the line, swinging ominously back and forth.

The torpedo was no longer in danger of escaping its cargo sling. However, the transport stress opened up a joint in the torpedo between the clockwork guidance system and the compressed air motor, and the edge of the reinforced canvas sling jammed into the split. As the oscillations slowed and stopped, the newly minted Petty Officer Weber judged the timing, and had the men wrestle the uncooperative package through the loading hatches. Fortunately, those same massive doors hid the last, less-than-stellar delivery from the gathered throng who would have misjudged the abilities of the sub-mariners; the near disaster was not their fault.

I slid down the ladder to assist, but found Weber was already examining Stewart. The remaining two men guided the nose of the weapon toward the steel ready rack.

"Bugger all!" Jonas exclaimed, as the torpedo refused to settle onto the steel frame. The canvas sling was still firmly wedged into the joint, blocking the device from perching in its proper place, and both sections of the Whitehead torpedo were completely fouled.

The day started far too early because sleep had once more eluded me. I arrived at sunup and discovered that the Thames shipyard was bustling with activity as the double shift of men completed their night's work. Unlike the smaller repair facility, which could easily be flooded, the much larger construction dock was built above the waterline and the complete riverside wall would have to be removed. The night before I had watched twenty men begin the long, laborious task, and they were still at it now. Teams of men were hauling away sections of the barrier. Ten more men from the launch crew were just starting their job, affixing polished iron rails to the steel runners the boat rested on. Steam powered jacks would soon force iron wedges under the frame, raising one side of the boat until the force of gravity pulled the entire thing sideways into the Thames. The channel had been dredged several times over the years to ensure the water was deep enough to launch the largest gunboat, and another dredging operation had taken place during the night to remove any silt that might have accumulated.

My plan was to take a quick tour of the preparations, then finish work in my office until the festivities started, but too many people wanted my attention. I barely got back to the offices before visitors started arriving. By 1000 I was in Captain Wilson's office staring out the window as chaos literally spilled from the main gates, slowly spreading to the river.

I did my best to ignore the conversation behind me, but the buzzing whine of the argument drilled into my brain. Since I was not a party to the matter, I endeavored to distract myself by studying the growing crowd. I picked up an antique spyglass from the bookshelf by the window. Training it on the front gate, I spied the arrival of Mr. Barney Monroe from the *Times*, accompanied by his cameraman. Word of our endeavor was printed in the previous day's paper and must have stirred up some interest, as every newsman in London seemed to be following him. I imagined I could hear the howls of protest at the gate as the marine guards kept the tide of reporters at bay, allowing only Mr. Monroe and Petey into the compound. I lowered the instrument to rest my eye, and found my mind dragged back into the argument.

"The Honorable Mr. Gestlehum would like to know why his

recommendations have been ignored," said a fussy little man in a charcoal grey morning coat. He had repeated the sentence three times.

Captain Wilson promptly attempted his third politely bland evasion. But this time, the fussy men interrupted by waggling a disdainful finger at him. The Captain stopped, regarded his visitor, and spoke sharply. "Because the recommendation is flat out stupid," he said to the man standing in front of his desk. This officious man represented a member of Parliament who had nothing to do with the Admiralty, had no experience of the navy, and had never served in the army. However, since he had read history at Cambridge, he considered himself a military genius. His recommendation had been to fill the abandoned target hulk with gunpowder to guarantee an impressive explosion. As I recalled the meeting where this idea had been proposed, I raised the spyglass and turned it to the ship in question. It was a wooden-hulled frigate that had been hastily fitted with a steam engine, as well as a small turret assembly, and was run aground during launch. A steam tug tried to drag it off the sand bar, but the ill-conceived, top-heavy structure made it so unstable that the hull started to crack under the strain. It had since been stripped of what was useful, and the rest had been sitting there for nearly three years, a hazard to navigation.

"You cannot," the man paused, "call a member of parliament stupid."

"I most certainly can," the captain countered. "But in this case I did not, as I am unfamiliar with Mr. Gespunch, or whatever his name is." He sat up straighter and stabbed a finger into his desk. "But the idea is ludicrous! The men we invited to this demonstration, the men we need to impress," he jabbed his finger at the short man. "Those men know what it looks like when a ship is hit by a torpedo. If there is a mass of secondary explosions, they will know we have rigged the test. If they believe we have rigged the tests, they will assume we expected it to fail, telling them we have no confidence in our own weapon. And that would be completely counterproductive." He sighed and displayed a plainly artificial smile on his saltwater-tanned face. "But please, convey my respects to Mr. Gustpump." He turned his chair back to face the desk, picked up a folder, and began to study the contents.

Hiding a grin, I went back to staring out through the spyglass. I watched The Royal Navy brass band unload instrument cases and sort out where they should assemble. The drum major was strutting around waving his baton at the bandsmen, seemingly upset that they were not already playing as worthies began to arrive. Barney Monroe had not disappointed me. His purple prose could give Edward Bulwer-Lytton a run for his money, and as a result, we had far more dignitaries than at our previous launch. A gaggle of foreign naval officers had arrived early and were wandering around, keeping a suspicious watch on each other. Kapitän Mueller of the German Empire had the largest entourage, but it was rivaled by the Czar's naval attaché, while the American naval attaché, together with the US ambassador to the Court of Saint James, was only accompanied by Messrs. Roosevelt and Greer. Mr. Roosevelt seemed to be the only one comfortable with all the important visitors and I watched him move through the crowd eagerly shaking hands, appearing to be sincerely happy to see everyone.

The silence behind me took on an ominous tone, and I chanced a glance back to see what had transpired. Wilson was still writing at his desk as Mr. Gestlehum's parliamentary assistant glared at him in impotent rage. He finally realized he had been summarily dismissed, so he snatched his top hat from the table by the door and stomped out.

I turned my scope back on the crowd, zeroing in on Herr Kapitän. My new study of our Prussian visitors revealed three of the accompanying German officers also wore the emblem of the white escutcheon with the thin black cross around their necks. I resolved to ask Lieutenant Graf about the meaning of the symbol.

Once our parliamentary annoyance was safely out of earshot, the captain looked up from his desk and interrupted my train of thought.

"One more bloody recommendation from a half-wit politician and I shall improve the demonstration by tying him to the target."

I chuckled at his outburst, relieved that I didn't have to deal with these people, or the populous in general. Not only were the throngs of invited guest milling about the pier, but hundreds of people turned out on the opposite shore to watch. An entire detachment of marines was employed to keep prying noses out of the danger zone behind the day's target.

"I thought he'd never leave," Cooper-Smythe remarked, entering the room and carefully locking the door behind him. He was dressed in a proper black morning coat, and a particularly flamboyant necktie, and carried a fine silk top hat.

Wilson drummed his hands on the desk. "We are a trifle busy today. Could you be so kind as to play your games another day?"

"Reggie Ross is an invited guest," Cooper-Smythe pointed out. "But there are events you should know about. The American, Thomas O'Connor, is giving up what he knows."

My ears perked up at the words.

"He still insists the attack on the *Ram* was all his idea, but before that, he was selling information on the shipyard to the priest. And he is certain that whoever he is, the priest is not German."

"Based on?" I asked.

"Based on his accent," Cooper-Smythe replied. "O'Conner says it is very convincing, but fake. He asserts he worked with many different Germans in American shipyards, and this guy sounded odd."

"Did he give a description?" Wilson asked.

"Claims he never saw the man. Their only face-to-face meeting was in the confessional of a Catholic church, and they spoke through a screen, of course. Since then, they planned locations for leaving messages. We clandestine types call that a dead drop."

"So he is a real priest and spy?" Wilson said with a sigh.

"Doubt he is clergy, but he is a spy, and a good one. After our altercation in Limehouse, I ran down some information. The priest has been buying up gambling debts of British officers, paying a premium, and offering to erase the debt for information. If that doesn't pan out, he resells the debt at a loss to one of the local gangs."

Captain Wilson said, "So, we *know* he is a spy, instead of being very certain he is a spy, and we know that he may, or may not be a German— not very much progress."

Cooper-Smythe turned his lips in a very predatory grin. "It never seems like much, right up until we put the rope around the man's neck." He retrieved his topper, smiled his most empty-headed "Reggie Ross" smile, waved in an ostentatious manner, and let himself out.

The captain, noting my presence, checked his watch. "Shouldn't you be out there showing our guests around?"

"Yes, sir," I answered reluctantly, like a child reprimanded for procrastinating. I put off the inevitable just a few extra minutes by stopping in the washroom to groom myself for the day's activities. My face in the mirror reflected my exhaustion. The odd bare patch of skin around my head wound was covered with a slight stubble, and I again resolved to keep my hat on as much as possible.

At the entrance to the building, my junior officers stood in a casual clump waiting for me. When I joined them, each one reported on the special tasks assigned for the morning festivities. In turn, I nodded my approval before sending them all away, except Lieutenant Graf. "I have a confidential question for you." I motioned him closer. "I noticed the other day that Kapitän Mueller had augmented his medallion and you didn't seem to approve very much."

"The medallion you refer to is known as the Knight's Cross. It is the amalgamation of the Teutonic Order and the Knights of Jerusalem. It is a very traditional award."

"And the augmentation?" I pressed.

He worked his upper lip so his mustache wiggled left and right. "That shield is the actual coat of arms of the Teutonic Knights."

"I didn't know any of those medieval orders still existed."

"The orders evolved into social and charitable organizations until they were completely suppressed by Napoleon, but I have been hearing rumors that a small group within the army and navy has taken to wearing the symbol to indicate they have become very close with Crown Prince William the Second."

"Sort of an inner circle?"

"I hope that is all it is," he said.

"What do you mean-"

"Nothing," he interrupted sharply. "I will leave rumors and gossip mongering to Bartley." He saluted and strode off.

I nodded to myself, took a deep breath and waded into the throng to greet the dignitaries. It was Kapitän Mueller who first admitted he noticed the apparatus on my arm. He strode towards me and, similar to his behavior at the theater, unabashedly grabbed it and held it up for inspection.

"I wish to say, commander, how enthralled I am at your devices. Does it truly function?"

As before, I was discomfited by the Prussian's grasp. It was every bit as intrusive as if he had seized my natural hand, but I maintained a neutral expression and made a demonstration of working the fingers. I chose not to coordinate those movements with my thumb, leaving it slightly bent out of the way. I was uncomfortable letting him know the full extent of my abilities. I made the smallest of talk with the Germans until I could break away and spent the next hour making my way through the crowd, introducing myself to the emissaries I had not previously met, shaking hands, and making polite noises to those I knew. Mr. Roosevelt pushed his way through the crowd, accompanied by a handsome woman that I took to be his new wife, although he neglected to introduce us. A very guarded-looking Mr. Greer followed them.

The strong American politician shook my hand with great vigor. "It is good to see you today, good indeed! Adam has apprised me of your adventures." His eyes gleamed at me with infectious excitement. "Tell me sir, are you and that craft truly ready for such a historic launch?"

"Absolutely," I declared, reflecting his enthusiasm.

"Bully!" he exclaimed, pumping his fist in the air like a victorious prizefighter. "Just bully!"

A young messenger tugged at my sleeve. "Captains compliments, sir. He requests that the invitees advance on the reviewing stand." He pointed at the temporary structure adjoining the nose of the new boat. I waved a farewell at Mr. Roosevelt, nodded to his wife in lieu of tipping my hat, left them behind, and pushed my way toward the stage.

Climbing up the temporary structure, I saw Admiral Wainwright of the First Fleet conversing with a somewhat homely young lady. He had a protective hand upon her shoulder. She was shorter than the admiral, but seemed tall due to her pencil-thin shape. Not even a fashionably bustled gown could round out her figure.

I ignored them and crossed the stage to the rough railing just three feet away from the bow of the *Thunderbolt*. This close, her plated skin seemed garish, but still I marveled at how the clever coating made the boat seem so smooth. I had to look closely to discern the division among the hundreds of plates that made up her hull, and the tiny points of shadow that revealed the thousands of rivets. Only the permanently placed handholds stood out from the gleaming hull. They climbed vertically up her sides and divided the craft into four equal sections.

"She's a beauty," Captain Wilson said as he stood next to me.

I looked around and noticed that the rest of the invitees had clustered at the other end of the reviewing stand around Admiral Wainwright.

"I suppose you have been aboard her?"

"I just completed a walk-through with the admiral."

I stood silent.

Wilson stepped to the rail and placed his hands firmly on the rough wood. "The plaque in the conning tower was a nice touch."

"Sir, I can explain."

He tilted his head back and laughed. "No, you can't," he replied with a chuckle. "It's the men who give you a nickname, and God knows how they decide on the right one, or why one sticks and another doesn't. Don't be upset about it, Ian. I believed that you would go down in history as Commander Ian 'Stumpy' Rollins, but 'Commander Claw' is the one that stuck. Better than being known as "Tug," I can tell you."

"I've always been a little curious about that."

"I was a junior officer, trying to get another battleship to come alongside properly. The captain couldn't seem to manage, and I got frustrated and yelled out to him, 'Do you think it will help if I give it a tug?' and that was it."

I changed the topic, and waved in a general way towards the assembling crowd. "Who is the young girl with Admiral Wainwright?"

"That would be his niece. She has been chosen to sponsor the boat."

I had assumed something like that upon seeing them together, but I felt compelled to voice a mild objection.

"I would have thought that Miss Tesla would have been a, well, more appropriate choice." The sponsor was generally an unmarried woman who was somehow close to the ship or its crew.

"I think you might be a bit prejudiced . . ."

I fear I reddened a bit.

"Even though naming her the sponsor would be politically awkward, the Admiralty did consider it. But it was actually Miss Tesla who objected. She thought it might lead to too many questions." He inclined his head and used his chin to indicate the stairs. "Speaking of our brace of Serbian savants . . ."

I turned to see Nicola Tesla strut up to the stage, followed in a more decorous manner by Danjella, who was carrying another new walking stick. This one was a blond wood, oak or ash perhaps, with a mother-of-pearl inlay and a silver handle. The pair was pursued by Miss Raymond and the imposing figure of Mrs. Livingstone.

Wilson consulted his watch. "We have about five minutes, then I shall introduce you before the speeches, which should give you ample time to make your escape."

I took a deep breath and let it out slowly as my mind went through all the steps I needed to take over the next hour to make everything work. As soon as the crowd knew who I was, I would leave to watch the christening from a steam tug in the harbor. Immediately after the launch, that tug and its partner would move in and take the mooring lines of the submersible. Lieutenants Graf, Bartley, and Hanley, and I would board her, along with Petty Officer Grant and a full crew to man the torpedo room and the four ballast stations. We were expected to get the forward loading hatch open, and three torpedoes on board and ready to fire, before the crowd lost interest. I touched the brim of my hat in an informal salute. "Then, sir, I have one thing to attend to . . ."

Turning away from Captain Wilson and the *Thunderbolt*, I tracked the crowd until I saw Danjella and her companions, made my way over to them, and touched the brim of my hat, saluting each of them in turn, without actually showing my head.

"Mrs. Livingstone, I assume since you're here that Jenkins is doing better."

She regarded me with hostile eyes. "Fat lot you care. You've been at home three times, but only stopped in once to see 'im."

I started to respond, but Danjella interrupted. "He's doing quite well, actually. Robin and I stopped by to see him last evening and he was well enough, so I invited both he and Mrs. Livingstone for today. But he declined, pleading he did not want to appear frail in front of people who might know him." Her tone was pleasant, and her face was set in a cool smile, but there was something in her eyes that I could not understand at that moment.

I saluted the ladies again and rejoined the admiral for the day's festivities. Half an hour later, I was wrestling a torpedo into its rack.

Jonas pulled at the sling, but the reinforced canvas did not budge. Weber rushed beside him, squatted low to put the weight against his back, and keep the 120-pound cylinder from falling out of the rack. Stewart clambered halfway up the loading catwalk scaffold and waved for the crane to lower enough slack to undo the cargo hook, and release the derrick.

"Get something to cut that away!" Weber shouted. "Even if we get it in the rack with that stuck, there's no telling where the fish will go if we launch it!"

The other men carefully closed the loading doors, engaging the rather ingenious watertight system of locks. I studied the offending sling. The material had rubbed against the torpedo as it was being loaded and I realized immediately how this had occurred. The sling was in exactly the same place for this torpedo as for the previous two, but this one had a live warhead which made it a good twenty-five pounds heavier than the others. Suddenly, I hoped that the men who set the depth clockwork had kept that in mind.

Jonas was still having no luck with the canvas obstacle. I stepped forward and seized it with my mechanical hand to jerk it from the dividing joint. Instead, a sharp metal edge from one of the finger plates caught the material, and cut it in a ragged slice. I continued using my device to cut the cloth away until my efforts left only a trace of frayed canvas jammed into the joint.

"That should do; we'll fire the bloody thing."

I stepped back and sighed with relief. Then I noticed how badly using my hand thus had chipped the plate and flaked off plating. Danjella would not be pleased.

"Commander Claw," Jonas muttered drolly under his breath,

"That's enough of that," Weber snapped at him. He addressed me, "Beggin' yer pardon, sir."

I frowned, nodded sharply, then quickly turned, and scaled the ladder so they could not see my smirk. I guess I could live with "Claw." At the top, I grabbed the handrail above the open watertight hatch and swung myself onto the solid deck of the command center. My mind raced, trying to sort out how I was going to keep the great display from fizzling. I informally waved Lieutenant Graf out of the captain's chair so I could personally supervise the torpedo loading. He stepped smartly to the first officers' duty station.

I drummed the fingers of my right hand on the lightly padded chair arm. I looked straight ahead, but I listened intently for the chime of the ship's Chadburn telegraph which would alert me when the all hatches were sealed. It seemed an eternity before I heard the alarm, but, checking my watch, I noted that it had only been twenty minutes since we had come aboard. Without hesitation, I grabbed the speaking tube, eschewing the whistle mouthpiece as the men at the ballast stations were awaiting my call.

"Ballast one-quarter," I ordered. Each of the four ballasting stations situated in the *Thunderbolt* had a glass tube with a floating brass ball that indicated the amount of water inside. We calculated that one-quarter ballast should allow the stationary sub to settle about ten feet under. That was deep enough to provide a realistic firing of the torpedoes, but shallow enough that the two oceangoing steam tugs could control us. The boat began to rock gently from side to side as it began its uneven settling to depth.

I pushed myself out of the chair, feeling the vessel sway under my feet as I walked to the prismatic telescope. Through the eyepiece, I determined the tugboats had done their job keeping us situated in the exact correct position. From beside the optical device, I drew down the speaking tube that connected directly to the torpedo room.

"Status!" I demanded.

A strong voice replied, the actual words distorted by a hollow bass echo. I was able to identify the speaker as Weber and heard him say, "Tubes one and two loaded, locked, and flooded. Fusing torpedo number three now."

"Very well, prepare the pair to fire tube one at my mark. Immediately load torpedo three; do not wait for my order," I said. These were unnecessary instructions for men who had worked this drill nearly one hundred times in the last two days.

"Aye, aye, sir."

I consulted my watch. "Fire tube one." There was a slight rumble beneath my feet. The large craft gave a tentative shudder as the torpedo left the boat.

"Torpedo away," came the hollow voice on the other end of the tube.

I fixed my eye to the prismatic telescope. I watched the trail of bubbles that revealed the course of the Whitehead torpedo, and I counted slowly in my head. When the fish was three-quarters of the way to its target, I ordered, "Fire tube two." The boat shuddered again and I returned to the eyepiece, grasping it with both hands and refocusing just in time to see the first dummy torpedo slam into the side of the abandoned ship. I determined that the second torpedo was on the correct path. I held my breath, counting, waiting for word from the torpedo room. I had reached twenty-five, and felt panic rising in my chest when I finally heard Petty Officer Weber's excited voice boom from the speaker. "Tube one loaded, locked, and flooded."

"Fire," I replied instantly, ignoring protocol, and the boat shuddered a third time. I steadied the scope and anxiously locked my eye on the trail of the torpedoes as the second one hit the side of the wooden-hulled wreck. The third torpedo had me nervous as it was coursing somewhat more to port than I intended, running several feet deeper than its fellows. I feared that it would pass under its target, although that would not be a catastrophe as it would still explode when it hit the sand bar that held the wreck fast. But the splash of an underwater explosion would not be as effective a demonstration as a solid hit blowing a hole through the hull. No, the direction of travel concerned me more with each heartbeat, as a complete miss could turn into disaster. I mentally willed the torpedo to correct its course and depth. The fish continued on, unswayed by my mental efforts, until it finally managed to catch the very back of the ship, running just shallow enough to blow a very satisfactory hole in the stern.

I allowed my chin to sink to my chest and let out a relieved sigh. The rest of the sub was dead quiet. Although we felt a gentle rumble at impact, I realized I was the only technical witness. I picked up the speaking tube. "Congratulations; three direct hits."

Undisciplined whoops bellowed from the forward section and I allowed myself a moment to share their enthusiasm. But that was the only respite I allowed before returning to the captain's chair and making mental notes about improvements to the system. First of all, the damn telescope needed handles of some sort. Gripping the eyepiece to my face was undignified at best, ineffective at worst.

I grasped the speaking tube, and bellowed, "Blow all ballast!" The boat rocked gently to starboard as port reacted slowly, but the boat righted itself and quietly broke the surface. I stood up, nodded in response to the congratulations of my officers, and walked to the ladder. I was buoyed by the stellar performance of my weapon's crew as I climbed up to the main hatch, undogged it, shoved it open, and clambered out onto the gently rocking deck of the conning tower. Even without MP Gestlehum's gunpowder, the target ship was in flames and slowly collapsing into the Thames. I looked behind myself and observed the crowd standing in silent awe, not knowing if they should cheer or be afraid.

I was deep in concentration when I was startled by a knock on my open door frame.

"Come in," I responded. My tongue was not paying attention and I fear the words sounded slurred, as if thick with sleep.

"Sorry to wake you, Commander Ian," Danjella said. Her voice was polite, but she had an angry fire in her eyes.

"I was not asleep," I replied.

"You were snoring." She waved her new stick in my direction, pointing it over my head.

"I do not snore." I noticed a quirk at the corner of her mouth and realized she was teasing me. The humor on her lips did not, however, diminish the blaze in her eyes.

I glanced at my open watch on the desk and realized that I had been 'contemplating' over an hour more than I thought. "May I help you?" I inquired, hoping that her fury was not directed at me.

Her brow creased and she allowed her whole being to project the rage inside.

"I have arranged a celebratory dinner at officer's mess, for officers and crew of the *Thunderbolt*."

"Yes, I'm looking forward to it."

Her eyes flashed. "I am excluded from it, and will not be allowed to dinner and celebration, unless I am properly escorted." Her lovely face twisted in scorn.

"Is that all? Have Nicola take you," I suggested.

"He not go; he's shy."

"Then, ask that stick guy."

"He knows nothing about submersibles," she snapped. She then continued after an awkward pause, "I want to be at dinner with someone I can talk to, intelligently." She placed two firm hands on her walking stick, leaned forward, and raised her chin. "You must take me."

I sat up straighter. "I would like that, but I . . . ."

"The dinner is at seven. You will meet me here at six." Her chin raised just a touch, as if daring me to protest.

I nodded in surrender and then noticed her gaze had shifted to my apparatus. Her eyes narrowed as she scrutinized the chip in the fingerplate.

"Already?" she sighed.

"It is just a—"

She quieted me with a raised hand. "Spare parts will not be enough; we make a spare. You wear one, we fix one." She rubbed her nose in contemplation. "Is strong, but not doable? Durable!" She smiled. "That is the word I meant. You meet me here, yes?" Without waiting for me to even nod, she swept out of my office.

I looked at my watch and decided that I was too tired to go anywhere, so I leaned back in my chair for more contemplation.

Chapter Twenty-four

Awkward would be the mildest way to describe how the evening started. I was only vaguely aware of how I ended up as Danjella's escort for the event. Since the Serbian lady was still staying with her minder at the Admiralty, transport was a secondary concern. Jenkins, having become restless with his role as patient, clattered around the flat, positively irate that I would not let him fetch a carriage from his brother-in-law and act as my coachman for the evening. I consoled him by allowing him to serve as my barber, shaving me quite close and trimming my hair unfashionably short so the stubbly patch the surgeon left did not stand out so much.

"Well then," he said a bit petulantly, "If yer will not be needin' my services, I'll be escorting the lovely Mrs. Livingstone to a temp'rance lecture."

I pulled my head away from his shears and stared at him. "Really?"

He nodded, but I sensed his heart wasn't in it. "Taking the pledge?"

He sighed and shook his head vehemently. "Lord love yer, no. But I'll sit through the thing to spend time with 'er."

I bit my lip to refrain from an ill-advised retort. Instead, I leaned back in the chair and allowed my valet to finish his work. Well-groomed and with my bowtie perfectly knotted, I hired a hackney for the night and set out for the Ironworks in the warm evening air.

Danjella arrived from her admiralty quarters with a respectably attired Miss Raymond, whose dark green dress with a compact bustle and high neckline made her look quite elegant. Danjella herself was dressed in the same maroon gown she wore to the theater, but she had covered the interesting décolletage with a gauzy shawl, and was still carrying her new walking stick. She breezed in, and simply waved for me to follow her. I soon found myself with her and Miss Raymond alone aboard the lift to the laboratory.

"I would like to replace that damaged plate before we go to dinner," she said, absently flicking a finger at my mechanical hand. "I do not want you looking broken."

"It's just a chip."

She silenced me with a glare and I meekly followed her out of the lift to her desk. She laid her walking stick among the tiny cogs, gears, and what appeared to be a miniature bicycle pump. Out of curiosity I picked up the item and looked at it.

"Part of my project for the Reilly Company. Do you realize this thing only pumps air when you push?" She mimed using the pump, "But not when you pull? Is that not a waste?"

I failed to see how we could do otherwise as you have to draw air into the cylinder before pressing it out, but I held my tongue. I put it down and picked up the extremely feminine cane, feeling it had as much heft as the previous one. "More lignum vitae?" I inquired, puzzled by the pale wood under several heavy coats of vanish.

"No, is finished oak, but is loaded." Without fanfare, Danjella adroitly pushed her bustle up so she could sit on the bench, then bade me bring my hand to her. I put down the stick and complied. She whipped out a jeweler's loupe, screwed it into her eye, then produced a tiny screwdriver. In less than a minute, she pried the damaged plate from a retaining bracket and replaced it with a new piece with a much smoother edge.

She patted my hand, her touch lingering for just a moment on the cool metal, "There, you look presentable." She turned and addressed Miss Raymond who was settling herself down at another desk. "Robin dear, will you be comfortable?"

The minder produced a thick book from her carrying bag and nodded.

"She's not coming with us?" I blurted, suddenly feeling exposed.

Danjella twisted her mouth sideways in an expression I could not read. "Unlike my other companion, Robin is loose with the . . ." she wiggled her fingers.

"Leash?" I offered.

Danjella's brow furrowed, and she seemed offended. "No, like range? Rainy? Some word like that for horses. You think I'm a dog?"

My mouth worked, but no words came out. I stopped trying and bowed my head to her. "I apologize. That was not my meaning."

Danjella nodded and regarded me with a tight smile. "I should not take offense. She trust me, and she even trust you." Her voice softened, "She thinks we would be more comfortable on our own."

I looked at the minder, and for a second, I thought she winked at me.

Without another word, Danjella briskly stood and moved towards the elevator, expecting me to follow. Once again I found myself alone with Danjella in that singular conveyance, so close to her I noticed a subtle fragrance, simultaneously spicy and floral. With the doors closed, Danjella looked back at the gate as if she could see the laboratory beyond. "I do wonder about the girl," she said. "When we talk alone, she has such a sharp mind. I suspect she is as much a secretary as I am."

The door opened on the ground floor, and we hurried to the hackney. The sun was a red ball hanging in a deep blue sky; a rare sunset in London. Steady winds in the afternoon had cleared out the factory smoke, leaving a freshness and clarity that brightened my mood.

When the two of us reached the officers' mess, we were directed to a banquet hall on the far side. Most of the ship's crew had already arrived. Our good seamen had already availed themselves of the potables provided for the dinner, and the wine and beer put them in good spirits. My lieutenants all seemed to be enjoying the event, except Lieutenant Graf. He was pacing with his hands clasped behind his back, as if he expected something to go wrong at any moment. I escorted Danjella to her seat and went to see what my lieutenant was fretting about.

"I do not like this familiarity," he said. His uniform was as crisp as ever, with a starched collar that forced him to keep his chin up, and a tightly knotted bow tie with ends equalized to within a one-sixteenth of an inch.

"Don't fret," I replied calmly. "It will be over soon and in less than twelve hours, you will be taking your crew out on the first river trial."

He pursed his lips and twitched his mustache. "If I can find enough of them sober."

"I'm sure the coxswain is keeping your men out of the punch bowl. They should sleep off a few beers and be bright-eyed in the morning." I changed my tack and attempted to be sociable. "Is your lovely wife in attendance?"

"I was unaware you'd met my wife," he said hotly, as if he were looking for some excuse to be offended.

"I haven't," I replied, flustered.

He stood straighter for a second, which I think was the closest he'd come to admitting he'd overreacted to something.

"Elsbeth is over there." He pointed his chin toward a very beautiful woman in a light blue gown.

"I should be introduced, don't you think?"

His lips twitched and he finally seemed to relax a bit, releasing his hands from behind his back. "This way."

As we were introduced, Elsbeth smiled at me in a truly friendly fashion, and was generally much more outgoing then her stiff and proper husband. I accepted her proffered hand. She wore very minimal amounts of rouge and powder and I observed the faint white scars along her temple line. I furrowed my brow and look sideways at Lieutenant Graf.

He stood stiffly and almost seemed to be preening. "He has noticed your scars, my dear."

She casually raised her left hand and used the middle finger to trace the longest of the three faint scars along her brow. "My fault, I fear. Sometimes when my arm gets tired, I drop my point, putting my opponent inside my guard."

"I was unaware women participated in the Mensur."

"Oh, yes," Elsbeth said. "The suffragettes don't seem to know what to make of us. Some days, they cheer because the men allow us to participate, and at other times they protest that we get injured. Anyway, it is how Henry and I met . . ."

Heinrich shuffled uneasily at the casual nickname.

"And it was love at first fight." Elsbeth pointed to the scar on her husband's brow.

Graf flushed a bit, making the scar stand out.

I was about to respond when a hush fell over the room, replaced by the gentle clink of a butter knife blade striking the rim of a crystal goblet. Captain Wilson had arrived, accompanied by Sir Hastings Reginald Yelverton. The captain's young aide, Robeson, was using the customary signal to announce them.

"If I may have your attention for a moment," Robeson said. Everyone turned their eyes to him and he bowed to Sir Hastings.

I nodded my apologies to Mrs. Graf and headed back toward my table. Lieutenant Bartley was keeping Danjella company in my absence and, as he spotted me, he rendered a casual salute, nodded to Danjella, and left for his own place.

"I will let you return to your festivities, in a moment," Sir Hastings said, in a reedy voice with only a small quiver of age. "I've just dropped by to congratulate all of you on a successful launch." Genteel applause interrupted him "And to deliver papers, to Captain Arthur Wilson. These orders establish him as commander of Her Majesty's Royal Navy submersible squadron. In addition to the two submersibles currently in service, he will be appointed a flagship destroyer, two more destroyers, and a supply ship which will serve as support and tenders for them."

More robust applause filled the hall.

"Additionally, Captain Wilson will be asked report to the Admiralty on Wednesday of this week to accept the promotion to admiral."

This time the applause was beyond robust. Many men and junior officers jumped to their feet in raucous approval. Hastings bowed to the assemblage, and said something I could not catch from my location. Hastings clapped Captain Wilson on the shoulder, shook hands with him, then retrieved a top hat from the table, and made a quick departure. I rushed up, along with the other junior officers to congratulate our new flag officer.

After that, I have to confess I do not remember much of the dinner. I shared a glass of wine with Miss Tesla and I recall we chatted most amicably. But the steward kept refilling my wineglass. After a toast to the queen, a toast to Captain Wilson's upcoming promotion, a toast to the successful launch, a toast to the upcoming trials, and a toast to my health, I was quite well toasted. Additionally, each of my junior officers presented me with a cup of punch, even Lieutenant Graf unbent enough for tradition, and I drank of mouthful with each for the sake of fellowship.

The week had been long and I had been unable to make up much sleep before the dinner party. I found my head nodding over dessert. I was suddenly aware Danjella had a hand on my shoulder shaking me. I sat up quickly; hoping no one else noticed I had fallen into a doze.

"I think, Ian," Danjella said softly, "we should make our departure and let the others have their fun."

I nodded blearily and stood up. She joined me and placed a steadying hand on the inside of my elbow, still making it appear as if I were escorting her. I was too muzzy at the time to marvel at how natural her hand felt on my arm. That hand, strengthened by hours of work with welder and springs, firmly directed me toward the door of the banquet hall. She grabbed my hat from the rack by the entrance, shoved it under my arm, and led me out toward the warm night air. A crisply starched steward intercepted us and advised us that the carriages had been removed around to the other side of the building. He led us across to a short hallway and pointed for us to cross to the open parlor rather than go outside.

We were almost to the door when a rasping voice called out, "Good God man, have you no shame? Staggering drunk through the officers' mess with some strumpet to hold you steady?"

I shook Danjella's hand from my elbow. An unaccustomed rage burned in my breast and I turned to face Lieutenant Gaither. He was staring at me with an outraged twist to his mouth, his rail thin body taut as a hawser under load.

Captain Clarke sat in a wingback chair a few feet away and took in the scene.

I took a belligerent step toward Gaither, the wine in my head stoking the fire that burned in my chest.

Danjella laid a restraining hand on my left shoulder, her grip like iron. I noticed she also laid her walking stick casually on her other shoulder. "If you'll excuse us, Commander Rollins is feeling ill. We should be going." She used her grip on my shoulder to turn me back around. Turning made the ground sway beneath my feet. Suddenly a strong hand on my other arm helped me settle my stance.

"I would like to apologize," Captain Clarke said, and then changed his tone at my astonished glance. "Not to you, stupid." He turned back to Danjella. "This lady is not responsible for your depravity, and it is impolite of my colleague to address her with less than respect." He turned a withering eye on Gaither, who just stood there. Clarke turned his attention back to Danjella. "Please, allow me to assist him into a carriage before he pukes himself."

Clarke dragged me through the parlor and out the door; Danjella acted as a guide to keep me from colliding with the furniture. We arrived at our hired carriage, and they loaded me into the rear of the hackney. Everything still swayed as I collapsed on the seat.

Captain Clarke said in a cool aristocratic tone, "I trust he keeps a manservant who can drag him into his quarters?"

"I still have Jenkins," I declared.

"I am concerned," Danjella replied. "His valet has . . . taken ill." Her eyes darted to the left and right as she tried to find a way to explain herself. Abruptly, it dawned on me that she was attempting to convince Clarke to see me home. I raised my head to voice a protest, but vertigo overcame me and I fell back on the seat with a groan.

Danjella peered at me with concern. "Good captain, I am under a curfew and must meet my chaperone at the Ironworks."

"Your chaperone is at the Ironworks?" Clarke frowned in confusion, his face grim.

"I am employed there." Danjella touched him lightly on the shoulder and looked at him with her big brown eyes and a sad smile. "May I prevene?" She shook her head, her faced pinched in concentration. I tried to send her the word by thought and she seemed to get it, her head snapped up. "No, prevent? No, prevail! That is word I want. May I *prevail* upon you to escort him safely home?"

He glared at me, sighed, and nodded at Danjella. "For such a gracious request, I will deliver him."

Again I tried to protest, but any movement made me dizzy— unnaturally dizzy. I tried to recall just how much I had to drink. My head was accustomed to hard liquor and my stomach was full of good food. Even with all the refills of my wine glass, I could not have consumed more than three full glasses of wine. It dawned on me just how unnatural a condition I was in. Once again, I opened my mouth to say something, but only a groan came out.

"One minute, please," the captain said, and strode back to the club.

Danjella climbed into the carriage and laid a cool hand upon my cheek.

"Ian, you look so dreadful," she said, her eyes warm with concern.

I fought to respond, to tell her my suspicions, but once again I barely managed a moan.

She touched my brow with the back of her hand. "Relax; rest now. I fear for your head in the morning."

The carriage jerked as Clarke entered wearing his cocked hat. "I told the driver we need to deliver you to the ironworks, is that correct?" he asked, still dubious.

Danjella moved from me and sat straighter. "Yes, that is good; my chaperone will meet me there."

Clarke frowned at the odd circumstance, but held his tongue.

I struggled to sit up, but this time the vertigo was even stronger, and the world went black.

"Get up, you drunken sod. I'm not going to carry your sorry arse up to your flat."

I understood the individual words, but the context escaped me. Aggressive hands shook me until my teeth rattled; bringing me to consciousness, if not comprehension. Somehow I thought myself back at university, wrapped in the golden glow of post-game revelry; tired, sore, and drunk after a victory. But that feeling quickly drained as bits of memory fell into place, forming at best a half-completed puzzle.

"Come on, I see you're awake," said a familiar, but harsh, voice. Strong hands yanked me from the carriage by my lapels. On the sidewalk, my companion released his grip and I staggered a few steps, the clear night air clearing a part of my brain. Then I vomited.

I bent over as my stomach purged itself. I stood there gasping for breath between heaves. My mind cleared.

"I'm not drunk," I declared, although I was uncertain of how my protest sounded to Clarke.

I heaved again, then stood and took deep, cleansing breaths, each lungful serving to clear my head. "I'm not drunk," I said again, this time my mouth formed the words correctly. "I've been poisoned."

Clarke stepped to me, grabbed my lapels and pulled me to him.

"You've been poisoned, I grant, but by overindulgence. You disgrace us all. Get up to your quarters and sleep it off."

"We'll take it from 'ere guv'ner," an Irish voice said from behind the captain.

Still holding on to me, Clarke stepped out of the way to reveal three men brandishing cudgels. One young thug with a broken nose said, "'ey, there was 'sposed to only be one uf dem."

"So?" retorted an older tough. He wore a billycock hat, a sort of shallow bowler with a broader brim. "There's three of us."

Clarke peered at the trio. "What is your business with this man?"

"Bugger off," Billycock jerked his thumb at the carriage. Clarke puffed up.

The hackney driver, having been paid in advance, did not want any part of what was about to transpire. He cracked his reins and drove off.

The man raised his cudgel and waved it at the captain. "I means business boyo. Bugger off."

I took a deep breath and tried to stand up straight, "They're working for a German spy." I said.

Clarke looked at me, then at the men, his face distorted into a disbelieving frown.

"This sod owes us money." The lead tough spat back at me.

Clarke sighed in disgust and pushed me away with a flick of his wrist. "Oh, good God, sir."

I stumbled and nearly fell to my knees. "No, they're working for a German spy."

Clarke grunted in revulsion, and slapped his hands together as if he were dusting them off. "Right then, you boys deal with him."

"Dammit, Clarke!" I shouted. "These men work for the man who blew up your ship!"

That got through to him. With fierce eyes he glared at billycock, then back at me, clearly weighing my trustworthiness. His mouth formed a grim line. After an interminable pause he spoke slowly. "On second thought, I have some questions for this man. So, you should bugger off."

Clarke assumed a pugilist's stance; which should have looked threatening, but with his chiseled features and a pose that looked like an engraving out of the Marquis of Queensbury manual, he looked unreal, almost comical.

Billycock snorted, "Oh, I'm scared now." He shot a humorous glance to each of his fellows. "Big bad sailor may hit me. Well come on, mate."

He charged at the captain, swinging his cudgel in a slow feint to the head. When the captain moved his arm to block the blow, his assailant jerked the strike down to the knee; a knee which was not there. Clarke anticipated the attack and stepped into the man's advance and they collided. Clarke held his ground while the other man stumbled back half a step. From this vantage, Clarke had his hands back in the pugilist pose and delivered a lightning jab to his opponent's jaw, which sent his cheap hat sailing.

I remembered the captain's nickname was "Jab." "Oh, *that's were that comes from.*" I charged one of the other men. The last one, the young man with the broken nose, just stood there.

Charged may be a bit strong of a term, but I stumbled purposefully toward him. My adversary seemed caught off-guard, but before I could close the gap, he swung his cudgel for my head. I easily blocked the shot with my left hand, flinching as I heard a crunching sound. We were face to face, and in desperation, I smashed my forehead into his nose. Blood flowed freely as he staggered back, and I brought my knee up between his legs. His eyes clenched as he bent over, blinded by the pain. I hit him with a right cross that whipped his head to the side. He staggered again and hit the gravel. I looked back to see how Clarke was faring. He stood alone holding Billycock's cudgel. While I gasped for breath, I noticed the three of us were alone, the other men had fled. My foe recovered his footing. If he moved toward me my next stratagem would be to throw up on him. Fortunately, he turned away and took off at a sprint. I promptly heaved, but nothing came out.

"Good gad, man," Clarke scolded me. "Kicking him in the jubilees? There are rules, sir."

I gasped for breath as the vertigo came back, and I collapsed to the sidewalk.

I woke lying on cushions with a cool rag over my face.

"Captain, sir," I heard Jenkins's voice from far away. "I think 'e's comin' round. This time for certain, he is."

I pulled the cloth from my eyes and tried to sit, but a firm hand on my chest pushed me down. "Now, you just lie quiet, sir," Jenkins said.

"Jenkins, let me up." I sat up without opposition.

I was in my own sitting room on a couch. Captain Clarke sat at my table before a hot cup of tea, a plate of bread, cheese, and a few biscuits.

"Your landlady is quite generous," Clarke said as he politely nibbled at a bit of cheese.

"More tea, captain?" Jenkins inquired.

"Yes, please, and bring a cup for Commander Rollins." He pursed his lips and considered me carefully, "Maybe something stronger."

"Tea will be fine." I buried my face in my hands and became aware of the taste in my mouth. "In fact, tea would be a blessing."

"Your valet seems to agree that you were poisoned," Clarke said, holding his cup out as Jenkins refilled it from the pot.

"Chloral hydrate, from the look of it," Jenkins added. "The admiral got dosed with that in Singapore. Given the right dose, you just sleeps it off. Too much and there is a lot to clean up."

"He does make a good case," the captain admitted. "I have to agree when he says you are enough of a drunkard you couldn't have been so sick so early."

I looked up and noticed it was quite dark. "What time is it?" I asked, then remembered the blows to my hand. I examined it for damage, noting a dent and a crack in the plating at the base of the thumb.

The captain regarded his watch. "Near four bells," he replied, snapped his watch shut and glared at me. "Now what about German spies and my ship?"

I accepted tea, and a plate of bread and cheese from Jenkins.

"I am violating the official secrets act telling you, but the Admiralty determined someone on board the *Indomitable* was a saboteur. You are still beached because everyone is a suspect."

He bristled. "Everyone but you."

"I was cleared because investigators were able to clearly determine my whereabouts at all times. I was never in a position to cause the fire."

He chewed on that for a moment.

"Since then, the spy's men have attacked me several times."

Clarke snorted. "You make it sound as if it is all about you."

My head jerked up as a terrible thought dawned on me. I put the heel of my right hand to my forehead, trying to rub away the pain behind my eyes. "Of course—it is all about me, that right bastard Graf. He as much as said so." I shook my head in frustration. "They're not trying to sabotage the program, or slow it down, they want to control it!"

"What are you talking about?

"The submersible," I said as comprehension dawned. "They got rid of Waite, and Graf was sure he would be the commander, and have all of the boat's secrets. Hell, he could sail the damn thing right out of the harbor. Damn, he still could." I scrambled to my feet, grateful that the floor stayed still. "I have to get back to the Ironworks."

"Now?" Jenkins and Clarke said almost in unison.

"Graf is to take the *Thunderbolt* out on a simple trial this morning, in about four hours, and he poisoned me to keep me out of the way."

Chapter Twenty-five

I silently vowed to never again offer a London cabbie a crown to go as fast as he can. He can go much faster than I want.

After realizing the poisoner's intent, I paused just long enough to leave the soiled dress coat with Jenkins and grab my work a day. Captain Clarke followed me out into the pre-dawn darkness.

"Where do you think you're going?" Clarke demanded, keeping at my heels.

"The Ironworks." I lengthened my stride.

"You intend to walk?"

"If I have to," I said, "but I think we should find a cab near Regent's Park, even at this time of night."

"If we do, the driver will be drunk."

It was well past the hour when they extinguished the lamps, and we had to pick our way along the black streets. The mild weather was holding, but the air was heavy, and unseasonably humid—enough that sweat dampened my collar by the time we reached Park Square. We discovered a hansom cab parked by a dark lamp. I ran to the rear and smacked my flat metal palm on the side of the driver's bench. "You sir," I yelled with as much wind as I had left. "Are you for hire?"

The driver visibly started, then peered through the gloom trying to identify who accosted him. "Who are you?" he demanded, as his breath enveloped me in a gin haze.

"Are you for hire?" I repeated.

The man shook himself awake. "That I am, sir." Despite the air of gin, his words were coming sharp and clear. It seemed he may have had just enough to ward off a chill.

"Good, then I'll give you a crown added to your fare if you get us to the Thames Ironworks and Shipyard at Leamouth as fast as you can."

A wicked gleam appeared in the cabman's eye. "Done sir, just mind yer step."

We maneuvered into the front of the hansom. The driver cracked a whip over our heads and we were off. Minutes, later we were flying down the cobbles and I gripped the rail in front of me with both hands, one white in the knuckles, while I fought the impulse to squeeze the metal one tighter for fear of crushing the wooden bar. The dent by my thumb had damaged a control link, and the digit tried to tighten three clicks when I intended one.

I was pleased to note that Captain Clarke also had a death grip on the wooden bar, although his features, under his cocked hat, were set in stoic lines that revealed nothing. It seemed the lurching ride went on for hours, but in fact, the reckless cab driver had us to the main gate in less than twenty minutes. Once I extracted myself, I dashed for the entrance with my former commander on my heels. I passed through without stopping, ignoring the marine guard's salute, although Captain Clarke paused long enough to return the gesture. I fully expected a lecture about *standards* later.

I was shocked to find Petty Officer Grant and most of the men selected for Graf's crew milling about the wharf, and further shocked to see no trace of the *Thunderbolt*.

At my approach, the coxswain called the men to attention, starting to salute.

"Where the hell is the damn boat?" I blurted out, waving away his formality.

"The boat, sir?" Grant replied. He jerked his thumb at the river. "Out for trial, just like you and Captain Wilson ordered."

"No one ordered such a thing," I snapped. "Not at this hour."

Grant cocked his head to one side, and shook it. "Beggin' yer pardon, sir, but you was a mite unsteady last night so's you may not remember . . ."

"I was not drunk, I was poisoned," I snapped. I raced to gaze at the empty pier. "Graf is stealing the boat."

The petty officers mouth worked, but nothing came out. "Are ye' certain of that?" he finally managed.

"Very."

The petty officer looked to Captain Clarke for some sign of confirmation, or an indication that I had not slipped into madness. That worthy nodded his agreement.

Grant said, "Lieutenant Bartley told us, that Graf said you and he met with Captain Wilson and decided since we could only use the river until noon, that we was 'sposed to double up on trials."

My eyes narrowed. "Where's Bartley?" I demanded, suspicious of even him at that moment.

I'd never seen Grant shaken before, but now he seemed very uncertain about everything as he shuffled his feet before responding. "Graf said he wanted a skeleton crew, for a short cruise. Bartley's with him."

Of course, I thought, *easier to control a few men when they realized what was happening.*

"Bartley was in a bit of a tizzy, if you don't mind me sayin' so. He said Graf didn't want him along, but that he gave in when Bartley pressed the matter."

I could imagine that discussion.

"He's also got Smith, Jonas, and young Bell with him, sir." He grimaced. "If we've been 'ad, sir then I suppose you don't know about the other matter."

"What other matter?" I demanded. "Spit it out."

"They said you arranged it, but had to pretend you didn't know about it."

His tone set off alarm bells in my brain. "About what?"

"The woman, sir, Miss Tesla, they are supposed to give her a ride in the boat, on the quiet, sir." He seemed mortified at the admission. "They said it was yer doin'"

I fought the urge to scream at my Petty Officer, but I knew he was only guilty of following orders. Orders that might otherwise have been suspect were allowed to pass in the recent atmosphere of rushed schedules and irregular proceedings. "How long have they been gone?"

"Not more'n a quarter hour, sir."

I clenched my jaw and looked out over the water. "Send a signal to every boat on the river to stop the submersible, by any means possible."

"You don't mean to sink her?" he replied, aghast.

I shook my head. "I don't mean to, but it's worth my life, and yours, to keep that weapon from the enemy." But a small voice inside my head asked, *Is it worth Danjella's?*

I shook the thought away. "Is there anything here with a hot boiler?"

"No, nothin' I knows of. But there is one other thing, about the signal to the other ships—in the dark, I don't think anyone'll see the boat. It submerged, sir."

I sighed and fought the urge to tear what was left of my hair out, "Submerged? You didn't think it odd? The orders have been posted for days for surface trials."

"I knows sir, but, they was already a couple of hundred yards from the dock and I thought they was taking the opportunity to show Miss Tesla —"

"Never mind," I interrupted, accepting that the fault lay in a chain of command that had been acting so erratic that good sailors had no choice but to do as they were told, and trust their leaders.

"Send the signal anyway." I sighed fatalistically as I peered out into the black river.

While he gathered runners, I stood there at the edge of the pier, my workaday uniform unbuttoned. I stared at the smooth surface and tried to divine the enemy's actions. I concentrated on the pewter grey of a forthcoming sunrise, but neither river or sky surrendered a clue. If they ran submerged and gained access out to the North Sea, there was no way to stop them, but until they reached the depth of open water, the sub would have to travel slowly. The south channel of the Thames was deep enough, but they would need to steer clear of sand bars in the turns, especially the sharp bend just before the narrow part at Gravesend. But even if I had a boat ready to go, how could I stop them? I thought for a moment about chasing them with a steam launch and when I caught up, taking a big mallet and smashing the top of the prismatic telescope. An amusing thought, but impractical on so many levels.

Sapient thought is a very mysterious process. Sometimes it seems as if a part of my brain has already made decisions, solved problems, developed answers, and is just waiting for the rest of my mind to ask the right question. Everything I needed to know came to me in one clear moment. I had a boat, ready to go. Smaller, faster, and just like that, I had a plan.

"Weber, you and Frank Bell get down to the *Holland Ram*." I turned to Grant. "Who is your fastest runner?"

"I just sent him off to send the signal."

"Fair enough, second fastest? Whoever that is, just send him to the equipment lockers, fetch me a diving helmet with a tank, and get it down to the *Ram*."

"It won't fit in the hatch."

"Doesn't have to. Tell him to get some rope to secure it to the lift bolts behind the conning tower."

"What are yer goin' to do?"

"Lead a mutiny," I called out as I sprinted to the HMS *Holland Ram*.

I consulted my watch; ten minutes had passed before we were aboard the *Ram* with the power up. The entire boat was bobbing vigorously from the rapid movements of the crew and the two men affixing the diving apparatus to the outside. One of them knocked a signal on a view port. Without waiting for them to clear, I gave orders to move the sub, leaving the men on the outside to scramble off the conning tower, barely catching the gangway before it fell into the water. I ignored their plight and turned the *Ram* out to the river.

As soon as I dared, we were moving at full speed, with the boat as deep as I could take it and still see out the view port. We did not have time for dead reckoning.

"Weber, how fast do you think we can make Gravesend?" The controls felt good in my hands and the firm grip with my left gave me much better handling that I'd expected, even without my brass adapter.

His brow creased in concentration. "Three quarters of an hour, if we don't slow down."

I considered this information, uncertain if it would be fast enough to overtake the *Thunderbolt* and beat it to its principal constraint.

"Can we go faster?" I asked.

Weber looked the whining electric motor, wiped sweat from his eyes and shook his head, "The engine is at maximum capacity now."

I raised an eyebrow. "Is it?"

He looked back at me and his mouth turned up. "Well," he conceded, "not the real maximum, if you know what I mean. It's regulated."

"Regulated, for the most efficient and safest operating parameters?" He bit his lower lip. "That it be, sir."

"I would suspect that a clever new petty officer would know how to goose a few more horsepower out of it." I fixed him with my eye.

He scratched his head, "I suppose I could, but it will use more of the battery, and well, sir, frankly it could burn the thing out."

"I'm willing to wager neither will happen before we get past the sharpest bend in the river."

"Aye sir," he agreed reluctantly.

"Make it so."

Weber quickly undid a cover plate to his right and loosed the tools clipped to the backside. He immediately went to work on the wires inside with a screwdriver and a pair of pliers. A blue spark lit the interior of the craft and Weber cursed, waving burned fingers. "Sorry, sir,"

Even as the words of apology left his lips, the craft surged forward. "Good work," I called out.

We continued in silence for twenty minutes as I scanned the water through the view port, straining my eye for a glimpse of the prismatic telescope sticking out above the waves. I saw something odd just ahead and it took several seconds for me to understand its significance. Two small silver waves glinting in water, creating a V shape pointing away from us. I still could not see the matte black telescope against the steel grey of the dawn sky, but the wake was giving away the location. They were staying right in the middle of the deepest part of the south channel. As we edged closer I could finally make out the vertical height of the telescope itself, sticking a good ten feet above the water.

Graf wasn't being nearly as reckless as I imagined, running only ten feet below the surface, but as far as most boats were concerned, he might as well have been a hundred feet down since there was no realistic way of engaging the craft.

By my reckoning, he was making five knots, a respectable showing, and at the very upper limit of what I thought my plan could deal with. I had feared he might push a little harder, but I also fervently hoped he would slow down at the treacherous bend in the river.

Using the diving planes, I took the *Ram* deeper so that we were fully submerged and I could take advantage of the full capability of the overlarge propeller. If I could have, I would have crossed both sets of my fingers, hoping that Graf had his eye affixed to the prismatic telescope and would not catch a glimpse of us through the observation ports. As black as the river water was, I doubted he could see the smaller vessel's golden glimmer rushing by. Even so, I passed to port giving him a wide berth. When I determined I'd gone far enough, I brought the *Ram* back to awash position. I was leaning forward as if my posture could push it faster.

Ten more minutes found me well ahead, and I maneuvered around the sharp bend just before Gray's Beach. From there it was another five minutes until I arrived at the narrowest part of the river, just before Gravesend, where the Thames was a mere 600 yards wide and I positioned the *Ram* in the center of the south channel. At this point, the north channel was fouled by shifting sandbars, small scrubby islands, as well as treacherous rocks. I calculated that Graf would want to keep the most water beneath him so he would stick as close as possible to the very center of the deep water channel.

I brought the boat fully to the surface, cracked the hatch, and clambered out onto the gently swaying conning tower.

"Weber," I called down into the boat as I used my mechanical hand to make short work of the ropes securing the diving gear. "I want you to open the ballast tanks and take the *Ram* deep; I don't want anyone to see her. Raise her in half an hour. I don't suppose you can drive this thing?"

"Aye, sir," he said. "I've puttered around on the surface a time or two. What are you going to do?"

I strapped the awkward compressed air cylinder to my back. "I'm going to try for the lockout chamber on the *Thunderbolt*."

Weber's eyes bugged out. "Sir, no one in their right mind would try that with the boat moving. You pointed out yourself that it was too close to the propellers."

I glared at him for his choice of phrase. "Petty Officer Weber," I said, my voice firm, "never doubt that I am in my right mind, and never doubt my determination."

"Aye, sir."

I grabbed the helmet by the corslet, turned my head to work my cranium through the narrow opening, and settled my chin into the familiar pad. The sounds echoing through the hollow metal shell made it impossible for me to hear anymore. I gave Weber a "thumbs-up" sign, which he returned tentatively. I eased myself over the side and swam out from the boat. I was near certain about my calculation of the position, but had failed to allow for the current, which was stronger here. But I could use that to my advantage. A field of bubbles surrounded the *Ram* as air vented from the ballast tanks, and the reliable craft slid quietly under the waves, leaving me alone.

I cracked the air valve and allowed my body to drift with the current, conserving my energy for later, just kicking my legs enough to stay somewhat near the center of the channel and bob up out of the water to seek out my objective. I pictured the cross section of the *Thunderbolt*, twenty feet wide–not an impossible target. I should have a few minutes after I spotted the telescope to adjust my location and wait for her.

Another miscalculation, as it turned out. I did not have near as much time as I assumed to alter my position. Without seeing the silver sheen of the wake behind the upright shaft, I almost missed seeing the thing approach at all, so that out of nowhere the black prismatic telescope loomed over me, a little bit more to the north than I'd hoped. I kicked as hard as I could and stroked awkwardly around the unwieldy corslet.

The Thunderbolt Affair

Fortune did shine on me though, as the current lessened our relative speeds. I closed in on the starboard side and dropped below the water, but not far enough. My body's buoyancy, together with the air in the helmet, kept me from dropping more than a fathom below the surface. I sucked in a deep breath, intentionally dumped some air, and waved my arms to propel myself deeper.

Bright light gleamed through the viewing ports, they had the internal lights at the highest setting, which should make the ports on their side seem like mirrors, or at least I hoped so. This pale illumination revealed the railing atop the conning tower gliding toward me at four knots. I braced myself as if preparing for a flying tackle and allowed the bar to catch me full in the ribcage. The air exploded from my chest, but I managed to wrap my arms around the bronze railing. I struggled to keep the helmet upright and filling with air. As the water retreated from my face, I gasped to refill my lungs. Now that I caught a submersible, I realized I wasn't exactly sure what I was going to do with it.

I pushed uncertainty from my mind and I inched myself along the rail where I encountered a new setback. I was beginning to depend upon my new hand, but as I moved along, the damage to the thumb became more apparent and I could not adequately control my grip. I settled for leaving the thumb sticking out, locking the fingers in a loose curve that I used much like my hook. I pulled myself along to the stern of the conning tower using my right hand to slide along the rail.

At the teardrop point, I locked my legs around the rail, deliberately dumped all the air from my helmet and bent over, near upside down to grasp the ladder-like handholds positioned down the side of the boat. Soon, my lungs were burning from the effort as I clawed at a rung, finally catching firm enough to let go of the rail with my legs and slide them down to return me to an upright posture. I felt a twinge of panic counting the seconds until my helmet refilled with air. When my face was finally clear I took in great panting breathes, but that wasn't enough to slow my heart.

My knees shook in the cold water, leaving me barely able to move my foot down to the next rung. An unbidden thought entered my mind: I had already passed the point of no return. If I could not reach the lockout chamber, or if the crew had the wherewithal to secure it, then I was stuck with no way to let go of the craft without being drawn into the twin bronze propellers.

Gritting my teeth, I forced the fear somewhere down deep and continued to descend the rungs, mindful of the boat's moderate wake that would still sweep me off the side if I made a misstep. One foot, one hand at a time, I crept down the hull until I reached my goal across from the lockout chamber hatch, then nearly banged my head against the hull in frustration. Despite my hours studying plans, walking over every inch of the boat, my memory had played me false. I thought the chamber to be four feet from the rungs, but even in the faint light filtering from the surface, I could plainly see that it was closer to seven.

Geoffrey Mandragora

Through the thick glass of my helmet, I studied the hatchway, trying to spot any more details that had slipped my mind, this time looking for specifics that might aid me. The watertight door was the same round, two and a half feet in diameter as all the others, hinged at the top with grab bars to either side and below to assist divers. The handrails were each much longer than the rungs I clung to, but they did not stick out any more from the ship, giving me scant inches to work with.

My only option was not one I cared for and my legs nearly rebelled at my actions, shaking so violently it was challenging to bring them up. Once again, I dumped the air from my helmet, held my body parallel to the length of the boat, my faceplate flat against the hull, and let go of the rungs.

The wake carried me along the side of the boat as my legs drifted away from the hull, but I managed to keep both hands sliding along the cold gleaming surface. The first handrail caught me firmly in the gut, skimmed up my chest, and hit the bottom edge of my corslet with a heavy clang that jerked the helmet up against my lower jaw. Only the leather pad kept me from being knocked out. My fingers scrambled for the rail, but could not win purchase as I swept across the hatch, my legs feeling the prop wash drawing me away. My impact slowed me down enough to grasp the hatch exterior locking wheel with my right hand. I hurriedly snagged the left to the support bracket, pushed my head back upright, and refilled my helmet, the oil-tinged air tasting sweet to my desperate lungs.

I caught my breath, fervently wishing to just rest for a while, but I was diving without a chronometer, and had no idea how much air remained. So, I took one more deep breath, unhooked my left hand from the locking mechanism, and resettled it on the aft handrail, carefully locking down the problematic thumb for a firm grip. I checked the sight glass, relieved to see the chamber was in its default position, flooded, so I tried the wheel, spinning it with my right, and it moved easily.

Unlike all the other hatches, the hinge at the top of this one contained a powerful spring to counter the weight of the door, so when the wheel stopped turning, I gripped the handle at the bottom and was able to lift the ungainly thing up, slowly moving it through the resisting water. Every muscle in my body pressed against the current as I raised it enough to slide into the chamber, then pulled it shut behind me.

I still wasn't safe. An alert man in the engine room might hear me pressurize the chamber and stop it, and I would be caught in the flooded chamber, waiting for my air to run out. I spun the wheel to fill the space with compressed air, relieved when nothing interfered with the process. Finally the water receded past the safety level. I wrenched off my helmet, took great gulps of metallic air laced with the volatile fumes of engine oil, pulled open the inner door and ducked down through the tiny aperture to board the wayward submersible.

I was standing in an instinctive crouch, aware that there was almost a foot of space between my cranium and the deckhead above, but still feeling cramped. Before me was a three-foot-wide passage; to my left was the huge bulk of the starboard electric motor, to my right the bank of ceramic batteries that drove it, and six feet ahead was the intersection of the narrow central corridor. To the left, it led between the engines to the power controls, then the differential gear levers and the great gears themselves, terminating at the rudder control station. A right turn would lead me between banks of batteries to a watertight door opening to the electrolyte storage and charging station.

Trying to stay quiet, although I doubt I could be heard over the whine of the engines and pulsating whir of the gears, I slipped up to the corridor and looked left. One man was in there, laboring away at the rudder wheel as he pressed the speaking tube to his ear, listening to commands from the bridge.

"Smith!" I yelled and he turned to regard me, visibly shocked by my presence.

"Put down the tube," I commanded. "Release the rudder and help me stop this boat."

"And why would I be doin' that?' he replied, his eyes sincerely puzzled. He released the control wheel and walked toward me.

"Because Lieutenant Graf is stealing this boat," I said.

He nodded as he approached. "Yeah," he said slowly. "That's about the right of it." The former fleet champion raised his hands in a boxing pose, similar to the one Captain Clarke had struck earlier, but with his huge scarred fists, he looked far more menacing.

I had neither the energy nor the aptitude for a prizefight, so I launched myself at his knees in the most illegal flying tackle I'd ever attempted. Unprepared, he went down hard, but immediately kicked himself free of my grasp. His boot caught me first in the elbow, and then in the face as I jerked my head away. I clawed at his sailor's striped jersey with my metal fingers, but the thing simply ripped away, hanging in a great flap to reveal a schooner tattooed across his chest. As I fumbled to my feet, he scuttled back far enough to regain his feet even before I did.

"Why are you doing this?" I demanded.

"They don't pay a sailor shite," he retorted over the engine whine.

"But think of your country!"

For an answer, he spat on the deck. "'Sides the lieutenant says we be doin' the country a service, gettin' rid of this 'ere white elephant."

I brandished my mechanical hand at him, trying to imply that it was an effective weapon. He responded by stepping farther back, and before I could react, yanked the quick release on the metal shroud covering the differential gear.

I approached him and he threw the cover at me. The large piece of light gauge metal made a poor projectile and I easily batted it way, but it had served its purpose. It delayed me long enough for Smith to reach his objective, the gear spanner stored under the shroud, a very serviceable weapon made of carbon steel and three feet long. He held the thing in both hands as he charged at me, and I ran.

Well, as far as one could run in a submersible engine room.

I reached the shroud plate, picked it up, and clumsily threw it back at him, making it his turn to bat away the ineffective projectile using the spanner. I exploited the split second diversion to charge back at him. I grasped for the tool, and managed to clutch the steel bar with my right hand. I swung an awkward roundhouse punch with my steel hand. He dodged the ineffectual blow, effortlessly jerked the spanner back from me, and swung it at my head. I ducked, too slow to avoid all contact, but he only managed the barest graze along the side of my head. The blow still made me see flashing lights and put me on the ground. Smith failed to check his swing, however, and the tool smashed into the electric motor control box. A blue spark flashed, sending Smith dancing backwards, stunned.

Although he had been hit by a powerful shock, the direct current did not electrocute him, but burned his hand. The sight of the charred blisters enraged him and he flew at me. I crouched, raised my hands as if in fear, then at the last second, dropped them, turned my shoulder and leaned into a solid body block. He grunted in surprise and fell back.

Unwilling to give up the initiative, I followed him, intending another tackle, but he brushed me aside with a bellow of rage and a careless clout to the side of my head that sent me sprawling to the steel deck. The fight was taking its toll on him as well; he braced his arm on an overhead pipe and leaned his head on it to catch his breath. I tried to get to my feet, but my legs were like jelly and I found myself too unsteady to rise.

Smith recovered first, and balled his blistered hands into meaty fists. He turned toward me as if intending to use the damaged appendages to beat me into bloody broken pieces. He was unaware that the torn flap of his shirt fell into the differential gear he'd exposed. I watched in horrified fascination as the cloth was pulled into the giant meshed cogs.

His first inkling was a gentle tug and tearing sounds as the cotton jersey continued to rip up to the shoulder seam, but the seam held. Suddenly, the pugilist was dragged into the huge gear, his arm crushed in a second. His screams merged with the high-pitched whine of the electric motor as it revved up, overheating, trying to force the jammed gears.

I forced myself up and over to the gear lever, squeezed the locking handle, and shifted it to neutral. My intention was to separate the gears, and his mangled arm. But instead, opening the gap gave the drive side enough room to drag his torso into the machinery. He screamed one more time before his head was jerked through with a sickening crunch. His legs twitched once and went slack. The room filled with the stink of burnt copper as his blood boiled against the overheated gears.

The engine screeched and began to smoke. I hustled to the red power lever and threw it all the way to "off." The submersible was already slewing to one side, so I grabbed the other gear lever, unlocked it, and made it neutral. I shut down the power on the other side, as well.

I had control, but decided to take one more step for good measure. It was just a few steps to the twin battery banks where I opened up the maintenance box and threw the double blade emergency de-energizing switch. To de-energize the batteries under normal conditions, we would pump the electrolyte back to the charging and storage room, but in an emergency this switch shunted the power directly to the outer hull and the highly conductive plating, which in turn attempted to charge the seawater, draining the battery banks in minutes. The only effect it had outside was a stream of tiny bubbles along the hull. The water grounded the electricity so effectively that a person could be gripping the hull with bare hands and not even notice the operation.

Having finished one objective, stopping the boat, I collapsed on the cold steel deck and caught my breath. The terror of the moment was passing. So many parts of my body registered pain that I wanted to scream; strands of molten iron ran across my back to coalesce in my left arm until all I could do was drop my head into my arms, hold back sobs, and catch my breath.

"What sort of shite is goin' on down 'ere!" An angry voice rang out.

Chapter Twenty-six

I lifted my head to see Jonas clambering through the watertight door from the charging room. Upon seeing me, he froze in shock.

"Beggin' yer pardon sir. What da 'ell are you doing here?"

I sighed. My original plan assumed the crewmen were dupes, and I would lead them against Graf, but now I didn't know what to do. I was in no shape to fight Jonas, let alone Young Bell who followed him in.

"Where did you come from?" I demanded, while gathering what was left of my strength.

"Forward planes," Jonas replied, gesturing to indicate both men. "We was ordered to see what was going on when the motors went haywire."

"Who else is on board?"

The men looked at each other, "Just the lieutenants, Graf and Barkley, Smith . . ." Jonas paused as he finally noticed the legs hanging out of the gears. He crossed himself. I knew Bell to be a Methodist, but he crossed himself, as well.

The lights flickered as the batteries drained down to the last few minutes of charge.

"The ship is disabled," I announced. "I'm ordering you to abandon ship. There is a diving helmet at the lockout chamber, and more equipment in the gear locker. I want you off this minute."

The Chadburn telegraph rang in alarm—orders and inquiries from the bridge.

"What's going on?" Jonas's voiced betrayed honest confusion.

"Gentlemen, as sub-mariners, we work in a hostile environment, and sometimes we have to react to emergencies with obedience, not questions. I need you men on the surface to report our position to the Admiralty as soon as possible."

The two men exchanged a worried glance, and I suspect they thought I was not right in the head, but they saluted, responded with a chorus of "ayes," and hesitantly walked past me toward the lockout chamber.

The lights flickered once more and died. I counted to eight, spacing out the seconds with "Piccadilly," but still counted too fast as I reached ten before I heard relays click, echoing throughout the boat as little cones of yellow light appeared. "Thank you, Danjella," I said aloud. The emergency lighting with individual batteries was not only her idea, but she'd insisted on it even in the face of our abbreviated schedule.

I heard a metallic clang and turned to see the men had grabbed diving helmets and pulled them on over their striped jerseys. They both signaled encouragement with a "thumbs-up" and I returned the gesture. I levered myself to my feet, grateful my legs were following orders again, and walked over to ensure the men cycled through the lockout chamber. As my feet trod the cold steel deck, I noticed it tilted forward a few degrees, and I realized Graf must have trimmed the ballast bow heavy to produce more depth control using just the forward planes. Now, without power, we were moving deeper.

The chamber cycle completed and I sighed relief. I could not be certain either of them was knowingly involved, but if I was going to confront Graf, I didn't need an uncertain threat at my back. I stepped back to the main corridor to see another figure climb through the hatch. In the ghost light, I could not make out his features and mentally prepared myself for confrontation, until Bartley stepped into the light.

He stood there, looking crisp and proper in his sub-mariner's waistcoat, pressed trousers, and seaboots gleaming with polish, his mouth gaping in total shock.

"How? What?" He tried to steady himself, finally settling on, "Why?"

I was too tired to be anything but blunt. "Graf is stealing the boat."

His eyes widened in disbelief and he slowly shook his head. "No, no, no."

"Yes," I replied. "There was no meeting, no doubling the trial schedule, no order for a skeleton crew. You've been duped."

He straightened up as if I'd insulted him. "That can't be right."

"Where is Graf?"

"He's on the bridge." Bartley said, still shaking his head.

"And Danjella? I mean Miss Tesla."

"He, they, that is . . ." He cast his eyes around, and was still trying to come to grips with the situation when he noticed the dark shadow of Smith's legs. His head whipped back to me.

In frustration, I punched him on the shoulder. "Pull yourself together, man. I've sent men to the surface; soon there will be divers and support. But before that, we must secure Graf and ensure Miss Tesla's safety."

Finally, he nodded. "I left them chatting on the bridge. Graf sent me down when we lost power and no one answered the tube or telegraph."

"I don't suppose you're armed?"

He blanched. "No sir, I mean this was a river trial."

"Graf?"

"I don't think so; wouldn't that be odd?"

I glared at him.

He looked back at Smith's remains. "Are you sure about this? I'll

277

grant you Graf is right bastard, but a traitor?" He shook his head. "He's not wearing the waistcoat uniform, and I suppose he might be carrying a gun in his pocket, but so I can't really say. You?"

"As well armed as Cooper-Smythe."

I didn't explain, but pushed past him as he turned his body in the narrow space and followed me through the hatch. We made our way through the electrolyte chamber and the crew's quarters, and passed the galley and head, to reach the ladder rising to the bridge. The hatch was open, but with no light was visible, a black spot in the twilight of reserve illumination. The only sound was a sort of irregular, muffled thumping. I glanced back at Bartley.

He shrugged and whispered, "You want me to go first?"

I shook my head, "No, I want you at my back." I locked my left hand into a hook and climbed the ladder up to the dark bridge. The ladder was situated so I emerged from the opening to face the control center.

Things must have changed quickly after Bartley left. Only one emergency light was on, directly above the captain's chair. Danjella was seated on the deck facing me. The thumping came from her heels as she kicked against the deck, struggling against the ropes binding her torso to the chair back. Her new walking stick was tied across the back of her shoulders, her hands bound at each end, the rope passing around her neck, and a handkerchief stuffed in her mouth was bound with the same rope. Graf sat stiffly in the captain's chair, staring straight ahead, in his full uniform with his service cap on his head.

At the sight of me, she began kicking wildly, making guttural noises from her throat. I held up a finger to silence her, but that only increased her agitation.

Forgetting stealth, I pushed myself up on the deck, ran past Danjella's writhing figure, intent on throttling Graf, only to discover someone had beaten me to it. His face was purple, his tongue protruded and a glint of bright steel wire dug an ugly trough around his throat. Realization dawned on me and, confused, I turned back to the hatch. Bartley had not yet appeared.

"I do not know why my associate tried so hard to avoid killing you," a harsh, raspy voice said. I turned to see a thin figure step out from the shadows from behind the prismatic telescope. The familiar voice of my old shipmate had taken on an oddly distinct German accent.

"Gaither," I snapped.

"Grüber, actually," he corrected me as he stood with his hands calmly behind his back, "Erik Grüber." A muted clang behind me announced the belated arrival of Lt. Bartley, and I whipped around to see him rising from the hatch with his Webley service revolver pointed at me. He emerged onto the deck and then sealed the hatch behind him.

I glared at Grüber. "So, you are the priest?"

He waved his forefinger between him and Bartley. "We both are.

Bartley does my voice very well."

Danjella redoubled her squirming efforts.

"So Gaither—"

"Gaither died of a tropical fever in India; it was pathetically easy to replace him." He made a sweeping gesture to Bartley, "Especially when ones shipmate is eager to tell the story of how much my appearance changed over the course of my illness."

I glared at Bartley. "Why?"

"Money, of course," he answered simply. "I don't know how to be poor."

"But you're rich."

"My family is rich," he clarified. "As soon as they learn I can't go through with a certain arranged marriage they will at least disinherit me, if not cut me off all together."

I shook my head, not able to comprehend. "Because you're seeing an actress."

"No, old boy," Bartley said, "seems I picked up the French disease from some Hindu whore; no way to hide it from a spouse, don't you know."

I also knew syphilis could drive men mad.

"But the *Ram*, the explosion."

"Good God, don't be simple. I set up that fuse myself. Despite what I said, we had at least ten minutes, plenty of time for me to point it out to you if you turned out to be thick-headed."

He flicked his pistol at Danjella who was making progress against her bonds. "Stop that," he ordered.

"Oh, leave her alone." Grüber sighed as he approached. "It is sort of entertaining. Besides what is the little girl going to do? Hit us with her stick? Her first attempt was as sad as it was pointless."

Danjella made a noise of rage behind the gag.

"Now what?" I demanded.

Grüber addressed Bartley. "You still don't have the stomach for killing him."

Bartley raised the gun menacingly. "I will if I have to, but I prefer not." He looked at me, "I actually do like you. I don't suppose you'd care to join us?"

"Don't be stupid." Grüber snapped. "As if we could trust him? Since we've already sold Miss Tesla, he will make an acceptable hostage."

"For what?" I said. "You're sinking."

Grüber glanced at Bartley.

"I can fix the damage. We are past the hard part. Two men can get this tub out of the Thames, if we run like monkeys."

I was aghast at the level of his betrayal.

Grüber made a circling gesture. "Turn around; put your hands behind your back."

Danjella screamed as loudly as she could through her gag.

Seeing no immediate options, I complied.

Danjella was six feet to my right, and her efforts were making headway. She'd inched the tip of her cane across her back enough to free her left hand and was tugging at the rope around her neck. Mentally, I cheered her on, but knew it was a useless gesture. She could never get all the ropes undone in time to stop me from being trussed up like a Christmas goose, and then they would tie her again, more securely.

Grüber moved up behind me, and Danjella clawed at the gag, screaming again. This time I understood. "Garrote!"

Reflex made me raise my *flesh* hand to protect my neck as the steel wire came over my head. Grüber's cast wasn't completely successful and I managed to catch the wire with my right forefinger. He gave the wire a violent wrench. His knee was in my back and he pulled harder than I imagined his wiry arms could manage. Even as I struggled, my air was cut off and the sharp wire threatened to amputate my forefinger before I died.

Bartley averted his eyes, and turned to consider the bulkhead behind him, his shoulders slumped in resignation. As ragged flashes of light began to encroach on my vision, I cast pleading eyes to Danjella.

Her hands were free now, and she was not even attempting to loosen her legs. Instead, she brought her cane around and grabbed it with both hands to firmly yank at the T-shaped grip. It pulled away from the shaft and for a second I thought she'd invested in a sword cane, but she merely rotated the grip ninety degrees and pushed it back in place. My eyes widened in complete shock as she fingered a small silver stud which now protruded from the stick, and, with her mouth set in a determined frown, sighted down the cane.

The report was about a quarter of what one would expect from a pistol as she shot through the rubberized leather tip. Later I learned that the Reilly air gun cane fired a .32 caliber bullet with a muzzle velocity comparable to a conventional pistol. It was considered deadly accurate within fifteen feet. Shooting from the side, the bullet caught him just under the armpit.

Grüber grunted in surprise and tried to pull harder, but I could feel him slumping as the strength flowed out of his body. I jerked my hand against the wire, ignoring the cutting pain in my finger as I ripped the wire from his dying hands.

Danjella franticly re-cocked her weapon as Bartley recovered from his astonishment and brought his gun to bear on her. I leapt at him, slicing at the skin and bone of his hand with the wire and steel of mine. The gun fell from his limp fingers, but he surprised me by twisting his body toward me, and landing a vicious left-handed punch to my solar plexus.

I doubled over and he shoved me away. I slipped in the pink froth gushing from Grüber's mouth as I fought to regain my balance. Apparently Danjella's bullet had pierced both lungs but missed his heart, which now pumped out the results of his wounds. Mercifully, he was senseless and would not feel himself drowning in his own blood.

For some reason, Danjella chose not to shoot again, but desperately wrestled at the knots binding her legs. Bartley turned from me and scrambled awkwardly across the deck to retrieve the Webley revolver with his left hand. Suddenly the boat jarred and quaked as it hit the bottom. The motion threw him off balance just enough to allow me the chance to launch my body at him as he brought the pistol to bear once again on Danjella. I seized his left hand with my right before he could take aim, swung him around, and clutched at his throat with my mechanical left hand, timing the grab so the fingers stopped as soon as they wrapped around his neck. I hastily added two clicks to hold him firm and he continued to struggle in my grasp.

"Drop the gun!" I shouted, and tightened my steel grip one more click. He struggled harder. I feared his gun hand would soon slip my natural grasp, and he would succeed in shooting Danjella.

But abruptly, Danjella was behind me. She brought the tip of the cane over my shoulder, leveling it directly at Bartley's right eye. "Drop it now," she said.

Instead of complying, Bartley repeatedly pulled the trigger as fast as he could. His first shot struck the three-inch- thick quartz glass of the port observation window, blasting a huge chip out of it. The second shot cracked the tough glass from side to side, and the third shot created a shatter pattern which began to bead water.

"Stop!" I cried, tightening my grip one more notch. I intended the action to be just enough to make him obey, but the damaged thumb slipped and ratcheted further. I heard a sharp snap; Bartley stopped firing, and the Webley tumbled from his slack grip. The body in my steel grasp began twitching uncontrollably, and I dropped the dying man to the deck.

Another loud crack rang out as the shattered port gave way, and the Thames flowed into the conning tower.

I slogged through the rising wet to reach the port and fought to shove the watertight cover over the opening as water poured into the chamber. I did not have to give any instructions to Danjella, but she was immediately beside me, lending her strength to close the floodgate. The watertight cover had been designed with this type of scenario in mind and the sliding movement was intended to resist the push of the water as it sliced off the flood. But theoretical design is one thing and practical application is another; as my mind was imagining a ratcheting wheel with mechanical advantage to replace the manual labor, my body finally shoved the piece into place, and Danjella spun the wheel to lock it.

Either the exploding glass or the bullets warped the sealing surface so the hatch did not completely stem the flood, but reduced it to the flow of a mere fire hose. I stumbled from the port in water rising above my knees. I grabbed the rail in front of the prismatic telescope and caught my breath. The water by that time was almost up to Danjella's waist, and rising.

"Why didn't you shoot?" I asked over the sound of the rushing water.

"Cane has air for five shots, but only one bullet," she shouted back. "To reload you must muzzle it." Exhaustion and stress made her accent thicker.

"Muzzleload," I corrected her.

"I am making the Reilly Company a four-shot prototype, but is not yet done."

"We're on the bottom," I announced. "There is a procedure."

"I know," Danjella replied hotly. "And if Captain Arthur listen to me, I would have practice." Her English unraveled in the tense atmosphere.

I left her at the rail, waded through the flood to a wall panel marked by four red stripes, and tugged a hidden release, exposing four sets of escape bottles. Selecting one for me and another for her, I slogged back through the rising water and handed over her bottle. She took it and set it aside, securing it by wrapping the retaining straps around the now-submerged rail.

"Think you can manage it?" I asked.

"I manage or I don't. Does no good to think too much."

I nodded and said, "Danjella, there is something I want to tell you, need to tell you, about me, about us. I have trouble . . ."

Her eyes grew wide. "Now?" she snapped. "Now? You want to have this talk now?"

"I thought . . ."

Her voice crackled with an intensity I never imagined. "You think too much, except when you think too little!" She took a calming breath. "We have talk. I am distracted now." She looked around the flooding compartment, then back at me, her gaze focusing on my eye. "Very long talk, I am thinking, but for now, I summarize." She grabbed me by the shoulders and kissed me on the lips. The actual contact was as brief as the time our lips touched at the theater, but this kiss was a firm statement, and a promise.

She looked me in the eyes. "Is understanding?"

"I'm not sure, could you repeat?"

She rolled her eyes, her lips twitching with amusement in spite of herself. She pressed her wrist to her mouth as she surveyed the rising water. "Now, I need you to get me out of distress."

That seemed an odd way for her to put it. "I shall endeavor to rescue you."

Her face screwed into an angry scowl, and her eyes sharpened. "You are not listening," she enunciated carefully. "I need you to get me out of *this dress*." She almost laughed at the expression on my face.

"This dress, weighs fifteen pounds, dry. I cannot image how much is wet." She swayed gently from side to side, to make a point. The heavy folds of fabric moved sluggishly in the chest-high water, and definitely did not float.

"I see," I replied.

She turned around and moved her hair from the back of the neckline. "Please."

There must have been over forty tiny cloth-covered buttons. I tried with my right hand to pick at the material. Frustrated, I grabbed handfuls.

Sensing my intent, Danjella said over her shoulder, "Go ahead."

I yanked hard and tiny buttons flew everywhere. A snort of laughter rose up and I tried to strangle it.

"What was that?"

"Nothing," I replied, reluctant to admit this was very near something I'd wanted to do since I was fourteen.

Free, she pulled her arms from the sleeves and I helped her peel the soggy garment off her body. I was relieved (disappointed?) to discover she had on a light cotton shift over her corset. And even as water made her garment near transparent, it clung to her frame in a way that revealed more layers beneath.

She retrieved the flotation belt and fastened it lightly around her waist, slung the oxygen bottle on her arm, then pointed to the damaged port. "May as well open it."

"Are you sure?"

"Given choice of standing in cold water for thirty minutes, or getting out in ten, I choose the latter."

I also strapped on my belt, put my arm through the bottle strap, and paddled over to the port. I looked at her one last time. "You can swim, right?" I asked, and at her nod, opened the cover. The flood of water was so intense it was difficult to swim back to her; by then it was so deep Danjella could not touch bottom and was crouched on the rail.

She pushed off the rail and swam a side stroke, her right hand propelling her through the water while her left hand pushed along the top of the conning tower over to the ladder ascending to the main hatch. I joined her and together we let the rising tide take us up the remaining inches.

I spoke slowly as my voice reverberated in the small closed space. "When you take a breath from the bottle use your hand to keep the tube in your mouth; it will try to blow free."

She nodded, and mimed using the bottle.

I fought back panic, not for me, but for her safety. I twisted open a small vent aperture on the cover, and a fierce hiss of escaping air assaulted our ears. By the time the noise abated, the pressure began to take its toll. We were huddled in the well of the hatch ring, waiting until we could take that last unassisted breath. I felt the pressure building behind my eyes as the blood rushed in my ears and Danjella screwed her eyes shut.

"Swallow air," I shouted. "It helps."

She released one hand from the ladder, held it to her face, and screamed.

From behind, I wrapped my arms around her and pulled her tight, although our floatation belts kept our bodies from actually touching. She shivered in the cold water and yelled something that was lost in the rush of air. And then it was time to take our last free breath.

I nudged her aside and shoved the hatch open, floating out first. I turned to assist her, but she was already out taking her final breath from the bottle. Without hesitation, she kicked off from the top of the conning tower to the surface, her white shift floating around her, giving her form an otherworldly, nearly angelic shape.

I took my breath and made up my mind to pursue.

Epilogue

I stood in the washroom down the hall from my office at the Ironworks, staring in the mirror. On the shelf was a small wooden box, six inches long by two inches wide which Nicola Tesla had given me that morning. His farewell gift, he called it, as he was leaving in few days to America, "to electrify the world."

Four dimly glowing glass orbs sat cushioned in velvet. He had said, "One to use, one to be ready, one to be charging, and another because you break things."

I selected one at random, rinsed it with water, and gingerly pressed it into my empty socket, immediately blinking rapidly as the unaccustomed object stimulated my still-active tear ducts. Tesla worked with a craftsman to make it look something like an eye, but the iris was a brass plate and the pupil an experimental filament. Following his directions, I took my finger, pressed on the front, and the light shone out in a narrow beam. I pressed to turn it off. Nicola assured me that with practice I'd be able to operate it with my eyelid. He also said I'd get used to the feel, but I suspected that would take some time.

Someone knocked impatiently on the door. "Well?" Danjella's voice carried through the heavy oak door.

It was two days after our escape from the sunken *Thunderbolt*. Of course, she had no trouble exiting the sub and we easily rose the 120 feet to the surface. *The Ram* was a few hundred yards away, but the men saw us thrashing about and soon we joined the other refugees from the *Thunderbolt*. We sat on the conning tower, awaiting another boat.

After being plucked from the Thames, we were allowed a day of rest, but before that I had one wretched duty. Captain Wilson offered to take my place, but Commander Heinrich Graf (posthumous promotion) had been under my command and it was my responsibility to inform his wife and two daughters of their father's courageous death. He had allowed himself to be tied up to protect Danjella, and was garroted after he was helpless.

After sleeping most of the next day, Danjella and I met for dinner under the watchful eye of Miss Raymond, and we have yet to have the promised long talk.

But today we were back at the Ironworks for a complete debriefing.

Nicola grabbed me when I entered the building and pressed his gift on me. "Only light," he said. "But maybe one day I make one shoots lightning. I will send to you."

Coming from anyone else . . .

A knock at the door cut through my reverie. "Ian?" Danjella called again through the stout door. "Does it work?"

I still felt uncomfortable with the vaguely unnatural appearance of the orb, so I replaced my eye patch, concealing the addition. "Yes, it works," I replied as I stepped out of the door.

She cocked an eyebrow at the sight of the patch, then reached up and pulled it away.

"Ah," she said in admiration. "Looks good on you."

"I'm not so sure." I reached to take the eye patch back from her, but she snatched it away with her right hand and deftly caught my elbow with her left, then tugged me down the hall. "We show the others, they waiting."

The earlier part of the day had consisted of a debriefing and going over events multiple times in Captain Wilson's office. In attendance with the soon-to-be admiral were Mr. Cooper-Smythe, back in his somber clothing, the muttonchops growing back nicely, and Adam Greer, looking unusually jovial.

It was Cooper-Smythe who started the meeting with an unexpected announcement. "We received a communiqué directly from Kaiser Freidrich. It states that he would like to clarify communications from the Crown Prince and, since the safety of the waters off the Cape of Good Hope is of mutual concern, he would invite us to join the security force already there. However, he is sorry that he would be unable to allow us port privileges anywhere on the continent of Africa."

"Of course," Wilson had said, then turned the conversation to immediate concerns. "The salvage divers tell me that the *Thunderbolt* will be raised tomorrow. You will need to detail a crew to bring it back for repair. You have thirty days, and then the *Thunderbolt* submersible squadron will sail for the Cape." The group went on to discuss details.

After the meeting finally finished, Danjella had insisted on seeing Nicola's gift. Now, she dragged me back to the office.

"Gentleman," she said as we entered the room. "Is it not, magni . . . magna, not English then, *magnifique*?

"*Tres magnifique*," Cooper-Smythe said.

"Why's that thing glowing like that?" Greer asked.

I endured a few more wise remarks as the group broke up. I found myself shaking hands with the man who had dragged me into this mess.

"I suppose that growing back the muttonchops means no more disguises for a while," I said.

He brushed his knuckles through the curly hair. "My wife likes them, so I grow them when I can."

I blinked in surprise. "I didn't know you were married."

His face took on a more somber expression. "I do not advertise the fact. Knowledge of my family can make me vulnerable."

I nodded. "Still, I suspect you have a most interesting wife. I should like to meet her sometime."

He smiled, walked a few steps, and looked over his shoulder at me. "You already have," he replied. He continued talking as he walked away. "And I am supposed to remind you that you have an appointment on Thursday."

The End

Please continue for an excerpt from
"The Eidlerland Incident"

An excerpt from the new novel,

The Eidlerland Incident

Coming from Rosswyvern Press, December 16, 2013

Prolog - January 1888

    The freezing bitter wind stung the general's face through the thick woolen scarf wrapped around his nose and mouth. Leather pads that were meant to keep the tin goggles from freezing to his skin had hardened into brutal lumps in the icy temperatures and scraped his face whenever he blinked. The general gingerly lifted the goggles to his forehead and attempted to shelter his face with his right arm as he peered through the telescope mounted on the edge of the observation basket at the very front of the airship. Since he was below 10,000 feet it was not necessary to lug an oxygen bottle around. Even so he cursed the low altitude and yearned to take the giant airship back above the clouds into more stable air. For the time being however, this was not to be. While he was in command of the mighty dirigible herself, he was not in command of the expedition.

    He squinted through the eyepiece, unending white gleaming in the not really night of Antarctic summer. "Take note, Hans," he yelled in German, raising his voice to be heard through his thick polar gear as he used small knobs on the telescope to lock it into a rapidly approaching point on the horizon. "I have spotted the island again. It is volcanic. There appears to be liquid water along the south shore."

    Hans raised a hand in acknowledgement.

    "Do you think you can signal the sealer again?" The general called out.

    "I can try, Herr General, we are awfully low." This comment earned a frown from the commander that Hans could sense, even through layers of wool, fur and leather. "But I will try."

    Hans moved to the powerful signal lamp. Its formidable arc light was only to be used in the open air of the observation gondola, away from the service cabins and the twenty giant hydrogen bladders that kept the 120 meter craft into the air. Hans flipped at the handle attempting to acquire the attention of a seal hunting expedition on the edge of the ice shelf, a spot on the horizon that was only identifiable when its own carbon arc signal lamp was on. The intermittent contact with the sealer was the only way to relay messages, through a Yankee whaler back to the dirigible's supply ship and base.

From a dark edge on the horizon, a tiny dot of light responded.

The general grunted. "Good. Send him our position, course and speed, and I'll go find out what that idiot wants to name *this* damn bit of rock."

Hans did not reply. In fact he appeared not to have heard the remark at all, a valuable trait when Officers in the *Reichsheer,* the Imperial German Army, clash with their civilian masters. But somewhere deep in his heart Hans agreed: the man was an idiot.

The general clambered up the ladder to the catwalk and worked his way back to the Command cabin. Muffled thuds reverberated beneath his heavily wrapped feet as he stepped along the aluminum walkway. He pulled back the fur-lined hood of his coat as he entered the outer door, divested himself of the thick woolen scarf, and brushed off the ice crystals formed by his breath on it in the frigid, dry air. He opened his coat, without removing it, and left the tin goggles hanging around his neck, dangling just below the old style *ritterkruez* he wore on a silk ribbon, just peeking out from his uniform tunic. He left the foot wrappings in place, anticipating either going back to the observation gondola or making an inspection tour of the engines after reporting to Herr Eidler. He stepped in the significantly warmer air in the forward command cabin, the first of a string of six cabins that served as the work and living spaces aboard the airship. This cabin was also the only one equipped with special sealed vats of caustic soda to heat the air without open flame or spark. The general nodded to the helmsman as he passed.

"Ah, Herr Graf von Zeppelin," the officious little man who commanded the Empire's great Antarctic expedition greeted him in friendly tones that, as usual, managed a touch of suspicion especially as he pronounced the Noble title.

"*Generalleutnant"* the general corrected absently, wiping frost from the full beard that sprouted from his face at an aggressive angle.

Ignoring the correction, Herr Eidler continued, "You should join us in a cup." His assistant, Wechsler, a jittery young man who didn't enjoy leaving the ground, was preparing coffee. The general watched with a carefully measured gaze as the young man's hands shook so badly that he had to grip the pot with both just to pour.

Eidler changed his language to English for the benefit of the British visitor with him and waved for the General to join them. "We were just discussing the intriguing theory," he tapped his chin with his forefinger, "that the Earth is hollow." Wechsler grimaced and turned away from the group. Eidler paused as if waiting for the General to reply, but the officer had learned that thoughtful comment only encouraged Eidler to go on.

Eidler used his mug to indicate the white landscape beyond the lightly smoked port observation window, "you know, for centuries natural philosophers have thought that out there," he waved the coffee mug in a grand gesture, "Out there, is the entrance to a purer world."

In spite of his determination not to provoke useless discussion, the General grimaced. He found that he had a distaste for most things Eidler described in terms of their "purity." The odious man could go on for hours about "pure blood" and "race hygiene," and, of course, the "curse of the *untermenchen.*"

"The speculation is intriguing," the Britisher joined in.

The general eyed the Britisher with the sort of politeness one gives to an uninvited guest. When the new Crown Prince, Wilhelm the Second, announced the expedition, the fledgling Kaiserreich Geographic Society invited an international committee to join in the flight, but they were rebuffed. The only country willing to send a representative was Britain and, in Graf's mind, they hadn't sent their best. Or at least, not their most *straightforward*. The British representative was a minor noble, a dilettante explorer seeking the attention from the Royal Geographical Society. The man talked in bluster and the crew speculated that he was nearly as feebleminded as Herr Eidler, but the general wasn't so sure. His first impression had been of a man of military bearing with a strong chest and back. The Britisher's skin was weathered and his face craggy as if from long exposure to the elements; he had the appearance of a man of action, but when he spoke the Britisher was all bombast and silly grins. Nonetheless, the general thought he saw something in the man's eyes, some hidden shrewdness, it was just enough to put him on his guard. The general nodded to the guest. "Sir Reginald."

"Oh, Reggie, You must call me Reggie," the man replied in English, his voice a strained tenor as he punched the air. Had he been close enough, the playful blow would have landed on the General's upper arm, again.

At the beginning of the voyage, the passenger demonstrated a clumsy knowledge of German; and rather than indulge in long stilted conversations, the General communicated with him in crisp, lightly accented English.

Herr Eidler, whose ability with the language was not quite as fluent, with an accent so thick it sounded like caricature, nevertheless tried to follow suit, "Yes, Ferdinand, you should call him Reggie, we are all friends here, *ja?*"

But the General shook his head toward Herr Eidler. "I have only come to inform you we have found another of the islands you are so concerned with. I must proceed to the chart room."

"Volcanic?"

3

"Yes, with liquid water on the Southern face. Also, as you asked us to look for, it is an elongate crescent shape."

Herr Eidler eyes narrowed, suddenly all serious, "The crescent facing north?"

"*Ja*, and with two peaks, the eastern one much higher than the other."

Eidler nodded vigorously to himself. "Excellent, I shall have to come up with a name. Do we have any flags left?"

The General turned to the helmsman standing before the front window, "Ignatz, any flags?" he inquired in German. This was the eleventh island they'd encountered during the flight, not to mention the flags dropped on the continent itself.

Exploration was Germany's ostensible reason for the trip, but dropping flags over the frozen continent was Herr Eidler's brainchild. It was his attempt at the most massive land claim in the planet's history. Of course, they couldn't sail the entire continent dropping his ludicrous little flags, but that was no business of the General's. The airship successfully dropped four hundred of the sixteen inch flags with weighted bases over a wedge of Antarctica, claiming the area as Kaiser Wilhelm Land. Eidler publicly announced that he believed the International Convention would recognize a claim of the marked territory, although privately he thought the Empire might push a claim for the entire continent. The General did not care. The scheme had made his concept-airship into a reality much sooner than he ever hoped. He was currently riding in the design he had begun soon after his first voyage in a tethered balloon from whence he observed the American Confederacy during their ill-fated struggle.

Ignatz did not directly answer, but reached for a speaking tube and relayed the question. He held the device to his ear and nodded after a moment. "There is a handful that caught in the release netting. Maybe as many as two dozen total."

The flags gave rise to another scruple in the Generals mind. Only half the banners were the official flag of the Kaiserreich. The other half bore a white escutcheon and thin black cross imposed upon a field of red. It was the banner of the old Teutonic order that, since the assassination of Kaiser Wilhelm, was evolving into a political organization calling itself the "Nationalistische Arbeiter Partei." With its brown shirted "security force," it was fiercely loyal to the crown prince and wielded a power over the Reich that seemed to grow stronger each day.

"Are you certain it is an island?" Eidler demanded.

The General puffed out his cheeks, sighed and gave the same answer as the last three times they sighted one of these volcanic mounds sprouting out of the ice. "The charts say we are now over the ice shelf, therefore the land jutting up should be an island, but with the ice. . ." Eidler's face contorted in concentration, "I do not want to name it an island and have some future expedition call me a fool. It is always easy for those that come after to disparage the vanguard. We shall call it. . ."

His face screwed up in deliberation.

"It's obvious," Sir Reginald chimed in, his grin turned up a degree. "It is high time you named something 'Eidlerland.'"

The General kept his face impassive as the remark grated on his nerves. Herr Eidler shook his head in mock humility, barely keeping a pleased grin of his own off his face.

"I insist," Ross continued, and pointed imperiously at the General. "Please have the discovery logged."

The general pursed his lips and relaxed his shoulders. The thought of "Eidlerland" offended him somehow, but realistically he didn't care if they called it *Katzenarsch*. "*Ja,*" he replied in a tired, resigned voice. He nodded to the expedition commander. "Herr Eidler," he said by way of dismissing himself, and walked a few feet away to the helmsman. The island was just coming into view through the forward window.

"Ignatz," he addressed the helmsman standing before the great ship's wheel, then changed his language to German. "Steer for the Island and order ballast moved forward to direct us low enough for the drop. And send orders to the crew to gather the remaining flags."

"*Jawohl, mein herr.*"

"You will be able to reach me at engine station one, where I will direct the operation."

The general walked past the other men and left them to their discussion, their mood very animated at the upcoming drop, except Wechsler who nervous mood seemed to sink into near panic at the imminent maneuver. Leaving the compartment he made his way to the attached chart room to ensure that the coordinates and name of "Eidlerland" were officially recorded. From there, The General returned to the command cabin and walked hastily toward the exit, not wishing to be caught up in the current discussion, which seemed to be about something called "vril," whatever that was.

Regaining his woolen scarf from the peg by the door, he wrapped it across his face and stepped out into the bitter cold. As it would take several minutes for the crew to prepare, the General took the indirect route to the engines, making an inspection pass through the forward interior. He was especially concerned with the two pairs of *blaugas* engines, and the reserves of the gaseous fuel, so he climbed the ladder up to the long axial corridor walkway.

Small electric lights illuminated the dim interior of the ship, their feeble light shining off the translucent skin of the gas cells. As always, each time he crossed the great expanse of the interior frame, he inspected the hydrogen cells above, and the more compact blaugas cells below, for any sign of shrinkage or unusual wear. The hundreds of thousands of sheets of goldbeater skins, actually the outer lining of cow's intestines, that made up the seven layer thickness of the cells were joined together to make a theoretically impermeable barrier, but the General was by nature a cautious man and he studied the smooth texture of each cell carefully.

The disaster happened so quickly he had little time to consider the danger, and even less to act. Something ahead sparked, like a high voltage electrical short and he tried to run toward it. Before he could take a step, the hydrogen cell above the spark shivered, and fiery red lines covered the surface as the expanding gas broke free and exploded through the interior. Flaming tendrils stretched their destruction to the remaining cells. *Generalleutnant* Ferdinand von Zeppelin held his breath, dropped flat on the catwalk and buried his face in his hands.